HUI GUI
A CHINESE STORY

HUI GUI
A CHINESE STORY

A NOVEL BY
ELSIE SZE

Library and Archives Canada Cataloguing in Publication

Sze, Elsie, 1946-
Hui gui : A Chinese story / Elsie Sze.

ISBN 0-9737210-0-6

1. China—History—20th century—Fiction. 2. Hong Kong
(China)—History—20th century—Fiction. I. Title.

PS8637.Z42H84 2005 C813'.6 C2005-900863-6

Produced with the support of the City of Toronto through the Toronto Arts Council.

Published by BTS Publishing House
P.O. Box 962 Station B
Willowdale, Ontario
Canada M2K 2T6

Printed and bound in Canada by University of Toronto Press.

This is a work of fiction, purely a product of the author's imagination.

Cover design and layout by Samuel Sze
Cover calligraphy by Benjamin Wong

For Ben, Sam and Tim,
with love

ACKNOWLEDGEMENTS

I am deeply indebted to my mentor Isabel Huggan who taught me the skills, guided and encouraged me throughout the writing of the novel, and never doubted that it would some day be published.

I am very grateful to my parents, Hon Ngi and Elizabeth Chin, and my late uncle James Liang, for the wartime stories they told. Many thanks to Peter Chiu, Thomas Fung, and Betty Tsang for their invaluable assistance in my research on Hong Kong. I am very thankful to Leanne Lieberman and Pansy Tan who reviewed early drafts of the manuscript, and my writers' group in Toronto whose constructive criticisms mattered a lot. My special thanks to Ania Szado who edited an early as well as the final draft.

A big thank you goes to relatives and friends in Canada, the United States and Hong Kong for their interest in the novel, contributions in matters of research, and help at various stages of bringing the novel to publication.

To my children, Ben, Sam and Tim, my heartfelt appreciation for their unfailing support, both moral and technical. To Sam, a special thank you for designing and formatting the entire layout of the book.

To Michael Sze, my husband and best friend, I owe the realization of this lifelong dream.

With deep affection, I remember my *amah*, Wong Kam Lin
(1919 – 2004)

CHINA

Locations of places cited in the novel

Beijing • Tangshan
• Tianjin
HEBEI

SHANDONG

Yan'an •

SHAANXI

Nanjing •
Shanghai •

Chengdu •

SICHUAN
Chongqing •

HUNAN
JIANGXI

Kunming •

YUNNAN
GUANGXI

Guilin •
• Tai Shek *
GUANGDONG
• Ka Hing *
• Guangzhou
•
Hong Kong

* Fictitious place names

GUANGDONG

Locations of places cited in the novel

HUNAN

Guilin

Tai Shek*

GUANGXI

GUANGDONG

Wuzhou

Ka Hing*

Guangzhou

Zhaoqing

Shenzhen

Hong Kong

Macau

SOUTH CHINA SEA

* Fictitious place names

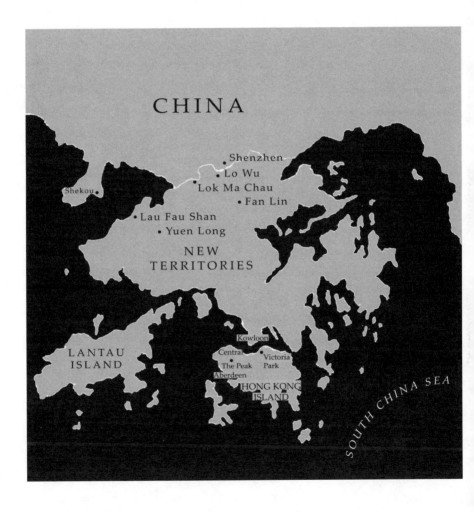

HONG KONG 1997

Locations of places cited in the novel

CHINA

Shenzhen
• Lo Wu
Lok Ma Chau
• Fan Lin

Shekou•

• Lau Fau Shan
• Yuen Long

NEW
TERRITORIES

LANTAU
ISLAND

Kowloon

Central   • Victoria
The Peak   Park
Aberdeen

HONG KONG
ISLAND

SOUTH CHINA SEA

Glossary of Transliterated Words
(from the Cantonese dialect, unless specified Mandarin)

Ah	definite article sometimes used in front of a given or last name
amah	hired household servant
ayaa	exclamation of dismay
bo bo	treasure
charsiu	Chinese barbecued pork
cheg	approximately 13 inches
cheongsam	Chinese one-piece national dress with mandarin collar
chi fan	sticky rice roll with fried dough centre, food from northern China
Ching Ming	spring festival for paying respects to ancestors at the cemetery
Chung Yeung	ninth day of the ninth moon in lunar calendar, a day for paying respects to ancestors at the cemetery
dan (Mandarin)	approximately 110 pounds
dim sum	appetizers served in Chinese restaurants
erhu (Mandarin)	two-stringed instrument
fook	good fortune
ga so	daughter-in-law
gai lan	Chinese broccoli
gor	older brother
go tsung	upper secondary school, the last two years of high school
goy wui	oh my!
guanxi (Mandarin)	connections
gum mo	flu
gun	approximately 1.1 pounds
Guomindang	Nationalist Party
guzheng (Mandarin)	stringed instrument
gweilo	foreigner
har gao	shrimp dumpling
hui gui (Mandarin)	returning home, a term used by the Chinese to refer to the return of Hong Kong by Britain to China in 1997

kung hay fat choy	Chinese New Year salutation, wishing prosperity
kung kung	maternal grandfather
kungfu	martial arts
li (Mandarin)	approximately one-third mile
liang (Mandarin)	approximately 1.76 ounces
lin	water lily
lo fan	foreign or foreigner
lo sze	teacher
lo yeh	father-in-law, old master
mahjong (Mandarin)	game with small tiles, played by four
makwa	long pants worn under *cheongsam* by men and boys
min	noodles
mou	one-sixth of an acre
mui tsai	household maid, bought into family
pak	uncle (father's older brother), respectful form of address for an elderly man
peipa	stringed instrument, shaped like a lute
po li	a black Chinese tea
poh poh	maternal grandmother
samfu	two-piece Chinese traditional outfit consisting of jacket and pants
siu bin	urinate
siu cheh	young mistress
siu siu	little son of the master
siu yeh	young master
suk	uncle (father's younger brother), respectful form of Mr.
sum	aunt (wife of father's younger brother), respectful form of Mrs.
tai chi (Mandarin)	form of Chinese exercise
tanka	fishermen's community
wei chi (Mandarin)	kind of Chinese chess, also known as *go*
wonton	dumpling
yeh yeh	paternal grandfather
yuan (Mandarin)	dollar in Chinese currency
zheng (Mandarin)	stringed instrument, also known as *guzheng*

'Tis fine, Papa. 'Tis fine. I will sit here with you for as long as you wish.

1

Prologue

I LOOK UP TO the wall above Papa's chair. My eyes meet his as he gazes out of the rosewood frame I have hung there. That typical half-smile, the well-defined jaw, his thick dark eyebrows and deep-set eyes giving an impression of outward composure and inner strength. His hair is grey at the temple, adding dignity to his years. He would be about sixty when the photograph was taken. A mole sits above the left corner of his upper lip, a small dark spot hardly noticeable in the photograph if one didn't know to look for it. But I see it, and memories flood my mind, even as I look. When I was a child, this round black blemish on my father's face worried me, until Papa told me it was his storytelling mole. Every time I touched it, he would be obliged to tell me a story. And I always wanted a story, and his stories were always about China.

"Imagine holding a *chi fan* to your mouth," Papa said in the rather dramatic storytelling manner he used when recalling his childhood in China. I was about four and fascinated with the idea of a tasty snack I had never eaten before. "Imagine taking a bite of it, munching it, and using your tongue to free the rice sticking to the roof of your mouth. Imagine the crunchy hardness of the deep-fried dough and the melting softness of the sticky rice that wraps around it."

I closed my eyes and imagined.

"You want to eat it slowly, savour every bite, make it last longer," he continued. "Then, suddenly this delicious treat is snatched from under your nose by a little beggar who runs away happily and devours it in no time."

I opened my eyes wide and looked with dismay at Papa.

"You are hungry and angry," he went on, "your eyes brimful with tears, and the adults will not get you another *chi fan* for the one so rudely taken from you. Serena, that happened to me when I was about eight, in our village of Ka Hing, before the Japanese came. It was a time when there was little food in China, and many hungry children of poor families were turned out into the streets to beg, yes, even to steal."

"Seenla," Ah Lan calls my name as no one but she would call it, "look at all the *hui gui* gimmicks they're selling on Temple Street! Tins of colonial air, bottles of colonial soil!" Her loud terse Cantonese rouses me from thoughts of my father. "Know what I saw today at the roadside stands near Central Market? Dolls with English flag behind and Chinese flag in front!"

I laugh. "Hong Kong people are some of the most enterprising in the world. We certainly know how to make the most of everything. I was at the Central Post Office today and saw all these beautiful *hui gui* commemorative stamps and coins in 24 karat gold. I was tempted to get a set, but they're too expensive."

Ah Lan is watching the daily local television coverage of happenings leading up to Britain's return of Hong Kong to China, to take place in just thirty days, after more than 150 years of British colonization. More than 150 years of British imperial dominance, deemed servitude to the *gweilo* by some locals, perhaps more so in the earlier days of the colony, and, to others, a haven of safety from the dark force of Communism, ever since the Communist victory in 1949.

"Seenla, I never dreamed I live to see the day," says Ah Lan. She cocks her head slightly to one side, takes in a deep breath and sighs. "I suppose as Chinese I ought to be proud, but I don't trust the Communists." She glances at me with her small but still sharp eyes framed with age lines. "Young people like you should leave.

Old wood like me can stay."

Good old Ah Lan, my *amah*, my mother's *amah*. What has endeared her to us all these years is her uncompromising loyalty to my mother, and later also to Papa and me as we came into her life. In all her days of active service before we retired her from manual labour much against her will, she belonged to that now-defunct school of *amahs* who kept the least desirable parts of the meat for themselves and ate leftovers from every meal. Until she fell victim to her arthritic joints and progressively porous bones, she would walk a good mile and back to the herbalist down the hill for medicine when one of us was under the weather – *gum mo*, as she called it in Cantonese. When Papa was on night shift, she stayed up for him so Mummy could get the sleep she needed.

At eighty-two, Ah Lan is a mere ninety-pounder, reduced from her prime-time five-foot straight to a bent four-foot-nine. She wears her hair short these days, having cut her long queue some thirty years back. But for all her stooped posture and shrunken frame, her mind is as alert as ever, her memory intact. She still has the worry-free look of a simple, straightforward, can-think-no-ill-of-anybody soul. Except for what she calls railroad tracks on her forehead and chicken feet around her eyes, she does not look her "almost-seven-dozen" as she describes her years.

A sudden streak of lightning illuminates the night sky for one brief moment, followed by crashing thunder. The ceiling light in the sitting room flickers. Ah Lan gets up from the sofa and stretches.

"This rain makes me sleep good. I go to bed now, Seenla."

My old *amah* shuffles in her loose slippers to her room. I remain on the sofa alone, idly watching a late-night broadcast of Hong Kong marketers cashing in on the approaching handover. Sleep is far from my thoughts. Perhaps I am being drawn into the exhilaration, apprehension, uncertainties, and conflicting emotions building up here in Hong Kong, pride in its reunification with China and fear of the Communist regime, as the clock ticks away the days, hours, and minutes. Or perhaps I am thinking of the changes coming for me after *hui gui*, of dreaded sad farewells – and an exciting new beginning. A paradox of emotions. Like Hong Kong.

Soon, Hong Kong will be returned by its surrogate parent to its motherland. *Hui gui*, we call it, returning home.

"When you were a little boy in China, Papa, did you have lots of friends?" I was sitting beside him on the sofa, holding his hand in both my own and playing with his big thumb, my feet swinging back and forth above the parquet floor.

"No, I didn't have many friends back then, but there was one boy who played with me all the time. His name was Ah Chu."

"You had only *one* friend?" How lucky I was to have so many friends in the kindergarten I attended in Hong Kong and to have invited six of them to my last birthday party, when I became four.

"You see, the kids from the village and the farms didn't like to play with me because I was a landlord's son. They thought I was not one of them," Papa explained, looking at me with arched eyebrows, the way he sometimes looked when he conversed with adults, which made me feel important. "But Ah Chu lived with us because his father and mother worked in our house. He was two years older than I, like a big brother to me."

Ah Chu. What a name! It sounded like someone sneezing, but even worse, in Chinese, the sound *Chu* designates the word for "pig." Immediately I conjured in my mind the picture of a fat boy with a snout for a nose.

"Was Ah Chu your *best* friend?" I had lots of best friends.

Papa stroked the back of my head and smoothed my two pigtails that Mummy braided every morning.

"Yes, he was my best friend," he answered after a moment. "Let me show you a picture of me and Ah Chu."

He took from his room an old red photo album. He turned to a picture of two young men in front of a pair of Chinese lanterns and strings of firecrackers hanging from a store. I recognized

Papa as one of them, although he was a much younger version of himself – same gentle smile, same bushy eyebrows, same kind eyes looking at me. The other young man was taller and thinner, with a wisp of hair covering one eye and a lot of teeth showing as he smiled into the camera, not in the least like the porky image I had of Ah Chu.

"Where's Ah Chu now?"

"He's in China. I have not heard from him for a long time."

"Why have you not heard from him for a long time?"

"It's a long story, Serena. I will tell you some day, when you are older," Papa replied in a particularly gentle voice, but I guessed he did not want to talk anymore about Ah Chu. I was silent for a short while, but soon came up with another question.

"Papa, what is a landlord?"

"A landlord is someone who owns land." Papa was always patient with me. "When I was young, there were many landlords in China. They rented out their land to farmers. Some of them were very mean to the farmers, but my father — your *Yeh Yeh* — was a good and kind landlord."

"Is *Yeh Yeh* still in China?"

"Yes."

"Will you take me to visit him some day?"

"Some day," promised Papa, nodding slowly and putting a hand on my shoulder. "And some day, Serena, I'll give you a very special story about China."

Papa's story, written in his firm-handed style of calligraphy with a Chinese brush and ink on rice paper and bound between red hard covers with a gold trim, my greatest treasure. I have kept it for years in my nightstand drawer. He wrote it for me. I love it not only for what it tells, but also for its style of writing. I have sometimes thought that, under different circumstances, Papa could have been a professional writer. Indeed, he had, on more than one occasion, expressed his dream of writing. I have read his story many times, but not for a while. I will read it again. Tonight. I turn off the television. I retrieve Papa's book from the nightstand, make myself comfortable on the bed, sitting against two propped-up pillows, and turn to the first page. The columns of characters seem to step out to me with a life of their own, graceful dancers clad in black, with long and willowy arms, their expressive movements conveying meaning and telling a story.

2

A Chinese Story

For My Daughter

Hong Kong, July 5th, 1960

My beloved daughter, on this auspicious day of your birth, I pick up my brush and begin my story for you. It will be my gift to you, to keep and treasure, and to pass on to later generations. I want you to know and remember the past, that you may understand the present, and build the future. I will simply call my story *A Chinese Story*.

3

A Chinese Story

The Year of the Dog 1934

WEEKS BEFORE THE FIRST day of the first moon, the whole household was busy with preparations for the celebration of the most important event of the lunar calendar. I suppose it was the same preparations, the same excitement every year, but that was the first New Year I remember, the Year of the Dog. I was five.

"Why are the *mui tsai* sweeping all the floors in the house this morning?" I asked Ming Suk, our manservant, as we walked through the moon gate in the inner courtyard.

"Because we need to clean up the house to welcome the New Year, Young Master," Ming Suk replied, smoke puffing from his lips as he spoke, for it was a very cold morning. "Besides, no one sweeps the floor during the first moon of the year."

"Why?"

"Because we may sweep away the prosperity and the good fortune as well."

I followed Ming Suk into the big kitchen to watch Ah Fong prepare the New Year food. Ah Fong was our servant. Her position was unlike that of the *mui tsai*, for we did not buy her; we paid her. She supervised the *mui tsai* my father bought from poor families in nearby villages. My father said this way he could aid the poor and have more household help. Indeed, owning *mui tsai* seemed to be the correct thing to do. As I grew older, I would become aware that it might not have been right to buy and own people, but, by then, the times had changed, and *mui tsai* were no longer a part of our lives.

My mother had her own *mui tsai*. She had to be waited on because of her frail health and her once-bound feet, the "three-inch golden lilies." Her feet had been bound at the tender age of three.

"With your small feet, you will marry well, for no rich respectable family wants a daughter-in-law with big feet," her mother had said.

My mother told me that every night she cried in excruciating pain when her old servant unwound the binding cloth to wash her feet and afterwards bound them again, tightening the cloth as she wound it around each bruised and sore foot, in the same manner Ah Fong tied rice cakes wrapped in lotus leaves with strong reeds. Over time, the bones of her feet became twisted and their growth stunted. She could hardly stand. She tottered whenever she took a step. Then, one day, when she was about the age of six, her feet were unbound never to be bound again.

"Big feet are not so bad after all," her mother said. "Nowadays, good families will take girls with unbound feet for their sons." But the damage had been done, and, even though her feet had grown since their unbinding, they had a distorted shape, and she walked with a weak and uneasy step.

At eighteen, my mother married my father, who was looking for someone to fill his empty chamber after his first wife died. She wanted to bear my father a son, and her wish was fulfilled when I was born. My mother had a hard time carrying me, and she remained in poor health after my birth.

Every morning, I went into my mother's quarters to pay my respects. I enjoyed talking to my mother while I watched her comb her shoulder-length hair into a bun which she neatly secured in place at the back with long pins and a hair net, a daily chore she could perform with her eyes closed. Secretly, I preferred her with long hair, for it made her look younger and prettier, but she said it was only proper for married women to wear their hair up in a bun. She had a sweet and gentle voice, which I was sure she could not raise even if she tried. Indeed, I had never in my recollection heard her scold. In spite of her wealthy family background and her marriage to a rich landlord, she was never rude to the servants and *mui tsai*. Every year, she let them go home to their families for a few days and gave them red packets of lucky money on their birthdays. Very few mistresses were as kind in those days. And she was very proud of me.

"You will succeed in everything you do, Tak Sing," she said. "I pray every day for you. The Lord Buddha is looking after you."

My mother prayed all the time. Every day, she walked and sat in the garden of the inner court of our big house, with Buddhist beads in hand. And on the first and the fifteenth day of every moon, she went to the village temple in her sedan chair, to pray for my father and me, she said, and for a good harvest, and to give thanks to the gods.

That morning before the New Year, as Ming Suk and I entered the kitchen after I had greeted my mother, Ah Fong and two *mui tsai* were grating long white turnips, chopping preserved meats, and kneading dough for dumplings. I sat down on a small stool out of everybody's way. Several wood stoves were lit. Basins of turnip cake mixture were lowered into cauldrons of boiling water for steaming, and so were the seven-layered sweet rice cakes, decorated on top with red dates and sesame seeds. Of all the New Year food, I liked especially the deep-fried dumplings filled with sweet red bean paste. I watched Ah Fong's fat but nimble fingers kneading the dough made from glutinous rice flour, forming it into boat-shaped hollows, filling each with a spoonful of the red bean paste before pinching it shut in a wavy edge. A few, she made into funny shapes, like round balls each with a little spout. I did not know at the time they were intended to bear a resemblance to the male organ.

"What is that funny shape?" I asked her.

With a smile of one who knew but would not tell, she said, "That is for good fortune, that the family may have many sons."

And I felt proud, because I was a son.

Ming Suk's son, Ah Chu, came into the kitchen, pulled up

another small stool and sat down beside me. Ah Chu lived with his parents in a small white stone house within our family compound. He was two years older than I, and, for a long time, I only reached to the top of his ears. I have always remembered him as a tall, thin boy, with a whiff of hair in front almost covering his eyes, which he kept brushing off his forehead. He had a bony face, narrow but alert eyes, and a slight overbite which, instead of making him look ugly, made him seem wise. I looked up to him as to a big brother, and he was my constant playmate in those early years.

Ming Suk was very strict with Ah Chu, and there was not one day I could remember when he had not reprimanded him for one reason or another.

"Stop sniffling. It is bad manners," Ming Suk would say.

"Don't run with the Young Master. He may trip and fall."

"Clean out your bowl, Ah Chu. If you leave rice in your bowl, you'll marry a pockmarked woman!"

"Yes, Pa," Ah Chu would answer every time in a respectful manner and immediately obey, although he never seemed to remember his father's words for long.

I had never considered Ah Chu's name as a real name, like mine, but for a long time that was the only name he had. When he was born, Ming Suk and his wife, Ming Sum, decided to name him Ah Chu, meaning "the pig". This way the gods would not be jealous of him, thinking he was a pig, and would not harm him, for, in spite of their supernatural power, the gods were simple-minded and believed easily what they heard.

"*Siu Siu*, I have a secret to tell you," Ah Chu said as soon as he sat down, addressing me as the young son of the master, for he was taught not to call me by name even though we were friends. "I heard Pa tell Ma this morning he had permission to take you to the village with us on New Year's Day to watch the lion dance."

I was very excited about finally going to the village with Ah Chu, especially on New Year's Day, but I was worried about the lion. I only hoped it would be a lion from the south, a kind and

11

happy one which, according to the tale Ming Suk told, swallowed all the flood water of the southern provinces and thus saved many from drowning and famine. In any case, if it was a dancing lion, it could not be ferocious.

Just then, Ah Fong came over with two freshly fried boat-shaped dumplings filled with red bean paste for us. Ah Chu took his eagerly and finished it in no time. I considered mine, and hesitated.

"Ah Fong, may I have one of those sons instead?"

Ah Fong looked at me strangely for a moment, then, with a smile of recollection, said, "Young Master, we need to save those for the New Year, for good luck."

The sounds and smell of firecrackers filled the air as we approached the village. We had started out soon after the midday New Year meal of preserved pork and liver sausage, preserved duck, and a vegetarian dish. Ah Chu and I both ate more than we should have had, especially Ah Chu. With our full bellies, we were glad for the long walk along footpaths cutting through paddy fields before reaching the village gate. The fields were empty; not even the water buffalo were out. The farmers were all celebrating the Year of the Dog in the village or in their houses on the edge of the fields, red paper posted on their doors to welcome the new spring and good fortune. I had on a new blue *cheongsam* and matching *makwa*, a blue ceremonial cap, and new black felt shoes. Ah Chu wore a new padded short jacket his mother had made, and pants lengthened from the year before, but they looked good because he had only worn them on important occasions.

We passed through the village gate and found ourselves on a busy street, treading on ground covered with red confetti blown off the lit firecrackers. Even the water in the gutters was red as blood. We inched along the crowded main street. It was lined with shops all decorated with red lanterns and red paper posters with words of good fortune on them. I was especially attracted to a toy stall displaying dragon masks, swords and daggers. We held on to Ming Suk's hands, except when he stopped at food stands to buy us each a big sesame seed ball filled with ground peanut and sugar, and thick molasses on a stick. The cold air hardened the molasses, keeping it from running down the stick onto my hand, and making it last longer.

"Ming Suk, *Kung Hay Fat Choy*. I see you have brought the Young Master along," a short, fat woman in a bright red jacket with a mandarin collar called out from behind.

"*Kung Hay Fat Choy*, Cheng Sum. The Old Master has asked me to take the Young Master to see the lion dance."

"I'd say this is all an eye-opener for the Young Master," Cheng Sum said, looking at Ah Chu and me busily licking the molasses, and waving her hand as she talked, as though there were some invisible flies in front of her. "Your son is so lucky to be a play companion to the Young Master."

"The Old Master teaches his son well. The Young Master is not spoiled like some of the other landlords' brats. He and Ah Chu play well together," Ming Suk said, nodding at us.

The sounds of drums, cymbals and gongs rose above the noise of firecrackers and the crowd, and soon I was staring at the gigantic head of a lion, with huge bulging eyeballs rolling around and around in their sockets, long brush-like eyelashes attached to eyelids flapping up and down, and a mouth so big it could easily engulf a man's head. With quick movements, it twisted and turned, its bright red and yellow satin body trying to follow its head which kept changing direction every moment. As it moved to the right and left, the head bobbed up and down, following a dancer in front, whose mask was an enormous round painted face of a laughing boy. The masked dancer finally stopped in front of a wine shop. The shopkeeper lit a string of firecrackers hanging from the doorframe, just as the lion approached.

"That is to chase off evil and welcome the new spring," explained Ming Suk.

From the eaves of the store high above the front door was hung a head of green lettuce topped with a small red packet, like those containing money my father and mother passed out every New Year's Day. The beating of the drums became louder and faster, and I could feel the thump in my heart vibrating to the pounding of the drums. How could the lion eat the lettuce and get the red packet? Unless it could stretch. Then, as if in answer to my thoughts, the lion's body grew longer, as an acrobat came out from the crowd and disappeared under the bright red and yellow satin covering it. The lion reached up to the lettuce. The lettuce was eaten, its leaves shredded and scattered on the ground in front of the shop, and the red packet torn from the hanging string and held in the lion's mouth before it disappeared within. The lion then followed the masked dancer again, and the crowd cheered and followed to the sounds of drums, cymbals and gongs, until it stopped in front of the herbalist's shop. I looked up and saw hanging from the eaves green lettuce topped with a red packet.

"Wherever it stops, the lion will bring good fortune to the place," said Ming Suk.

Both Ah Chu and I were dead tired by the time we passed through the village gate to walk the good distance home. Our steps were becoming slower and heavier. After a short while, Ming Suk bent down, told me to climb on his back and gave me a piggyback ride the rest of the way home, while Ah Chu quietly dragged his feet beside his pa, till we reached the big house.

4

A Chinese Story

Before the Storm

LONG BEFORE I WENT for the first time to the temple beyond the west end of our village, I had heard of the monster statues inside, with eyes that followed you no matter where you stood. I was full of dread at the thought of seeing them.

"Why do I have to go to the temple, Mother?" I asked, not long after my outing to Ka Hing on New Year's Day.

"I think it is time I take you there to present you to the gods, Tak Sing, for they have given you to me, and you are the biggest reason for my gratitude to them," my mother answered. "They may be offended if I don't take you to the temple soon."

Adults knew best, and they decided everything. Besides, I did not want to make my mother unhappy, so I asked no more. I felt better when my mother later told me Ah Chu would be going with us.

We went in two sedan chairs, my mother's in front, each lifted by two coolies. Ah Fong and a *mui tsai* walked beside my mother's chair, while Ah Chu walked alongside mine. Ah Chu's presence somewhat eased my mind about coming face to face with the monster statues; there were two of us they had to contend with. As we went past our village and up a small hill to the temple, I peeked out from behind the curtains of my chair at Ah Chu. Soon, we were signing to each other and laughing very hard, watching Ah Fong from behind as she walked with difficulty up the hill, swaying a little to the right and a little to the left, for she was a fat woman. She and the *mui tsai* had big feet, and they could walk a long way. How I wished I could jump out and join Ah Chu on the ground, but I knew my place was inside the sedan chair.

The Four Heavenly Kings were gigantic, two on each side within the entrance hall of the temple, guarding the temple and all it contained. Dressed in ancient armour of war, they had snarling teeth and big bulging eyes, and held weapons and beasts that could kill. Ah Chu came up and we stood in silence for a long while, in the centre of the entrance hall, as though a slight movement or noise from us would rouse the Four Heavenly Kings and spur them to action. I was very thankful when I heard my mother calling my name.

Ah Chu and I joined my mother in the courtyard outside the entrance hall, and we entered the incense-filled main temple. I gazed on a tall goddess sitting with bare feet, crossed and upturned, on a golden lotus in the central shrine, and with a gold crown on her head. She seemed to be looking with downcast eyes at her own hands held together in a praying position. Her fingers, from which hung a string of gold beads, were long and graceful. Her small red lips wore a gentle smile, and her face was peaceful and kind. In spite of her height, almost to the ceiling, I was not afraid of her.

"Who is she, Mother?" I asked in a whisper.

"She is *Kuan Yin*, the Goddess of Mercy," my mother replied in her normal voice, as she planted lighted joss sticks in the huge urn at the base of the altar. "Before you were born, I prayed to *Kuan Yin* for a son, and she granted my wish. I am very grateful to her."

"She is so beautiful," mumbled Ah Chu, not taking his eyes off the goddess' face.

"There is a story about her. I'll tell you boys some day," my mother said.

"Tell it now!" we both begged.

My mother soon sat down on a bench against a wall of the main hall, beneath pictures of the eighteen *Lohan* gods as she called them, and told us the legend of *Kuan Yin*.

16

"In one of her mortal lives, *Kuan Yin* was a beautiful maiden. She was also kind and good and everyone loved her. One day, her parents told her they had betrothed her to the son of a neighbouring family. Now, she did not like this boy. She begged her parents to free her from the promise of marriage to him, but her parents would not listen to her plea. In the end, before her wedding day, she jumped into a pool and drowned herself. Soon after, a beautiful white lotus flower emerged from the pool and floated on the water."

"That's why she is sitting on a lotus flower," I concluded, glancing up at the big statue.

"The parents were so cruel to force her to marry," Ah Chu said, knitting his brows and looking very serious. "They were the ones who killed *Kuan Yin*. When I grow up, I will never make my daughter marry someone she doesn't like."

"Come now, I'll buy you boys each a joss stick to light for *Kuan Yin*," my mother said. "Pray to *Kuan Yin*, that she may help you grow up to be tall and strong."

Ah Chu and I soon bade our silent farewell to the fair goddess, went through the entrance hall where the Four Heavenly Kings stood guard, and, without daring to look at them again, made our exit from the temple to where the coolies were waiting with the sedan chairs in the shade of a tree. My mother and I sat in our chairs and were hoisted up again to start our journey home. I looked out at Ah Chu walking beside my chair.

"I need to *siu bin*!" I called to the coolies carrying my chair. "I can't wait till we reach home!"

"I'll tell them in front to go on first," said one of the coolies.

My chair was soon lowered, and I got out. I ran over to a clump of bushes to relieve myself. Ah Chu made use of our sudden stop to do the same. We soon felt a lot better and laughed the rest of the way home, squeezed into the seat of my sedan chair.

My father, Lee Wing, was a good landlord. Our family had owned five thousand *mou* of land outside the village of Ka Hing in Guangdong for over a century. In his youth, Lee Wing had worked on his own land. He had sweated and laboured alongside his hired hands, and realized their hardships and appreciated their toil. He built the big house after his first marriage, moved in there with his wife, and left all his land to tenant farmers to plough. He had a son by his first wife, but the boy, who would be my half-brother, died of complications from a fever at the age of ten. My father and his first wife took the death of their son very hard. A year later, his first wife died, whether from a broken heart or some illness I did not know. Two years after the death of his first wife, my father married my mother.

In times of plenty, my father received as many as five thousand *dan* of rice a year from his tenants, plus other cash crops. But in lean years, he expected them to pay only whatever they could, no more and no less. For this reason, they loved him, especially since other tenant farmers were forced to sell their sons as labourers and daughters as *mui tsai* to pay their debts after bad harvests.

From the time I was four, my father hired a tutor, Fu Tze, to teach me to read and write. On my first day of school, I remember kneeling in front of a picture of Confucius and repeating after Fu Tze verses from *The Book of Three Characters*. Later, I had to recite Confucian ethics from *The Four Books* and *The Five Classics*. I did not mind the studies. Perhaps some day I could be a scholar too, and I would write things for people to read.

"Your knowledge is my best legacy to you, son," my father often said. "Gold and silver, and even the land, others can take away, but no one can take from you what you have stored in your mind."

My days until the age of eight were divided between my lessons and roaming the grounds of the big house and beyond, in the fields my father owned. And on my wandering, Ah Chu went along as my companion and bodyguard. Often we stopped at farmers' houses, where the farmers' wives would give us a flour cake or a sweet potato baked in a stone oven. Sometimes we listened to gossip of matchmakers' successes and failures, and occasionally idle talk among the farmers about the Communists who had made their homes in the caves in Yan'an. And always there were worries among the villagers of a full-scale invasion by Japanese troops already present in Manchuria and northeastern China. However, both the Communists and Japanese seemed very remote to me. They could not possibly invade my world, where I lived protected by my father and surrounded by everyone and everything dear to me.

Nestled in my father's land was a lotus pond shaded by a huge willow tree. Ah Chu and I went there often to catch the frogs that lived among the lotus pads. We took along a woven reed basket and a big net. We gave the big frogs we caught to Ah Fong who cooked them with rice, which made a delicious meal. We kept a few of the smaller ones in a tank. Every day, we hunted for food for them: crickets by day, fireflies by night. Ah Chu was very skillful at catching fireflies with a swoop of his bare hand. Since fireflies still glow for a flicker of a moment after they are swallowed, we loved watching the frog light up in the dark for a second after it had eaten a firefly, like a house aglow with a lamp inside.

One early autumn afternoon, when Ah Chu and I were walking home along a dirt path after catching crickets in a field, I tripped upon a rock and fell. The glass jar holding the crickets hit the ground and broke. The crickets escaped and the frogs lost their supper. Then Ah Chu cut his thumb on a piece of the broken glass and it started to bleed.

"Ah Chu, I have a grand idea," I said, looking at the blood oozing from his cut. "Since you've cut your thumb, if I draw some blood from mine, we can pledge to become blood brothers!" I was thinking of stories Fu Tze, my tutor, had told me of friends becoming brothers by mixing blood.

"That's great!" said Ah Chu, all excited.

"According to Fu Tze, some blood brothers slash their own hands and let their blood drip into a bowl. The blood is mixed, and they take turns drinking it."

"Let's just join our bleeding thumbs and skip the drinking," Ah Chu said.

"Yes, our pledge should still hold." I nodded, sounding authoritative, for I wasn't too keen on drinking blood either.

The excitement over the idea marred my fear of the pain I might feel. Carefully, I picked up a piece of sharp glass and, without a second thought, jabbed my thumb with it. A little blood spurted out. No pain after the first hurt. We crossed our bleeding thumbs. Recalling the pledge of blood brothers in a story Fu Tze had told me, I asked Ah Chu to repeat after me:

"We, Lee Tak Sing and So Ah Chu, swear to the heavens that, from this moment on, we are sworn brothers. We will never forsake or betray each other. We were not born in the same year, the same month, on the same day, but we wish to die in the same year, the same month, on the same day."

I was seven and Ah Chu nine.

New Year's Day, the Year of the Ox, 1937, we did not go to Ka Hing to watch the lion dance. The festive mood of previous years was gone. There was less New Year food to eat, although we still had preserved pork sausage and the traditional vegetarian dish. That winter, I did not have a new padded jacket. Everyone was concerned about the drought in the northern provinces, followed by famine.

"There is so little food up north, people are eating tree bark," my father told us. "We should be thankful we still have rice for every meal and meat for the table to celebrate the New Year. But let us be frugal, for we never know when such misfortune from the heavens may befall Guangdong."

That winter was a very cold and damp one. I remember my mother becoming sick not long after the New Year. Her cough stayed with her for so long that, for a while, I was told not to visit her in her chamber in the morning, for fear I might become sick too. With the Ching Ming Festival, the warmer weather finally brought my mother's recovery. I remember going with my father and mother in sedan chairs to the family burial ground to pay respects to our ancestors. The *mui tsai* took along food for the ancestors, a piece of roast pork and a few mandarin oranges, and joss sticks to burn at the graves. What I liked best was that we took the food home to eat afterwards. I remember helping Ah Fong and the *mui tsai* fold gold and silver paper money for the dead the night before Ching Ming. I was fascinated with the paper houses and paper boats, paper hats and paper shoes. How these items could reach the dead when they were all to be burned to ashes was a mystery to me. There were many things I did not understand and the adults could not explain to my satisfaction.

The summer and autumn of 1937 brought more disturbing news from the north, of Nationalist forces battling Japanese troops around Beijing and Shanghai and losing ground in northern and central China. By the end of July, the Japanese had controlled Tianjin and Beijing, and, by late autumn, Shanghai. Even though the fighting seemed far away, our villagers were worried that the Japanese would sooner or later attack Guangdong.

"What will happen to us if the Japanese come?" my mother asked my father.

"We won't wait till they come. If I see any real danger, I'll take you and Tak Sing to a safer place. There's no need for you to worry, Wei Fan."

On the thirteenth day of December, Japanese troops entered Nanjing.

5

Bo Bo

I LOOK UP FROM Papa's book as Ah Lan peeks in.

"*Aaya!* Seenla, one in the morning and still reading?" Ah Lan asks in a raspy voice, her eyes squinting from the glare of my lamp. She usually gets up a couple of times in the night.

"I'm not sleepy. I want to read tonight."

"Don't stay up too late."

"I'll be okay. Tomorrow's Sunday."

The old *amah* closes my bedroom door, mumbling to herself. Good old Ah Lan. She has been a mother and grandmother to me for as long as I can remember. I love her almost as much as I loved my mother. Sound of shuffling, another door closing, then quiet again, except for the constant humming and occasional snorting of the refrigerator in the sitting-dining room, and the continuous hiss of rain beating against the windowpanes.

I stretch. Something falls out from between the pages of Papa's book – several loose sheets of notebook paper. They are covered with Chinese handwriting I know to be my own, nothing like Papa's refined calligraphy. They contain stories Ah Lan told me in my early years of high school, about her life, and more importantly my mother's as a young child. I was going through a "writer phase" at the time and recorded everything Ah Lan said. Looking back now, I see the seed of trouble planted in Mummy's young life, sheltered but for the war. Ah Lan narrates in these pages, although a lot of her Cantonese colloquialisms are lost in my paraphrase. I pick up the sheets, arrange them in order as numbered. For years, I had kept them in my private drawer, but

ever since Papa gave me his book after Mummy died, I have kept
these sheets with it. Papa's book is the common ground where
our souls meet. Mummy never left me anything as tangible.
Unlike Papa, Mummy rarely talked about her youth. The stories
I recorded on these loose pages are the only window to my
mother's childhood. As I set them in a pile beside me on the bed,
my eyes are compulsively drawn to the first sheet.

*At eighteen, in 1933, I left Guangzhou for Hong Kong to find work.
I was the oldest of eight. My father was a coolie at a riverfront godown
in Guangzhou, and my mother was a seamstress. We were very poor. I
had heard about rich people in Hong Kong hiring servants from China.
With free meals and lodging, I would be able to send most of my monthly
wages home t:o help my folks. Sure enough, after three days in Hong
Kong, I was hired by the Poon family. My job was to be a baby's amah,
my charge, a month-old baby girl.*

*My master, Poon Kwok Wing, was a successful doctor. The other
servants said he had studied in England. They said his grandfather,
Poon Ka Lung, was a favourite minister of the Empress Dowager,
Cixi, and had been an ambassador to France and Russia. My mistress,
Rosie Kwan, was the daughter of a shipping tycoon. I heard all about
their courtship and wedding from the other servants. The Mistress was
introduced to the Master at a party. He courted her with a lot of gifts,
and on New Year's Eve, 1931, he gave her a three-carat diamond ring.
Believe me, that rock sparkled like a tiger's eye at night. As the saying
goes, their doors and numbers matched, for both came from rich families.
Their wedding in 1932 at the Peninsula Hotel was attended by many
Hong Kong big shots. After the wedding, the Mistress became a lady
of leisure, entertaining and attending parties with her husband, and
playing mahjong.*

*Your Mummy was born under a lucky star. They named her Kit Lin.
They also gave her the English name Lily. To me, she was always Siu
Cheh. From the time she was a month old, I took care of her. I bathed her,
changed her, washed her clothes and diapers, rocked her to sleep. I got up*

in the night to give her a bottle. When she first started to eat solid food, I prepared a mashed mixture of soft rice and ground meat for her every day.

Even though they were busy people, your Kung Kung and Poh Poh spent as much time as they could with their daughter. Every Sunday afternoon, from the age of two, your Mummy went with your Kung Kung and Poh Poh to the Botanic Gardens. Your Kung Kung would put her on his shoulder, where she sat like a princess, as they walked home from the park.

Siu Cheh was a lovable little girl, with large round eyes, dimpled cheeks, thick long hair combed into two doggy ears tied with bows. Your Poh Poh dressed her in the smartest samfu of silk and satin. Pink was Siu Cheh's favourite colour. She was beautiful, and, most important, she had a kind heart.

Your Kung Kung called her his "bo bo". When he came home in the evening, he always spent time with her.

"I saw the beggar again today, the one with one eye and holes all over his shirt," she told him one time.

"Oh yes, and did you give him some money?" Your Mummy shook her head, and your Kung Kung then said, "Ask Ah Lan for ten cents to put in his cup next time. We should help the poor, for we are luckier than they."

"Daddy, why don't we share everything with them?" Your Mummy looked seriously at her father.

The Master just smiled and did not answer.

My mother must have had a charmed existence as a child, doted on by her father and mother. There was however not a single photo of my maternal grandparents at home. And I had never met them.

"I lost touch with your *Kung Kung* and *Poh Poh* before you were born. It was very unfortunate," Mummy would say every time I asked about them when I was growing up.

"Do you miss your father and mother?"

"Yes, I miss them very much."

6

A Chinese Story

Flight

GUANGZHOU FELL IN OCTOBER, 1938. The adults in the big house, on the farms, and in Ka Hing were worried that the Japanese would advance westward toward Zhaoqing, only sixty *li* east of us. Everywhere Ah Chu and I went, we heard news of Japanese atrocities, tales of tortures and killings. While the fighting might still seem distant, we were feeling the pangs of war in the shortage of food all around, and the fear that the Japanese would sooner or later come to our village.

My father summoned me into the main parlour of the big house one day in the spring of the following year. My mother was sitting mutely in a high-backed ebony chair beside my father, wringing a handkerchief in her hands.

"Tak Sing, I have made a decision," he said in a slow heavy voice. "We are going to leave our home for a short time, and travel to northwest Guangdong. There, we will be safe from the Japanese."

"But what about all our things here, Father?"

"We will place our house, land, everything we have here in the protection of the gods. The thirteenth day of the third moon is the earliest auspicious day for traveling. We will leave on that day. We will only take our essential belongings."

Every word added weight to my spirit. The reality of the situation suddenly gripped me, and I feared for the first time my world was crumbling. I glanced at my mother who had started to cry.

"Will we go in sedan chairs, Father?"

"There will be no sedan chairs, son. In this time of unrest, everyone must look after himself. We cannot ask to be served. Ming Suk and Ming Sum are coming with us, but I have released the *mui tsai* and told them to return to their families. Ah Fong, too, will not be coming with us. This way we have fewer mouths to feed," my father said, looking older and more tired than I had ever seen him.

My only consolation was Ah Chu would be accompanying his pa and ma. We would journey about sixty *li* to the border between Guangdong and Guangxi not far from Wuzhou. From there, we would continue north in Guangdong for another hundred *li*, to the remote village of Tai Shek, near the junction of the three provinces Guangdong, Guangxi and Hunan. An uncle of my father lived there, and he would give us shelter. To reach our destination, we would cut through mostly rural country, crossing rivers and paddy fields.

The preparation to leave was as emotional as the departure itself. Most of the things my father and mother held dear had to be left behind: the fine china from Emperor Kangxi's time, the porcelain vases painted with designs of peonies and beautiful ladies of the court, black lacquered screens studded with jade, coral and mother of pearl, and scrolls of brush paintings done by famous old masters.

"The gods will look after the house and all the things in it, Wei Fan," my father consoled my mother, who was reluctant to part with anything, including clothes I had outgrown. "If we are fortunate, the Japanese may pass us by and leave the house and the land unspoiled. For now, we must think of our safety. Think of Tak Sing."

The first stage of the journey, my father had arranged for a lorry transporting some goods to Wuzhou to take us west as far as the border with Guangxi. There, my father would look for further arrangements to continue north. As the lorry carrying us exited through the main gate of the compound, I cast a last longing look at the house and its surroundings, and said a silent farewell to the place where I was born. The house now looked strange and mysterious, with its bolted red doors and closed brown shutters. I hoped the Japanese would spare our house, our land, our village, so that when the war was over we could return and go back to the life I had known. Little did I realize the day we departed for remote northwest Guangdong, I left behind my childhood, along with the house and the land.

My father sat in front with the driver of the lorry. The rest of us, including Ah Fong who was going to Wuzhou, were in the back, squeezed between big boxes. It was a bumpy ride along country roads bordered by paddy fields, and quite uncomfortable since there was little room for us, but Ming Suk said we ought to be thankful we did not have to walk.

We got off at a village called Shan Kai close to the Guangdong-Guangxi border, after saying goodbye to Ah Fong who was continuing on to Wuzhou.

"May you two grow up to be fine young men and be a joy to your parents. Ah Fong will not be around to cook and do the housework. You will have to help your parents and take care of them," Ah Fong said to me and Ah Chu. I knew I would miss the seven-layered rice cakes and dumplings with red bean filling she made for the New Year, and I touched her old puffy cheeks and wiped some tears away.

We stayed in Shan Kai for several days, hoping a lorry heading north would stop at the village. In the meantime, a group of students from Guangzhou traveling to Kunming stopped at Shan Kai for the night, and spread news the Japanese might be heading west to Liuzhou and north to Guilin. If this was true, they could be passing very close to Shan Kai. The students reported seeing farmers flee from their farms just west of Guangzhou. They had witnessed bridges burnt down by local villagers so that the enemy troops could not cross. They had seen fields of sprouting crops set to flames by farmers before they left, so that, when the enemy troops arrived, all they could find would be a barren charred land.

"We will leave here before the Japanese arrive," my father said firmly. "We will not waste another day. We will walk north, to Tai Shek."

The next morning, we started out. We each had a sack of rice tied to the back, except for my mother, because of her frailty and her weak step, and Ming Suk, because he carried my mother on his back. We trod along narrow paths between paddy fields and fish ponds, with farmhouses and hills in the distance. Trees were laden with the white blossoms of spring, and there was a sweetness in the air, mixed with the smell of turned earth and animal dung, not totally unpleasant, except when we passed vegetable plots recently fertilized with composted human excrement — and then I wished I had never been blessed with the sense of smell. We rested whenever Ming Suk had to rest, and that was not very often, as he was a big strong man, and my mother was a small frail woman weighing not more than seventy *gun*. In the evenings, we looked for villages where we could spend the night. Most of the time we had no difficulty finding some kindly farmer to give us shelter for the night. Many farmers still lived on their land, holding out as long as they could. Occasionally, we spent the night in a deserted farmhouse, where Ming Sum would cook a simple meal with rice and salt on its brick stove.

There were times when night had fallen before we found a place to sleep. Ming Suk taught Ah Chu and me a verse for walking in the dark:

> *Black is mud,*
> *White is stone,*
> *A shiny patch a puddle*
> *Reflecting the moon.*

After that, we seldom walked into mud or puddles.

One time, however, I lost my balance on a narrow path between paddies and landed ankle deep in the muddy water flooding the rice fields. My canvas shoes were soaked. For the next half *li*, I waded in the paddy field, for the mud was cool and soft. It was not until I had to walk on dry land again in my damp shoes that I felt an uncomfortable sensation in both my feet.

"Father, my feet are itching all over, and I can't wiggle my toes."

"Try to make it to those houses, Tak Sing. We can all rest, and I can look at your feet," my father said.

As soon as we reached the community of some five or six farmhouses, I sat down on a bench and took off my shoes. What I saw filled me with stiffening horror. On both feet, around and between the toes, were slimy, dark brown leeches, each about the length of my little finger.

"You picked them up when you were wading in the rice fields. They love the warmth of your feet, especially between the toes," said Ming Suk, as though it was not as big a disaster as I thought.

Ah Chu was the first to come to my rescue. He pinched one of the leeches with two fingers and pulled it away from my toe. Detaching it from my foot was not hard, but it left a thin trail of blood, my blood, where it had sucked. I was horrified.

Ming Suk took a joss stick from a tin urn by the front door of a house and one by one applied it to the leeches. Blood trickled from where the suckers had left their marks. In all, I counted fifteen leeches, eight on one foot, seven on the other.

I could not tell the number of days we traveled before we finally arrived at Tai Shek. There were others going the same direction, but they usually overtook us. I recall one fleeing family walking alongside us for some distance, the man with a bamboo pole on his shoulders, from which hung two big baskets, one at each end, the woman carrying a baby strapped to her back in a cloth carrier. The baby was crying most of the time. The man walked in front, the woman behind. Curious, I ran alongside the baskets and peered in, expecting to find clothes and pots and pans, perhaps even some precious items such as the ones we left behind in the big house. In one basket were two sacks, the larger one, the man told me, was rice, and the smaller one, salt. I looked into the other basket. To my utter surprise, I saw a little boy, much smaller than Ah Chu or I, asleep on top of some blankets. Rice and salt, and their two children, the older one too young to walk the long distance. Those were their treasures.

We crossed the Lian Jiang, rowed across by fishermen in two sampans. On this last stretch, we met Chiu Hong and his wife, both students from a university in Guangzhou on their way to Chongqing. Chiu Hong would continue his studies there. The woman was going to have a baby. Any time, she told my mother.

On the morning of the second day after we met Chiu Hong and his wife, when we were in a wild deserted field away from the paddies, Chiu's wife suddenly gave out a cry, as though she was gasping for breath. She whispered urgently to Chiu Hong, who called to Ming Sum.

"It's a sure sign the baby is coming!" cried Ming Sum excitedly. "We can't move her now. Let her lie down on the soft grass in the field. I'll put a blanket under her."

Ah Chu and I were told to sit in the shade of some trees a earshot's distance away, with my father, Ming Suk, and Chiu Hong. There we sat for a long time, while my mother and Ming Sum stayed with Chiu's wife. Not a whisp of smoke from a distant farmhouse was in sight, not a soul passing us by. Waiting seemed especially eternal when there was little to do. Ah Chu and I amused ourselves with making grasshoppers with blades of long broad grass. We watched our shadows shrinking and growing as the sun traveled across the sky. Gradually, we heard whimpers, then screams coming from Chiu's wife. We noticed the anxiety on Chiu Hong's sweat-covered face, but, no, he was told by Ming Sum that giving birth was strictly a female matter, and he must not see it.

The sun was almost on the western horizon when we

finally heard the cry of a baby, followed by Ming Sum's loud proclamation: "It's a boy!" At that, Chiu Hong could control himself no longer and hurried to where his wife was in the field. Ming Sum scampered over to us, opened one of our bags, took out a porcelain rice bowl, and ran back with it to the birth scene. I asked my father and Ming Suk what the rice bowl was for and got no answer.

The baby's birth brought everyone some joy, a feeling I had forgotten since we left home. My heart was lighter the rest of the way. That evening, we did not find a farmhouse to spend the night. Instead, we came to a deserted shed, where Chiu Hong laid down his wife whom he was carrying on his back on the earth floor, and Ming Sum laid the baby, wrapped in a small blanket, beside his mother. The women slept in the shed, while we men folk slept in the open, on the dry hard earth, wrapping ourselves in the blankets we brought with us. It was the first time we did not have a roof above our heads in the night since we left home. Ah Chu and I thought it was wonderful, sleeping under a thousand stars, a night fragrance brushing through our nostrils, the cool air filling the pores of our skin, and the sound of crickets forming rhythmic music in our ears.

The next day, we parted with the Chiu family. We continued toward Tai Shek, and they caught a lorry that would take them to Guilin and on to Chongqing. They named their son Tien Sun, meaning "born in the field."

Later, my mother explained to me and Ah Chu the rice bowl was smashed in order to use its freshly cut raw edge to sever the cord of life joining the baby to his mother, for it was sharp and uncontaminated.

7

A Chinese Story

Tai Shek

TAI SHEK WAS A SMALL TOWN with a population of about three hundred at the northwest corner of Guangdong, with Hunan to its north and Guangxi to its west. A wall surrounded the little town nestled against a hill on its north side and facing a small river, the Wen Sui, to the south. In the course of our stay there, we were to see students going by, students who had left Japanese-occupied cities to journey to the free cities of Kunming or Chongqing, some even further to Chengdu, to continue their studies in the universities there. Soldiers of the Nationalist Army passed through on their way to join up with other platoons, some hauling machinery to Chongqing where Chiang Kai-shek had fled before the fall of Nanjing.

And some stopped by on their way north to Yan'an to join the Communists.

There was not much of anything in Tai Shek, just a main street paved with slabs of cement, cracked and broken in many places, with some twenty or thirty buildings lining both sides. The buildings all had two storeys, businesses on the ground floor, homes upstairs. Two town gates marking the eastern and western ends of the main street closed at dusk, except for a small door by the side of each gate to let pedestrians through. I remember distinctly a medicine shop managed by a herbalist whom everybody consulted for all kinds of ailments, and a barber shop whose entrance was marked with an old barber's sign above the door frame, its stationary spiral red, white and blue stripes encased in a broken glass cylinder. There were a few food stores and shops selling sundry items, and a teahouse. Wild dogs roamed everywhere, sniffing for anything that could pass for food.

As we dragged our tired feet down the dust-blown street on that first afternoon of our arrival, nothing could endear me to the little community that would be our refuge as long as the war lasted. We stopped at the teahouse and my father asked for directions to Second Grand Uncle's house.

"Lee Kuan lives about three *li* east of here. Just exit through the eastern gate. Follow the footpath on the left. You'll see his house beyond the burial mound," a waiter said.

Leaving the town, we walked along the northern bank of the Wen Sui, passing a few wooden houses scattered along the edge of small paddies. We went over the burial mound, but there were no stone tablets inscribed with the names of the dead. It was only a small low hill covered with dirt and grass, and yellow wildflowers here and there. Walking over what were probably the decayed flesh and broken bones of the unknown dead gave me an uncomfortable feeling.

About two *li* beyond the mound was a small one-storey house of white stones, no bigger than the one Ming Suk and his family occupied in our family compound. Around the house were plots of vegetables and corn. Some chickens were pecking grains from the dirt. On one side of the house was a wooden canopy from which were hung strips of red meat. Here, finally, was the home of Second Grand Uncle.

Second Grand Uncle was very surprised but pleased to see us. He had told my father he would have a place for us if the Japanese came, but we had arrived ahead of the letter my father sent him. Since Second Grand Aunt died some years earlier, he had lived alone. He had been to our house once when I was younger, for I remembered the red packet he gave me even though it was not the New Year. My mother explained later that, because it was the first time he saw me, the red packet was for good fortune. This time, his gift was shelter from the war.

The shelter was not much, but my father said we should

be very grateful we had a roof over our heads in an area the Japanese would most likely leave untouched, for Tai Shek and its surrounding country were not close to a major town or railway line and had not much cultivation except what the locals grew to feed themselves. There was nothing for Japanese troops to pillage, nothing for them to live on.

Our house was about a half *li* further on from Second Grand Uncle's house, and a little brook ran between the two. It was built of wood, square in shape, about forty *cheg* on each side. There were two storeys, if one could call the attic a storey. Ah Chu and I wasted no time in climbing up the stepladder to the opening in the ceiling of the lower floor, and soon found ourselves on the upper level which was divided into two rooms with a wood screen and no door. There were no windows on the upper level, but air and a little light passed through the chinks where the slanted roof met the external walls.

Below, there was only one open space. A long wooden table and four high-backed wooden chairs were in the room. Two oil lamps sat on the table. There were four windows, one on each side of the house, without glass panes, just wooden shutters hinged at the top of the window frames that opened out from the base. A spittoon was in a corner of the earth floor, and, in another corner, a charcoal burner like the ones we used back home in the winter. Cooking was to be done outside the house, under a canvas canopy extending from the side.

I whispered to Ming Suk that I had an urgent need to *siu bin*.

"Come, I'll take you to the outhouse by the common field," said Second Grand Uncle, reading my body language. He led me across the yard at the back of the house to a small shed at the edge of an uncultivated field. It was our house toilet as well as a public latrine for passersby. The shed was made of wooden boards on all sides and thatched with straw mats on the top. The smell was even more potent than the newly fertilized vegetable plots we passed in the country. I pushed open the latchless hinged door and could just make out a big hole in the ground, framed with wooden boards. Flies hovered all around inside the shed. Pursing my lips and trying hard not to breathe, I stood on the boards and urinated into the opening in the centre. I could hear no sprinkling, just the thud of liquid splattering on soft earth. In the dwindling daylight, and especially in the dark shelter, I could not see to the bottom of the hole. It was just as well, for what I would see there in the days ahead were human faeces infested with thousands of squirming white maggots.

At first, we all slept upstairs. My parents and I occupied one room, and Ming Suk, Ming Sum and Ah Chu took the other. There were no beds; we lined the floor with reed mats. It was spring going into summer when we first arrived, and we did not need blankets at night. But we needed a chamber pot, one in each room, for it was very trying, especially for my mother, to climb down the ladder in the night. It was easy passing empty chamber pots up the ladder every evening, but the task of reversing the route with filled chamber pots in the morning was a challenge. Every morning, Ming Suk would take them to the outhouse to empty and rinse at the brook. The sleeping arrangement upstairs was far from ideal. It was too crowded and overly stuffy. After a few days, Ah Chu and I moved downstairs and slept on wooden beds which doubled up as benches during the day.

On the flight to Tai Shek, my father, Ah Chu and I had been scratching, but it was not until we had settled in our new place that I discovered little white insects lodging in the folds of my elastic waistband.

"Body lice all right," said Ming Suk. "They are white. Harder to find. You must have picked them up from the farmhouses."

Somehow, Ming Suk seemed to have profound knowledge of the unwelcome creatures that had tormented me since we left home. First leeches, and now body lice. At least, this time, I had companions in my misery. Our infested clothing was boiled in a big cauldron of water. After we had given ourselves a thorough scrub in hot water, Ming Sum gave us some ointment she had brought with her from Ka Hing to soothe the skin bitten by the lice. One consolation was we had no head lice, so we did not have to suffer the humiliation of being shaved on that account.

Our first trip back to the town of Tai Shek was just the day after we arrived at our new home. I went with my father, Ming Suk and Ah Chu to purchase food and other necessities.

Just inside the east town gate, a wild dog was engaged in a losing battle against three other dogs trying to seize its hollow old bone. I picked up a stick and threatened the attackers, and they backed off one by one, leaving the defender alone.

"Young Master, don't go near those wild dogs. They may bite! And they may have rabies!" Ming Suk called.

Next to the teahouse was a food store. I pointed in shock to what looked like huge rats, dried, preserved, and smelling like the ducks we had back home at New Year's time.

"Yes, they are rats. They are good to eat and nutritious," said Ming Suk. I winced. "They are caught in the paddies. They can be eaten because they feed on rice, not on rubbish."

"No, thank you."

To my dismay, my father added a couple of the rats to our purchases. We picked up some fatty pork which Ming Sum would fry at low heat in a wok to extract lard for cooking. The chewy fried pork drained of the fat would be used later for a stew with vegetables. We got some salted eggs and some fresh duck eggs – a better value than hen eggs because of their size – and oil for the lamps in the house.

That night after our trip to the town, my father, mother and I went over to Second Grand Uncle's for dinner. To welcome us to Tai Shek, Second Grand Uncle cooked us a delicious meal of stewed chicken, preserved pork, steamed beaten egg, and fried white cabbage. I had not eaten so well since we left home. I thought of Ah Chu who was having a simple supper of rice and green vegetables with Ming Suk and Ming Sum, and wished he were there to share my food, but servants were never invited along with their masters to dinner. Apart from occasions when my father took us to teahouses in Ka Hing, and our eating together out of necessity on the flight to Tai Shek, Ah Chu and I never shared a meal. Back home, he ate with his parents and the other servants in the kitchen, after my parents and I had eaten. Since there was only one room on the ground floor of our house near Tai Shek, Ming Suk, Ming Sum and Ah Chu ate after us at the same table. I had come to accept such unfairness as a way of life.

At dinner, Second Grand Uncle told my father about the elementary school in Tai Shek. Later, my father said to Ming Suk he would send Ah Chu to the school with me, for he believed all young people should have an education. Ming Suk thanked my father for giving his son the chance he never had, while Ah Chu was elated at the idea of going to school.

After that, Ah Chu and I walked to Tai Shek six days a week to attend school. We crossed the brook, trudged over the burial mound and along paths between paddies before reaching the eastern gate of town. Our school was halfway down the main street, next to the post office. It was a small school serving children in and around the town. My teacher, Wong Lo Sze, was a tall, gaunt, serious-looking man with hair that parted in the middle and dark-rimmed glasses sitting on the tip of his nose. He always wore the same navy blue *cheongsam* that reached down to his ankle. Since I already knew how to read and write, I was taught Chinese history and passages from the classics. Ah Chu had a different teacher, Tong Lo Sze. His lessons were very elementary at the beginning, and he studied with the younger children.

I was happy for the time spent with Ah Chu. In a way, it seemed we had gone back to the old days, but somehow we were no longer as carefree. Perhaps it was the war, and perhaps, too, we had become older. Since we left home, Ah Chu had grown quieter and more sober at times, as if he had something on his mind. It troubled me to see him brooding, for it seemed he was not telling me everything that came to his mind as he used to back home. I became jealous and feared I was losing my best friend.

"You know, *Siu Siu*," Ah Chu said to me in one of his talkative moments sitting among the unmarked graves on top of the burial mound, for we had become used to the idea of the dead beneath it, "when I am older, I will join the army. I will fight for China."

"I'll help my father with the land," I said, "but I'll tell you my secret wish. I'd like to be a writer some day."

"What will you write about?"

"To begin with, I'll write about my father, the kindest and fairest landlord."

"That's good, but it's more important that you write about the poor farmers who are suffering under greedy landlords, and children sold into rich men's homes, and girls forced into blind marriages."

"And about women with big feet, the better for standing and walking?" I laughed. Ah Chu was becoming too serious.

"*Siu Siu*," said Ah Chu after a while, "I wonder if we will still be friends in the future."

"Of course we will, Chu. We are blood brothers. Haven't we made that pledge long ago?"

8

A Chinese Story

The *Zheng* Player

E VERY TIME WE PASSED the herbalist's shop, we could hear beautiful music coming from the open window above. The music was like water from a flowing mountain stream, smooth and continuous and clear. Sometimes it was spirited, reminding me of the dance music of the Yi people from southwest China who passed through Ka Hing one time before the war and danced for us in the open square. But more often, the music was melancholy, as if telling the story of a sad and lonely person.

Wong Lo Sze said the music came from a *zheng*, but he did not tell us who the player was. Perhaps he didn't know. Many times I looked up to the window, hoping to catch a glimpse of the *zheng* player, but had no luck. Finally, Ah Chu and I came up with a plan that, if it worked, would let us see the player, possibly even talk to her. I never had any doubt the player was a woman.

One day after school, we stopped below the window of the *zheng* player. As soon as the music stopped, Ah Chu, being the braver of the two, cupped his hands to his mouth and shouted upwards, "*Zheng* player, we enjoyed hearing you play! Will you come to the window and let us see who you are?"

We waited quietly. Then our mystery lady appeared at the window, looking down at us. I was somewhat disappointed with her looks, for she seemed a plain and older woman, with hair combed back into a bun. I could not see her face clearly from the street.

"Thank you for listening, little friends. If you would come up, I will play a tune for you." Her voice was soft and inviting.

I could not contain my eagerness and nudged Ah Chu to say yes. Before we could change our minds, we had walked up the narrow dark stairs beside the herbalist's shop and through an opened doorway into the *zheng* player's home.

She had one room and a tiny kitchen. The room contained a bed with a mosquito net in a corner, a small square table and a chair against one wall, and a low cupboard on which were placed a thermos flask and a cup. The walls were bare, except for one picture of a scene in a black frame above the table. The *zheng* sat on a low narrow rectangular stand not far from the window, a long flat dark wooden box with strings across the top, tightly stretched all the way along its length.

She introduced herself as Ho Sau Yuk, originally from Jiangxi. I studied her face, trying at the same time not to seem rude by looking wide-eyed and innocent. She was younger than I had thought at first, about my mother's age, with small eyes and thin, semi-circular eyebrows, like those of ancient court beauties. Perhaps she had been one in a previous life, for Fu Tze had told me women of the court all played some musical instrument, whether it be the *peipa*, the *zheng* or the flute.

"This is a *guzheng, zheng* for short," she explained, pointing to the instrument with her long index finger. "I have played this instrument for twenty-two years. I learned it when I was a young girl."

Ho Sau Yuk played us two pieces that day. The first was a lively tune entitled *Festival of the Gongs and Drums*, which, she said, originated from Shandong Province. The second piece was called *Song in Praise of Lushan*. It was about a very scenic area in Jiangxi, she explained, where the Tang Dynasty poet Li Bai loved to visit. It was a beautiful but melancholy melody that left me with a heavy feeling of longing for my own home. Ho Sau Yuk too must have been homesick for her native province, for as she played, her eyes had a faraway look, and her face looked sad. For a moment, she seemed to have forgotten herself, forgotten our presence, for she bit her lower lip and let tears trickle down her cheeks. I felt very sorry for her. As she plucked the strings of the *zheng* with the metal pieces she wore on her fingertips, she was plucking at my heartstrings and, I knew, Ah Chu's.

As we got up to leave, my eyes fell on the picture above the table. It was a very attractive painting of stately golden roofed pagodas against a dark blue sky, amid a sea of white clouds and topped by a cone-shaped, snowcapped mountain towering over everything in the picture, except the white crescent moon. Seeing how interested I was, Ho Sau Yuk leaned over the table to take down the painting and showed it to me at close range. On the upper right corner of the painting were characters written in black ink: *"In our future society we will find our paradise."*

"This painting is of Shangri-La, a place in a book written by an Englishman several years ago," Ho Sau Yuk explained. "A close friend of mine read the book in the English language and told me the story of Shangri-La. It is a place hidden in high mountains, ruled by lama monks. It is a peaceful place where no war is fought, no crime committed. Time does not age the inhabitants. They live in harmony, obeying the laws set down by the lamas. The valley is fertile and lush, fed by clear water from the mountain streams and protected from the bitter winds and snow by the mountains all around. Food is plentiful. No one is in want of anything, not even the abundant gold found there."

"Do you think such a place really exists?" Ah Chu asked, looking more interested in what Ho Sau Yuk said than in the picture.

"It is a paradise, but we can always dream," Ho Sau Yuk replied with a smile. "Before he left Jiangxi, my friend gave me this painting. This and my *zheng* were the most precious belongings I took with me when I came here."

Very politely Ah Chu and I thanked Ho Sau Yuk and made our exit. As soon as she closed her door, we ran down the stairs to the street. Great was our sense of accomplishment that we had at last seen the *zheng* player. Yet, it remained a mystery why she ended up in wartime Tai Shek, alone but for her *guzheng* and the painting of Shangri-La.

9

A Chinese Story

The Two Wars

THE FIRST FEW MONTHS in Tai Shek, I thought a lot about home. I missed the big house, the village, the fields and farms where Ah Chu and I spent many sunny afternoons. However, gradually those images began to fade into the background as I became occupied with the immediate realities of life around Tai Shek, not in the least the scarcity of food.

One afternoon in the spring of '41, by the east town gate Ah Chu and I saw two men grabbing a white dog and forcing it into a cloth bag, despite its frantic struggles and heart-rending yelps. Before I could react, Ah Chu had pinned me to the gate.

"They are taking the dog to the river to drown, because they probably have not eaten for days, and they need food," he said. "It is not for us to stop them even if we could, *Siu Siu*."

Angrily I freed myself from Ah Chu's grip, but I was helpless in doing anything to save the dog. Deep down I knew Ah Chu was right. I also knew then why the wild dogs were fast disappearing from the town. I turned my back on the scene I just witnessed, and sulked all the way home. In one way or another, the war made monsters of us all.

The summer of '41, some university students and soldiers passed through Tai Shek on their way to Chongqing. By then, I was twelve and had more freedom. Even though there was no school in the summer, I still walked to Tai Shek almost every day, for there was little to do in and around our little house.

As I sat outside the post office with Ah Chu one afternoon, a few of the university students, two men and two women, came by, singing a patriotic song.

"Your song makes me feel like marching on, to defend China against the enemy," Ah Chu said to the students.

"It's called *The March of the Volunteers' Corps*. We sang it with the soldiers, just to keep up morale," one of the students said.

The students sat down beside us and started talking, more to Ah Chu than to me, for, at fourteen, Ah Chu was quite tall and looked older than his age. Certain things about him never changed though, and he still had the strand of hair in front of his forehead which he kept brushing aside, the same overbite showing as soon as he parted his lips to talk or smile. The students told Ah Chu they were traveling with the soldiers mainly because of the food.

"We were hungry until we met up with them," one of the two women said. "When we first left Guangzhou, we stole from deserted farms. We would pry open doors in the ground and enter storage cellars, but whatever the farmers could take with them, they'd already taken. The grains and beans left in the cellars were mostly seeds for the next year's crops, stored there in case they could return, but we took them anyway, for we were hungry."

"And the soldiers have food to spare?" I asked.

"They barely have enough, but the army gives a small ration to every soldier and every member of his family. We are registered as soldiers or members of their families, so we get the rations as well."

"Why do the soldiers let you travel with them?" asked Ah Chu.

"We have connections," replied one of the students. "One of our classmates from Zhongshan University has an uncle who is the commander of a division." As an afterthought, he added, "Besides, we do some translation work for them."

"Do you have meat every meal?" I asked.

"Rice and vegetables and, if we are lucky, a little pork fat are all we have, and all the soldiers have. The commanding officers are the ones who have good meat every day. Rumour has it a division would register five thousand men when in fact it may have only fifteen hundred. The rest are phantom soldiers, just names, to claim rations for five thousand. The money for the nonexistent soldiers goes right into the commanding officers' pockets. But we are not complaining. At least we are not starving."

I was upset. Ah Chu looked infuriated.

"If this is the case, there is no hope for the Guomindang," he muttered.

With the warmer weather and sunny skies, Ah Chu and I sometimes wandered around the countryside and talked to farmers. Mostly we heard about villages burnt and peasants killed near the front lines by the Japanese. In one story, the Japanese pumped poison gas into a maze of underground tunnels between villages dug out by peasants as shelters and escape routes, killing everyone inside.

"Then there is the *other* war," one farmer said.

It was the *other* war that seemed to interest Ah Chu most, the clashes between the Guomindang and Communist troops.

"Some three thousand Communists were killed by Guomindang forces in the mountains near Maolin," an indignant farmer told us when we wandered into his field one day, not long after we talked to the students. "I call this cold-blooded murder by the Guomindang. Why are we killing ourselves when there is a war to fight against the Japanese?"

Later, when I told my father about the farmer's censure of Guomindang action against the Communists, he was very angry.

"Tak Sing, the Communists are our enemies as much as the Japanese, more so because this is their country. The Japanese will leave someday, but not the Communists."

"But the Communist soldiers are decent men, Old Master," Ah Chu spoke up. "They always pay for what they take from the towns and villages they pass through. They don't take advantage of the poor farmers, unlike the Nationalist troops. The Communists don't raise taxes on poor farmers. They teach them

44

to help each other by sharing labour, tools, even animals. Old Master, why do you say the Communists are our enemies?"

I was frightened by Ah Chu's barrage of words and dreaded my father's reaction.

"Ah Chu, there are Communist sympathizers everywhere, and they are trying to brainwash you boys because your minds are fresh, like twigs that can bend with the wind. The Communists are out to confiscate our land and make life miserable for us all." In a sterner voice, my father continued, "Tak Sing, from now on, I forbid you to talk to the farmers. And Ah Chu, I hope you have the sense not to let the Communists work their way into your head."

From that day on, for the rest of our stay at Tai Shek, the word "Communists" was dropped from our household.

Late that summer, I became ill with malaria. For days, I alternated between shivering under piles of blankets and sweating in my bare skin. I suffered from such serious vomiting and diarrhea that at times I wished I were dead. The fact that the outhouse was a good distance behind our house was no help to me in my condition, and Ming Suk ended up running to the outhouse to empty the chamber pot several times a day, a very unpleasant job for the dear man, but he never complained. Luckily for me, my father was able to buy quinine in Tai Shek, though at very high cost. My life was spared.

During my illness, my mother nursed me and tended to all my needs. Ever since we left home, and especially since I fell ill, I had felt more than ever her tenderness and care and understood how much I meant to her, for back home we had the servants and the *mui tsai* to take care of us. For hours, she would sit by my bedside in the ground floor room, prayer beads in hand. Life had been hard on her ever since we left our home, but she had not uttered a word of complaint to my father. "Marry a rooster, follow the rooster; marry a dog, follow the dog." It was a crude expression among the farmers, but my mother believed and practiced

45

wholeheartedly the sentiment that went with it.

News of the Japanese air attack on Pearl Harbour early in December 1941 swept through Tai Shek in no time, followed by news of the entry of the United States into the war against Japan. With the Americans on our side, the war should soon be won. Throughout that winter, my father, Ah Chu and I frequented the teahouse mainly to listen to the radio news of the war.

Our hopes were dampened when news came in late December that the British had surrendered Hong Kong, and then Singapore the following February. In April, we heard the Japanese had taken Lashio, an important stop on the Burma Road linking Kunming to Rangoon, China's main route to and from the outside.

The end of the war seemed nowhere in sight.

10

The Worst of Times

MUMMY WAS EIGHT WHEN the Japanese occupied Hong Kong. Many adults who lived through that period are dead, the young then are old men and women now, unless, like Mummy, they never lived to become old.

Of the stories Ah Lan told about my mother as a young girl, the ones during the three years and eight months of Japanese occupation of Hong Kong were quite terrifying. Instinctively I pick up the pages I have placed on the bed beside me, on which are recorded those stories.

The world turned upside down when the Japanese came in 1941. They bombed Kai Tak Airport, crossed the Shenzhen River to the New Territories, and advanced on to Kowloon. The lo fan retreated to Hong Kong Island, waiting for outside help. I was supposed to visit a friend in Kowloon that day, but thanks to Kuan Yin and Buddha, I had a bit of gum mo and decided not to go. If I had crossed the harbour, I might not have come back that day, or for many days, or ever! The ferry service was stopped. Families on different sides of the harbour at the time were separated. Some were foolish enough to cross the harbour in hired sampans. Some made it to the other side, but others never did, their boats sunk by the Japanese. From the waterfront on the Hong Kong side, I could see Japanese soldiers patrolling the Kowloon waterfront, their flags of the red sun flying high from the pier at Tsim Sha Tsui. The crackling sounds of gunfire from Kowloon made my heart stop. We knew sooner or later the Japanese would land on Hong Kong Island.

As a child of seven or eight, your Mummy said her happiest times were Sunday mornings when she went to her parents' room, jumped into their bed, and wiggled her way between them under their blanket. Her parents called her "the middle person."

Christmas morning, 1941, just as Siu Cheh was knocking on the Master and Mistress' door to be let into their room, Japanese soldiers were stabbing patients in their beds at Chun Wah Hospital with bayonets. They had landed a week earlier on the east end of Hong Kong Island. Later that morning, when the Master received a telephone call from Sai On Hospital where he worked, telling about the massacre at Chun Wah, his face turned as white as a ghost's.

"Were there no doctors and nurses around?" the Mistress asked in a shaky voice, after hearing the news.

"Yes, there were one doctor and six nurses. They were all… brutally murdered."

The Mistress cried. The Master was careful not to let Siu Cheh hear what had happened.

"Don't go to your hospital, Kwok Wing. Just lie low for a few days, please!" the Mistress pleaded.

That same afternoon, the Governor formally surrendered Hong Kong to the Japanese.

Your Kung Kung and Poh Poh would not allow your Mummy to go out much in those days, because the Japanese soldiers had done very bad things to girls of any age. Some girls were so afraid of the soldiers, they disguised themselves as boys or smeared soot on their faces when they went out, so the soldiers would think they were ugly and leave them alone.

I have never forgotten the day I took your Mummy to the herbalist on Wyndham Street in the spring of '42. She had been running a fever for days, and your Poh Poh wanted the herbalist to take her pulse and prescribe some herbal medicine. I was just waiting with your Mummy for the herbalist to fill the prescription, watching him measure each herb carefully with his little balance, when suddenly we heard loud, angry cries outside the shop. An old man picking pomegranates from a tree by the roadside to give to his young grandson was seen by a Japanese police officer. In those days, all civilians had to stand aside, hats removed, and bow when Japanese soldiers or police officers passed through. Hearing the policeman's threatening shouts, the old man quickly climbed down the tree, picked up his grandson and ran. The officer shouted some more, but the old man kept on running, for he was probably scared out of his wits. The officer took out his gun, aimed it at the old man and shot him in the back. He fell to the ground, his grandson falling with him. The officer took a sword from one of his men and walked toward the wounded old man who lay moaning and writhing in pain. As the officer got close to him, the old man shielded the boy with his body. The officer raised the sword and, with one hard blow, chopped off the old man's head. Blood splattered on the boy's face, as his grandfather's headless body slumped over him. The boy screamed in terror, while the officer kicked the old man's body aside. Holding up the sword stained with the old man's blood, he stared at the boy who was no more than four. He paused, and I was afraid he was going to harm the boy, but instead he lowered his sword and walked away. All this your Mummy saw from the herbalist's shop. She did not talk or sleep for three days. She did not even cry. She never talked about what she saw that day. It was as if it never happened.

The Japanese occupation was hell for all of us. We kept out of the way of the soldiers. Every time we went out, we could be stopped and questioned by Japanese sentries. If for any reason or for no reason at all they were not happy with you, they beat you, or arrested you and locked you up for torture. We were very careful to obey the curfew, for if they saw you out during the curfew, they would shoot you on the spot.

There was little food. We lived on six and a half liang of rice ration a day and sometimes a sweet potato. Meat was very scarce and expensive, and when we managed to buy a little, it was very poor cuts. Some people survived on cassava flour and tree roots. I knew a woman – Ah Wong was her name – who was a garbage collector. She used to live on leftovers people gave her, and any food she could find from the garbage. But during the Japanese occupation, there were no leftovers and no food in the garbage. This poor woman had to eat banana skins, and insects and worms she scraped out from the dirt. Her body was so undernourished and filled with poison that, after the war, her hands shook constantly, and she could hardly haul the garbage.

During those three years and eight months of Japanese occupation, because of food shortage in Hong Kong, the Japanese forced many local residents into the mainland – the areas not occupied by the Japanese – only to let them starve there. But the Master stayed on in Hong Kong with his family. Doctors were in high demand, and the Japanese knew when they saw a good one. The Master was treated with respect by the enemy.

By the time Japan surrendered, and the English returned to govern Hong Kong in 1945, Siu Cheh had grown into a blossoming thirteen-year-old.

11

A Chinese Story

Liberation

WHEN THE WAR FINALLY ENDED in August, 1945, we had been in Tai Shek for six years and four months. I turned sixteen that January, and Ah Chu was eighteen. At last, we were going home. Much as I was anxious to return to our big house, I dreaded the devastation that might be awaiting us there. And always, I had a nagging fear that life at home would not be the same as before.

"Come back with us, Second Uncle," my mother said before we departed. "We can look after you back home."

"My good nephew's wife, my roots are here, and here I will live out the rest of my days. It is regretful I have no son to look after me in my old age, but I will manage. The townsfolk know me, and they will take care of my needs."

My father had arranged for a lorry to take us all the way to Ka Hing. Before we left, Ah Chu and I went to say goodbye to Ho Sau Yuk. That day, instead of the dark colours she was accustomed to wearing, she had on a deep red *cheongsam*, and her hair was let down, long and straight, almost reaching to her waist. She seemed ten years younger.

"You look different, Ho Sau Yuk," I said, with quiet approval.

"You see, any day now, my fiancé may come for me," she said dreamily. Then noticing our silent curiosity, she added with more spirit than I had ever seen her, "I never told you my story, did I? If you have time, I'll tell it to you now."

Ever since we knew her, Ah Chu and I had wondered what brought her to Tai Shek, but we did not dare to ask, lest we conjured up sad memories. She might even be offended by our inquisitiveness.

"I was the daughter of a silk merchant in Lushan, Jiangxi Province," Ho Sau Yuk began, as we sat down on the edge of her bed, while she pulled up the chair for herself. "When I was twenty, I met and fell in love with a young man who had graduated from Zhongshan University in Guangzhou. He had returned to Lushan full of high hopes of serving his province and country. He told me secretly that, disillusioned with the corruption of the Guomindang and at the same time attracted to the discipline and order of the Communists, he had visited the Jiangxi Soviet and joined the Chinese Communist Party. I assured him his political affiliation and my bourgeois connection should not stand in the way of our regard for each other. Before long, we were engaged, and we were to be married in the spring of the following year, 1935. We kept his party membership from my parents, however, because he feared their opposition to our marriage if they knew he was a Communist."

"Would your parents have objected to your marriage?" Ah Chu asked.

"They would indeed. Late in September, 1934, my fiancé confided that the Jiangxi Soviet had to be dissolved because of Guomindang attacks, and he felt it was his duty to join his comrades in their withdrawal across China to a safer place further north where they could reestablish themselves. I wanted to go with him, but he said it was too dangerous for me to make that trip across rough terrain and wild rivers, with Guomindang troops in pursuit. The plan of the Communists was to reach Shaanxi to the north by way of the southwest, where the Guomindang defense lines were weak. Our own personal happiness could not be realized yet, he said, but he would send for me as soon as the situation allowed. However, if war broke out with Japan, I was to go to a small town in the foothills of northwest Guangdong where he had once stopped over. The town was Tai Shek.

"'Wait for me there, Sau Yuk,' my fiancé told me, 'where you will be safe from the Japanese.'

"He had painted a watercolour picture of Shangri-La as he imagined it after reading the book *Lost Horizon* an English friend at the Zhongshan University gave him. Before he left, he gave the painting to me.

"'Whenever you begin to lose hope, look at the painting and dream of the society awaiting us when all the hardships are over, and China is united again in peace and plenty. Sau Yuk, I *will* come back for you,' he said.

"Soon after, on a mid-October night, he left Jiangxi and joined his comrades on the Long March."

Ah Chu and I were very quiet when she finished, perhaps paying a silent tribute to the young Communist who sacrificed personal happiness for his country. My eyes wandered to the painting on the wall, which had kept the hope alive in Ho Sau Yuk all those years, as she waited for her lover's return, blinding herself to the worst possibilities.

"You should be very proud of him, Ho Sau Yuk," Ah Chu finally said in a solemn, almost reverent, voice.

"Will you go back to Jiangxi now that the war is over?" I asked the practical question.

"No, Tak Sing. I will stay in Tai Shek. Eleven years have gone by since my fiancé left me to go on the Long March. He must know I've come to Tai Shek." She rested her eyes on the picture of Shangri-La on the wall for a few good seconds. "The seasons come and go, and night ends with every break of dawn, but he will come home to me some day. I will wait for him. He will come home. He *will* come home." Her voice ended with a shrill laugh, alarming for a moment, her eyes lighting up briefly only to fall back into their usual listlessness.

"I will miss you, Ho Sau Yuk," I said.

"I will miss you both too very much. May happiness and good fortune go with you always." As she stood up, she added in a strong and clear voice resounding with hope, or hiding the lack of it, "My fiancé's name is Wang Tien. If you ever see him, tell him Ho Sau Yuk is waiting for him in Tai Shek."

We left her flat for the last time, my heart crying for her. Two lines I learned at the school, written by an anonymous poet long ago, echoed in my head as I thought of Ho Sau Yuk, a lonely desperate soul clinging to a dream:

Pity the bones that lie beside some riverbank,
They belong to one in an inner chamber's dream.

The next day, our lorry took us through the main street of Tai Shek, past all the familiar buildings that had come to be a part of my life for the last six years. As we passed the herbalist's shop, I looked up to the second floor window, hoping to catch a glimpse of Ho Sau Yuk and wave to her, but she was not there. Neither could I hear the *zheng*. The roar of the lorry engine would have drowned the music even if she was playing.

The lorry passed the school Ah Chu and I attended for six years. Our teachers would stay on, dedicating their lives to saving rural children from illiteracy, and perhaps inspiring a few to pursue education in the cities. Soon we had left Tai Shek behind, journeying south in the direction of Ka Hing.

12

A Chinese Story

Ka Hing

A S OUR LORRY PUT distance between us and Tai Shek, the countryside became bleak and barren. The fields were empty not from harvesting, but from burning. Everywhere I saw charred remains of dead trees and broken sheds, and land reduced to an ashen grey. We passed farmhouses whose doors and windows had been smashed, roofs fallen in, bearing no sign of life in any form. Mansions which had once been the stately homes of rich landowners were scorched, some razed to the ground. Rural Guangdong had become an ugly wasteland, and, as if in sympathy with the remnants of war, the sun did not shine for a single moment during our journey home. Only the distant hills gave a little colour to the bleak landscape, for where the trees had not been destroyed, leaves had turned a rusty gold.

"Did the Japanese cause all this?" my mother asked my father.

"Hard to say, Wei Fan. The peasants themselves might have torched their fields before evacuating. Pitiful, pitiful." My father shook his head.

We were quiet most of the way. I sensed a tension building up in all of us as we got closer to home. Or was there still a home? And what of our land, the land we left behind with our tenant farmers? What of the farmers? As our lorry bounced on the winding dirt road that was the last stretch of our journey, my heart was thumping violently, from fear of the sight awaiting us when we would finally turn the corner onto the straight road leading home. Yet, there was a faint hope that, in spite of what

55

we had seen on the way, our house had remained the same, with closed shutters and doors the way we left them, and the tiled roof undamaged – hope against hope, hope against all odds. We passed a stagnant duck pond thick with fallen branches and dead leaves. We saw the battered remains of rice threshers and wooden winnowing machines by the edge of the fields. There *were* some signs of life though, not men and women working in the grey and barren fields, but a few children playing outside white-walled farmhouses, and a few dogs sniffing for food. I held my breath as the lorry wound round the last bend before heading on the straight road to our house.

The house came into clear view. *It was still standing.* From a distance, it looked the way we left it, with its red walls and roof of green tiles. The lorry took us closer and closer to the house. Gradually I saw broken tiles on the roof, fragments of which had fallen on the ground. Smashed shutters revealed shattered windowpanes, and shards of glass were scattered on the ground. Large patches of red paint were scraped from the walls. The lorry came to a standstill in front of the house. The latch was broken, and the front doors were half open.

"Well, it is still here," my father broke the silence, surveying the front of the house from the lorry. "We still have a home."

I helped my mother alight. We followed my father through the red double doors into the front courtyard which was full of dead leaves and dirt accumulated over time. Flowerbeds were overgrown with tall weeds. We proceeded into the front hall of the main building. Immediately I smelled damp, stagnant air, reeking of mold and decay. My father's favourite scroll painting of eight galloping horses was still on the wall, slit lengthwise in the middle. We entered the sitting room. Furniture was broken, porcelain vases smashed, the ornaments of jade and semi-precious stones all removed from the cracked ebony screens and cabinets. Whatever could be taken was gone, whatever was left behind destroyed. I stood in front of the family altar, gazing grimly at the smashed wall stripped of the ancestors' plaques we had taken with us.

"Who did all this, Father?" I finally found my voice.

"Japanese soldiers or our own, I don't know." My father turned to comfort my mother. "The most important thing is we are alive and together, Wei Fan. Come, the worst is over. We will rebuild our home and our lives."

The day after our return, my father called a meeting of all his tenant farmers to assess the condition of the land. He was informed two of the older farmers had died from illness, and two of the younger farmers who had been drafted into the Nationalist Army were killed in the war. The rest had returned, to salvage whatever they could.

"Old Master, my family have rented your family's land for three generations and gone through good and bad times with you and your father and grandfather. You have been generous and kind to us, and we are very grateful. We welcome you back and are prepared to work hard in the fields again," said Cheung Fook, the spokesman for the farmers. "However, many of us had to leave our ploughs and our threshers behind when we fled, and we came back to find them either damaged or gone. Those of us who owned water buffalo had to either sell or slaughter them for food before we left. We have lost our instruments of livelihood."

My father looked thoughtfully at the farmers gathered before him. His voice was full of compassion when he spoke.

"When I left for Tai Shek, I took with me a gold reserve, not a lot but enough to be converted to cash loans to you. With the rapid devaluation of the paper note, we must waste no time. Come to me if you need help, and we will work out a loan agreement that will help you stand on your feet once more. My good men, we are all survivors of the war. When spring comes, work hard on the land. If it is any comfort for you, the ashes from the burning enrich the soil. Good harvests will return to us, if not next year, then the next."

And Cheung Fook said, "Old Master, we won't forget your kindness. We wish there were more landlords like you, but sadly this is not the case."

My father hired workmen to repair the house. The damaged rosewood furniture was replaced with pine. The newly whitewashed walls remained bare of the paintings that had either been looted or damaged. The broken Qing Dynasty crystal chandelier in the dining room was replaced with a five-candle fixture with milky glass shades.

"The house is not what it used to be," I said to my father.

"Times are changing. We cannot hope to live the way we did before the Japanese came, and not because of the Japanese. The Communists have control of most of the countryside in the north. They are abolishing land tenancy, confiscating the landlords' land and redistributing it to the peasants. I fear the ill winds of Communism will sooner or later blow south to Guangdong. We have to be prepared."

Early in 1946 came the disturbing news of landlords being beaten and some killed by peasants in Shandong, in retaliation against the landlords' cruelty and injustice. I was sure my father would not share the fate of those landlords if and when the Communists came, for his tenant farmers loved him, and could not possibly wish him ill or do him harm. Justice had to prevail.

About that time, my father told me he was sending me to Guangzhou the following autumn to attend a secondary school. It was his wish I continue on to a university afterwards. As for Ah Chu, Ming Suk had wanted to send him to Guangzhou to learn a trade, but changed his mind because of the political unrest in the country. Ah Chu was to stay home and find work on the farms.

"I'll be so homesick when I'm in Guangzhou, I'll want to come home the minute the term is over," I said to Ah Chu as we walked to Ka Hing for the celebrations of the Year of the Dog, 1946.

"You remember the last Year of the Dog, *Siu Siu*, when Pa took us to Ka Hing to watch the lion dance?" asked Ah Chu.

"Don't I remember! I was scared of that lion," I said, "but I loved the food your pa bought us. It was one good day. Twelve years ago today. So many things have happened, Chu, so many changes, more bad than good."

"Better days are ahead," said Ah Chu with conviction. Then, in a quivering voice that surprised me, he continued, "*Siu Siu*, I want you to know and remember no matter what holds for you and me in the future, I will always think of you as my brother. I hope you will think of me in the same way."

"Hey, what's come over you, Chu, talking as though something's going to happen to us!"

We entered the village gate and mingled with the crowd in the square. Some people were having their pictures taken in front of a shop, against a backdrop of firecrackers and lanterns.

"*Siu Siu*, let's have our picture taken," said Ah Chu, surprising me again with his unusual display of sentimentality.

We posed for the camera, standing side by side, each with one arm on the other's shoulder. Best friends. Blood brothers. It was our only picture together. I had two copies made that day, one for Ah Chu, one for myself.

13

A Chinese Story

Ah Chu

ABOUT A MONTH AFTER the New Year, one cold, damp morning in March, 1946, Ming Suk and Ming Sum scurried over to the big house looking for me. They seemed very anxious.

"Young Master! I am afraid something has happened to Ah Chu. He's gone! I found these two letters on his bed," Ming Suk said, handing me two envelopes with trembling hands.

One letter was addressed to his parents, and the other to me. I opened the one for Ming Suk and Ming Sum. It was in Ah Chu's rather immature style of handwriting, but the content was plain and clear. With nervous apprehension, I read aloud:

5th March, 1946

My dear Pa and Ma,

When you hear this letter read to you by Siu Siu, I will have traveled many miles from home. The truth is I have decided to go to Yan'an to join the Communists, because only the Communists can free our people from oppression and poverty. Forgive me, Pa and Ma, for being an impious son in leaving you. Please understand that in serving my country, I will bring honour to you and my ancestors. I will always be grateful to you both for giving me life and caring for me all these years. Do not cry for me if I die

*fighting for the Communist cause, but be proud. If we win
and I am still alive, I will come back to see you.*

Your son,
Chu

"My son! I have only one son! Why do they have to take him
from me?" Ming Sum wailed, holding up her tight fists and
looking up to the heavens, and crying as though her heart would
break.

"Even as a child, he had shown a lot of interest in them living
in the caves of Yan'an. I suppose I can't blame him, for he has
heard so much about the greed and looting of the Nationalist
troops, and the government's corruption," said Ming Suk quietly,
controlling whatever emotion he might be feeling. "To him, the
Communists must seem like saviours of the poor."

I wanted to read Ah Chu's letter to me in private, but realizing
how much Ming Suk and Ming Sum wanted to know its content, I
read it in their presence, first silently, and then aloud to them:

5th March, 1946

Siu Siu,

*I am at last going to Yan'an. It has been my intention
to go there for a long time, for I admire the discipline and
goodwill of the Communists everywhere they go. I am
joining the Red Army to fight for a strong and united
China in which people need suffer no more from hunger,
poverty and submission, and our country will have peace
again under a new Communist government.*

*Think kindly of me and remember me as I will always
remember you, as a friend and brother. My greatest regret*

is I cannot be there to take care of my pa and ma in their old age, but China needs me, and my country must come first. I can only hope they understand. Please tell the Old Master and Mistress I am truly grateful to them for all they have done for me all these years. They have treated me as their own son. I shall never forget.

Your friend and brother,
Chu

I realized from that moment I had lost Ah Chu. We would be taking different paths that could never meet. His letters did not come as much a shock to me as to Ming Sum, for in the deep recess of my subconsciousness, I had long read my brother's mind. When my father was told about Ah Chu, he was at first very angry. Later, he stopped mentioning his name altogether. To him, Ah Chu was as good as dead.

14

A Chinese Story

At War With Herself

THE COMMUNISTS WON THE PEASANTS' support in northeastern China in the months following the surrender of Japan. But for a while in 1947, the Guomindang forces rallied, and they recaptured Yan'an from the Communists. We had not received any news from Ah Chu since he left. Ming Sum cried every time one of the villagers asked about him, and when news of the Guomindang takeover of Yan'an came, she was beside herself with worry for her son's safety. Ming Suk managed to hide his anxiety and busied himself with his household jobs in a quiet way, as if he was placing his son's fate in the hands of the gods. My father never asked about Ah Chu, but I believed he still cared for him and grieved for his faithful old servant, for his profound loss. As for me, in the first two years after Ah Chu left, I often thought of him and wondered where he was and what he was doing, and every time I heard of a Communist setback in the north, I feared for his life.

In the autumn of 1946, I enrolled at Sun Kwong Secondary School in Guangzhou and became one of the few boarders there. My years of studies with Fu Tze as a child and later with Wong Lo Sze in Tai Shek had qualified me to enter *go tsung*, the last two years of secondary school. It was the first time I was away from home on my own, and I was very homesick. Often in the still of the night, after I had finished the day's studies, and long after the last electric light in the building had been turned off, I sat at the window above my bed and looked out into the quiet deserted street, dimly lit by a single gas street lamp, thinking of home. A night-soil carrier usually passed by, balancing two big covered wooden buckets on his shoulder pole. Sometimes, a bat flittered under the street lamp, and often I could hear a flute playing sweet melancholy notes of solitude that broke the silence of the night. Some nights I could see the moon high up in the sky. I recalled a verse by the poet Li Bai I learned as a child:

> *The bright moonlight above my bed*
> *Shines like the frost upon the ground;*
> *I raise my head to see the moon,*
> *Drop it in thoughts of my hometown.*

I was home for three weeks the following spring. During that time, my mother fell sick and had bouts of hard coughing causing pain in her chest. My father sent for the herbalist from Ka Hing who came to our house several times to see her. The house stank of the bitter black medicine Ming Sum boiled in a small earthen medicine pot. By the end of my holidays my mother seemed better and my father looked happier. I returned to school with a lighter heart, knowing she was going to be well again.

By mid-1947, the Communists dominated Shandong and recovered some of their lost grounds in the north, and in the spring of '48, they controlled most of the northern countryside and recaptured Yan'an. From then on, it seemed the Guomindang would lose the war, which was to end with their complete evacuation from the mainland.

In the autumn of 1948, I was admitted to Zhongshan University in Guangzhou, much to my parents' pride and joy. But that winter my mother fell ill again, and my father took her to Zhaoqing to see a doctor of western medicine. She was diagnosed with tuberculosis and put on a strict regimen of medication. When I went home in February of the following year, I was alarmed to see how thin she had become. The paleness in her sallow cheeks and dark rings around her sunken eyes filled me with apprehension. The three weeks I was home, I spent almost every minute with her, entertaining her with stories about my life in the big city and at the university.

"When you are well again, Mother, I will take you to Guangzhou. I'll show you the city and the university, where I live and where I study, and where I spend time with my friends," I said, as if my words might coax her back to health.

"I shall love that," she said, with a faraway look in her eyes. And then, focusing on me and appearing embarrassed, she asked, "Tell me, Tak Sing, among all your classmates at the university, is there someone you especially like?"

I realized then my mother was anxious that I have a girlfriend. I was only nineteen, but in my father's generation men were already married at that age, or even earlier. I had long decided whomever I married was not going to be someone chosen for me, as my mother had been for my father. Her sudden and unexpected question filled me with relief that it was not her intention, or my father's presumably, to arrange a marriage for me. But, just then, I had to disappoint my mother.

"Mother, I have made friends with many girls at the university, but there is not one I am particularly fond of. I am still young. I have plenty of time."

"Don't wait too long, son," my mother said, smiling sadly into my eyes.

The civil war continued into 1949, with the Communists gaining ground, first in the countryside, and then in the cities as well. In April, the Communists entered Nanjing, and a month later, Chiang Kai-shek, who had moved his capital to Chongqing during the Japanese invasion, left the mainland for the island of Taiwan.

I went home for the summer and was relieved to discover my mother's condition had stabilized. The doctor in Zhaoqing told her and my father that with the medicine he prescribed, plus rest and fresh air, she could recover. Her appetite improved, and I was able to take her on short walks outside our family compound.

A week before I was due to return to Guangzhou for the opening of the new term in September, on a beautiful day that was sunny with a touch of crisp autumn air, I went with my mother on one of our morning walks. As we walked slowly on the gravel path outside our house, with my mother leaning on my arm, she said as if half to herself, "How I wish you were not going back to Guangzhou, my son. I'll miss you very much when you are gone."

"Mother, if it makes you happier, and healthier, I'll talk to Father about delaying my return to Guangzhou. Besides, with General Chiang in Taiwan and the Guomindang losing every inch of the way, who knows what is going to happen to us here. I'd want to be close to home, and to you and Father, if the Communists take Guangdong."

That night, when I brought up the subject with my father at supper, giving my reasons for wanting to stay at home, he looked disturbed.

"Tak Sing, I appreciate your concern for your mother and for me, but you must know soon there will be no place for landowners in this country. After more than a hundred years of living off the yields of the good earth, the Lee family is about to lose all the land we own," he said, putting down his chopsticks and rice bowl, and folding his arms on the table. "Your education is the only means you have to break away from the land and find a new life in the city. Son, you have to finish your studies, and the sooner you do so, the better."

I felt the urgency of my father's words and realized he was right. I glanced at my mother who was looking at her food with downcast eyes.

"I will go back to Guangzhou," I said quietly.

15

A Chinese Story

The People's Republic

I WAS IN THE STUDENTS' common room the afternoon of October 1st, 1949, when Mao Zedong and his comrades in power stood on the viewing stand at Tiananmen Gate and declared the founding of the People's Republic of China. My fellow students and I hovered around the radio to listen to Mao's speech.

Every drama has a prologue, but that is not the climax.
The Chinese people's revolution is great, but what follows
will be a longer and more difficult journey.

Thus spoke the leader, followed by the radio announcer describing the hoisting of our new national flag, five stars on red.

From this moment on, we will be insulted no more.

The new national anthem was sung. It called to the people to rise up, to refuse to be slaves, to build a new Great Wall with their blood, with their lives. I remembered the song, for it was *The March of the Volunteers' Corp* I had first heard sung by the students and Nationalist soldiers who passed through Tai Shek. I never dreamed then that the song would one day be used by the Communists as China's new national anthem.

About two weeks after the founding ceremony in Beijing, Red Army troops led by Lin Biao approached Guangzhou, where Guomindang forces put up a defense outside the city. I was in the university library the afternoon my classmate Weng came excitedly to tell me the Guomindang troops had surrendered and Guangzhou was at last in Communist hands. That evening, the university auditorium was packed with students, talking about the relatively peaceful entry of Communist troops into the city, and discussing the university's stand in the immediate days ahead. The next day, big red banners were posted at the main entrances of all university buildings, inscribed with the characters *Long Live the People's Republic of China!* Some students participated in a parade along the Pearl River waterfront two weeks later, carrying banners and portraits of Mao and other Chinese Communist leaders, as well as the Russian leader Stalin.

I was not a participant in the celebrations. All I could think of was my father and mother back home. I was worried about them, since the new government had no sympathy for the landowning class. I could visualize Communist cadres and soldiers going in the middle of the night to the big house, banging on the door, and demanding in the name of the People's Republic of China that they be let in. Ming Suk would get up to open the door, and they would push him aside. They would march into the main sitting room and order my father and mother to appear before them. They would decry all objects in the house as sins of landownership, crimes against the poor, and they would confiscate the house and all our land and turn my parents out into the cold dark night with only the clothes on their backs. My mother would not survive the treatment, and my father would die of a broken heart. Such horrifying thoughts filled my mind by day and my dreams at night, and left me with not a moment's peace. I was dying to go home, and yet I stayed on until the midyear examinations were over.

In the first two months after the "liberation of Guangzhou" as the Communists called it, the general atmosphere in the city, as in the rest of the country, was one of excitement and hope of better things to come, of salvation from the destitution that had plagued the country for the last hundred years. The Communist government guaranteed personal freedoms and equality to all, except those it considered a threat to its well-being and to its professed principles of freedom from bondage, servitude and poverty. It showed no leniency to its political enemies, the Guomindang members who could not or would not leave for Taiwan, where Chiang Kai-shek had set up his Nationalist government. It showed no tolerance to the rich factory owners in the cities who had exploited the workers, or the landlords in the countryside who had made the lives of peasants miserable beyond repair. As a result, many were executed.

Life in the university was not affected. Classes continued. The students were generally in a state of euphoria, as hope in the Communist government ran high. They believed the new government would rectify social evils and improve the condition of the peasants and workers.

"There's going to be a public execution of ten enemies of the State in Nan Hoy Square this afternoon," my classmate Weng told me about a month after Guangzhou fell. "Are you going to watch?"

"I don't think so. I don't enjoy seeing people die, whether they deserve to or not," I said.

But as the morning wore on, I became quite restless with the thought of the impending execution, the first of many to follow, I had no doubt. I might as well get used to the new regime's system of justice. I could not concentrate on my studies, my mind wandering to images of the condemned men about to be publicly executed. What were their crimes? Did they have a fair trial? Did they really deserve to die?

I found myself cycling down Wende Lu with some of my friends toward Nan Hoy Square, to witness with the big crowd gathered there the ritual of a public execution. About twenty minutes before three, an open army truck transported the condemned men to the square. Every prisoner's hands were tied behind him, encircling a long and narrow wooden board that extended up his nape and above his head. Words written on the boards stated their crimes. *Guomindang traitor. Guomindang running dog. Murderer. Traitor to the country and the people. Rapist. Extortionist.* They were pushed down a plank from the truck by soldiers and led to the execution wall.

To this day, I have not forgotten the expressions and reactions of these men in those last moments of their lives. Whether they were guilty or not for the crimes they were dying for, I did not know. Some went berserk with fear as they were led to the wall, screaming and struggling, with the wild look of trapped animals. One man was crying and wetting his pants as he was pushed forward. A soldier kicked at another condemned man, who threw up and fell on his own vomit. One prisoner, no more than my age, fainted and had to be dragged to the wall, where he was cruelly revived with a bucket of cold water. Another in his late twenties or early thirties calmly walked to the wall, his eyes staring ahead, his ashen face bearing a harsh and fierce expression. As he walked, he shouted, "Down with Communism! Long live the Guomindang! Long live General Chiang!"

The condemned men were made to kneel facing the wall, and ten soldiers lined up with rifles behind the prisoners. The crowd was subdued. Some were crying quietly. A woman beside me covered her young daughter's eyes and ears with her hands. A command was shouted. The soldiers took steps toward the condemned men until they were only a few feet behind them. Then each soldier took aim at the back of one man's head. I looked away, my heart pounding, my legs weak. Another command. Shots rang out and it was all over. I kept my eyes down, afraid to look. Then slowly I turned my head, my eyes daring to scan the execution wall about a hundred yards from where I was standing. I saw motionless bodies slumped forward on the ground toward the wall, and red matter, blood or brain, splattered on the wall at the level where their heads had been.

For the first time in my life, I stared death in the face, in all its nakedness, with no room for human decency or dignity. The execution is as disturbing now as it was when I witnessed it with a throng of onlookers at best curious and at worst bloodthirsty.

How senseless the cruelty and pain human beings can impose on other human beings, be they perpetrators of crime or ministers of justice.

A few days later, I heard the family of each executed man was charged the price of a bullet.

16

A Chinese Story
Landlords' Plight

I LEFT GUANGZHOU IMMEDIATELY after the midyear examinations and caught a ride that would pass through Ka Hing on its way to Wuzhou. I was aching to be home, but instead of being excited as I was in times past on my journey back, I felt a dull sense of dread gnawing at me all the way. I reached the big house in the fading twilight of a clear and cold day in late January. As I walked through the front double doors into the courtyard, the whole place seemed unusually quiet. Some dried leaves from the magnolia tree were still on the ground, blown and gathered against the walls. A bare branch from a sapling close to the main building rattled against a windowpane, like a lone ghost wanting to be let in. There was no sign of Ming Suk or Ming Sum. I became anxious at the sight of a padlock on the wooden door of their little stone house. The door to the entrance hall of the big house was ajar. I crossed the threshold and walked briskly through the corridor peeking into the sitting room as I passed it. No one was in sight. The house felt cold and damp, as though it had not been inhabited for some time.

I found my father in his study. He was standing with his back to me, looking out of the window into the inner courtyard, his hands behind his back. As I entered, he turned and I was alarmed by his drained countenance. He seemed to have aged ten years in the five months since I saw him last. He was also noticeably thinner. His face had the look of one consumed with worries.

"Father," I began, but could not continue. I went up to him and embraced him, and, as I did so, tears welled up in my eyes.

"My son, all is lost, all our land, even this house," my father said in a deep broken voice. A pause, then he continued slowly, as if weighing every word he uttered, "I'll always remember this house, grand, beautiful, orderly, the tall magnolia trees, acres and acres of rice fields."

He sat down with me. He told me three members of a work team from the township party committee came by about two weeks earlier and handed him a written summons to appear at a meeting of the Peasant Association formed by all the tenant farmers within the township. When my father went to the village hall in Ka Hing for the meeting on the appointed day, two other landlords were there, Li See and Hui Pak Lok. The three of them stood in front of the work team and representatives of the Peasant Association. Tenant farmers and villagers from the area were present in the hall. The chief cadre who headed the work team told my father and the other two landlords that, because of a land reform law under the new government, all the land they owned would be seized and redistributed to the inhabitants of the township.

My father said Hui Pak Lok uttered an angry protest. Two members of the Peasant Association dragged him out of the building, thereupon he was beaten by farmers who claimed they had suffered under his brutality and greed. One farmer whose fifteen-year-old daughter was kidnapped and raped by him took a butcher's cleaver and severed Hui's manhood. Later, my father found him unconscious, drenched in his own blood on the ground, and no one would help him. He died there that day.

As for Li See, my father said he was accused of exacting rent payment in full from his tenants when the harvests were bad, causing them to sell their sons and daughters. As punishment, not only was he stripped of all his land and his house, but he would also have to beg for work as a labourer, that he might know how it felt to be poor and hungry, and to be at the mercy of someone else. He went on his knees in front of the Peasant Association, begging his tenant farmers to have mercy on him in his old age and to put in a good word to the work team for him. But no plea from him could change the decision of the committee. That night, Li See went home and hanged himself.

My father closed his eyes, knitted his thick brows together, and heaved a long, deep sigh. I noticed, more than ever before, age lines deeply entrenched in his forehead. His tall and proud stature seemed to have been reduced to an insignificant smallness.

"All of the five thousand *mou* of land my family has owned for the last hundred years, gone like a wisp of smoke," my father said slowly, as if to himself. Looking at me, he continued, "I was told this house would be used as the headquarters of the local cadres. Tak Sing, in three days they will be here to take over the house. All the things in it that have survived the war will also become the property of the State."

"You were such a good landlord, Father," I said, unable to comprehend the reality of the situation.

"The chief cadre told me the work team had reason to believe I had been a decent landlord, although being a landlord gave me bad blood. He told me our family of three would be allotted one acre of land to farm, for land was to be distributed according to the number of heads in each household."

"Father, what has our country come to? What has happened to everyone?"

"I don't know, Tak Sing, I don't know." My father shook his head. He sounded very bitter. "I have tried to live by the rules of reason and decency all my life. I never dreamed in my old age when I should be enjoying having my son and grandchildren around me that I would be reduced to a state of nothing."

"How is Mother taking all this?"

"She does not know everything. I told her about the redistribution of the land, but she does not know about the violence suffered by the landlords. The knowledge of such cruelties would kill her. Go to her now. She has been sick with worry about you."

I found my mother asleep in her rocking chair in her chamber.

She had become much thinner since my last visit home. As I walked close, she opened her eyes, and her face lit up as soon as she saw me. She put out her hand, and I took it immediately in both my own. I knelt down beside her.

"Son, with you home, I will not be afraid of anything. I have been worrying about your safety in Guangzhou," she said, gripping my hands as if she was afraid I would disappear if she let go. "Have the Communists treated you badly? We haven't heard from you these three months, but your father said the postal service had been suspended. Tak Sing, I am *so* happy you are home." She looked contentedly at me for a long time, then collecting herself she said with a feigned laugh, "Your father told me we would be moving in three days to a farmhouse half the size of Ming Suk's house here, and I haven't even packed. I don't know what to take with us."

I looked around the room and out into the inner courtyard.

"Where are Ming Suk and Ming Sum?"

My mother sighed. "They were ordered to move out of our house and told they were servants no more. They were given their own piece of land down by their home village of Man Tao, about seventy *li* south of here. They left about ten days ago.

"Before they left, Ming Suk said he regretted very much he had to leave us after having served in our household all his life. He and Ming Sum kowtowed to your father and me, and your father bent down and helped them up on their feet. Ming Sum and I were crying."

I rested my head on my mother's knees, my heart too full for words. My mother touched my head comfortingly.

"I will miss them very much," I managed to say.

"Your father and I went over to their place to see them off. Your father gave Ming Suk a gold bar, one of the few he has hidden in the house, and he said, 'Ah Ming, this is for you. Hide it well. It may be useful to you some day. I wish I could give you more, but I have run into hard times. I will never forget how good a servant you have been all these years, especially the years at Tai Shek. We could not have survived there without you and your good wife. If our paths do not cross again in this life, I hope in the next life we will meet again, not as master and servant, but as equals.' Your father then embraced Ming Suk."

"Mother," I said, holding her hands, "I have decided to stay home and help Father in the field. We won't starve as long as we work hard. I am not returning to the university."

"But what about your education, Tak Sing? You should go back. Your father and I will manage here," my mother said, but I knew it was not what her heart wanted her to say.

"Your mother is right, Tak Sing." I heard my father's voice and turned to see him in the chamber, his figure silhouetted in the doorway. "I want you to go back after the spring holiday. You will fulfill your filial duty to us by going back to the university and finishing your education."

I knew that voice of my father's, the voice of authority. But for the first time in my life, I was determined to contest him.

"Father, I have always respected your sound judgment and obeyed you, but if I return to Guangzhou, you will be left alone to plough the field. Even though it is not much land, it is hard work, and you have not worked in the field for a long time. And Mother who has never worked in her life will now have to do all the housework. Father, allow me to stay home and help you both, if not for your own sake, for Mother's," I begged. Then, to add weight to my plea, I added, "At least, for now, let me stay. My education can wait. When times are better, I will go back."

My father was silent as he looked out into the courtyard. I looked at my mother, so thin and frail, and her once-bound feet so deformed. How could she manage all the work Ming Sum used to do for us? My father was turning fifty-five in a month's time. I could not let him toil in the field without help. He turned to me, and his face was etched in sorrow.

"My son, I grew up in a farming community. Although my father was a rich landlord, I was sent to the local village temple to learn reading and writing for just a few years. When you were born, I vowed this son of mine would be given every opportunity to pursue a full education, that he might bring honour to our ancestors. Above all, I wanted you to have the chance to break away from the land and pursue your own destiny. If you give up the university now, Tak Sing, you will be tied to the land all your life, like me and your grandfather." My father took a deep breath, then continued in a firm voice, "That is why I want you to go back to the university at the end of the holiday. I don't need you here. I worked on my father's land when I was young, and I can work again on the little they give us. On no account are you to stay home. It is my wish and my command." He ended with a tone of finality I had known throughout my years growing up, and I knew no pleading and reasoning with him at that moment would do any good.

Yet I could not go back to Guangzhou.

17

A Chinese Story

Purged

WHEN WE LEFT THE BIG HOUSE in 1939 to escape the Japanese, we hoped and expected to return. Tai Shek was a sojourn we regarded as a haven, a refuge from a worse predicament if we had remained in the big house. But in 1950, when we left at the order of the Communists, we knew we would never return. I had a strong aching sense I was saying a permanent farewell to the house and all it embodied, a life forever gone, an era that was no more. We packed the few belongings we would take with us. And we cleaned the house meticulously those last days.

"I want to remember the house the way I have always known it, except of course for the time when we came back after the war," my father said, as he compulsively and vigorously polished the shiny white marble framing one of several moon gates. "I want it to be in a perfect condition for as long as I can help it." His face contorted into a bitter smile.

We left most things behind in the big house, loading only necessities – clothing, blankets, an iron wok, a couple of pots, and some bowls and dishes – into a pushcart. On the morning of our departure, a mail carrier from Ka Hing arrived on his bike, signaling the resumption of the postal service. He handed me a letter. I looked at the writing on the envelope, and my heart beat faster. It was a letter from Ah Chu, addressed to me. Tears came into my eyes, as I felt an unspeakable relief that Ah Chu was alive. Quickly I put the letter into my pocket as my father called me from inside the house.

Soon we were walking through the front gate onto the dirt

road beyond, I pushing the cartload of our belongings and my father carrying a hoe and a rake on his shoulder, with my mother walking slowly beside him, often leaning on his arm for support. I stole a glance at my father. He wore a stony, determined expression on his face as he set his eyes on the road in front of him. Slowly we walked on, none of us saying a word, and the only sounds we made came from the rattling of the objects in the pushcart as it bumped forward on the rough path. We reached the end of the road and turned in the direction of our new abode. My mother was crying quietly. My father never once looked back.

We made very slow progress, partly because of the heavy pushcart, but mainly because my mother could not walk fast. We rested many times by the roadside and finally reached our little grey stone house with a black tiled roof in the late afternoon. It was smaller than our house near Tai Shek, on the acre of land allotted to us, in a far corner of what used to be the land one of my father's tenant farmers rented from him.

When we had unpacked everything into the house, my father stood at the edge of his plot, looking at the vast expanse of land in front of him, land once his, but now divided into small segments so that every man, woman and child in the township could have a share. My mother went up to him, and he put his arm around her shoulders in a protective way. They stood together for a long while, watching the sun go down behind the distant purple hills.

I read Ah Chu's letter as soon as I had a private moment. All these years, I have saved it, along with the letter he wrote me when he left for Yan'an.

January 5, 1950

Brother Tak Sing,

In the four years since I left home, many events have taken place that have changed the course of history and

79

our country's destiny. I have been very honoured to have taken an active part, no matter how small, in the shaping of our country's future. The time is now ripe for everyone who calls himself Chinese to do his part for the good of the People's Republic of China.

When I left Guangdong four years ago, I made my way to Yan'an through Guangxi, Guizhou, Sichuan. It took me three months to reach Yan'an, because I had to go through Guomindang territory, often hiding from Guomindang soldiers by day, and passing mountainous terrain and crossing rivers by night. Although the route was dangerous, I was happy to be following the footsteps of the Long Marchers. When I reached Yan'an and saw the cave city, I was overcome by the undaunted spirit and patriotic ideals of the Communists in face of extreme hardship and poverty. I knew there was hope for China yet.

I received military training in Yan'an while attending regular school there. Our classroom was in one of the caves dug out of the hills. When the Guomindang took Yan'an in 1947, I had to flee for my life. I made my way with some of my comrades to Shandong and joined the guerrillas in the hills in the southwest part of Shandong. Soon after the Communists recovered Yan'an in 1948, I returned to Yan'an and enlisted in the army. When Commander Zhu De led his troops to the north bank of the Yangtze before the takeover of Nanjing, I was there. I was with the troops entering Nanjing when it fell. Since the establishment of the new government in Beijing, I have been assigned to the party committee for the countryside just outside Nanjing, as an assistant to the chief cadre.

Even though I have not written until now, I have had news of you all. I will not write separately to my pa and ma, for this letter is as much for them as it is for you. I entrust you to visit them and read this letter to them. Tell them it is my wish to see them again some day. As for you,

*my friend, the fact that you are from the landowning class
will be a hindrance to you wherever you go, but if you serve
the new government well, you will eventually be forgiven
for what you had no control of, and you will advance.
China needs people like you.*

I shall end here. I wish you and your family well.

So Kwong Wah

*Postscript: I have cast off my old name, for it was a
reminder of the superstition and servitude that had stifled
our country for centuries. We need to purge China of such
social evils.*

What was in a name? As I finished reading Ah Chu's letter, it
meant all the differences between the past and the present, old
feudal values and new Communist principles. For me, Ah Chu's
change of name was a personal loss. Carefully I folded the letter
and put it back in my pocket. I believed, below the surface, he
was still the Ah Chu I knew and grew up with, my friend and
brother. He must *want* to say he missed us, his parents, me, my
father and mother. He must *want* to say to his parents, "I love you,
Pa and Ma." Why was he not saying it in the letter? What was he
afraid of? Could memories and feelings nourished through all the
years of our growing up together mean nothing in the face of a
political ideology? Was there no room for family ties and personal
relationships in a social order born of revolution? I noticed from
Ah Chu's letter his writing had improved tremendously. He was
a bright fellow and it was likely the government had plans for
him.

Ah Chu wrote only to me. He wanted me to visit his parents
and bring them his unspoken message of love, on the pretext I
should read his letter to them. Ah Chu knew I would fill in for
him the feelings for his parents he could not express on paper.

His letter must have been screened, like all our activities, our belongings, our thoughts. A few days before I was due to leave for Guangzhou, I told my father I was going to visit a friend about thirty *li* southwest of Ka Hing. I caught a lorry heading for Maoming. I got off at the village of Man Tao and soon located Ming Suk and Ming Sum. They were overjoyed to see me and showered me with questions about my father and mother, about Guangzhou and the university. They did not bring up the subject of Ah Chu until I took out his letter and read it to them.

"Tell Pa and Ma I love them and miss them very much. In serving China well, I will be honouring them," I added.

"I always knew he was a good son. I am so proud. Such an important position, too," Ming Sum said tearfully.

Before I left, I said to Ming Suk, "I am not going back to Guangzhou. Mother's health is poor, and soon Father will be out in the field. I am needed at home."

"If only Ah Chu would think the way you do, Young Master," said Ming Suk, shaking his head.

"He thinks bigger thoughts. His motives are selfless and honourable."

"One cannot be honourable without piety to one's father and mother, Young Master."

"Ming Suk, call me Tak Sing from now on. If anyone hears you addressing me or my father in the old way, we will be in trouble."

My holiday was coming to an end. I needed to confront my father with my decision not to go back to Guangzhou. Soon, the spring rain would arrive and the earth would be soft enough to plough. I was worried about my mother. The coughing and fever had come back. Just three days before I was due to leave for Guangzhou, my mother coughed up blood. Later, after she had fallen asleep, I went into the front room where my father was sitting on one of the hard pine chairs, smoking his water pipe, the one luxury he brought with him from the old house. Knowing how determined he was to promote my welfare even at the cost of self-sacrifice, I decided to approach him with a different point of argument.

"Father, I know you have always wanted me to earn a higher education and make a life for myself away from the farms. But since the new government took over, universities have mostly become the powerhouse of Communist thought. The days of the freedom of expression in the pursuit of a liberal education are gone. My thoughts will be controlled and my mind stifled in no time if I go back. Father, I cannot survive in such an environment."

My father looked out of the window at the grey sky, with an expression of anger mixed with resignation.

"Son, it grieves me to see the hope I have built up in you over the years vanish with the Communist takeover. I am growing old, and I will accept and bear whatever comes my way in the remaining years of my life. But you, Tak Sing, have a whole future in front of you, and I will not be appeased if I see your life destroyed at the hands of the Communists." My father said the last sentence in one breath, his voice rising to a loud crescendo of anger as he finished. I noticed for the first time tears trickling down from the corners of his eyes. I remained silent, staring at the floor, while he recollected himself. After a while, he said in a quiet but determined voice, "Perhaps you should stay home for a while, but don't you think for a moment this is to be your lot in life."

The spring holiday came to an end. I remained at home, taking care of my mother, doing the best I could to make her feel more comfortable. When the Ching Ming festival arrived, and with it a south wind that brought warmth and humidity, I helped my father till the soil of our one acre of land and grow green cabbage, turnip, and yam. We were part of a mutual aid team of farmers, pooling our equipment and sharing our produce. Most of the farmers in our group were once my father's tenants, who remembered him kindly, and they repaid him with consideration, treating him as one of their equals. Other landlords were not as lucky, nor were they as deserving of kindness.

On one of my trips back to Ka Hing, I heard about the frightful trial of a landlord in the village of Kiu Tow about twenty *li* from us. The man was led to the open village square, with a long wooden board behind his back reading: *Wang Hong, Murderer and Extortionist.* More than a hundred villagers had assembled and Wang Hong was made to kneel in the middle of them. One by one, his tenant farmers came forward to accuse him of crimes he had committed.

One distraught woman said her husband could not pay him the full rent in grain when the harvest was bad three years earlier. The beast, as she called Wang Hong, raided their home one night with his men, all roughnecks who did his dirty work for him. They ransacked the house, overturning everything including the small altar to honour the family's ancestors, looking for grain and money that were not there. They found a few sweet potatoes and a small sack of flour in the rice bin, whereupon Wang Hong accused the woman's husband of hiding food that should go to the rent. He ordered his men to take the little food they found and beat the woman's husband to unconsciousness, amidst the frantic hunger cries of their month-old son. Her husband died a few days later and neighbours helped dig a hole in the field where she buried him without a coffin. Soon after, the baby became sick with vomiting and a fever and died within a month of his father's death. The woman wrapped her child in an old rice sack and buried him in the field beside his father. Alone and destitute, she tried to kill herself jumping into a river, but was rescued by a neighbouring farmer, who took her in and asked her to nurse his infant daughter, for his wife had died at childbirth.

"You killed my husband," one of the villagers quoted the woman as saying to Wang Hong. "My baby would have lived if it were not for you. My milk would have been used to nourish my own child, instead of another's. You are worse than a beast, not worthy of the dirt I walk on. You deserve to be condemned to the ninth level of hell!"

The Peasant Association condemned Wang Hong right there

and then to be executed amidst the angry frenzied shouts of all the peasants there. There was so much hatred for this man that, when the local party committee sentenced him to be shot immediately, the peasants shouted loud opposition to the method of execution. They wanted him to die a horrible and lingering death. He was tied to a scaffold and flayed alive by a farmer who was expert with a butcher's knife. As Wang Hong screamed in excruciating agony, a kinder farmer stepped up and ended his suffering by plunging a knife into his heart.

I was stunned by what I heard. Such was the cruelty of many landlords. Such was the passion for revenge and more cruelty among the peasants. Many atrocities were committed by peasants on landlords that year, but we were spared.

18

A Chinese Story

Leaving Home

IN THE WINTER OF 1951, just as the civil war ended, and people were hopeful of peace, China was sending troops into Korea to help the Communists in that country's civil war. The war was to result in the loss of many Chinese lives.

In the meantime, my mother's condition worsened, and by January, she was confined to her bed most of the time.

"Tak Sing, you are now twenty-two. Many men your age already have children of their own. I know you want to marry someone you like, but you should do so soon," my mother said on one of her better days, her head resting on her hard black lacquered pillow as I stirred the charcoal in her brazier.

"Mother, I'll know when the right girl comes along. I can assure you she will be somebody you approve of, somebody as good as you. I will not let you down," I said, my heart heavy with the realization she would most likely never get to see her daughter-in-law. I added quickly, "We still have to go to Guangzhou when you are better, Mother."

But my mother never got better. Her breath became laboured and difficult, and the cough that kept her awake in the night was a drawn painful one. On the rare occasions when she felt more comfortable, she would sit up in bed, her head leaning against the wall, and watch me intently as I sat by the window reading or writing. When the damp southerly breeze came, my mother's bad days far outnumbered her good ones, and her life soon became one long continuous ordeal, in and out of consciousness. It grieved my father and me to see her suffering so. Two days before

Ching Ming, my mother died, not knowing we were there with her to the end.

We buried her in the family's ancestral plot two *li* north of Ka Hing. I sent word to Ming Suk who came back for the funeral. There was no procession with flutes and cymbals, just a simple Buddhist ceremony as my father and I, with the help of Ming Suk and our former tenant farmer Cheung Fook, carried her coffin to the grave site and laid her to rest. On her tombstone were these words I composed:

> *Greatness needs not come from heroic deeds*
> *That rouse the heavens and rock the earth;*
> *It can manifest itself in the silent love*
> *Of a virtuous wife and a good mother.*

For the next six months, I wore a black cloth band on my arm as a symbol of mourning. My father placed a photograph of my mother on the small altar to our ancestors in the tiny front room of our house. We put a couple of Xinhui oranges on the altar whenever we could, for my mother loved those oranges. Every morning, as soon as I got up, I lit some incense at the altar for her. I remembered as a child seeing her light incense to *Kuan Yin* in the temple. My mother had become my *Kuan Yin*. As for my father, even though he was not disposed to an open display of emotion, he became gloomy after my mother's death, and I caught him once wiping a tear as he looked at my mother's picture.

That spring and summer, my father and I worked hard in the field, ploughing not only our own plot, but also the common land that was part of our cooperative. For the time, there was enough to eat, three meals of rice a day. Often, I found my father in deep thought looking out to the fields and the hills beyond. Perhaps he was thinking of my mother. Or better days when he was lord of all he surveyed.

On the night of the Mid-Autumnal Festival, I sat with him outside our little house, drinking a green tea we drank only on

87

special days, and admiring the perfect circle of the moon. He was silent for a long time.

"Tak Sing, I have been thinking seriously of late about your future," he finally said. "There is nothing for you here. This is no life for a young man like you. For this reason, I want you to go to Hong Kong. I know what you are going to say, but hear me out. I have a lot of hope in you. Only when I know you have every chance of living up to my expectations will I be at peace. Go, son, and find your new life in a free land. Only in doing so will you fulfill your filial duty to me and to your mother."

I knew my father was right. And deep down I knew I wanted to leave. After my mother's death, my father was the only reason I was staying in Guangdong. How could I oppose him convincingly when I knew I should go, that I wanted to go, as much as he wanted me to? And yet, I could not bear the thought of leaving him in the winter of his life, him who sired and raised me, him who would not hesitate for a moment to give his life for me.

"Stay with me till after the harvest, Tak Sing, then go," my father continued quietly, "before it is too late."

I stayed on and helped my father with the harvest. And when I had threshed the last stalk of rice on the common land and dug up the last sweet potato from our own plot, my father and I both knew it was time for me to go. I tried hard to remain busy, to find work to do on the land, plucking the last weed from the field, sweeping the grounds around the house over and over again, and cleaning the farm tools even though I had already cleaned them for the winter. In short, I wanted to stall for time, for I dreaded the moment when my father would say, "Son, it is time for you to go." Or was my father also trying to avoid the moment of parting?

One afternoon about two weeks after the harvest, I walked to the family's burial ground to visit my mother's grave for what I knew would be the last time. I knelt in front of her tombstone for a long time.

"Mother," I whispered, "I shall not disappoint you. I shall make you proud."

When I reached home that evening, my father had prepared a sumptuous supper of a whole chicken soaked in wine, and a pond fish – food I had not seen or tasted in a long time. He placed the dishes on the little altar.

"Tak Sing, come pay your respects to your ancestors and your mother. She loved you dearly in life. She will guide and protect you on your way."

I lit some incense and kowtowed in front of my ancestors' plaques and my mother's portrait. Afterwards, my father and I sat down at the table and ate the food for supper, the best meal we had had in a long, long time, our last supper together. But I could not enjoy the food. It seemed, with every bite, I was severing a bit of my connection with the past, of my ties with family and country.

"Tak Sing, I have hidden three gold bars behind the stove," my father said after we had eaten. "I want you to take them with you to Hong Kong and use them well. They will keep you alive until you find means to support yourself. Tomorrow, at dawn, I will go with you to Guangzhou and see you off on the train to Hong Kong."

He removed a brick in the wall behind the wood stove, took out the gold bars, each about the length of my index finger but twice as wide and weighing five *liang*, and handed them to me.

"These are all we have left," he said. Without another word, he went out of the house to the edge of the field to smoke his pipe. I packed my belongings into the black vinyl suitcase I bought in Guangzhou, the few clothes I had, including my only pair of foreign-styled pants and a shirt from Guangzhou, a few photographs including one of my mother and father in front of the big house, and the one of Ah Chu and me taken in Ka Hing shortly before he left for Yan'an, and his two letters.

I wanted so much to go up to my father and tell him how much I would miss him when I was gone, but something kept me back. Unlike my mother, my father was not one to whom I could freely express my feelings. That night, I put on the cotton *samfu* I would be wearing for the journey the next morning. I hid the three gold bars inside my waistband and slept with them.

Before the first twitter launched the orchestral morning birdsong, before there was the slightest hint of red in the eastern sky, my father and I walked to Ka Hing along the dirt road. Neither of us spoke, as though all we could think of was to reach the end of the road, and from there go on to Guangzhou. I was unusually aware of the limpid country air on my skin, a cool, luring caress touching my senses. I took deep breaths. Funny, the air never smelled so sweet as on the morning of my departure, that country smell of newly-turned sod moistened with dew drops in the night, before it hardened and cracked under the scorching sun. Somewhere a cock crowed, the first of the heralds of dawn.

We reached Ka Hing just as day was about to break and boarded a lorry loading produce to take to Guangzhou. We sat in the back among the crates, and as we left Ka Hing on the gravel road, I turned back to look at my home village, while the lorry put distance between us. Ka Hing looked humble and insignificant in the morning haze. Yet, if there was a place where I'd rather be on the face of the earth, it was Ka Hing.

Gradually the sky reddened in the east, and clouds took on all shades of pink and orange, and the countryside unraveled on all sides about me. Anxiously I took mental pictures of farmhouses, duck ponds, and chicken coops, of harvested fields, willow trees and distant hills, things I hardly noticed growing up because they were too familiar. The lorry bumped on toward Guangzhou. And all the while, I felt untold heaviness in my heart.

We arrived in Guangzhou and were dropped off at the train station in the early afternoon. The platform was crowded as we made our way to the train. I held onto my suitcase and ticket. My father followed me closely.

"These are for you, Tak Sing, in case you get thirsty on the train," I heard him say just before we reached the train.

I turned around and saw him taking two Xinhui oranges out of the inner pockets of his jacket. I could not contain myself any longer.

"Father, I don't have to go. I want to stay with you."

Putting one hand on my shoulder, he said in a steady voice, "Tak Sing, listen to me. I will be miserable the rest of my life if you stay. I will feel my life is a total failure if I cannot give my son a chance to be free, to break away from this hopeless situation we are in. If you go, I will end my days in peace, without any regret. Go for my sake, if not for your own."

"I will come back to see you, Father," I said between sobs. "I will come back."

"Leave that to the future, my son. Look after yourself. Find a good job. Continue your education if you have the opportunity. Remember what your mother said – get yourself a good wife. And always bear in your mind whatever you do, do it well, do it straight. As for me, I am still strong, and the gods have blessed me with good health. I will have enough to eat, and I won't be lonely since I have my friends nearby. Just write sometimes." He patted me on the back and with a firm hand pushed me forward toward the ticket officer standing at the base of the steps to the train.

I looked at him through my tears. He embraced me then, for a brief moment, before letting me go. I boarded the train and found my seat. Slowly the train ground its way out of the station, bound for Shenzhen and the border with Hong Kong. I scanned the platform to catch one last glimpse of my father through the foggy glass of the window but I could not find him in the crowd.

19

No Money Can Buy

THE FLUSHING OF THE TOILET, then the shuffling of feet, and Ah Lan peers in.

"Seenla, four o'clock, and you are still up!"

"I'm reading Papa's book. Whenever I open it, I don't want to close it until I've come to the last page."

Ah Lan's stern face softens, and gradually there forms a faraway look in her eyes.

"The night he came home from the hospital, after visiting your Mummy and seeing you for the first time, he took out his inkwell, brush, paper, all the writing stuff. I had often seen him writing in his free time, but," Ah Lan pauses, and, looking at me with raised eyebrows, continues, "after a long day at the hospital waiting for you to be born? I asked him what he was doing. And he said: 'Ah Lan, I cannot afford to buy my daughter an expensive gift, but I'm going to give her something no money can buy. I'm going to give her a story, that she may know her heritage.' And for the next three years, whenever he had some spare time, he was writing the story for you."

20

A Chinese Story

Hong Kong

THE TRAIN STOPPED AT SHENZHEN, a small border town with bungalows and shops, cyclists and pedestrians, mostly farmers judging from their attire – black *samfu*, farmers' wide straw hats with black fringes, and straw sandals. Several lorries full of baskets of vegetables and one packed tight with squealing piglets in wicker cages were parked near the train station. I changed to another train for Hong Kong. Throughout the whole journey, I thought only of my father, missing him, worrying about him as he traveled back to our village alone, wishing more than anything in the world to turn back and be at his side for as long as he lived.

As we neared the border at Lo Wu, I saw the British flag flying above the guard station marking the entrance to Hong Kong. It was the first time I set eyes on the Union Jack. Years later, when I was with the Hong Kong border police, guarding against the influx of refugees from the mainland, I would look back at the moment of my first crossing into Hong Kong and feel how lucky I was that the border was open when I stepped over.

The train passed more paddy fields and farms. I could still imagine myself in rural Guangdong. Then the landscape gradually changed, as the train neared Kowloon. I saw buildings two, three or four storeys high, and streets with more cars than bicycles. By the time the train pulled into the Kowloon-Canton Railway Terminus, it was dark under the clear October sky. Retrieving my suitcase from the rack above my seat, I made my way to the door of my car and stepped down to the platform. It

ELSIE SZE

was bustling with people alighting from the train, and people welcoming relatives and friends to the British colony. I looked up and down the platform lit with bright fluorescent lights under a long white canopy. I was alone in the crowd. A desperate sense of loss and loneliness gripped me.

I was jostled to the station's main entrance, one hand holding tightly my suitcase, the other hand feeling the three gold bars tucked safely inside my waistband. Breathing the cool evening air outside the station, I realized how bad the air had been on the train, where three, sometimes four, passengers were crammed into hard seats intended for two. Standing on a front step of the station entrance, I looked up to see a tall tower above me, its big clock lit up like a full moon beneath a small white dome. I clearly remember it was half-past seven when my Hong Kong life began. As I stepped onto the street, I began to feel the reality of where I was, the desperate urgency of my situation. I needed some Hong Kong money to buy food and find a place to sleep. Several young beggars followed me closely as I walked away from the station, on a street lined with low dark buildings and lit by gas street lamps. I had nothing to give them, so I walked briskly, hoping to lose them. After a short while, they turned away to beg from another.

I crossed the street and came to an enormous, brightly lit, tall building. In front of the building was a huge illuminated fountain. Red carpet covered the front steps leading up to an entrance facade of polished stone, shiny metal and sparkling glass. The place was the Peninsula Hotel, unknown to me at the time. To this day, I have had no occasion to walk through its doors.

Soon I came to a livelier part of the city, where suspended garish neon signs almost met each other in mid-air across narrow streets, above honking cars and jostling pedestrians. I walked along a pavement, suitcase in hand, finding it hard to believe just that morning I was still in rural China. I could never have envisioned a place such as Hong Kong, and my first experience of it thrilled and awed me beyond words. I passed a dried seafood shop displaying a big dried sail-shaped fin of a shark. In the window of a medicine shop was a huge coiled snake preserved in a glass jar. In another window was a photograph of a man whose long bushy beard was a nest for bees, an advertisement for the products of a local honey farm. Street vendors laid out their wares on the pavement – watches, jades, Chinese artifacts of wood, pottery and stone – commanding crowds attracted to the merchandise as well as the bargain price. Nearby, inside the window of an ivory shop, a little old man with a goatee and wearing a black *samfu* was seated at a workbench, carving dragons into a multi-layered ivory ball the size of a peach. Displayed in the window were miniature elephants of various sizes, all made of ivory. Sitting on a wood stand was a yard-long tusk carved with imperial scenes of palaces and gardens, and court ladies on bridges under willow trees. I had never seen so many shops selling so much exotic merchandise, not even in Guangzhou.

Then there were the eateries. I passed noodle houses with huge signs displaying the character *Min*. Inside the front open windows, cooks were ladling noodles and dumplings from steaming pots into big soup bowls. I passed a barbecue shop where roast ducks and strips of red roasted pork hung at the window, dripping juices and grease into a pan. Food and more food. I was very hungry. Then I remembered the two oranges my father gave me. I could not eat them on the train, where I was sitting squashed between two women arguing with each other over a family matter. I took them out of the outside pocket of the suitcase and, sitting down on a concrete step below a billboard indicating *Beauty Parlour*, started peeling them.

As I sat there, eating my oranges and trying to decide my next move, my eyes fell on a shop across the street, its entrance brightly lit with a neon sign saying: *Tai Lee Gold Merchant*. I picked up my suitcase and crossed the street. It was a jewelry store, displaying a glittering array of gold rings, bracelets and chains in its showcases. At the entrance was a smaller sign, "99% Gold. Today's price $250 per *liang*." That might be a good place to sell one of my gold bars. As I stepped in with my suitcase, the shopkeepers looked at me in a manner that made me feel I had no right or reason to be there.

"What do you want?" asked a balding bespectacled man in a brown Chinese jacket of silky brocade and matching pants. He looked at me with the haughtiness of a minister of an ancient emperor's court.

"Do you buy gold here?" I ventured in a hesitant voice.

"Yes we do. Why – you have some?"

"Actually I do," I said, sounding a bit apologetic for no reason.

"Well, let's see what you've got, and I'll decide if it's real stuff," the man said.

I asked to be excused, and going over to a corner of the shop, with my back to the people in the store, I loosened my waistband and took out one piece of gold. I presented it to the man who spoke to me. As soon as he saw the yellow bar, his countenance changed from disdain to disbelief. He took the bar with both hands almost reverently. He beckoned to me to sit down at one of the inner counters away from the entrance to the store and the inquisitive eyes of passersby. Using a hand balance he weighed the bar in my presence.

"Five *liang* of gold, 99% purity, at $250 a *liang*. We'll pay you $1250 for the bar," he said conclusively, but his manner had become reasonably courteous, and he looked as one about to do business with an associate. No question was asked as to the origin of the gold bar.

I was elated that the bar was worth so much and relieved the transaction was after all easier than I had imagined. With the money safely tucked in the inside pocket of my jacket, I found my way back to one of the noodle eateries and ordered a bowl of wonton noodles and a plateful of fried rice. I consumed both easily. Still not full in my stomach and seeing the people at the next table having a brown rolled meat that looked inviting, I asked the waiter what it was.

"*Chu tai cheung,* pig's large intestines. Our specialty. Very good."

I asked for a plateful to be brought to me. The waiter cast a curious glance at me, perhaps wondering if I had just come from a prison camp, or worrying if I had money to pay for all the food. The pig's entrails were the most delicious food I had ever tasted, boiled in soya sauce with spices and herbs. I savoured every bit of it. As I left the noodle shop, my stomach was satisfied, but I felt guilty at the thought that I was enjoying the food so much when I had only left my hometown that morning, where people had hardly enough to eat. Three bowls of rice and green vegetables made up my father's usual daily diet.

It was past ten o'clock by the time I walked back to the train station. I would spend the first night inside the station and look for a place to stay in the morning. I was content to lie down on one of the benches, using my suitcase for a pillow.

21

A Chinese Story

Squatters

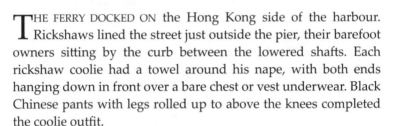

THE FERRY DOCKED ON the Hong Kong side of the harbour. Rickshaws lined the street just outside the pier, their barefoot owners sitting by the curb between the lowered shafts. Each rickshaw coolie had a towel around his nape, with both ends hanging down in front over a bare chest or vest underwear. Black Chinese pants with legs rolled up to above the knees completed the coolie outfit.

Feeling a tug on my pants, I turned around and saw a young boy wearing a fading black Chinese jacket and black pants too short for him. He could be no more than eight or nine years old. He looked up at me, and, for a split second, I thought I was looking at Ah Chu as I remembered him when we were children. He had the same thin and lanky build, and the same loose strands of hair over his forehead. But this boy had high cheekbones and a higher nose bridge suggesting he might have come from a line of northern ancestors. His eyes were as intent as Ah Chu's but lacked the latter's liveliness, and the forlorn expression on his sallow face seemed to tell the world he was missing out on the joys of childhood. He held out his cupped hand, and I realized he was a beggar. Because he reminded me of Ah Chu, I stopped in my step, put my suitcase on the ground between my legs, and fumbled in my pants pocket for a coin. I put ten cents into the dirty palm.

"Little friend, what is your name?" I asked.

He could have taken the coin and run, but instead he answered, "I am called Kay Chai." Looking at the money in his hand, he added, "Thank you."

"Where do you live?" I pursued, taking a liking to the image of Ah Chu.

"Up on the hillside, in Wanchai," he answered. "Where do *you* live?"

"I don't have a place yet," I answered. As an afterthought, I asked, "Is there a vacancy for rent where you are?" Wherever he lived the rent must be cheap, and I needed to conserve my money, for I had no idea how soon I could find work.

"I don't know, but my ma would know. Why don't you come home with me and ask her yourself."

Kay Chai's suggestion might not be a bad one. I asked if we should take a rickshaw to his house, but Kay Chai said, "They cost a lot of money. I usually walk here from Wanchai, but if you can pay for a tram-ride for both of us, I'll take you to a tram stop."

I was impressed by his sound financial advice. Picking up my suitcase, I walked beside Kay Chai. Soon we were on Des Voeux Road. We boarded a double deckered tram and sat in the lower level since the fare for the upper level was twice as much. The tram clanged on its track in the middle of the road between cars, bicycles, rickshaws and even pedestrians. It passed a gigantic billboard that extended the entire side of a three-storey building, with pictures of a beautiful couple and handsome watches displayed on it. I was amazed at the number of pawnshops we passed, their red gourd-shaped emblems hanging prominently above their entrances. Then there were the numerous teahouses, eateries and barbecue shops, much like the ones I saw the night before in Kowloon, except, in the daytime, the glitter, excitement and crowds were not there. The tram made frequent stops, its passengers getting on and off in the middle of the road, at the risk of being hit by cars failing to stop for them.

As I was watching the street drama unfold, Kay Chai told me to alight at the next stop. We were in Wanchai, he said. What I saw when I got off the tram confounded me, for covering the hillside in front of me were multitudinous shanties built with boards and plywood, and sheets of tin and plastic. I had seen many dilapidated houses of poor farmers in rural Guangdong, but never had I set eyes on anything the like of the hillside squatter huts confronting me. Smoke rose from various parts of the hill, where cooking was probably taking place. I could hear above the hum of traffic dogs barking and children crying. I followed Kay Chai along a gravel footpath going uphill. Toddlers in crotchless pants and barefooted school-aged children were playing outside the shanties, women were cooking on wood burners in the open, and some were hanging up washing on clotheslines tied outside the huts. The stench of urine assaulted my nasal passage. Perhaps we were nearing an outhouse, or perhaps the whole hillside was one big outhouse. Dogs were on the loose, sniffing around garbage piles for food. The hillside bustled with life, but it seemed to be wretched life, even compared to Tai Shek.

Kay Chai stopped at a shanty about two-thirds up the inhabited part of the hill facing the road below. It had wooden sides and a tin roof. Some washing hung on a clothesline strung from the hut to a tree nearby. Near the side of the hut on the dirt sat a wood burner charred from use, and a pile of dry wood. The door was open, and a piece of cloth the length and width of the doorway hung over the entrance, shielding the inside of the hut from view. On each side of the doorway was glued a narrow strip of red paper with words of good fortune.

"My ma is home today. Normally she would be working down in Wanchai," explained Kay Chai.

"What does she do?" I asked, wondering why she would let her son beg in the streets.

"She writes letters," said Kay Chai, looking up with pride. "Wait here."

Kay Chai went inside. He emerged after a few minutes from behind the cloth curtain with a small woman I judged to be in her thirties, with short straight hair, wearing a floral *samfu* and plastic slippers. She studied me suspiciously for a moment until her eyes rested on the suitcase.

"My son told me you are looking for a place to stay," she

began without any introduction, in the voice of one addressing a stranger. "There are some empty lots further up, but you have to pay."

I assured her I had no intention of not paying.

"The hill is really government land," she continued. "We don't pay rent to build on it, but we pay some people in order to secure protection from thugs who may steal our things and destroy our hut. This is still cheaper than anywhere else. If you are really interested, I can show you a good empty lot. The people collecting the protection money are coming today, and you can talk to them."

"I'd really be grateful, Ah Sum," I said, addressing her politely. "Your son has been most helpful. I wouldn't have known about this place without him."

On the mention of Kay Chai, she smiled faintly and said, "He is a wild one. No father to teach him. I am always working to earn us two bowls of rice and have no money to send him to school." There was regret in her voice as she looked at her son who was standing quietly by, listening to our conversation.

"Kay Chai told me you are a letter-writer."

"Yes, but today I am staying home because the people I told you about are coming to collect. I have to wait for them. If I don't pay when they come, we will not be protected. Who knows what will happen then to our hut and everything in it."

Telling Kay Chai to stay at the shanty, his mother led the way up the hill to a moderately flat spot off the main footpath, about fifteen feet long and ten feet deep. Some pieces of ripped cardboard and wood splinters were strewn here and there on the dirt. A darkened spot in the ground suggested cooking might have recently been done there. I could see the roads of Wanchai below, and trams moving at a snail's pace.

"Premium lot," said Kay Chai's mother. "The previous hut was razed to the ground just two days ago, because the people living here did not pay protection money. Thugs came in the middle of the day while the man and his wife were out, pulled the hut down, took everything worth taking, too. They were mainland refugees, that couple. Don't know where they went from here. The lot is all yours if you want it, but remember to pay your dues."

I thought for only a moment. I should make the most of the situation and build my home there. Kay Chai's mother told me the dues were thirty dollars every three months, a reasonable sum to pay for the safety of my hut, freedom from harassment, and peace of mind. So when the collectors came later that morning, I was ready with my money.

Four of them came, wearing western-style suits and black leather shoes. At first they eyed me with suspicion and demanded to know who I was. When I told them my intention of building on the vacant lot, they became quite friendly.

"Best lot on this side of the hill. Best view of Wanchai. Can't find anything better. We are here to protect your property from thieves roaming the hillside. Some come up from the city just to steal from you poor folks, and if they find nothing worth taking, they tear down your hut," said one of the men, presumably the spokesman of the group.

"I shall be happy to pay the dues," I heard myself saying.

Thus, I staked my claim to the lot. That afternoon, Kay Chai took me to a junkyard in Wanchai where I picked out usable wood, metal, plastics, and rocks. Kay Chai and I carried the salvaged materials uphill in several trips. By the time we had made our last trip uphill, the sun had set. I stopped at Kay Chai's hut to thank his mother for helping me find a home. Their family name was Wong. Wong Sum, as I would address his mother, was just getting supper ready and invited me to eat with them. I ate three bowls of rice with salted fish and pickled cucumber. I offered to pay for the food.

"We are neighbours now, and we should help each other. I will not take money from you for a little rice," Wong Sum said with a wave of her hand. "Who knows, Kay Chai may learn something good from you. I am ashamed to let him wander to the Star Ferry Pier to beg from strangers, but what can I do? I am never here in the daytime." Wong Sum sighed, looking over to her son who was washing the few dishes in a plastic basin of water. "Writing letters is a poor profession, twenty cents a letter, but at least it is respectable. On good days, I write as many as ten letters. But there are days when I get only two or three."

That night, I slept under a starlit sky on top of a wooden board on my lot. The next three days, I was busy building my hut. I had a piece of tinplate for the roof, cut at a hardware shop in Wanchai. I purchased some treated hardwood boards for the external walls and door. Some of the hillside residents lent me tools for driving the walls into the earth and attaching the roof which I erected in a slant to prevent rainwater from collecting on it. The scraps and pieces I picked up from the junkyard were used for the floor, a bed, a table and a stool. Having tied two corners of a plastic sheet to two trees on the side of my hut, and attached the other two corners to my roof, I had a canopy shielding me from rain and sun as I cooked below it. The hut was completed by the end of my fifth day in Hong Kong, and I was mighty proud of it. In truth, I believed I had the best hut on the hill, neatly assembled and partly made of new materials.

Kay Chai helped me as much as he could, within the abilities of a nine-year-old. He did not go begging at the Star Ferry Pier those few days, but I made it worth his while by paying him for his help. He was delighted with the few dollars I gave him and proudly presented the bills to his mother.

"Ma, I want to work, to earn money for you. This is better than begging."

His mother took the money and smiled at him appreciatively, then looked away with watery eyes. When he was out of hearing, she turned to me and said, "I wish I could send him to school. I teach him to read and write whenever I can, but without proper schooling, he will never get out of this dump and make a good life. His father left us four years ago, left us with not a cent. Life has been very hard. I don't care about myself, but I owe it to my son. Life is unfair, isn't it, Mr. Lee?"

"Yes it is," I answered, my thoughts wandering to my father.

I had spent more than I intended on the hut, but I now had a place to call my own, and I felt good. The first night after the hut was finished, I sat down at the table of cardboard boxes and wrote my father by the light of a kerosene lamp.

22

A Chinese Story

The Dance Hall Girl

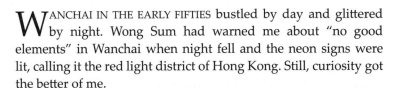

WANCHAI IN THE EARLY FIFTIES bustled by day and glittered by night. Wong Sum had warned me about "no good elements" in Wanchai when night fell and the neon signs were lit, calling it the red light district of Hong Kong. Still, curiosity got the better of me.

One evening, wearing my shirt and trousers, I strolled into Wanchai. Even though the streets were busy in the day, it was at night that they came alive with a different crowd looking for excitement and entertainment. There were numerous restaurants serving foods from different parts of China – Shanghai, Hunan, Beijing, but mostly Guangdong. I stopped in front of a brightly lit theatre showing an American film called *The Red Shoes*. The billboard displayed a picture of a beautiful ballet dancer with long thick curly hair, wearing a short red ballet dress and red ballet shoes. I could not read the English description, but I was fascinated with the dancer. I had seen one American film in Guangzhou, *Gone With The Wind*. I had thought of it for many days afterwards, and even dreamed of it at night. It had been a feast for my senses, but I did not like the female character Scarlet. I considered her a conniving and fickle woman.

I looked at the prices of tickets at the ticket booth; the cheapest was fifty cents for front stall seats. Too much to spend on entertainment.

I sauntered on to Lockhart Road on the waterfront where big old buildings three or four storeys high faced the harbour. I could smell the salty air and hear water lapping against the concrete sea wall. Nearby a peddler was selling roasted chestnuts, handing them to his customers in newspaper cones. For ten cents I could get a good handful.

My thoughts were suddenly interrupted by loud noises close behind me. I turned and saw two men scuffling with each other. One man drew a gun and aimed it at the other man. I looked desperately for a place to hide, and as I ran into the nearest stairway, I heard the loud pop of a gun. Frantically I ran up the stairs, through a half-opened door on the first landing, and only stopped when I had closed the door behind me.

For a minute or two, I stood still, for I was in pitch darkness. Then gradually, objects came into view as my eyes got accustomed to the surrounding. By the dim lights on several tables encircling a small round floor, I could see two or three couples on the floor moving to the sound of music coming from near where I was standing. I had barged into a dance hall, probably the kind Wong Sum was warning me about.

"Can I help you, mister?" A woman's voice sounded near me.

I jumped in nervousness and turned. Without looking at the speaker, I said agitatedly, "I think a man might have been shot on the street! Call the police!"

The woman immediatly spoke to a man standing nearby. Then she turned back to me.

"I recognize you," she began. Those words threw me into another frenzy. "I've seen you going up and down the hill. You live in one of the huts."

"I - I do," I stammered, still not focusing on her. "I'm sorry, but someone might have been shot out there, and this is the first place I could possibly get help."

"You have not disturbed us. In fact, you are welcome here. This is a dance hall. My name is Mimi. What's yours?" I saw the parting of red lips into a smile.

"Lee Tak Sing," I mumbled reluctantly. I looked at her then, and in the dim light, I could see a youngish woman in a red *cheongsam*, with long straight black hair, a white powdered face, and large dark eyes. I lowered my eyes. "I'll leave as soon as I know it's safe downstairs."

"Come, relax," she said in a coaxing manner, "I'll buy you a drink, or do you drink?" Before I could answer, she had taken me by the wrist and led me to a table. Sitting me at the table, she called a waiter and turned to me again. "Tell me what you'd like to have."

"I don't want anything, but thank you." I was beginning to feel very uneasy.

"We'll both have a Coca-Cola." She waved the waiter away. Then sidling up to me, she asked, "So tell me about yourself."

"I came recently from Guangzhou," I heard myself saying, although it was not exactly true, but I did not want her to know I came from rural Guangdong, that I was a country lad.

"So did I!" she said excitedly. "Now we have another thing in common. I live on the hill too, just lower down. I came to Hong Kong in '48. This is a great place to live, to enjoy life, to make lots of money, that is, if you have the right connections." She nodded at me.

I was silent. Did she have connections? Was she making a lot of money, and doing what? And if she had a lot of money, why was she living in a squatter hut?

The Coca-Cola was brought to us in two tall, cold glasses. On seeing my hesitant look, Mimi said, "It's free. Let's drink to our new friendship!"

I looked at my surroundings. A few other tables were occupied, each by a couple engaged in small talk. At one table, a man and a woman were kissing each other on the mouth, as the woman ran her hand over the man's hair. In shock and embarrassment, I looked away.

"You are in a dance hall. What you are seeing are very clean, common practices," Mimi said casually, following my gaze. "The dirty business is in those booths back there." As she spoke, she flung her head backwards in the direction across the dance floor.

My eyes followed the direction she indicated. It was then

I realized the hall was much bigger than I thought. Perhaps I was getting used to the lighting, for the room seemed to have expanded to include some booths behind the tables on the opposite side of the dance floor. They were high-backed booths, with the backs to us. I knew then what the dance halls really were – nests for prostitution. What would my father say if he knew I ever visited such a place? How would my mother feel if she could see me now?

"I think I'll leave now," I said in a low tone.

"I'm not sure if it is safe yet to go downstairs," Mimi said quickly. "Perhaps you can stay till I finish work, and walk me home. It's on your way, you know. On a night like this, I'd be afraid to walk back by myself."

She had me trapped. Inexperienced though I was with the opposite sex, I knew it would be inconsiderate and rude to allow a lady to walk home at night by herself, whether the potential danger was there or not, and of that there was little doubt in view of the evening's shooting. I felt responsible for Mimi's safety.

"Come, let's dance," and as she spoke, she stood up, pulling me up by the hand.

I started to protest, for I did not know how to dance. She put an index finger to my lips and led me to the dance floor. I stumbled after her. The music was slow. She took my arms and wound them around her waist, resting my hands just below it. She then put her arms around my neck. We started moving on the floor slowly while she steered.

"It wouldn't seem like I am working if we don't dance," she whispered into my ear. "They will call me away to another customer. Some of the customers are quite disgusting."

I felt her breath, and smelled her perfume, too strong, too intoxicating. I hated the situation I was in, yet could not free myself from it. I felt like one forced to smoke opium and afterwards unable to refuse it. She was so close her body touched me in places that sent electric shocks through me as we moved on the dance floor ever so slowly. Finally she rubbed herself against me just as her lips found mine. In that moment, I was thrown into a state of unspeakable pleasure and utter abandonment.

Mimi must have known what was happening to me. She must also know how green I was in the matter with women. Perhaps she could guess it was the first time I had ever been close to one. She drew herself a little away from me and was quiet the rest of the time we were on the dance floor. As soon as the music stopped, we returned to our table. By then, my euphoria had turned to shame and distress, and I wished the evening was nothing but a dream. I was thankful the lights were dim, but there was still the fear that the people in the dance hall might have seen through me. Perhaps they were making small talk about me, and laughing at me, at my inexperience with women. I was very uncomfortable as I sat at the table, waiting for the dance hall to close for the night, so I could take Mimi home. Mimi, however, did not entertain another customer that night. After sitting with me for a short time, while I squirmed in my seat, she left me to talk to a man who was presumably her manager, then came back to me with a shawl over her shoulders and clutching a small purse.

"I told Johnny I am leaving early with you," she said simply.

I rose thankfully. Slipping a hand through my arm, she walked out with me. The trouble on the street had died down. I did not know if anyone had been shot, and Mimi did not seem to be concerned with it. Perhaps such trouble was not an uncommon occurrence in that part of town. Once outside, Mimi took her hand off my arm. We walked silently along the waterfront. By then, I was feeling quite depressed over the events of the evening, hating myself and feeling ashamed for getting involved with a dance girl, one who sold her favours for a living. Mimi must have read my thoughts.

"Tak Sing, if I have upset you in any way tonight, I am sorry. I like you. I hope we will be friends from now on," she said shakily, stripped of all the confidence she showed earlier in the dance hall.

"I want you to know whatever took place in the dance hall

tonight means nothing to me. Tomorrow, I'll forget everything that happened in there," I said, intentionally insensitive to her feelings, and ignoring her invitation to friendship. The truth was I was as much annoyed with myself as with Mimi. Then, regretting almost immediately the harshness of my words, I added, "I don't think you should stay in that profession for a long time. Find another job. That place will doom you if you don't leave."

"It is easier said than done," Mimi said quietly. "You don't understand."

I stayed away from the vicinity of the dance hall after that night. But Mimi and I became friends. We never talked again about that evening.

23

A Chinese Story

Hawker

November 20, 1951

My dear Father,

Today I looked at the calendar and realized over a month had gone by since we parted. I am quite well. I like the little hut I have built. Though small, it is sufficient, and it is mine. I am still earnestly looking for work, and though I haven't had much luck so far, I am hopeful I will find a job soon, for I believe opportunities will come to those who try hard enough. Although I have used up much of the money from the sale of the first gold bar, I expect to have found a job before I need to sell the second one. Food is plentiful here. Every day, meat, and fish, and fresh vegetables from the New Territories are sold in markets. I eat frugally, mostly rice and vegetables, and salted fish, but I will be able to take better advantage of what the markets have to offer when I have a job. Winter is almost here. I think of you all the time and hope the coal brazier will keep you warm. Take good care of yourself, Father, and may the gods protect you and grant you good health and peace.

Your dutiful son,
Tak Sing

I wrote my father every week, but kept from him the desperate reality that the squatter hut was only one degree better than homelessness. The damp cold air made living on the hillside very uncomfortable at times. I missed the charcoal braziers we had. In cold weather back home, I used to carry one of those portable warmers wherever I went, outdoors as well as in the house. However, I did not want to put anything of that nature in my shanty, for I had heard about the terrifying fires that swept entire squatter hillsides, leaving their occupants homeless and destitute. So I wore my padded jacket and thick socks to bed. My most costly investment so far, other than the hut, was a blanket stuffed with thick cotton batting. My biggest luxury was curling up under the blanket at night. By early morning, it would have formed a soft warm pocket which was very hard to leave.

I left my personal belongings still packed in the suitcase, for Wong Sum had said the squatter area residents were always prepared to evacuate their huts at the first sign of a fire or landslide. I just hoped if such a disaster should occur, I would be home to take my suitcase out. The gold bars and the money I still had from the sale of the one bar, I kept with me all the time, in a cloth pouch I wore inside my clothing. I would not leave them in the hut even though I had a small padlock on the door, and had paid my protection dues, for Kay Chai told me he recognized one of the thugs who tore down a hut as one of the men who came to collect the protection money. Only his outfit was different, for the man wore a *samfu* and rubber shoes on his mission to loot and destroy.

I looked for work in many places, knocking on doors of shops and restaurants, but everywhere I went, I was given the same cold answer, that they were not hiring. I wrote a couple of short stories about rural China set in the time of the Japanese invasion, and took them to one local newspaper after another, only to be told each time they were not the type of material the newspaper was looking for.

"My brother is a licensed hawker in Kowloon," Mimi said

to me when I met her outside her hut one afternoon, before she went to her night job. "He sells fruit near the licensing office. He could pick up a license for you. All you'll need is ten bucks for the license and a little capital for your merchandise. Want to give it a try? It's better than nothing."

Being a street hawker was indeed better than not working at all. Meanwhile, I could keep on looking for something more to my liking. So I had a photo taken in a studio and gave it to Mimi, along with the fee for the license. A week later, she knocked on my door holding a hawker's license with my name and photo on it. I was happily surprised I was able to secure the license so easily and quickly.

"My brother used his address on your registration," said Mimi, "since it's impossible to give an address here."

"I am grateful to your brother," I said to Mimi. "Tell me, why don't you live with him? Maybe you could find some other kind of work in Kowloon."

"You don't give up, do you, Tak Sing," Mimi said with a laugh. "It is very hard for me to live with my brother, because he and his wife rent a small room in a flat. She's a waitress in a third class café. Her job may be more respectable than mine, but she makes next to nothing. Besides," Mimi added, lowering her eyes, "she and I don't get along."

The Mimi I met the first time was a woman hiding behind her make-up and the pretense her job demanded. But in the light of day, I saw a different person. Her eyes were keen and lively without the black pencil lines and long eyelashes that made them look like those of blinking porcelain dolls. She had a naturally fair and smooth complexion that rouge and face powder only served to cover up. When she was not working she tied her long hair in a ponytail which, together with her disarming smile, gave her an air of youth and freshness. How I wished she would keep the natural look about her all the time. It was unfortunate that when night fell, harsh reality would set in and the Mimi I liked was transformed into a plaything of men.

113

With the hawker's license, every morning before sunrise, I took the tram to the west end of the island. By the time I arrived at the fruit market, the city was just beginning to stir at the first touch of daylight. Before the market opened, I bought my breakfast at a roadside food stall nearby. I always ordered *congee,* for I found the steaming gruel of rice in the early morning most satisfying to my stomach. I sat on a high stool, savouring the *congee,* intermittently taking a bite of the greasy crusty fried dough that came with it, while I watched crates of fruits and vegetables brought to shore by bare-chested coolies from sampans along the waterfront. I listened with fascination to the coordinated coolie cues and chants as, two by two, they balanced crates between them on shoulder poles, on the last leg of transportation of the farm produce to warehouses nearby. I could smell whiffs of salt sea air mixed with rotting garbage in the water lapping against the cemented shoreline. In those moments, I would have an unspeakable sense of satisfaction, conscious that there was an orderliness in my life, while at the same time I was in the midst of an adventure whose bounds were yet unknown.

As soon as the market opened, I picked out the fruits I would sell for the day. Depending on the shipments the market had received, there could be Xinhui or Sunkist oranges, Delicious apples, or bananas from the Philippines. I was told there would be more variety in the summer months – mangoes, lichees, persimmons, watermelons, and sometimes even honeydews from the United States. I had put down most of the remaining cash I had from the sale of the first gold bar for the baskets and the fruits on the first day. Since then, I was able to pay for the fruits every day with a good part of the cash from the sales the day before. My biggest challenge was walking up the gradient streets of Hong Kong, balancing the two baskets full of fruits on a shoulder pole.

I met Ching Hoy Tin as I was waiting the first day for the fruit market to open. Like me, he was a fruit hawker, but unlike me, he had no license. It was Ching Hoy Tin who told me about the best areas to sell.

"The best places are the residential areas on the hill, and I don't mean where you live." We laughed, for I had told him I lived on the squatter hillside of Wanchai. He offered to take me to where rich Chinese lived, so I followed him all the way through Pokfulam Road, Caine Road and up to the elite heights of Robinson Road. The higher we went, the more we sold. That day, I had oranges and bananas, and Ching Hoy Tin had Chinese pears. He taught me the hawker's street cry:

"Oranges! United States Sunkist oranges! Ten for a dollar! Sweet Sunkist oranges!"

And then there was bargaining. Everyone bargained. According to Ching Hoy Tin, whom I called Ah Hoy as we got to know each other better, the trick was to make the buyer feel good about the price he or she was paying, while at the same time making a sound profit. I was never very good at bargaining, and often I sold the fruits at prices more agreeable to the customers than to myself. However, I usually sold everything in my baskets, for I believed it was better to do so at lower prices than to have fruits left over. Occasionally, I had a few items left at the end of the day, and I would take them home after depositing my baskets and pole in the warehouse where I had rented a storage space for the night. Kay Chai was always happy to see me with a bag, for I would give him and his mother some of the fruits I brought home. On one of those occasions, he walked up the hill with me to my hut, eating a banana I had just given him.

"Sing Gor," he said, addressing me as his big brother, "I was in Theatre Lane behind the Queen's Theatre today. People coming out of the shows are usually in a good mood, and many gave me a few coins. But you know what else I noticed? There were a few shoeshine boys polishing shoes for the American sailors. I'd love to have a shoeshine box of my own and make a bit of money shining shoes. I asked the boys where they got their shoeshine boxes, but they just yelled, 'Go eat dung, you dirty bum!' and chased me out of the lane. If only I knew where I could get one of those boxes and shine shoes to make some money, Ma wouldn't have to work so hard."

Kay Chai's good intention stayed with me. A cobbler on my usual hawker's route told me I could apply for a shoeshine kit from the Urban Council Office. I did so, not without cutting short two of my hawking days. I was able to obtain a shoeshine kit for Kay Chai for a cash deposit. It was a rectangular wooden box with a handle doubling up as a footrest for the customer. Inside the box were brushes of different sizes and cans of polish of different colours and shades. Armed with the kit, I headed home feeling very pleased with myself. Eagerly I hurried up to Kay Chai's hut. He was not home, but Wong Sum was just carrying a bucket of water back from the public tap near her hut.

"Tak Sing, I am very grateful to you for being so good to my son," she said, moved to tears when she found out what I had done.

"When I see Kay Chai, I see my childhood friend who is now lost to me. I want to help him in some way."

Just then, Kay Chai appeared, breathless from running and with blood on his face.

"I got into a fight with those shoeshine boys in Theatre Lane, Ma," he said through bruised lips. "They wouldn't let me even beg there. They said it was their territory."

"You may not have to beg anymore. Look what Sing Gor brought you," Wong Sum said, as she prepared to wash the dirt and blood off her son's face.

I produced the shoeshine kit from where I had hidden it outside his hut. Watching his expression of utter surprise changing to wonder and joy was all the thanks I needed. He went over to the shoeshine kit and touched it as though it was something sacred. Slowly he opened the lid and looked inside, wearing a controlled smile on his swollen face. He took out a few of the items, looked at them, and carefully replaced them. Then he came quietly over to me, and hugged me without a word.

Kay Chai never went back to begging after that day. He took his shoeshine box to the Star Ferry Pier and solicited business from ferry passengers. He charged twenty cents for a pair of shoes, the same price his mother did for a letter. But the difference was his customers could afford to tip generously, and often did, charmed by his upturned appealing face.

December of 1951 was the first time I saw Christmas celebrated with the pomp and excitement of the Chinese New Year. I passed shop windows decorated with fake snow and beautifully wrapped gifts with pretty bows. I had never observed Christmas in China, not even during the time I was in Guangzhou before the Communists took over. So I was surprised when Mimi knocked on my door on Christmas morning and presented me with a long thin box wrapped in silver foil paper topped with a red bow. I was shy about taking it.

"You are supposed to open it in front of the giver," she said.

I unwrapped the box very carefully so as not to rip the paper. It was a dark red necktie with small faint blue dots.

"I have nothing to give you, Mimi," I said with embarrassment. "Here, I want you to have these Sunkist oranges. They are only from yesterday. Very sweet." Then I added, "Thanks for all you've done for me, especially the license. My greatest wish for you is you'll find another job. You deserve something better."

She forced a smile. "To tell you frankly, I am so used to my work it would be hard for me to do anything else. Tak Sing, it isn't easy for a woman who cannot read and write to make a good living in Hong Kong."

"I hope I'll have an occasion to wear the tie," I said, changing the topic. "Would you like the bow back? It will look nice on your hair."

February 6th, 1952. The day King George VI, the British monarch, died. Princess Elizabeth was called back from Africa where she was taking a holiday to become Queen.

That morning, Ah Hoy and I took our usual route up to Robinson Road. Then Ah Hoy suggested we should go up another level, to Conduit Road, and hit the really wealthy. We never sold together on days when we had the same fruits. But when we had different fruits, we liked to go together, for the companionship. That day, I had Chaozhou tangerines, and Ah Hoy had Guilin pomelos.

"Chaozhou tangerines! Big, sweet and juicy Chaozhou tangerines! Seven for a dollar!"

"Pomelos! Fragrant Guilin pomelos! Three for a dollar!"

We were making good sales. In a short time, my baskets were empty. Ah Hoy had a few pomelos left. One or two more sales, and he would clean out his baskets too. We decided we would go for *charsiu* rice after depositing our baskets at the warehouse. Life was good. The King might be dead, but his death meant nothing to me; it was just another day, perhaps a better day than many others, for I had sold everything by two o'clock.

As we were leaving the front gate of a residential complex on Conduit Road, we had the misfortune of running into a policeman, who stopped us and demanded to see our licenses. Quickly I produced mine, but Ah Hoy had none to show.

"I'll have to take you back to the police station. It's against the law to sell on the street without a hawker's license."

Ah Hoy pleaded with the policeman to let him go, beads of sweat forming on his forehead, his hands trembling visibly.

"I have been nice many times to you people, but you keep coming back," the policeman said, shaking his head at Ah Hoy. "I'm sorry, I have to book you."

If only we had not come up Conduit Road, if only we had turned into another building, we would have called it an early day and gone happily for our intended *charsiu* rice. Life was often unpredictable and unfair. Was there no way out? What I did next surprised even myself, for I approached the policeman.

"Mr. Constable," I began, "I know you may be risking your own job if you let my friend go, but you seem to have a kind heart, and no one needs to know if you spare him. As a token of our gratitude, allow me to give you part of my day's earnings." Immediately, I took out a five-dollar bill and, holding it in a fist, offered it to the policeman. He stepped back and looked insulted. At once, I regretted my words. What did I think he was, that he would accept the money? Now he would book me as well for attempting to bribe an officer of the law. I dreaded the worst.

"You who have a license, I suppose you must have paid big bucks for it. If I let your friend go, I am putting myself in jeopardy of losing my job. I better have a really good reason to let him off this time."

Without hesitation, and with relief, I took out another five-dollar bill and, holding both notes in a fist, attempted to pass them to him. This time, he took the money.

"Next time, I'll book you for sure. I won't spare you again," he said in a threatening voice of warning to Ah Hoy as he started walking away.

We waited in silence until he was out of sight. Balancing our baskets on the bamboo poles, we walked downhill in the direction of the fruit market. Ah Hoy was quite shaken. Finally he broke the silence.

"Ah Sing," he said, "I'll pay you back as soon as I can spare the money. My wife is due any time, and I'll need money, but I won't forget the debt I owe you. I'll pay you back."

"Actually, Ah Hoy," I said, "you should get a hawker's license, even though it's going to cost you. Just think, you could have got yourself a license with the money I gave the corrupt fellow today."

"You are talking nonsense, Ah Sing. What do you mean ten dollars for a license? It's more than ten times the amount, and even if I had the money, I probably could never get it for there is such a small quota for licensed hawkers. People pay black money for it. Well, *you* must know, for how else could you have got your license so easily?"

"The brother of a friend got it for me. I paid ten dollars," I said quietly, in a tone not even convincing to myself.

"Well, it's the most ridiculous thing I've ever heard. Ah Sing, you are very naive to believe this, or else you are hiding something from me, but I don't blame you," Ah Hoy said.

I felt as if a stone had dropped into my heart. I was silent the rest of the way, thinking how I would confront Mimi. Ah Hoy must have taken my silence to be an admission that I had bribed my way to the license. We did not go for our intended meal. As we parted, Ah Hoy repeated his words of gratitude to me, promising to repay me when he could, while I burned inside with anger, shame, and insult, thinking how Mimi might have secured me the license.

I walked fast up the hill to Mimi's hut. I knocked loudly on her door. She opened it, looking as though she had just woken up. She saw the expression on my face and must realize something was very wrong, for she looked frightened.

"Explain to me how I got my license so easily when it took everybody else a long time and a lot of money to get it!" I looked fiercely into her eyes.

"Tak Sing," Mimi said, her small voice quivering, "I wanted to help you. I just happened to know somebody in the licensing office. If I told you the truth, you might not have let me help you."

"All this about your brother is a lie. You make me feel dirty and cheap. I will not live on your charity. I will not have you sell yourself for me, no, not on my account. I don't thank you for this, and I don't need your help. So here, take back your damn license!" I threw the license at her and stomped away, back to my own hut.

I went to bed without supper. I could not sleep for a long time. I hated what Mimi did for a living. I hated her for doing what she did for me. I hated her. I hated myself.

I woke to faint daylight, feeling very tired from a restless sleep. Then events of the previous day came back to taunt me. For the first time since the shocking discovery about my license the day before, I thought about Mimi's feelings. I began to regret having hurt her. Then I realized I was in no hurry to get up, for I did not have the license anymore. I lay in bed for a long time, staring at the tin roof of my hut. I thought of my father, to whom I had been writing every week without fail. I would have to tell him I had lost my hawker's license in the next letter. I would have to get up and look for work. My hand went to the pouch I was wearing even to bed, and felt the two remaining gold bars on my stomach. I might have to sell one of them soon.

Then I noticed something on the floor, apparently slipped through the door. I got up to pick up a creased water-stained envelope with no writing on it. I ripped it open and found my hawker's license inside. I sat down on the bed and stared at the small piece of paper bearing my name and photograph, protected with a transparent plastic holder. I thought of the price she probably had to pay to get it for me. Was I so important to her? On the other hand, someone could have given her the license without her personal favours, someone who worked in the licensing office, who liked her well enough as a friend, and not as an object of pleasure. I stood up and pocketed the license. It was not too late to go pick up the produce for the day at the market.

I never formally apologized to Mimi for my outburst. I just found it extremely difficult to talk about it especially since I did not know what to believe of her, and I was afraid to hear what might be the dreaded truth. She did not seem upset by my behaviour. If she showed any emotion about the incident, it seemed to be relief that I had decided to keep my means of livelihood. When I looked back later, I realized what an ungrateful idiot I had been, blinded as I was by my judgmental high-mindedness. My behaviour toward Mimi was unforgivable.

After my discovery of the origin of the license, I was on a constant lookout for other opportunities. It had been my intention from the start to upgrade myself and make a better living, and the issue about the hawker's license spurred me in that direction. Above all, I wanted to do something meaningful for myself and for the city that had given me refuge.

The opportunity came in the autumn of 1952, when the Hong Kong Police Force was looking for new men to join its ranks. Up till then, my only dealing with the police was when I bribed the policeman to save Ah Hoy from arrest. One policeman accepting a bribe had not diminished my respect for the profession. After all, I was as guilty in offering him the bribe, although I had had no scruples about it, for there was no other way out for Ah Hoy, and his family depended entirely on him. When I read about the police recruitment in the *Sing Tao Daily*, I was quite excited about the opportunity. I had the physique and youth the Force required. So, I registered for the written examination. On the morning of the examination, I met Kay Chai as I was walking downhill to catch the tram for Central. Surprised to see me leaving at an unusual hour, and wearing my shirt and trousers instead of my Chinese jacket and pants, he asked where I was going.

"I am writing a test today," I confided. "If I pass, I'll treat you and your mother to tea. Let this be our little secret, and wish me luck!"

I had not taken a test since my days at Zhongshan University almost three years ago, but the common sense questions were quite easy, and the essay test was not a problem. Still, I dreaded receiving the results that came two weeks later. I had given Ah Hoy's address in my application, just as I had given his address to my father. So when one morning Ah Hoy gave me a letter from the Hong Kong Police Force, I opened it immediately, trying hard to conceal my nervousness. It took me just seconds to read the most important line in the letter, saying I had passed the police examination, and I was to report for an interview. I shook Ah Hoy's hand vigorously many times, as though he was the one to be congratulated.

"I won't have to worry about being booked for hawking without a license from now on," Ah Hoy said in jest.

"Don't try to bribe me if you run into me when I am a policeman!" I laughed, but I also knew I meant what I said.

A week later, I found out in a second letter I had passed the interview and would be admitted into police training school for six months, at the end of which I would become a constable.

"Constable Lee Tak Sing," I sounded it out. I liked it.

The day I got the good news of my acceptance to police training school, I suggested to Ah Hoy that we have something to eat at a nearby restaurant after we had deposited our baskets at the warehouse.

"We'll have the *charsiu* rice we never got to eat," I said, reminding him of his close shave with the law.

"Yes, let's celebrate the end of the hard life of a hawker, and the start of a respectable profession for my pal," Ah Hoy said.

Ah Hoy and I each had a heaping plate of steaming rice topped with reddish roast pork at the Ko Shing Restaurant, and shared a few more moments of camaraderie. I paid for the meal, and then took the tram home.

I reached Mimi's hut. It was only four thirty, too early for her to go to work. But surely she would be up by then. I knocked on her door. After a long minute, she opened the door. She was surprised to see me, for it was not my habit to call on her.

"Well, what brought you here, Mr. Lee?" she asked, delighted.

"Mimi, I have some good news, something to celebrate. Why don't you call in sick tonight. I want to take you out to supper."

What I said in one breath was probably too much for Mimi to take. If ever there was heaven on earth, Mimi looked as though she was in it then. She was all smiles.

"Can I go like this?" she asked, looking down at herself.

"You look great, better than in those skimpy dresses you wear to work," I said, meaning every word, for she looked radiant without makeup, in her blouse, blue jeans and with her ponytail. How I wished she wouldn't have to hide her natural beauty every night with heavy cosmetics, short tight dresses, and forced smiles.

She hurried to make her phone call at the store at the foot of the hill, while I used the public shower on the hill, and changed into my shirt and trousers. When I picked her up at her hut a little later, she looked a bit shy and coy. I liked her that way. We took the bus from Wanchai to Causeway Bay, to a restaurant serving food from the north. The restaurant was Mimi's choice, a modest place, but its spring chicken was the best on the island. There was a natural glow on Mimi's cheeks, and I thought from the liveliness in her eyes and her bubbly enthusiasm that she had never been happier in all the time I had known her, or prettier. She was eager to hear what I had to tell her, and full of anticipation of it. Finally, I broke the news of my new job to her, as she was eating a drumstick she was holding between her fingers.

"Mimi, I've been accepted into police training school," I said.

At my words, her hands froze in mid-air, and she looked at me in disbelief. I detected a fleeting hint of disappointment in her face, as though the news I gave her was not in her expectations. Then the moment of initial shock passed, and she recovered herself.

"I cannot be happier for you, Tak Sing," she said earnestly. "Being a policeman is so respectable. Better money and lots of prospects." Then putting on her working voice, she added with affection, "Just don't come and raid the hall where I work."

"Mimi, thank you for looking out for me," I said, not responding to her last sentence. After a moment of silence, I asked, "Tell me the truth, how did you really get the license for me?"

"Tak Sing, what I did with my clients was all part of my job, had nothing to do with you. But it certainly helped to know people with connections," she said, lowering her eyes. I regretted bringing up the subject, so I let it drop as quickly as I brought it up.

We walked along the shopping district of Causeway Bay after supper, weaving our way slowly through crowds of window-shoppers, past the garish entrance of a cinema packed with people waiting to attend the nine o'clock show, beneath brightly coloured neon signs. Mimi put her hand around my arm, as we walked beside each other, but I did not hold her hand. When she got tired, we took the bus home.

"Tak Sing, thank you for tonight," Mimi said when we reached her hut. "I haven't had such a good time in a long, long while.

Good luck with your new job. Things are looking great for you. You certainly deserve something better than this shitty dump."

Under the moonlight, I could see the glitter of tears in her eyes.

24

A Chinese Story

Constable Lee

"**S**HUN AT ALL COST corruption and bribery!" This principle was hammered into our heads at police training school. "You will otherwise be violating the trust of the people you set out to protect, encouraging and condoling crime, committing a crime against the city you serve, against your own integrity, the worst crime of all."

I wrote my father and briefed him on my progress at police school every week. Three weeks into my training, I received a letter from him, in care of Ah Hoy, who brought it over. My father had written me only once before since I left home, to give me his paternal blessing for the New Year, and to assure me he was managing well without me. Nervous and excited, I ripped open his second letter. My father was no man of letters, but his few years of temple schooling had enabled him to read and write reasonably well. It was a short letter, in his usual brief style, but I could read a lot into it.

November 5, 1952

Tak Sing,

I am very happy to know you are going to be a policeman. Two words you must remember always:

VIRTUE and INTEGRITY

*They were given you the day I named you Tak Sing, and
you should take them with you in all you do, all your life.
I am well. Do not worry.*

Father

My six-month period of training ended, and on a dull and
damp day in March, 1953, I was officially admitted into the Hong
Kong Police Force as Constable Lee Tak Sing. I sent my father a
photograph of me in uniform. It gave me much satisfaction to
imagine how proud he would feel when he saw it.

My first assignment was foot patrol in the Causeway Bay area
on Hong Kong Island. For a month, I went out with a corporal
named Yu Choy. On the first day, Yu Choy stopped for lunch at a
café in our patrol area, taking me with him. When I attempted to
pay for my rice plate, Yu Choy laid his hand on my arm.

"Don't bother. The lunch is free. It's the least they can do to
thank us for keeping law and order around here," he said.

I felt very uneasy, but since he was my supervisor, I believed
he must know his business. For the next two days, we ate meals
in cafés and food stalls without paying so much as a cent. Finally,
I made up my mind not to go with Yu Choy for meals. When he
next suggested we stopped at a noodle shop for lunch, I told him
I had an upset stomach from eating out too much, and I would
simply get a bun at a corner store. The rest of the month, every
time Yu Choy ate at a restaurant, I would buy something to eat at
a nearby convenience store instead.

"Ah Sing, let me give you a word of advice," he said on our last
day of patrol together. "To succeed in the Force, it is not enough
to serve and protect the public. You must cooperate and conform.
Do what the rest of the Force does. Get on the bus! Do not attempt
to be different, for we are one big family."

After the first month, I was on my own. On several occasions,
I came across unlicensed hawkers selling their produce on

residential streets. When they saw me in the distance, they would pick up their baskets and hurry away. I never gave pursuit, just pretended I did not see them. When I did confront one, I would give him firm warning not to let me see him selling again, and let him go. How could I arrest a hawker and deprive him of his meager means of livelihood when I had borne a hawker's burden and perspired a hawker's sweat? But to thieves in any form, I showed no mercy. In my first month of patrol, I apprehended a good number of pickpockets, shoplifters, and thieves, including one young woman I caught taking money out of a blind old beggar's cup.

I took Kay Chai and his mother to tea on the Sunday after I received my first pay. Kay Chai had never been to a teahouse for *dim sum*, and he was beside himself with excitement and anticipation days before we were set to go. I enjoyed seeing him happily munching on *charsiu* buns and *har gao*. Watching him eat, I could almost see Ah Chu eagerly gulping down the preserved duck and sausages, the red bean dumplings and rice cakes we had for the New Year back in Ka Hing. I decided there and then to find Kay Chai a school that would offer a free education.

I gave my hawker's license to Ah Hoy, who was able to have it transferred to his name. When I told Mimi what I had done with the license, she was very pleased.

That September, I enrolled in Sun Kwong College, a night school, to study English, for I was aware I would need some knowledge of the language in order to advance in my police career. Two nights a week after my day shift, I was to attend the night school in Causeway Bay. The first night I went to my English class, Serena, was the first time I saw your mother.

25

A Chinese Story

The English Teacher

O N THE NIGHT OF THE first class, as soon as she walked into the classroom with her arms full of books and papers, and dropped them on the desk in front of me, I found it hard to take my eyes off her. She was more beautiful than the images of the goddess *Kuan Yin* I had seen. She had large clear eyes, and a most captivating smile, framed by a dimple on each cheek. Her fair complexion suggested she could have come from the north, where people were usually fairer of skin, yet she had the mild soft features of the southern Cantonese. Her wavy hair which barely touched her shoulders was tucked behind one ear, exposing a tiny pearl earring, while covering the other ear loosely. The manner she arranged her hair, and her full upper lip, gave her a slightly flirtatious look at odds with her severe long-sleeved white blouse, gathered into a full red and grey skirt. She looked about my age, perhaps younger, for the skin on her face and hands was smooth as ivory.

I was so entranced by her presence I did not know she was addressing me until I realized she was looking at me the way a teacher would look at a student, with inquiring eyes. At the same time, students sitting in front of me had turned their heads in my direction.

"Please introduce yourself," Miss Poon said kindly, probably for the second time.

I recollected myself and said not without a measure of pride, "I am Lee Tak Sing, of the Hong Kong Police Force. I came from Guangdong two years ago."

She nodded, smiled, and looked for a few seconds at me with somewhat clinical interest, before turning her attention to the student on my left. For the rest of the evening, I watched her every movement, every gesture, every expression. If I was being rude, I was not aware of it, nor could I help myself. She was the most beautiful girl I had ever seen.

During the first half of that evening, every time she accidentally met my penetrating gaze, she seemed momentarily confused, quickly averting her eyes from mine, while her cheeks coloured. Was I imagining it, that I was making her nervous? I told myself I could not be affecting her composure, I, a refugee from Guangdong, who had spent most of my life in the country, whose feet, as the crude saying went, had been steeped in cow's manure.

At a quarter after eight, the class had a recess. I stayed in the classroom to look over the lesson the teacher had just taught, and also to await her return. She came back before most of the students, with a stack of paper to give out to the class. She must have felt my presence in the room as she entered, for she appeared a bit uncomfortable. Perhaps I had annoyed her with my staring throughout the first half of the class. As she started to put some sheets on each desk, I stood up and went over to her with the intention of offering to help. Just then, she stepped back and lost her balance against a chair. I caught her just in time from behind. For a few seconds, she was nestled in my arms, her back against my chest. Then we were apart, as she regained her balance. Without looking at me, she murmured an apology and continued to distribute the sheets. I asked in a soft voice if I could help.

"Certainly. Thanks," she said somewhat curtly, as she handed me the stack of paper without looking at me.

For the rest of the evening, I found it hard to pay attention to the vocabulary being taught. All I could think of was her falling over and over again into my arms and the electrifying sensation it evoked in me.

Since the first class, I had looked forward to Monday and Thursday evenings. Miss Poon was always courteous to every student, treating us as her equals, yet she seemed to purposely avoid my eyes after the first day.

One Thursday night in early November, I made a bold move. I could not be admiring Miss Poon from a distance forever. If I knew she had no interest in me other than as her student, I would stop torturing myself with fantasies of her. I might even change to another night school and not see her again. I planned to stay back after class one night and wait for her to leave the building. I would then invite her to join me for a late supper.

"Goodnight, Tak Sing," she said when she saw me in the hallway. She sounded like a teacher, quite superior. I lost heart. We walked out of the building into the cool air of a clear autumn night. The street was full of people, and restaurants were still open, though many shops were closing.

It's now or never, I told myself. With my heart pounding, I heard myself say, "I am going for a bite to eat since I haven't had supper after work. Miss Poon, will you join me?" It was the first time I spoke to Miss Poon in Cantonese, for she wanted the students to converse in English at all times in class. I tried to sound as casual as I could, as though my invitation was an unpremeditated one, out of politeness.

She hesitated in her step, looked down at her watch for longer than it would normally take to check the time, then, tilting her head to one side and looking up at me, said in a disarming manner, "Why not? I'm famished."

We walked along Leighton Road, passing several cafés serving European food, and *wonton* noodle joints, but Miss Poon did not seem interested. We wove through the crowds, beneath sparkling neon signs. I could not believe my good fortune, that she would agree so easily to having supper with me. Most likely, nothing would come of the evening, but for the moment I was walking on clouds, knowing I was monopolizing an hour of her life, commanding her undivided attention while it lasted. We turned from Leighton Road onto a small busy side street where the smell of stir-fries filled the air, of garlic, ginger, and black beans in heated oil. Miss Poon's face brightened as she noticed some roadside food stalls. Male cooks were preparing food for customers seated on wooden benches at tables in front of hot woks and pots that were above charcoal burners, under bright light bulbs.

"Tak Sing, I'd love to eat there," Miss Poon said, her head nodding in the direction of the food stalls, and looking at me almost imploringly.

It was obvious she had never eaten at such a place, for food stalls were mostly patronized by coolies and manual labourers, and those who found restaurants above their means. I feared she would be uncomfortable there, looking so foreign in her pink sweater set and fitted grey skirt. But her pleasure was my primary concern, so I walked her over to the stall closest to us. We sat down at the long wooden table, next to a man in a *samfu*, who had taken his thongs off and was sitting with one bare foot on the bench, his knee raised to the level of his face, and loudly slurping soup from a bowl. We ordered sampan *congee* and fried dough. While we waited, Miss Poon kept looking in the direction of the next food stall, where people were eating mussels in black bean sauce.

"How I'd love to have some of those," she said, watching the cook at the next stall dumping more mussels into a heated wok sizzling with steam.

I went over and placed an order for the mussels, and later brought them back to our table, to Miss Poon's delight. And then there was stinky tofu whose smell was as bad as its taste was good. I asked Miss Poon if she would like some, but she said she had never tasted it. Off I went to the street vendor who was frying the tofu in a wok of boiling oil, and brought back two squares of it, wrapped in newspaper. Miss Poon was at first a little hesitant to taste the tofu, for it gave off a smell like fried rotten egg. But she bravely took a bite, and another bite, and she liked it. I had always thought it was heavenly.

"It's such a thrill to have a chance to eat here," Miss Poon said with enthusiasm. "I've always wanted to try out these food stalls. Have you eaten at such places before?"

"I used to have my breakfast at a food stall every morning in the west end, before I became a policeman," I said quietly, "when I was a hawker."

On hearing that, she appeared genuinely interested in my past. While we enjoyed the steaming *congee* afloat with shrimp, squid and fish balls, I told her the main events of my life. I was reticent about my hawker experience though, for I wanted to keep my association with Mimi from her. Tears welled up in her eyes when she heard the story of Ho Sau Yuk, the *zheng* player of Tai Shek. When I told her about my father, living alone and working in the fields, and how sad I was leaving him, she laid her hand on mine for a moment and squeezed it lightly with her fingers.

"He ought to be very proud of you, Tak Sing," she said softly.

It was the first time she touched me, and I remember the moment still. After a while, she took off her outer sweater, laying it on her lap.

"The *congee* is making me sweat," she said with flushed cheeks. She removed the flesh of a mussel from its shell with a chopstick and popped it into her mouth. "This is wonderful! See what I have missed all these years?"

So far I had been the one doing most of the talking. I knew nothing about her, and was not about to ask, for I was aware of my position as a student, and did not want to sound intrusive. Yet, I did not want her to think I was not interested in her.

"Have you always lived in Hong Kong, Miss Poon?" I asked rather casually. She could say as much or as little about herself as she liked in response.

"Yes, I've lived here all my life," she said as she licked her fingers and wiped them on a handkerchief. "I was born in the Nethersole Hospital in 1933. Yes, I am twenty. I know what you are thinking," she laughed, "that you are older than your teacher, but there's a lot in life you can teach me, for you have experienced so much, while I have lived a sheltered life, like a frog looking up from the bottom of a well."

"So you were in Hong Kong during the Japanese occupation?"

"Yes, I was eight when the Japanese landed. I had to stay home mostly other than going to school during that time. Believe me, it was an awful time, very unpleasant, but our experience was probably better than what you went through during the war and when the Communists came. My family was lucky to have survived the war relatively unscathed."

"Where do you live now, Miss Poon?" I was becoming a little bold.

"On Seymour Road," she said simply. "I live with my parents, and Ah Lan."

"Who's Ah Lan?"

"My *amah*. She's been in my family ever since I was born. She helped my mother take care of me. She is as dear to me as my mother, but of course I won't say it to anybody at home. It would hurt my mother to hear me."

I was flattered Miss Poon should confide in me feelings she would not impart to her family. She seemed to be enjoying herself, the food, the experience of eating at a roadside food stall, and my company. The evening was turning out better than I had dared to expect. We sat at the table to talk after we had finished eating, for by then there were few customers and the cook didn't seem to mind us taking up the space.

"And where do you live?" Miss Poon asked.

I had dreaded the question, but thought she should know the truth about me from the start.

"I live in the squatter area of Wanchai. It was the cheapest solution when I first arrived."

"I admire you for that," she said, looking seriously into my eyes. "It must be very tough living there."

"You just get used to it."

When we got up to leave, it was past eleven o'clock. On the way to the bus stop, she stopped at a corner store to make a telephone call. I asked if it was too late for her to go home by herself, wondering if she would let me take her home. She said someone would meet her at the bus stop near her house.

"By the way, Tak Sing," she added, "you can call me Lily, except in class."

Just then, I was the happiest man on earth. So she would see me again outside class! And her name!

"I like your name," I said, trying to focus on her name rather than the encouragement I believed she was giving me.

"My Chinese name is Kit Lin. The English word for *lin* is 'lotus,' a kind of 'water lily.' That was how my parents came up with the English name Lily. Have you ever read the classical piece *In Praise of the Lin Flower*? It's one of my favourites."

"'*Many beloved are the plants from land and water. The Chun Dynasty scholar Tao singled out the chrysanthemum. Since the time of Tang, people have favoured the peony. I alone love the lin flower because it arises from the soil and yet is pure and untainted,*'" I began confidently, secretly blessing Wong Lo Sze, my teacher at Tai Shek, for making me painfully memorize those classical pieces back then.

"'*It blooms atop one straight hollow undivided stem. From a distance, it gives out a sweet fragrance. Elegantly it stands alone, to be admired from afar, not touched up close,*'" Lily continued.

I got off the bus at Wanchai, and it sped on toward Central District, taking Lily with it. *I alone love the lin flower because it arises from the soil and is yet pure and untainted.* If I had been infatuated with her before that night, I was now hopelessly, irrevocably in love.

26

A Chinese Story

Lily

EVER SINCE I SAW the advertisement for *The Red Shoes* at the cinema in Wanchai two years before, I had wanted to see the film, and it happened to be showing again at a third-run cinema a week after I had supper with Miss Poon. I waited after class till all the other students had left and we were alone in the classroom, and boldly asked if she would see the film with me.

"Yes, I would love to. I missed it when it was first out," she said, her face lighting up. Obviously she wanted to see *The Red Shoes*, or, as I preferred to think, to see it with me.

We met outside the small old rundown theatre in Yaumati on the Kowloon side. The seats were hard, and the air was stuffy inside the theatre in spite of the ceiling fans. But I did not care about the discomfort; neither did Lily seem to. She told me she had taken ballet lessons for many years, and she was looking forward particularly to the dance sequences in the movie. The film was about a beautiful ballerina for whom dancing was her life, until she fell in love with a young man and married him. But her happiness with her husband was short-lived. Torn between her love for him and for her art, and unable to resolve the internal conflict tearing her apart, she put on her red ballet shoes for the last time and gave the best performance of her career, until the final moments of her dance and of the film, when she suddenly leapt from a great height to her death. When it came to the scene where she lay dying in her husband's arms, I heard sobs coming from Lily beside me.

Instinctively I put my arm behind her, and drew her to me.

She allowed her head to rest on my shoulder while wiping her eyes with a handkerchief. We sat in that position for a while, she leaning on me for comfort, and I thrilled by her physical closeness, until the lights went on in the theatre.

As we walked out into the busy streets of Yaumati under the evening sky, Lily was unusually quiet, perhaps still mourning in her heart the tragedy of the ballerina whose life, like that of a flower plucked in full bloom, was extinguished prematurely by love. We walked in silence toward the pier to board the ferry back to Hong Kong Island. Our hands accidentally touched, and I took hers in mine. She did not object to our public show of intimacy, and let her hand remain in mine until we reached the pay booth.

Christmas Day, 1953. A fire broke out in the evening in the squatter area of Shek Kip Mei in Kowloon. It spread quickly across the entire shanty-covered hillside. In the night, the fire could be seen from Hong Kong Island, like an electrified centipede crawling its way slowly across a dark hill that formed part of the backdrop of the lighted city of Kowloon. The fire brigade's efforts were hindered by the dry wintry air and a wind that fanned the fire to new grounds. Police reinforcement was called in from Hong Kong Island. I remained on duty on the Hong Kong side until four in the morning. When I did arrive home, many of the squatter residents on my hill were still up, agitated and frightened by what was happening to their fellows across the harbour.

The Shek Kip Mei fire spurred me to look for another place to live. By then, I had been in the Wanchai squatter area for over two years, and had long grown accustomed to life on the hill, to the point that I could draw some simple, inexplicable pleasures out of the wretched lifestyle of the squatters. I had developed an attachment to my hut, and had a soft spot in my heart for my neighbours. But since I started asking Lily out, she had been persuading me to move. She feared the Wanchai squatter area would sooner or later suffer the ill fate of Shek Kip Mei.

On a windy, dreary day in February, 1954, I packed up my

belongings, dug up the gold bars I had buried in the ground under my bed ever since I started my police job, and moved into a room in a flat in North Point I rented from an old couple. The monthly rent for the room, about ten feet square, was forty dollars, a sizable sum for a police constable, but I had access to a flush toilet and tap water, and cooking facilities in the tiny kitchen I shared with my landlord and his wife. To me, those were luxuries only the upper echelon, the "men above men," could enjoy. Even in Guangzhou, I had never used a flush toilet. Needless to say, the squatters in Wanchai had to resort to the few public latrines on the hillside.

Saying goodbye to Kay Chai was not easy. He was sulky for days when he found out I was moving. I felt I had betrayed him and my other neighours, deserting them for a better life. However, two months after I moved, I was able to find a free school for Kay Chai, managed and taught by members of a social welfare club. Five mornings a week, Kay Chai attended school. When I visited him and his mother a few months later, Wong Sum told me he still took his shoeshine kit to the Star Ferry Pier some afternoons in the hope of making a dollar or two, but he would never do so at the expense of his schoolwork.

I never said a proper goodbye to Mimi, for when I stopped at her hut three days before I moved, she was not there even though it was only four in the afternoon. Neither was she there the next day, or the next. At the time, I felt it was just as well, for I did not want Lily to think I was ever associated with Mimi other than as a casual acquaintance who lived down the hill in Wanchai's squatter area.

27

A Chinese Story

Not a Primrose Path

I WROTE MY FATHER telling him I had met a girl who was as good as she was beautiful, someone he would approve of, someone my mother would have liked. Within two weeks I received my father's letter, and, in his usual brief manner of writing, he expressed his joy at the news, and asked me if I had set a date for my wedding.

That Lily loved me, I had no doubt. When she was alone with me, her face was mostly radiant. There was a certain feminine fragility about her, both physical and emotional, that made me want to take care of her, to protect her. She seemed, however, a little forlorn at times, but whenever I questioned her about it, she would always deny anything was wrong. Yet, I sensed she was hiding something from me, and I believed she must be trying to protect our relationship from harm.

Often we took the tram to Victoria Peak, and strolled along the lovers' lane encircling the top of the hill overlooking the harbour and the island coastline on all sides. It was one of the least expensive places for couples without the luxury of a car to be alone. On one such occasion, Lily told me about a dream she had.

"Last night I dreamed you and I were alone on the moon. It was a crescent moon, and we were sitting on it, like carefree children with our legs hanging down. There was a long ladder stretching all the way from the earth to the moon. We must have climbed up on it. We were so happy up there, no troubles, no worries, nothing to keep us apart." She had a faraway look in her eyes, as if she was looking into eternity. Then she said in jest, "What I should have done in my dream was push the ladder off the moon, and let it fall back to earth, so we could stay up there forever."

"Lily, no matter what happens, we can be together if we set our minds to it." I said, gathering her possessively to me.

I soon suspected why Lily looked unhappy at times. Her parents must not approve of me. She talked very little about them. Although Lily and I had been seeing each other for about six months, she had not taken me home to meet her parents. Whenever we went out, she would meet me at a bus stop or the entrance of a cinema. Late at night, when I took her home, we would embrace behind a big tree across the street from her home, a stately two-storey white house on Seymour Road, with a garden in front and a black iron gate at the main entrance. When we finally let each other go, I would watch her cross the street to her house, and wait till a servant had opened the gate for her. She would look back in my direction longingly as she crossed the threshold, as if from my world into hers.

Lily continued to teach at the night school until she graduated from university in June, 1954. She would start at St. Agnes High School that September as an English teacher. For her graduation, her parents had planned a big party in their home.

"I want you to come to the party, Tak Sing," Lily said to me nervously two weeks before the event. "It will be a good opportunity for you to meet my family."

At last, I would meet her parents. I was determined to create a good impression, to let them know I was good enough for their daughter, even though I was poor. After all, I did come from reputable stock on the mainland, and my family had been rich once, but I realized my roots were meaningless in the context of Hong Kong. Ten days before the party, I bought a two-piece brown suit. Two days before the party, I bought a tin of *Fry's* chocolate-coated almonds to take to Lily's parents. I rehearsed in my head many times what I would say when Lily introduced me to them. If Lily was nervous, I was ten times more so.

The day before the party, I finished my shift at three in the afternoon. A typhoon that had been brewing for two days had bypassed the colony, leaving a trail of heavy rain and high wind. I got off the bus at my street corner, and was surprised to see Lily standing near the bus stop, under a verandah to take cover from the rain. She had no raincoat or umbrella, and her hair and clothes were wet. As soon as she saw me, she ran over, and almost fell into my arms. There was a frantic look in her eyes.

"Tak Sing, I had a quarrel with my father. I can't go back home. You are all I've got now." She blurted out between sobs.

I draped my raincoat over Lily's shoulders, and, with her on my arm, we walked to my place. That afternoon, surrounded by the stark white walls of my room, amidst the sound of rain pelting against the window panes, our only intruder, we gave ourselves to each other, loving each other with no holding back.

Later that evening, Lily told me the reason for her quarrel with her father. I was not welcome at the party her parents were holding for her. Her father told her he had invited a very eligible suitor for her, the son of a medical colleague. She was to show him every courtesy.

"Lily, listen to me. I want you to go back tonight and be a gracious hostess at the party tomorrow as though nothing has happened. If you stay here tonight, they will be out looking for you." I held her close, hurting at the very thought of her accepting the attention of another. "Be reconciled with your father. In time, he may change his mind about me."

28

A Chinese Story
Knots Tied and Untied

THROUGHOUT THE SUMMER AND AUTUMN of 1954, Lily and I continued to see each other. She never talked much about her parents' objections to our association, although I believed there must have been more unpleasant confrontations at home since the graduation party.

The one person in the Poon household who was sympathetic to our situation was Lily's *amah*, Ah Lan. Lily had long wanted me to meet her. On one of Ah Lan's holidays, Lily secretly arranged for the three of us to meet for *dim sum*. Ah Lan was a small woman who wore her hair in a single long braid reaching down to below her waist. For twenty years Lily had been her charge, even after Lily had grown up to be an independent young woman. Single all her life, she loved Lily as her own daughter. From the first time I met Ah Lan, I knew we had a lifelong ally in her, that she would never desert Lily, or betray us.

"Take good care of my *siu cheh*, Mr. Lee," Ah Lan said to me at our first meeting. "She loves you more than herself. You are very fortunate, for my *siu cheh* is the best girl anyone can find for a wife. I know, because I have looked after her from the time she was one month old."

For months I had not visited Kay Chai and his mother. One November day, after I finished my shift, I walked up the familiar footpath leading to Kay Chai's hut. As I passed Mimi's shack, a strange woman was hanging up clothes outside. I stopped to ask where Mimi was, and got a blank stare. I soon found Kay Chai.

142

He was overjoyed to see me. He was excelling in his class, and his teacher had told him she would try to secure a place in a regular government school for him the following term, tuition free, if he kept up his good record.

"I still have the shoeshine kit you got me, Sing Gor, but I haven't been shining shoes these days because I am too busy with homework," Kay Chai said.

I waited till Wong Sum came home and asked her about Mimi.

"She moved out about three months ago. I haven't seen her since August. Just left without telling anyone," Wong Sum said, shrugging her shoulders.

Back on the street, I found myself heading for the Wanchai waterfront. At the bottom of the stairs to the dance hall where Mimi worked, I hesitated for a moment and went up. It was only six o'clock, too early for business. A few girls were sitting around a table, chatting and giggling. They hushed up and looked over to where I was standing at the entrance when they saw me. Memories of my first experience there flooded back.

"Don't know where she went. Didn't give me notice. Just scrammed without a word of goodbye," a man I took to be the dance hall manager said when I asked.

I left the dance hall, full of worries about Mimi. Regardless of her work, she had been a caring friend. In all the months after I moved out of the squatter area, even when I returned to see Kay Chai and his mother, I had not looked in on her. At that moment I felt an awakened sense of moral responsibility toward Mimi, coupled with deep remorse for having turned my back on her. I had wronged her, not by a conscious act of betrayal, but by my inaction and thoughtlessness. Somewhere along Harcourt Road, I heard a voice from behind.

"Mister, are you looking for Mimi?"

I turned and saw a girl walking fast to catch up to me, wearing tight jeans, a thin white blouse and a pair of high-heeled thongs. She must have been one of the girls inside the dance hall.

"I know where Mimi is," she said as she came close. "She's wrapped up by a tycoon. She's on McDonnell Road, in a nice flat. I have the address and telephone number if you want."

My immediate reaction was one of relief knowing where Mimi was, but her situation troubled me. Did she in fact want to be *wrapped up*, in the jargon used by the dance hall girl, by some rich tycoon, usually an older married man perhaps even respected in society but with a weakness for young attractive women? The thought of Mimi being kept in a gilded cage, and then cast out and left in a ditch when her keeper's interest waned, distressed and enraged me.

When I saw Lily later, she sensed something was wrong. It was time I told her all about Mimi, and I did, about the hawker's license, and the predicament Mimi was in. Lily listened quietly, calmly. She did not reproach me for keeping my friendship with Mimi from her. Instead, she was concerned about Mimi, and disturbed by the fact that I had neglected her.

"Tak Sing, go and see her," Lily said, laying her hand gently on my arm. "I want you to see her."

Lily dialed Mimi's number, and when she knew she had Mimi on the phone, she put me on. I could hear the tremor in Mimi's voice when she realized who the caller was. I wanted to say a lot to her, but did not. Instead, we arranged to meet at a café in Kowloon one afternoon.

I did not have to wait long before she came, dressed in a *cheongsam* of pastel peach with a matching short jacket. Her long hair was coiled up above her head. Except for thin pencil lines defining her eyebrows and eyes, and a pale lipstick, she wore no make-up. She looked respectable, almost elegant.

For the first few minutes, we both seemed shy of each other, like a boy and a girl on a first date. I complimented her on her new look, and she asked me about my police work, while we waited for our coffee. Mimi was smiling, but I recognized in her smile the same façade she put on at the dance hall, not the unaffected

144

joy that had radiated from her inner being when I took her out to dinner. Seeing through her pretense, I was disappointed and hurt.

"I have been worried about you. I'm sorry for not having been in touch for so long," I finally said.

"I must say I was hoping to hear from you the first few months after you left, but then I consoled myself with the thought that you were probably busy, all that training and new challenges every day." She paused, looking down at her coffee cup. "As you know, I am with someone now — he treats me well, although he has a family to go back to on the weekends. I am not in want anymore. Tak Sing, you don't have to worry about me. Don't act like a big brother." She laughed her dance-hall laugh.

"I'll be around if you need me," I said.

"Thank you. Come, lighten up," she said, her lips curving into an impish smile. "Enjoy the moment, for old time's sake."

But we could not. The truth was our meeting was no happy reunion of old friends. It was rather an occasion for us to say the goodbye we never said when I moved out of Wanchai, and for me, it was a chance to tell Mimi and myself that I had not rejected her for what she was.

"You know, Tak Sing, I've come to compare myself to a pebble in the sea," she said philosophically, sipping her coffee. "A big wave carries it shoreward and it rides on its crest until the wave weakens and subsides, and takes it back a little toward the sea. Then another wave comes along and another. The pebble just goes with the rise and fall of the surge, but it remains the same, indestructible, for it was once part of a big rock. Eventually, it will wash ashore, after many waves, where, embedded in the sand, it will remain. I am such a pebble and I will survive."

"If you are a pebble, what am I?" I asked, fascinated by her image.

She paused for a moment, thinking hard, then broke into a faint smile.

"You are a little boy who looks for rare and exquisite seashells at the beach. But I am just an ordinary rough pebble, nothing fancy, so I will never be picked up by you."

Clever analogy, too precise for my comfort. I was feeling quite miserable. Worse, I had to break the news of my impending marriage to her. She would be hurt more if I didn't, and she learned about it later through wayside intelligence.

"Mimi, I'm going to be married soon," I said quietly.

Her reaction reminded me of the time I told her about my acceptance into the Police Force, an instantaneous stricken look almost immediately covered up with an expression of exaggerated delight. She asked a lot of questions about Lily, listening with intense interest to everything about her. Then, leaning forward across the table, with one hand around my neck, she drew my face close to hers. Before I knew what she was doing, she had kissed me gently on the lips.

"This is to send you off on your married journey, and to wish you and your bride happiness always."

As we left the café, I said to Mimi, "It looks like you and I will not be seeing each other again for some time."

Lowering her eyes, she nodded knowingly.

"Goodbye, Tak Sing," she said softly, holding my hand and squeezing it. Quickly she looked away and let go of my hand. She turned and walked from me, looking back once to wave.

On December 20th, 1954, Lily left her house, much like any other holiday when she went downtown. She told her mother she was doing some Christmas shopping, and meeting friends for dinner, and would be late. That day, at three o'clock in the afternoon, Lily and I were secretly married by a Justice of the Peace in a simple ceremony attended by two of my friends, Lui Wing Seng and Stephen Kwan, both constables, who served as our witnesses.

When we left the Supreme Court Building where we were married, it was raining hard, quite unusual for December. We called a taxi to take us and our two friends to a restaurant on Des Veoux Road in Central to celebrate the occasion. From the restaurant, Lily telephoned her parents. She was going to tell her father she was married, and ask for his understanding and forgiveness. When she rejoined me and our friends minutes later, I knew from the hollow look in her eyes and the stiff expression on her lips she did not have her parents' blessings. I held her cold clammy hand, rubbing it comfortingly. As we stepped out of the restaurant to hail a taxi to take us to my place in North Point, our first home, rain dripped down Lily's forehead and cheeks, so that I could not tell if she was crying.

Lily's phone call to her father that afternoon was the last time he spoke to her. She had broken her parents' hearts by her secret marriage, and, in turn, they had severed the natural ties binding her to them. From that time, she ceased to exist in her parents' world, except perhaps in the secret recess of her mother's heart. Not long after we were married, Lily and I moved out of our room in North Point into a one-bedroom flat on Caine Road, with a small servant's room adjacent to the kitchen. In time, Ah Lan left the Poon household and came to work for us. Her *siu cheh* was all she cared for, Ah Lan said, and she would serve her till the end of her working days.

29

A Chinese Story

Afterword

FOR A LONG TIME NOW, Serena, I have wanted to be a writer. But just as war and political upheavals changed my life, uprooted me from the good earth to which I belonged and transplanted me in new soil, circumstances have made me a policeman, a career I accepted out of necessity and have come to embrace with pride. However, being a policeman has not kept me from writing this story for you, my daughter. I regard these pages as my life's work, for, in writing about my past, not only am I fulfilling my dream to be a writer, I am above all imparting something valuable to you.

What I have written is my story up to the time I married your mother. Your mother and I are very much in love, and out of this love we gave you life. I want you to know about my past, because it is also your past – my roots are your roots. I want you to know my father and mother, the love they gave to me, and through me to you. I want to share the memories of my childhood with you. I want you to have a sense of the history that has shaped China in our lifetimes, the blood and tears shed by her people, the sacrifices they made in pursuit of political and personal ideals, and the wars that took away much that I held dear. I have been a part of it all. My daughter, you too are a part of it all.

30

Mummy's Torment

EVERY TIME I COME to the last page of Papa's book, I don't want it to end. It leaves me with an aching sense of closure – a mistaken notion, for the last page of the book is not the end of Papa's story. After all, Papa was only twenty-five when he married Mummy.

I close the book, carefully inserting Mummy's pages, and replace it in my nightstand. Through the window, I see the sky has taken on a faint blue grey. Soon I will hear birdsong and the rumbling of the garbage truck. Quickly I switch off the bedside lamp and turn in, before Ah Lan wakes and gives me another of her well-meaning chidings.

Today, June 1st, would have been Mummy's birthday. Ah Lan has put a fresh water lily in the bowl of water in front of Mummy's photo. The photo sits in its silver frame, on top of the black lacquered credenza inlaid with birds, peonies and chrysanthemums made of mother of pearl. Mummy is serenely beautiful, in a pink *cheongsam* and matching jacket. With lips curved into a faint smile, she looks poised, refined, controlled. It is her eyes that betray that perfect image, for they are tired, deep-set eyes revealing an intensity of love and an equal measure of pain.

Ever since I was old enough to remember, Mummy had had low-spirited moments when nothing could rouse her from her melancholy. Nothing seemed to excite her then. Even the smiles Papa and I managed to evoke from her were facial counterfeits to appease us and hide a troubled mind. As a child, I had seen her taking medicine. When I asked her what the pills were, she'd say, "They are happy pills."

"Your Mummy worries too much. I've told her so many times to be like me – when the sky falls, use it as a blanket," Ah Lan said once during one of Mummy's down times, soon after my fourteenth birthday. Mummy had gone to bed and she felt free to talk. "I remember not long after she and your Papa were married, she started having bad dreams of your Papa getting injured, even killed, doing his job. Whenever there was a crisis in Hong Kong, she'd go crazy. She'd stay up all night, waiting for him to come home from his shift. Like the summer of '55 when Typhoon Lucy killed thirty people. And the Double Ten riots in '56 when Communists and Guomindang members clobbered one another to death."

Papa, who was in the living room with us, looked up from his newspaper.

"My job had made it very stressful for your mother, Serena. And it wasn't just the danger from external troubles, but also the corruption within the Force."

"Tell me more about it."

"I remember one of the boys on my first beat saying to me back in '53, 'Police salary is poor, but there is no end to the money road, as long as you hop on the bus and take the tea money given you,'" Papa recollected. "Many times I had been offered money by my partners on the beat, money said to have come from – above. 'Consider it a bonus, Ah Sing. We work our butts off to keep peace here, and what do we get in pay? Not enough for two full meals a day. Think of your old lady.'"

"What happened when you refused the money?"

"There was always somebody who would take it. Several times, I found a padded brown envelope in my locker at the police station, from an anonymous sender. I could guess its content, but I left it unopened. A few days later, the envelope was gone."

"Wonder how much money was inside."

Papa explained a lot of the cash came from gambling halls under police protection. He had taken part in raids of *mahjong* houses that somehow had gotten wind the police were on their track, so that all the police found were a few tables of harmless *mahjong* for private parties, solely for amusement. No big stakes gambling. Everything looked innocent. And always, a few days later, the money was there in brown envelopes, for the boys.

"Mummy was worried because you refused the bribe?"

"Your Mummy was worried someone might want to harm me if I was suspected of reporting the corruption. You create enemies all around when you are the odd man out. I never told on my fellow policemen, just turned my back whenever they accepted graft money. It's never easy to be clean, Serena. I was lucky nothing really bad happened to me for refusing the bribes." After a pause, Papa murmured, "Sometimes, I wonder if I hadn't been a policeman, if it would have been easier on Lily."

Mummy recovered that time as she always had from her depression. But we never knew the day or the hour when something would set her off on another downturn on the agonizing road towards mental breakdown.

31

The Refugees

M Y MOST MEMORABLE TIMES growing up were spent with Papa, times still real to me, images still concrete, like yesterday. Like the afternoon we spent at Lok Ma Chau, overlooking the border with China.

I had no school that weekday in the spring of 1975. Papa also happened to be off, and we were supposed to be doing something exciting together. Lok Ma Chau in the New Territories, on the border with China, was Papa's idea of an exciting place.

"I want to show you a special view from the hill," Papa said, as we walked up a footpath canopied with the lime-green leaves of spring and smelling of damp fresh woodland air. A number of snails had broken out of the thicket onto the open footpath after the heavy rain the night before, their brown spiral shells pointed at one end and round at the other, like giant teardrops lying on their sides.

About two-thirds of our way up the hill, we came to a flat clearing with a small grassy mound affording a panoramic view of the country below. A river crossed the distant fields, and beyond the river was a small town against a backdrop of hills. In the foreground were fish ponds and flooded rice paddies where farmers and water buffalo toiled. I could faintly detect barbed wire fencing all along the far side of the fish ponds, separating them from the bank of the river.

"You see the river on the other side of the fish ponds, Serena? That's the Shenzhen River. Beyond the river is China." Papa stood beside me, one hand on my shoulder, the other pointing to the view.

"How come you know the place so well?"

"I had been here many times, when I was a corporal stationed in the New Territories with the border police in the early sixties. I used to take the bus from Fan Ling on my free days, and I would come up here and look across the river to China. Somewhere far behind those hills is Ka Hing."

"It seemed so long ago when Mummy took me there to see *Yeh Yeh*."

"It *was* long ago. You were five then. But I was happy you and Mummy got to spend a little time with my father." His voice cracked, and he was silent.

"Was it dangerous being a border policeman?" I changed the subject.

"Not so much dangerous as difficult. We were guarding the border chiefly against mainland refugees who were trying to cross over into Hong Kong," Papa answered. "There were many of them, but they were no threat to us. In fact, they were weak and helpless. The mainland people were suffering from acute famine and starvation following the failure of the Great Leap Forward, Mao's industrial campaign. You see those wire fences?" Papa's eyes and hand took a broad sweep of the land, the river, the hills. "Every day, famine victims headed for the border. They pushed down fences to come over, they swam the Shenzhen River, and they scoured the border in search of a weak spot overlooked by the Hong Kong Police."

"Where did they go when they had crossed over?"

"They made their way through the New Territories, over the Kowloon hills to reach the city. Some found relatives and friends, some just lost themselves in the city, in search of shelter and a living."

"And it was your job to prevent them from crossing over?"

"Yes," Papa said with some difficulty, "yes, it was my job, the job of the Hong Kong Police to stop them from crossing over. You see, the Chinese government did little to prevent the mass exodus. Some days, I could see them coming from my post, a stream of skeletons in rags, young and old and all ages in between." There was a tremor in Papa's voice. "I did what I was ordered to do, rounded up those caught crossing the border, herded them into police trucks to take them to a nearby building. They were given a meal of rice. Sometimes I watched them devour the food as though their lives depended on it. Often I had to look away, for my heart was too full. And when they had licked their bowls clean, they were transported to the Lo Wu Railway Bridge where they crossed the border on foot back to Chinese territory."

He paused, closed his lips tight, his eyes still looking ahead, his face stolid.

"Weren't they angry that you sent them back?"

"They were generally passive, showing only resignation," answered Papa, turning to look at me. "But many returned to the border, in the hope that perhaps one time they might get lucky. I remembered some of the faces, not just sallow hungry images etched in my mind, but faces of individuals who had crossed the border many times, only to be caught and turned back every time, after a meal."

"Perhaps, for some, that was what they had come for, the meal."

"Exactly. I was sending my fellow countrymen back to a wretched life of hardship and slow death by starvation. When I went home for the weekend, I said to your Mummy that I felt I had turned into a stone, without feeling, without empathy."

"You were only doing your job. You had no choice."

"Once I *had* a choice," he said, his eyes lighting up at the recollection. "One morning, I was jogging along the path that cut through the woods between the police quarters and the station a mile down. While I paused for breath sitting among the underbrush, I heard rustling not far from where I was. I parted the shrubs and the next thing I saw was the dark head of a man crouching low on the ground, ten feet from where I had sat. Just then, he looked up, straight into my eyes. He could not be more than twenty years old, bare-chested, very thin, with ribs showing under his skin. His hair was disheveled, and he had a wild and scared look about him. We stared at each other. Serena, in that moment, my life as a boy in China appeared before me. I got up, turned my back on the fellow on the ground, and walked back to my quarters."

"I hope he made it to Kowloon," I said quietly.

"I hope so," said Papa, and to my surprise he started to weep.

I wiped his tears away with my hand. I put my arm around him. Together, we looked across the wide expanse of land in front of us in silence for a long time, under the dark threatening sky.

Later that evening, I told Mummy the story about the young man that Papa let go when he was with the border police. Mummy nodded in recollection.

"I have my own story to tell you," she said. "It happened about the same time. I joined some teachers and students on an excursion to the New Territories, but in fact we were looking for illegal immigrants near the border, for we had heard some of them were hiding in the hills, and we wanted to take food to them. We divided into small groups." Mummy's eyes took on more life as she recounted. "My group found a family of five, all huddled together in a small cave. They were destitute, shivering in their dirty rags. When they saw us, they looked scared. Then they saw the food we brought, buns and apples and soya milk, and suddenly all their fears vanished. I guess when you are hungry, nothing matters, not personal safety or human dignity."

"I'm so proud of you, Mummy," I said, hugging her.

"We went back a second time three days later," Mummy continued. "We scoured the hillside looking for our family, but could not find them. Either they were caught and sent back, or they had made it to Kowloon."

32

Yeh Yeh

ALTHOUGH I WAS ONLY FIVE when Mummy took me to China in 1965 to visit *Yeh Yeh*, I have retained a vivid memory of the trip. Papa could not go. As a Hong Kong civil servant, he was not allowed to travel to Communist China.

"You'll be going for the two of us," Papa said to Mummy. "Father will be very happy to see you and Serena."

Mummy and I left on a muggy August day. Papa looked very miserable as he kissed us goodbye, and I knew he wanted more than anything in the world to go with us. I was excited, if only for the fact that it was my first train ride. But Mummy was quiet a lot of the way, as if her mind was elsewhere.

At Guangzhou, we got on a bus bound for *Yeh Yeh's* village, bouncing along on a bumpy road bordered by rice fields, until we stopped for a toilet break. I hated the toilet, a small hut in a field, for it was very dirty and stunk so bad. Mummy had a hard time helping me squat. We were both afraid I would fall into the hole.

Finally, the bus stopped on the side of the dusty road, not far from a small group of farmhouses. Mummy gathered up her suitcase and backpack. Holding my hand, she alighted with me. A small crowd had gathered and were staring as though they had never seen anyone from Hong Kong before. Then I saw a man coming out of the crowd and walking in our direction, a tall thin man wearing a *samfu* with the mandarin-collared jacket buttoned to the top. As he approached, I noticed he was almost bald except for a little white hair on the sides. I looked into his eyes with instinctive recognition. I sensed it was *Yeh Yeh*. He walked up to us, his eyes smiling, looking from Mummy to me. Suddenly I felt shy and clung onto Mummy's long pants.

"*Ga So*, welcome home!" *Yeh Yeh* said to Mummy, who later explained to me the name he called her really meant *wife of the family*.

"*Lo Yeh*," Mummy addressed *Yeh Yeh* in what she called the proper form of address for a father-in-law, "forgive me for not paying my respects to you until now. Man On, come greet your *Yeh Yeh*." Mummy seldom called me by my Chinese name. When I was born, Papa had written to *Yeh Yeh* asking for a name for me. *Yeh Yeh* named me Man On, meaning scholarship and serenity. Mummy gave me the name Serena from the second half of my Chinese name.

Mummy bent down and pushed me gently forward toward my grandfather. *Yeh Yeh* squatted down with open arms to receive me. Surprisingly, my shyness vanished, and I was not afraid to go to him. I embraced him as I had always embraced Papa, and when I looked at his face again, I saw tears streaming down his wrinkled cheeks. Mummy was crying too while she turned her face aside.

A boy came up and carried our suitcase. Mummy walked beside *Yeh Yeh* who was holding my hand all the way back to his house.

"Your father lived here before he went to Hong Kong," *Yeh Yeh* said at the threshold into the house. At *Yeh Yeh*'s insistence and in spite of Mummy's protests, we were to take the only bedroom in the house, a very small room just large enough for a bunk bed and a wooden chest. *Yeh Yeh* himself would sleep in Papa's old bed in the main room of the house that was kitchen and parlour, and even bathroom, for a tall wooden barrel-shaped bathtub stood in a corner beside a rice bin.

As soon as Mummy and I had washed our faces in the basin of water *Yeh Yeh* had prepared for us in the kitchen, Mummy boiled some water and made tea using the tea leaves she brought from Hong Kong. She poured a cup of the tea and, asking *Yeh Yeh* to sit down in the parlour, kowtowed to him. Presenting the tea to him with both hands, she said,

"*Lo Yeh*, drink tea."

Yeh Yeh looked very pleased. His face was beaming from ear to ear, his smile seemed to have come from deep down. He took the teacup with both hands and put it down on the little tea stand beside him. From the inner pocket of his jacket he took out a small crumpled red envelope, smoothed it with his hand, and gave it to Mummy.

"*Ga So*, accept this red packet as a token of good fortune." *Yeh Yeh* then took a sip of his tea and, sighing with contentment as though he had not tasted such good tea before, continued, "I have waited for this cup of tea for a long time."

Mummy then kowtowed three times in front of my grandmother's picture on the wall, and placed a cup of tea on the table in front of it.

When I asked Mummy what the fuss over the tea was all about, she said it was the custom for the daughter-in-law to offer tea to her husband's parents as soon as she was married into the family, as a sign of respect.

"I'm very late in paying my respects, but better late than never," Mummy said, smiling.

That evening, *Yeh Yeh* bled a chicken and prepared it himself. Mummy boiled a vegetable soup and steamed a pond fish. I remarked to Mummy afterwards that there seemed to be a lot of food in *Yeh Yeh's* house.

"I think *Yeh Yeh* has been saving up his food coupons for our visit. I don't suppose he had eaten chicken in a long time. He killed that chicken just for us," Mummy said.

I enjoyed my time with *Yeh Yeh*. He showed me the fields where Papa once loved to roam. He took us to the old village of Ka Hing. Unlike what I had imagined from what Papa had told me, it looked very poor and shabby. The stores were dirty and did not seem to have much to sell. The children in the village, with runny noses and grimy cheeks, stared at me as I clung to *Yeh Yeh* and Mummy for security and protection.

"*Yeh Yeh*, can we still get *chi fan* here? Papa told me about it."

"I'm afraid they don't make it anymore in the village," said *Yeh Yeh*, laughing. Then turning to Mummy, he continued, "Times have changed. For a long time now, the only snack we've had is the chewy rice crust stuck to the bottom of the wok. The man who sold *chi fan* came from Shanghai and settled in Ka Hing before the war, but we saw no more of him when we came back after the war. No more *chi fan*, Man On. But how about molasses? That was also your father's favourite, and *that* we still have. Guangzhou is famous for it, and *Yeh Yeh* has saved up some money to buy you a *whole* jar."

We passed the big house where Papa grew up. *Yeh Yeh* said it had become a Communist Party building. We looked at it from the outside. It was shabby, with broken windows and chipped paint, and *Yeh Yeh* said nothing had been done to fix it in all the years since the Communists had taken over.

"I can almost see Tak Sing and Ah Chu crossing its threshold every day to run wild and free all over the countryside," *Yeh Yeh* said to Mummy, while he held my hand and I pranced beside him.

During our stay, we went several times to pay our respects to my grandmother in the family's burial plot a little distance from the old temple on the far side of Ka Hing. Mummy brought some incense and fruit from the village every time, and I picked a bunch of wildflowers along the way. Mummy and I kowtowed in front of the tombstone. She copied down the inscription in her notebook for me:

> *Greatness needs not come from heroic deeds*
> *That rouse the heavens and rock the earth;*
> *It can manifest itself in the silent love*
> *Of a virtuous wife and a good mother.*

"I'll always remember these words," Mummy said to *Yeh Yeh*. "Amazing the paint hasn't faded all these years."

"*Ga So*, I've been coming here every day since I retired. I talk to Wei Fan a lot, and I can feel her talking back to me. I have kept the tombstone clear of grass and dirt, and I touch up the words with paint as soon as they start to chip." After a pause, *Yeh Yeh* said, "Tak Sing adored his mother."

Mummy nodded. "My own mother once told me that you could tell how well a man was going to treat his wife by looking at how good a son he was to his mother. So I know," she said softly.

As the last day of our two-week stay approached, *Yeh Yeh* was not smiling as much as when we first arrived. Mummy too looked gloomy at times. I did not want to say goodbye to *Yeh Yeh* and when I asked Mummy if he could come with us to Hong Kong, Mummy shook her head and looked as though she wanted to cry.

Two days before our departure, a visitor came to call. I went to the door on hearing a knock.

"*Yeh Yeh*, an old man is here to see you!"

Yeh Yeh got up from his chair in the main room and went to the door. His face lit up.

"Ah Ming! What wind blew you here? Come in! You've come at the right time! Come, come! I have a surprise for you!"

The old man entered the house. He was about *Yeh Yeh*'s age, perhaps older, for there was more of a hump on his back, and his hands shook a little as he steadied himself before sitting down.

"Man On, come and greet your Ming Suk Kung," *Yeh Yeh* called to me. Then turning to the old man, he said, "Don't you think this is what Tak Sing's daughter should call you? You are the grandfather generation, so calling you *kung* is appropriate."

The old man looked at me and smiled.

"Old Master," began Ming Suk Kung, "I heard about your visitors, for you know how news travels. I said to myself that if I didn't come and see Tak Sing's wife and daughter this time, I would probably never have another chance. So this morning I got a ride on a lorry to come here!"

Mummy heard the commotion from the bedroom and came out. She insisted on pouring tea for Ming Suk Kung. *Yeh Yeh* wanted him to stay for lunch. Mummy boiled wheat noodles and served them with pickled vegetables stir-fried with black mushrooms she had brought from Hong Kong. After lunch, Mummy showed Ming Suk Kung photographs of Papa in police uniform, and gave him a picture of the three of us in the Botanic Gardens.

Then something clicked in my mind.

"Mummy, is Ming Suk Kung Ah Chu's father?" I blurted out. "Papa told me Ah Chu's father was someone called Ming Suk."

There was a moment of strange silence, and then Ming Suk Kung said, nodding at me, "Yes, Man On, I am Ah Chu's father. Your father and Ah Chu were best friends once upon a time."

Yeh Yeh spoke immediately, as though he had wanted to ask the question for a while, "Ah Ming, how is Ah Chu? Have you heard from him?"

"He's married and has a five-year-old son, a handsome fellow, not taking after his father I'd say." He laughed. "I have only met my grandson once, when his grandmother died. I haven't seen Ah Chu since he came back with his wife and son for his mother's funeral three years ago."

"I'm very sorry about Ming Sum," Mummy said, looking a bit shocked.

"I was very sad when I heard about it from villagers," said *Yeh Yeh*, nodding gravely. "I wished you had told me at the time so I could attend the funeral."

"I appreciate your concern, Old Master, but it was too far for you to travel. I take comfort in knowing she is now at peace after a long illness," Ming Suk said, shaking his head slowly and staring at the floor. After a pause, he continued, "In recent years, Ah Chu has sent money home, not much, but it's what's in the heart. He doesn't write, for I can't read, and he probably doesn't trust anyone to read his letters to me, for you never know when someone would use them as evidence against him, ridiculous as it may sound. You never know what's going on in the Party."

"He must have a good position," said *Yeh Yeh*.

"Ah Chu is the chief cadre in Zhoudu, but his wife has been assigned to teach in Tianjin, so they leave the boy with her parents in Shanghai," said Ming Suk Kung.

"It's too bad the government splits up families," said Mummy. "Tak Sing still thinks of Ah Chu. He has told me a lot about him. They were blood brothers, as you know."

"Oh yes, I knew all about their antics. They were the best of friends," said Ming Suk Kung. "It is sad that it ended as it did."

The day arrived when Mummy and I had to return to Hong Kong. We got up soon after the cock crowed from a nearby barn. After a meal of *congee* and salted duck egg, *Yeh Yeh* carried Mummy's suitcase out of the house, and the three of us walked to the edge of the dirt road to wait for the bus that would take Mummy and me to Guangzhou. Mummy and *Yeh Yeh* were very quiet. When we reached the road, *Yeh Yeh* put down the suitcase and took me in his arms.

"Give *Yeh Yeh* a big kiss, and tell him you'll come back again to see him," Mummy finally said in an unsteady voice.

I put my arms around his neck and kissed him on both cheeks, touching the shiny bald patch on top of his head.

"Mummy, next time you cut my hair, save it. I want to send it to *Yeh Yeh* so he can stick it on his head."

This made *Yeh Yeh* laugh a loud hearty laugh, just as the bus pulled up. *Yeh Yeh* helped me get on the bus. As I stood at the top of the steps inside the bus, he turned to Mummy, still smiling, took her hand in both of his, and said, "*Ga So*, tell my son he has done well. I'm very pleased."

"*Lo Yeh*, we will meet again. Take good care of yourself," Mummy said.

No teary goodbyes, only a tableau of smiles and waves as the bus sped away, blurring with the dust the diminishing image of *Yeh Yeh*, Lee Wing, standing at the side of the road.

33

Typhoon

"*GOY WUI!* NUMBER 3 typhoon signal is up! What are they going to do tonight?" Ah Lan is thinking of the annual candlelight vigil which will commence at sunset in Victoria Park, to mark the eighth anniversary of the Tiananmen Square massacre of June 4th, 1989. I have gone to the vigil every year. Apart from its universal significance in recalling the tragedy of Tiananmen, the candlelight vigil holds a special meaning for me, for it was at the vigil in 1991 that I met Richard…. Tonight, I will go again to the vigil, the last before *hui gui*, unless it is called off on account of the impending typhoon.

There was a time when, as a child, I loved typhoons, for they were harbingers of a day off from school.

"Ah Lan, remember how I used to curl up on your bed in your little room when there was number 7 or 9 typhoon signal? You'd be ironing and mending, and I'd sip warm soya milk while I listened to your ghost stories and tales about Guangzhou. You remember?"

Ah Lan nods and grins, showing her gold front tooth.

"And if I finished my housework early because I couldn't go to the market, you'd beg me for a few games of two-legged *mahjong.*"

"I remember the *mahjong*! You trained me early! But we always had to play two-legged. Papa was usually on duty when there was a typhoon, and Mummy would be too worried about him to do anything else. Only once was I able to get them to play with us, that time Papa had a day off during Typhoon Linda."

"Oh yes, that time they played with us. You were a smart little elf – just six, but you remembered all the rules I taught you."

"Pong! Game! Four chips everybody!" Papa called out as he laid down his tiles.

"I've been calling for my card for a long time!" complained Mummy, pretending to be mad.

"Papa, you always win! It isn't fair!" I felt heat in my eyes as tears started welling up.

"In any game you play, Seenla, you should be prepared to lose like a good sport," Ah Lan admonished, gently tapping the back of my hand.

Outside, Typhoon Linda raged on as I sat with Papa, Mummy and Ah Lan at the square Formica-topped table in the living room, noisily arranging *mahjong* tiles. It was the first time I played the game with the required number of players. As I waited my turn to draw a tile, I glanced from Papa to Mummy and to Ah Lan, drumming my fingers on the tabletop. I shook my shoulders to the Beatles' incantation of *I want to hold your hand* over Radio Hong Kong. Papa and Mummy too seemed to enjoy the Beatles, while Ah Lan had developed a good-humoured tolerance for them.

I prayed the typhoon would last. I wanted the eye of the typhoon to cross Hong Kong! The stronger the gales, the better, for they would keep Papa and Mummy at home, especially Papa, unless he was called away because of an emergency. It wouldn't be fair if he had to go, since it was his day off.

We had rice with canned pork and beans and canned fried dace with black beans for supper that evening. Canned food was special, for it was only used for emergencies such as typhoons when Ah Lan could not go to the market, or as add-ons when unexpected guests finally said yes to my parents' insistence that they stay for dinner, after having politely refused the invitation a few times. Linda might have created havoc outside, but it had been a very good day as far as I was concerned.

A typhoon meant no fresh meat and vegetables for a few days, a situation my parents and I did not mind, but hardly tolerable to Ah Lan. In normal times, she would go to the market every morning with her empty wicker basket, and come home with it filled with fresh vegetables, perhaps a whole red snapper or sea bass, or a piece of red pork or beef wrapped in newspaper, and, on special occasions, a chicken newly bled at the market. She only bought for the day, every day, year in, year out, except on typhoon days.

The typhoon might prevent Ah Lan from going to the market several days every monsoon season, but it was the Frigidaire arriving in the autumn of '66 that undercut the necessity of Ah Lan's daily trip to the market.

"No machine will replace what is fresh and wholesome from the daily kill at the market," Ah Lan grunted.

Although Mummy tried to persuade her not to go to the market every day, Ah Lan still kept her old routine. As for me, I was very excited to be initiated into the refrigerator-owning class. The seven-cubic-footer was installed in the sitting-dining room, a showpiece and the most expensive item in our home. In the quiet of the night, when I awoke, I would listen to its humming and snorting, and feel reassured that all was well.

Nineteen sixty-six was a drought year. Until Typhoon Linda came, little rain had been collected in the reservoirs. Since late spring, there had been water rationing, taps turned on at four in the afternoon, for only four hours, every fourth day. Papa had brought home a five-foot tall metal drum, thirty inches in diameter, painted white on the inside, to store water for cooking, washing, and even flushing of the toilet. The drum took up most of the bathroom. And when the appointed hour of the fourth day arrived, Ah Lan would ceremoniously turn on the bathroom tap connected to the drum with a rubber hose, anticipating eagerly the gurgling sounds that heralded the first gush of the milky chlorinated water, right on the hour, as though it would take the entire allotted four hours to fill the drum. And indeed filling the drum was a time-consuming task, when every unit in the building had its taps turned on in one synchronous act.

The water shortage was a matter of serious concern, but what shook Hong Kong that summer was a by-product of the water rationing. Mummy read about it in the front page of the *South China Morning Post*: *GIRL, AGED THREE, DROWNED IN WATER BARREL.*

The girl, climbing into the empty barrel in her home, fell in, knocked her head on the bottom of the barrel, and passed out in the afternoon of a "water day." Unaware that her daughter was inside, the housewife turned on the tap, started filling the barrel with water through a connecting hose, then left the room, until the barrel was full, yes, until it was too late.

"I cannot even begin to imagine how the mother must feel. I would kill myself if I were the mother," Mummy said to Papa that evening. For weeks, she complained of sleepless nights, and bad dreams when she was finally able to doze off. Once, she came to my bedside and woke me in the middle of the night, saying, "I just want to make sure you are okay, Serena."

After the water barrel tragedy, I was forbidden to stand on a stool and look over the rim of the drum in our bathroom. As for Ah Lan, she always made sure she knew where I was before turning on the water of life and death.

The water crisis eventually abated with the summer rains, and by late August, we were able to enjoy a daily water supply for two hours in the morning and another two hours at dusk.

34

Riots

"Seenla, THE CHINESE ARE sending lots of troops over right after *hui gui*. You think they fear there'll be trouble?"

"You mean protests? I don't think so. If anything, there may be peaceful demonstrations. People here may be worried about the handover, and some are upset with the future government, but most of them are celebrating, at least, on the surface."

"I just hope nobody puts bombs on our streets like that time with the riots in '67."

"I don't think you need to worry. Nothing like the riots of '67 will happen."

I remember the riots. How could anyone living in Hong Kong at the time forget?

When the rioting started in Hong Kong in the spring of 1967, all I was concerned about was that Papa was in peril, as he and the Hong Kong Police Force worked to protect citizens from rioters. The trouble that began as a labour dispute soon became a political instrument used by supporters of the Cultural Revolution in China to instigate trouble in the British colony.

I was six when the Cultural Revolution started in 1966, and was happily ignorant of the ten-year power struggle in the Chinese Central Government that was to result in the arrests and purging of all who were considered a threat to Mao, whether Party members, cadres, or university professors. Toward the end of the ordeal, I began to have a vague notion of the horrifying nightmare experienced by the mainland Chinese, and the tragedy of the country being turned into a cultural wasteland as literary and artistic works were destroyed, and those accused of hiding such were punished. China fell and crumbled under the young Red Guards who were roused by the aging Chairman Mao. They lived only by his commandments expounded in the little red book of his thoughts, and interpreted them at the cost of destruction of lives and legacies. Many of the fervent followers of Communism from the beginning, who went with the young ardent Mao on the Long March, had died, and many who lived to see the Cultural Revolution begin did not live to see it end.

Papa was a police sergeant heading a beat in Central during the riots. As such, he led his men to the forefront of confrontations with demonstrators. He was a link in the passive human chain the police formed to keep rioters from marching on the Governor's residence. When the mob flaunted the little red books of Maoist "wisdoms" at the police, jabbing them in the eyes, kicking them in the groin, calling them "filthy British running dogs," Papa was there. He endured it all. And when he came home late at night, exhausted and demoralized, he turned to Mummy for comfort. Since I slept in a little cubicle partitioned off from my parents' room with a screen, I could hear them talk late at night when they thought I was asleep.

"Today we had instructions to strike back," I heard Papa telling Mummy one night. "One man shouted in my face when I arrested him: '*You have forgotten your roots! You yellow-skin pig! You are licking the ass of those white-faced dogs! You shame your country!*'"

"Don't let such insults get to you, Tak Sing," said Mummy. "You're only doing your job."

When the trouble first started, Mummy would listen closely to the news on the radio, and often watch it on our neighbour's television. But as the weeks turned to months, and trouble continued to flare up in different areas of the colony, she stopped going after the news, for she dreaded what might have happened to Papa while he was on duty.

The worst nightmare occurred one evening soon after my

seventh birthday. Mummy had turned on the radio to hear the news. That day, several bombs, both real and fake, had been reported in the colony. In Wanchai, one five-year-old boy was killed when a bomb exploded outside his home before a bomb disposal team could get to it. In Shaukiwan, another bomb exploded near a parked car, destroying the car and injuring several passersby. In Central, two policemen on patrol were surrounded by a mob. Rioters doused one with petroleum and set him on fire, while the other was beaten and forced to watch his partner turn into a human torch. The mob dispersed just before police reinforcement arrived. The burnt policeman was in a life-threatening condition, suffering from third-degree burns over most of his body, while his partner was hospitalized for shock and undetermined injuries.

Papa patrolled in Central. He had gone out with a partner in recent weeks because of the trouble.

Mummy called the Central Police Station. No one knew where Papa was. The names of the two victimized policemen could not be divulged. The name of the hospital where they were taken could not be divulged. Mummy was almost certain Papa was one of the two men, and it was only a matter of which of the two. She was rubbing her hands and breathing in gasps. I sat on the sofa with my arm around her as she stared blankly at the front door with a wild, vacant look.

The phone rang. My heart was pounding till it hurt. Mummy could not bring herself to the phone. In a weak voice, she called Ah Lan to pick up the phone. Wrong number – a cruel mistake. Mummy called the police station again and got the same answer as before. A few hours passed, like eternity. Finally Mummy told me to go to bed, much as I protested.

"Papa will be home soon. You'll see him in the morning," she said in a small unconvincing voice, as she kissed me on the forehead with feverish lips.

I heard Ah Lan say as Mummy returned to the sitting room, "*Siu Yeh* is probably very busy with so much happening today. *Sui Cheh*, why don't you go to bed too? I'll wait up for him."

Some time in the night, in my wakeful sleep, I heard the lock turn in the front door. In a second, I was out of bed and out of the room. Papa appeared in the doorway, looking very tired and haggard. Mummy fell into his arms, clutching him tightly, and broke into a paroxysm of uncontrolled weeping. I ran to Papa and hugged him as I stood waist-high behind him. The smell of his sweat at that moment was the sweetest smell on earth as I nudged my face into his back. Papa turned and enclosed me and Mummy in his arms, as he tried to kiss away Mummy's tears.

Throughout the riots of 1967 which dragged on till the year's end, not only was Mummy constantly worried about Papa confronting raging demonstrators, she was also anxious about my safety. Other than walking the short distance to and from school with Mummy or Ah Lan, I was confined at home, as were many of my friends during those months.

"Papa, will the Red Guards take over Hong Kong?" I asked. "Red Guards" had become household words.

"No, the Red Guards will not take over Hong Kong. We will fight to keep them off," said Papa. Then he added half to himself, "I only hope China will be free of them soon."

"Is *Yeh Yeh* going to be okay?"

"I hope he is okay," said Papa.

Looking back on that time years later, I realized people in Hong Kong had no real knowledge then of how people were living or dying in China during the Cultural Revolution, for all that came out of the mainland were the little red books of Maoist slogans, and media reports disguised as news, and, in the earlier days of the ten-year havoc, decomposed corpses floating down the Pearl River into Hong Kong waters.

We received a few letters from *Yeh Yeh* in that period. In every letter, he wrote he was well. He disclosed nothing of what life was really like in China then. Papa said the letters had more than likely passed under the censoring eyes of a cadre on a witch-hunt mission to seek out the rebels to the cause of the Cultural

Revolution. Nonetheless, we were able to draw some comfort from seeing my grandfather's handwriting, knowing he was alive.

35

Mimi

IT IS TEN IN THE MORNING of June 15th, 1997, just fifteen days to *hui gui*. My eyes follow the television cameras through some dirty back streets of Hong Kong, up a dingy dark staircase to emerge into a congested rooming flat. A reporter is going to interview the occupants of the flat, to get their views on the handover, men in cotton vests and boxer shorts, women in plain *samfu* and plastic thongs, barefooted children running in the narrow corridor, old people transfixed on their straw-matted beds, their beds their entire living space, this side of glamorous Hong Kong.

Small though our flat was on Caine Road, I felt I was in a mansion after I went with Papa the first time to one such flat in Kowloon, when I was about nine, to see Mimi. Years later, when I first read Papa's book, I was to know more about her, and what she meant to Papa, what Papa meant to her.

I held on to Papa's hand as we wound through side streets reeking of decaying garbage piled high against the curbs. The smell was made worse by the humidity and heat already upon us even though it was only May. I skipped gingerly along the pavement, careful not to step on an occasional rotten orange or blots of yellow spittle left on the grids of gutters. I barely missed the bloodied water someone in a butcher shop was pushing with a straw broom onto the street after hosing down its floor. Strips of raw meat hung by hooks over counters in meat shops, where butchers in bloodstained aprons were hacking away with cleavers on thick wooden boards.

We turned into Pun Lung Street, just another side street with the same stench of rotten garbage. Papa looked at the numbers above entrances to narrow staircases sandwiched between storefronts as we walked along the dirty pavement, and finally stopped in front of a newsstand. The number above the doorway adjacent to the newsstand read 102.

"Serena, this is the place. Just follow me, and watch your step. It's dark on the stairs," Papa said as he climbed up the wooden stairs with me at his heels.

We soon reached the first landing. A door on our left was open. We stepped over the threshold into a dark narrow corridor. Doors lined both sides of the corridor. I held Papa's hand which had become cold and clammy. A woman in a black *samfu* and wooden clogs emerged from one of the doorways and slouched toward us.

"Ah Sum, I am looking for Mimi. Can you please tell me where she is?" Papa asked.

The woman pointed with her head to a doorway near the end of the corridor and spoke, showing a big gap in her front teeth. "She's over there, in number two. A sickly one she is, never leaves her bed. The landlady says if she doesn't pay her rent, she'll get kicked out soon."

Papa walked toward the second last doorway. A thin cloth curtain hung over the open doorway, shielding the interior. Papa knocked on the wooden slide panel on one side of the doorway. No answer. After a decent few seconds, he drew the curtain aside to reveal a cubicle, with space only for a single bed, a wooden wardrobe with a yellowed mirror on its door, and a dresser with a thermos flask and a glass tumbler sitting on top. There was a bare window with dirty fogged-up glass that allowed some light into the room but no visibility to the outside. My eyes focused on the bed which was occupied by a reclining woman. A blanket in a faded, flower-patterned cover was draped over her. As she turned her head toward the doorway, I saw her dark-ringed, sunken eyes, her thin, pallid face. Papa stepped into the room, leaving me at the doorway, and knelt beside the bed so she could see his face.

"Mimi, it's Tak Sing."

It took her a few moments to register what she had just heard. Her eyes came alive as she put out her hand, just skin over knuckles, and Papa took it in both of his. Tears formed and trickled from the corners of her eyes as she attempted to sit up, gazing at Papa all the while.

"Tak Sing, you haven't changed much after all these years. But look at me. I'm sorry, so sorry you have to see me like this."

Papa helped her up so that her head rested against the wall at the top of the bed, and propped the pillow behind her head. All the time, her eyes never left Papa's face.

"I just felt I had to see you," she said between sobs. "I hope you are not angry with me. I didn't want to call your home. I asked around, and when I found out which police station you worked at, I had one of the girls who used to work with me write you the note."

"I would have come to you earlier if I had known about your condition. Mimi, why didn't you call me? Why did you wait so long?" Papa sounded upset.

"You are a married man, and I'm nothing but a whore." She sounded bitter.

Papa, looking a little disconcerted, glanced in my direction. The reason that brought us to visit that sickly woman was a mystery to me at the time, as was the word "whore," but I sensed it meant someone not deserving of Papa, someone Mummy was not. I felt very uncomfortable standing there in the doorway. I did not like the place at all, but could not leave without Papa.

"Mimi, you are a good woman, a decent person, and my friend. All these years, I thought you were okay. Why didn't you call me when you were in trouble? Why?"

"I never wanted to intrude." Her eyes rested for the first time on me. "Who's that young lady?" she asked.

"My daughter." Papa beckoned to me. "Come, Serena, and say hello to my old friend Mimi. She helped me find a job when I first arrived in Hong Kong."

I entered the room. Mimi gave me a weak smile and took my hand.

"She's very lovely – must be a combination of you and her mother." She let go of my hand, to my relief, and turned back to Papa. "I haven't been like this the whole time, you know. I was fine. Been with a few, none lasting more than a couple of years. But I was fine, until one got me hooked on opium. I was a sorry wreck when he left me. I needed the opium but had no money...." She seemed to want to say more to Papa but kept quiet. She turned her face to the wall and coughed, a hard and heavy cough.

Papa rubbed her back gently. I returned to my position at the door. After a while, Mimi's coughing subsided, and she was able to rest in a reclining position again.

"I'm worried about you, Mimi. Have you seen a doctor?" Papa asked.

Mimi paused and swallowed hard.

"I went to the government clinic in Sai Ying Poon. But every time I had to wait so long for the doctor and the medicine, I got too tired to stay. I tire easily these days. It's TB."

Papa looked alarmed. "I'm going to take care of you, Mimi. Don't you worry."

Mimi rested her eyes on Papa's face for a long while, too long for my liking. Who was this woman anyway? Papa seemed to be very much concerned about her. Before we left, she said to Papa words that stayed in my head and bothered me all the way home, "Tak Sing, I've seen you again, and if I am to die today, I'll die contented."

As soon as we got home that evening, Mummy was very anxious to know how our meeting with Mimi went. When Papa had finished telling her all that happened, she wept.

"Tak Sing, do whatever you can for her." She hesitated, and continued, "Next time, you don't have to take Serena with you."

That night, as I lay awake thinking about Mimi, I heard Mummy on the other side of the partition saying to Papa, "I misjudged Mimi's intentions, Tak Sing, when you showed me her note."

"A woman has every right to be jealous when her husband receives a note from another woman, asking him to see her," said Papa, in the soft voice he used with Mummy whenever they were alone, or thought they were. Then he added in a teasing tone, "I'd feel hurt if you hadn't sent Serena along to protect me."

"You know I trust you completely," said Mummy to Papa. "Seriously, Tak Sing, you've got to help her."

"My father gave me three gold bars when I left home. I sold one as soon as I reached Hong Kong, and that kept me alive until – until – Mimi got me the hawker's license. It is now time to sell the second one. I cannot put it to better use than helping Mimi with it."

Papa had Mimi placed in the sanitarium for tuberculosis patients. He visited her often, occasionally bringing me with him.

"This is the best time of my life, to be so well taken care of by the nurses and the doctors, and to see you so often. I don't know if I ever want to leave here," Mimi said to Papa one evening when I went with him to visit her.

"Don't be silly. There are happier times ahead when you are well. I'll help you find work, and you can start afresh," Papa said.

"I just don't know if there can be happiness for me on earth," said Mimi, shaking her head.

"Be optimistic, Mimi. I met a woman long ago in Tai Shek during the war, a *zheng* player. She was able to hold on when all seemed lost to her, by dreaming of a paradise called Shangri-La and hoping that some day she would get there. We should all hope and work for a better life, even if there is no real Shangri-La."

Mimi looked away and murmured, "I stopped dreaming the day you moved out of Wanchai."

Mimi developed pneumonia after she had been in the sanitarium for a couple of months. From then on, Papa visited her every day after work. On the night of July 7th, two days after my ninth birthday, Papa called Mummy from the sanitarium to say Mimi had taken a turn for the worse. Papa stayed at the sanitarium through the night. He came home in the morning, exhausted, with heavy and baggy eyes. He held Mummy close, and buried his face in hers.

"She's gone," he said in a broken voice. "I was with her at the end."

36

Mummy

I CAME HOME FROM SCHOOL one day in late November of '75 to find Ah Lan crying.

"*Siu Cheh* has gone to the hospital, and *Siu Yeh* is with her," she said between sobs.

"Why?" I asked immediately, imagining the worst, that Mummy was dead. "Why is Mummy in the hospital, Ah Lan? Is she going to be all right?"

"Your Papa will phone as soon as he knows her condition," Ah Lan said. After a pause, she continued, "You know your Mummy has got a sleeping problem for a long time, but lately it's been worse. Last week, she told your Papa that when she closed her eyes, she saw him as a headless corpse on the street. Another time, she dreamed that her father thought she drowned in the tub long ago, and that was why he never called."

"Why is she in hospital?" I was screaming, ignoring Ah Lan's account of Mummy's dreams.

"Those pills she's been taking to help her sleep, to stop the nightmares." Ah Lan pursed her lips, then continued hesitantly, "She had a bad night, so she didn't go to work this morning, and while I was at the market, she took too many – all she wanted was to get a good sleep – I know *Siu Cheh*, that's *all* she wanted to do." Ah Lan's voice turned to sobs.

I felt as though my world had ended. I was desperate to go to Mummy immediately. I was sure she needed me. I had to set things right for her. I must go to her, but Ah Lan said Papa wanted me to wait at home.

Mummy, hadn't I always been there for you when Papa was at work and you needed someone to talk to, when you felt sad, when you worried till your head hurt? I had tried to give you comfort and joy by being a well-behaved daughter and an exemplary student. I had stopped playing loud music ever since you said your nerves could not take it. I hadn't invited friends home in two years. What else could I have done? Why were you doing this to yourself? To me and Papa?

Papa phoned to say Mummy's stomach had been pumped and her condition was stable. That night, Papa came home looking pale and drawn. I hugged him and began to cry.

"She's going to be all right, Serena."

"She didn't really intend – did she, Papa?"

"No," Papa answered in a strong voice. "She's been depressed, but I don't think for a moment she intended to harm herself." He looked at me with conviction.

"Why Mummy…?" I sobbed, not convinced by his words.

Papa was quiet, looking sorrowfully at me.

"We won't ask why, Serena. The important thing is to help Mummy get well."

Mummy came home after two weeks in the hospital. She stayed on medication, and returned to her teaching at St. Agnes High School, and life was back to normal for us, as normal as it could be, for she was never quite the same. I became very sensitive to her moods, and could tell when she was bothered by the fears and worries that gave her sleepless nights and wakeful dreams. I still clung to her for motherly advice and emotional sustenance during her normal phases, but gradually I sensed a reversal of roles as I tried desperately to comfort and soothe her troubled mind. As for Papa, he was always attentive and patient. It seemed his happiness depended on Mummy's well-being. At times, Mummy would be herself, the loving and caring wife and mother. But as the years went by, the normal times were to become more infrequent, as she fought a gradual losing battle with the dark thoughts that rattled her mind, took away her rest, and stripped her defenceless against her own despair.

37

The Intruder

MUMMY ENJOYED A RELATIVELY LONG spell of mental wellness after her recovery in the hospital from the overdose and from depression. For my sixteenth birthday in July, 1976, she and Papa held a small party for me. I invited four close friends, Beth Wong, Mona Tavares, Josie Chan and Noriko Sugawa. Papa worked an early shift that day, and was home by four in the afternoon. All day, Ah Lan was busy in the kitchen, concocting her best dishes, including sweet and sour pork, "Seenla's favourite," she called it.

"Ah Lan, you're the best cook, the best *amah* anybody can *ever* have!" I bent to hug the aging woman who barely reached to my shoulders.

"I'm also making soya chicken, pineapple ginger beef and *gai lan* in oyster sauce, everything you like," said Ah Lan.

"Did you cook like this when Mummy turned sixteen?" I was amazed by the number of dishes she was preparing for one meal.

"When your Mummy turned sixteen, I didn't have to cook at all," said Ah Lan, brushing the sweat from her forehead with the back of her hand. "Your *Kung Kung* and *Poh Poh* had a caterer prepare the dinner for fifty guests. A few were your mother's friends, but mostly they were your grandparents'."

"I don't think I would enjoy such a party," I said.

Just then, Mummy came home with a cake box and hurriedly put it in the Frigidaire, which had kept its place in the sitting-dining room since the day of its arrival.

"I bet that's my birthday cake, Mummy," I said, hugging her.

"You can't see it. It's a surprise," she said, smiling and raising

181

her eyes up slightly at me, for I was a good two inches taller than she.

Mona, who was of Portuguese descent but spoke perfect Cantonese, gave me a life-sized poster of Robert Redford, my all-time heartthrob. Beth and Josie got me a T-shirt with *Sweet Sixteen* on the front, and on the back the words *The Whole World In My Hands*. Noriko, whose father was a Japanese merchant doing business in Hong Kong, presented me with an album of the Beatles' greatest hits.

After dinner, Mummy brought out the cake which was in the shape of a key, alight with sixteen candles. I blew them out in one puff.

"You hold the key to your future, daughter," said Papa. "Your mother and I are behind you all the way, but you are the one who has control over your life."

"Yes, Papa," I said, my eyes suddenly watering. I did not care if my friends were present, I went over to my parents and embraced them. When I finally let them go, Mummy's cheeks were glittering with tears as she busily set out plates. Papa put his arm over her shoulders.

"I wonder what Serena wished for before she blew out the candles," said Mona, ready for some teasing.

"I bet she wished Robert Redford was at the door," said Noriko.

No sooner had Noriko finished speaking than there was a tentative knock on the door.

"He's here!" exclaimed Beth, and the girls fell about in peals of laughter.

"He could at least have rung the bell!" Josie managed to say.

Ah Lan put down her plate of cake and peeked through the private eye in the door.

"*Siu Yeh*, it's a stranger," she told Papa.

She opened the door ajar, without releasing the door chain, and after a brief exchange with the intruder, she shut the door and called to Papa again.

"*Siu Yeh*, he's asking for you. He knows you by name."

Papa looked surprised and got up from his chair. My friends stopped their giggling, and we all glanced from the door to Papa, and back to the door.

"Who is it?" Papa called out.

A pause. No footsteps heard. He was still at the door. Then came a small voice.

"I am So Tak Ming. My father has asked me to find Lee Tak Sing."

Papa hesitated for a moment, then opened the door as far as the chain would let him, revealing a lean fellow about Papa's height, wearing a *samfu* that was too short for him, and tattered rubber shoes. There followed a mumbled conversation between Papa and the intruder. I kept my eyes on Papa the whole time he was talking to the man. Then, instead of closing the door on him, Papa released the chain and opened the door wide. Much to my dismay, he put an arm over the young man's shoulders and ushered him into the flat.

"Lily, Serena," said Papa, "come meet Ah Chu's son."

My first reaction was one of absolute annoyance. Couldn't he have picked a different day to arrive, if he was to arrive at all? I was so embarrassed in front of my friends that I was close to tears.

"Hi," I managed to say coldly, not at all worried if he caught the rudeness in my voice.

Mummy, on the other hand, seemed delighted.

"I met your grandfather in 1965 when I took my daughter to visit my father-in-law. He talked very fondly of you."

I was exasperated that my parents could be so excited about the unexpected arrival of the stranger, who had crashed my birthday party and spoiled the whole evening. Papa asked him to sit down at the table, and Beth and Mona hurriedly made way for him. I could not help staring at him as he squirmed in his seat and fidgeted with his hands, his nails encrusted with dirt.

"How did you arrive, Tak Ming?" Mummy asked as she stood

ELSIE SZE

behind Papa, her hands on his shoulders.

"I – I swam over," the party-crasher replied quietly. He sounded polite yet I could detect a hint of pride in his own accomplishment. Then, in a stronger voice, he continued, "Across the Shenzhen River, from Shekou to Lau Fau Shan. Last night was a moonless night, the best time to swim without being seen. I waited for low tide and swam across. At some points near the banks, the river was so shallow, I just waded."

Bragger.

"Wasn't it dangerous?" Mummy asked.

"I had to be very careful to avoid the oyster shells on the cement slabs that stuck out into the water, for they were sharp as knives, and could cut to the bone."

"How did you get *here*? How did you find us? Tell us the whole story," Ah Lan pursued, standing near Mummy, looking more excited than I wanted her to be.

"When I reached shore at Lau Fau Shan, it was morning and raining. I walked into the village, and up a narrow street with markets and restaurants on both sides." He looked less uncomfortable as he told his story, supposedly the feat of a lifetime. "The local people were just opening up their stores. I needed to get out of my wet clothes before a policeman saw me."

I looked at Papa, and we exchanged smiles. I glanced over to my friends. They were listening to the fellow's story, looking serious and intent.

"A man came up from behind and asked in a low voice, 'Did you just swim across?' I jumped, thinking that it was the end of my escape, the end of me. But the man looked friendly. I nodded, and he said immediately, 'Let's get you out of those wet things. Come into my store.' I followed him into the back room of a seafood restaurant, where I was given this to wear." He looked down at his outfit. "He told me his surname was Kwok. Mr. Kwok asked me to eat breakfast with him and his wife. I told him I was supposed to find you, Tak Sing Suk," he said, addressing Papa as his father's younger brother. Looking at Mummy, he continued,

"My grandfather had given my father your address from long ago, soon after your visit to the mainland, Tak Sing Sum." How I wished he would stop calling my parents his uncle and aunt. "My father was hoping I could trace you even if you had moved. Well, after eating, Mr. Kwok took the bus with me to Yuen Long. From there we boarded another bus to the terminal at Sham Shui Po in Kowloon. There he left me to take the ferry across the harbour to Hong Kong Island, and I finally made it here after asking my way."

"You did well, Tak Ming. Your father will be very proud of you," Papa said, nodding.

"Come, have something to eat. Today is Serena's birthday, and we are just celebrating a bit," said Mummy, going into the kitchen to get some dinner for the fellow. At Mummy's words, he turned to me, as though he had just discovered my presence.

"Happy birthday," he said, nodding politely at me. I nodded back, pursing my lips to pull a straight face, till my eyes met Beth's, and then I fell into a fit of uncontrolled giggles with the girls, and Ah Lan had to call me into the kitchen to give me a lesson on politeness.

My friends soon left, but I realized the uninvited guest would be staying on for a while. I would have to get used to this country bumpkin from the mainland. In spite of myself, I was beginning to feel a little sorry for him. Still, I wished he was staying somewhere else.

"Pa has asked me to give you a letter, Tak Sing Suk," Tak Ming said as soon as my guests were gone. He took out from an inner pocket of his jacket a folded letter wrapped in a piece of oilcloth wrapped in turn in a plastic bag.

Papa's hand shook a little as he took the letter from Ah Chu's son, his nervous look reminding me of the first time he took me to see Mimi. I realized, as I thought of both times years later, what they must have meant to Papa – the reclaiming of friendship gone awry, a reconnection to a buried past, as though Papa's long-lost shadow had caught up with him. He read the letter silently, soberly, then passed it to Mummy who read it aloud.

April 23, 1976

Brother Tak Sing,

If this letter reaches you, my son is safe. My heart is full. I have a thousand words to say, but do not know where to begin. I shall do my best; the rest, I shall leave unsaid.

Looking back, thirty years seemed to have gone by like a flowing stream, sometimes fast, other times slow, but never still. I can see us as boys again in Ka Hing, bound in brotherhood by the mixing of blood. The truth is, through all the years, I have not forgotten that time, the most carefree time of my life. Since then, I had wandered in pursuit of an absolute ideal, sacrificing the small self for the ultimate whole, only to realize sadly in the end that it was not to be. There is no Shangri-La, Tak Sing, only a mirage that has eluded me for thirty years. I have been defeated, a victim of an ideology that has been defiled and has undergone frightful mutations, so that I can no longer recognize it. Need I say more? But I want my son to live. To this end I send him to you, my brother, whom I trust more than any other living human being, yes, more than myself. I ask you in the name of what bound us together to give Tak Ming all the assistance you can to enable him to start a new life in Hong Kong, as you did when you left China. I shall be grateful every day of my life.

We have seen the worst of times, Tak Sing, but there has got to be hope for our children yet. I named my son after the two persons who had meant the most to me, my father and you. The day I left my home, your father's house, to embark on my journey to Yan'an, I left behind my heart, and all

that I held dear. If fate permits, we shall meet again; if not,
my brother, we shall meet in the next life.
Kindly extend my regards to your wife.

Always your brother,
Chu

The room was quiet when Mummy finished. I took the letter from Mummy. It was written with a ballpoint pen. The writing was decent, though not as beautiful as Papa's.

"Pa would be in big trouble if I was caught and the Chinese authorities got hold of the letter, but he said he didn't care anymore. He just wanted to tell you, Tak Sing Suk, what he had wanted you to know for a long time."

Papa nodded gravely, lifting his hand to brush off a tear from under his eye. Mummy put her arm around Papa's shoulders.

"Tell us about your life in China, Tak Ming *Siu*," urged Ah Lan, addressing him like a young master.

Tak Ming seemed ready to talk. "I was six when the Cultural Revolution began. I started school at seven, but for two years I learned nothing except Mao slogans and copying the slogans onto posters. Many teachers and older students were too busy beating up the anti-revolutionaries and capitalists." Tak Ming paused, as though it was difficult to put into words the things he was recalling in his mind.

He continued to tell us that the situation became a little better after 1968, and he was then taught a bit of reading and writing in school. He said that his maternal grandfather had been secretly teaching him arithmetic, science and history. At school, he would sing *East is Red* and participate in self-criticism, but at home, he would be reciting the multiplication tables, learning about the planets and the seasons, and hearing stories of past dynasties.

"You were living with your grandfather?" Ah Lan asked.

"My mother was sent away to teach in Tianjin when I was

187

two. For a long time, I lived with my maternal grandparents in Shanghai, and only saw my mother when she was allowed to visit us."

"Tak Ming, tell us more about your father. You said earlier that he was well," Papa prompted. Tak Ming must have told him so when they were talking at the door.

Tak Ming faltered a little.

"Well, he's been in reasonably good health, considering all that he has gone through. Pa was the chief cadre in Zhoudu, until – until they humiliated him publicly, made him confess to capitalistic sympathies. They stripped him of his post, and sent him away to a reeducation camp in 1967. The extreme radicals accused him of being a revisionist having gone astray. They branded him an enemy of the State."

"How could he be an enemy of the State? He gave so much to China." Papa looked disturbed.

"Those camps were like prisons – pitiful living condition, little food, and, worst of all, mental torture," Tak Ming continued. "Pa said he was ordered to admit to betraying the Party and confess to crimes of being a revisionist. When he was not self-criticising and attending re-indoctrination classes on Mao thoughts, he was doing hard labour in the fields. They threatened his family would suffer if he didn't confess to his capitalistic leaning, so he did. When Pa was finally allowed to return to Zhoudu after nine months, he was given a subordinate position as assistant to the Party Secretary in Zhoudu. It was very humiliating for him, but he took it without complaint. At least they didn't strip him of his Party membership."

Papa shook his head slowly, his thick brows knitted into a deep frown.

"How's your grandfather?" Mummy asked Tak Ming.

"He passed away two years ago. My father, mother and I were allowed to return to the village to attend his funeral."

"Ming Suk dead?" Papa's lips quivered. After a few moments, he continued in a strained voice, "He used to carry me on his back when I was tired. He looked after me as though I was his own son. He put the interest of my family before his own. Tak Ming, your grandfather was a second father to me."

"He left a gold bar for Pa to give to me. That was the only thing Pa gave me before I left, that and the letter," Tak Ming said as he produced a gold bar from an inner pocket. "I hid it in a cloth pouch sewn to the waistband of my pants. Pa told me the gold bar was given to my grandfather by your father, Tak Sing Suk."

"It's a humble token of my father's gratitude to your grandfather for his devotion to my family," Papa said. "Use it well. It's your grandfather's gift of love to you."

38

Ming

I WAS AT SCHOOL on the day of the open house, just two days after my sixteenth birthday, my eyes darting anxiously to the front entrance, unable to think of anything but the embarrassment to come. Papa and Mummy finally walked through the front door with Tak Ming, who was wearing a short-sleeved white polyester shirt, khaki trousers, and black loafers, an outfit Mummy bought him. It was not his clothes that tagged him as a country bumpkin, but his face: the thick crop of hair closely cut above his ears, with bangs covering part of his forehead, above his closely-knit eyebrows and high cheekbones, and the expression of amazement, and the unnecessary obliging look.

"Who's that guy with your parents, Serena?" one of the girls from my class whispered in my ear.

"Some boy whose father once knew my father," I said, and walked over to greet Papa and Mummy, ignoring Tak Ming.

"Serena, don't worry about us," said Mummy considerately. She probably noticed my embarrassment and knew Tak Ming to be the cause of it. "We know our way here. Just stay at your post and welcome the guests."

Relieved, I sauntered back to the other girls in the foyer.

"Serena, isn't that the boy we met at your birthday party?" my friend Josie asked.

"Yes," I answered, rolling my eyes and zipping up my lips into a tight smile.

I did not see Tak Ming in the school again until I was in the cafeteria where refreshments were served, platefuls of cookies and sandwiches spread out on a long table covered with a white tablecloth. At one end, two girls were ladling out fruit punch into small plastic cups, and at the other end, two other girls were pouring coffee and tea. Parents and students were standing in small groups, engaged in quiet conversations. As I was getting some punch, I heard whispering and giggles coming from a group of girls nearby, all looking over to a corner of the cafeteria. My eyes followed their gaze and, to my utter bewilderment, I saw Tak Ming sitting at a table by himself, with a plate heaped high with cookies and sandwiches in front of him. He was enjoying the repast, oblivious of the crowd and the attention he was drawing from the girls. I was burning with embarrassment, and vexed with my mother and father for leaving him alone.

"Look! He's wolfing it down like he just got out of a prison camp!" I was close enough to hear the third-form girls.

"He's walking over to the coffee station! Oh no! He's emptying a creamer into a cup! He's drinking it! He must think it's milk!"

"He's cute!"

"Why don't you go and ask him for a date?"

Giggles.

"Where on earth did he come from?"

"Stanley Prison!"

"Or Mars."

"Let's go over and check him out."

Two girls walked idly over to where Tak Ming was finishing his food. He looked up at them, chewing with his mouth full. I could not hear them, but Tak Ming soon stood up and walked briskly over to the coffee station. He took two cups and filled them with cream. Looking gallant, he took the cupfuls of cream back to the two girls who had been bending double with laughter behind his back but were now trying to pull a straight face as he came toward them.

Suddenly, I was not ashamed of Tak Ming anymore. I was mad at the way the girls were behaving, disgusted at their meanness shown to someone as innocent as Tak Ming. At that moment, my parents entered the cafeteria, unaware of Tak Ming's plight. Without hesitation, I walked over to Tak Ming, just as he was handing the cups of cream to the two girls. I took the cups out of his hands, much to his consternation, and put them on the table in front of the girls.

"I'd like to see you two drink this up."

The girls exchanged glances with a what's-wrong-with-her look, and with a shrug went back to their group who had become very quiet. Tak Ming was stunned by my action, but not displeased, for his instinct must have told him that I was defending him. I glanced at Papa and Mummy who had witnessed the scene. Mummy looked amazed while Papa smiled at me, as if to say, "Daughter, I am proud of you."

Tak Ming's name was soon abbreviated to Ming. He was to enroll at Ling Tao Chinese Secondary School in September. Although he had graduated from middle school in China, his years of schooling, which included immersion in Chairman Mao thought and two months a year spent in factories, had by no means produced someone on an academic par with a Hong Kong secondary school graduate. At Ling Tao, he would be repeating two years of high school. Although he had expressed an intention to find a day job and move into his own place, attending only night school, Papa would not have it.

"I'd rather you go to regular day school, to catch up on your lost time, Ming. As long as you don't mind sleeping on the sofa, we have room for you here. We want you to stay. Your father would want you to stay."

"So, Ming, what made you come to Hong Kong? Other than your father's wish, I mean," I asked one evening at supper, soon after the open house.

"I was in trouble with the government, and had to flee." It was the first time he confided in us about the immediate reason for his escape.

"What did you do?" Mummy asked, looking alarmed.

"It began in January when Premier Zhou Enlai died. You see, since last August, my mother and I had moved to Beijing where my father had been transferred to the office of one of the cadres. For the first time since I was two, we could be together as a family. I attended high school in Beijing. Well, in April, at Ching Ming, some of my classmates and I put a wreath of paper flowers at the base of the Monument to People's Heroes in Tiananmen Square, along with many other wreaths and banners placed there in honour of Premier Zhou Enlai. We returned to the Square the next morning to find no trace of the wreaths and banners, as if they had never been there. The police had removed them."

"How absolutely outrageous!" I said.

"We were very angry. We protested, and I joined the mob throwing stones at the soldiers called in to assist the police. There was a big crowd of protesters in the Square, and some even set fire to police cars. Many were arrested, including some of my friends. Their fate is still unknown. I was very lucky not to have been caught. For two months, I hid in the home of Pa's friend, a comrade Pa knew at the re-education camp. This man lost his Party membership because he was accused of corresponding with capitalist friends in Hong Kong. He now works in a butchery in Beijing. He had me smuggled to Guangzhou on a freight train, and from there I hid in the back of a lorry transporting pigs to Shenzhen."

"I'm glad you got out, but it must be so hard to leave your family," said Mummy.

Ming nodded. "I didn't want to leave, but Pa said I had no choice."

"The price of freedom can be very high," Papa said. "I realized that long ago."

"*Ghaaargh!*"

The noise came from behind. Immediately, I grabbed Ming's wrist and walked briskly, almost breaking into a run, bumping into a few pedestrians.

"What's the hurry?" Ming was flabbergasted.

I had slowed down by then. Walking abreast of Ming, I explained, "One of the rules of walking on a Hong Kong street is when you hear *ghaaargh* from behind, you run, before the *ptsoi* comes, because it always does, soon enough, and you don't want to be sprayed by some stranger's spit. My friends and I call the *ghaaargh* the prelude."

"You are funny, you know. In China, people don't run when someone spits," said Ming. "If they did, they'd be running all the time."

The scenario made us laugh as we meandered our way through the crowd into the night market on Temple Street. My mission was to take Ming shopping for some clothes.

"Now remember, Ming, bargain even if the price looks good. Only the foreign tourists pay the asking price," I counseled, as we wove through throngs of bargain hunters, local folk as well as foreign tourists, inching our way through the narrow street lined with stalls selling imitation Versace shirts, Pierre Cardin sweaters, Rolex watches, Italian leathers. It had been a sultry day, like any other in July, and night brought no relief. The heat emitting from the high wattage bulbs above each stall contributed to putting everyone, vendors and shoppers, into a sweaty steam bath. But nobody cared, as long as the sales were good, and the bargains were good. Suddenly, Ming's eyes fell upon a navy blue tie with a gold dragon motif.

"Twenty Hong Kong dollars each! Three for fifty dollars!" the stall keeper called out as his eyes followed Ming's admiring gaze.

"Handmade in Italy. A hundred percent silk!" Ming read from the label. "I only want the one with the dragon. How about ten dollars for that."

"No way. I'll lose money then." The vendor shook his head definitively. "These are nice silk ties. Imported from Italy."

I pulled Ming away.

"Seventeen!" the vendor called after us.

We kept walking away.

"Okay, okay! Fifteen!" The vendor wanted the business.

We returned to the stall.

"Okay. We'll take it. Italian silk tie indeed," I said.

"Oh yes, very good silk tie, imported from Italy," the vendor echoed, failing to read the sarcasm in my voice.

"We are no fools. How can a silk tie cost so little?" I challenged, as Ming took out his wallet.

"Well, what do you expect for fifteen bucks, Miss? So long as it looks like silk," the vendor immediately agreed.

I smiled. Ming was happy with the bargain, silk or no silk, Italian or not.

39

When The Earth Shook

WHAT GREETED US IN the *Sing Tao Daily* on the morning of July 28th, 1976 shocked us beyond words, and drove Ming into a frenzy. In the night, China was shaken by one of the worst earthquakes the world had ever known, in the city of Tangshan, northeast of Beijing. Damage was also suffered in Tianjin, about seventy miles east of Tangshan. Beijing felt it too, but Tangshan literally vanished from the face of the earth.

"Pa and Ma - " cried Ming, his colour fading.

"They should be safe in Beijing. It's Tangshan that's gone," Papa assured him.

"The Chinese government is not saying much," said Ming, still agitated.

"The Chinese have a way of keeping to themselves, even in times of natural disasters. They don't want foreign help," said Papa, scanning the newspaper. "They say they can manage on their own."

Six weeks after the Tangshan earthquake, early in September, came the news of Mao Zedong's death.

"I *knew* when the earthquake happened that Mao wouldn't last very long. It was a sign he was going to die soon," said Ah Lan as we watched the evening news.

"You know, I hated Mao for what Communism did to my family. Yet, he had good intentions in the early days. So many believed in him, including your father, Ming," said Papa, turning to Ming who was watching the news with us.

"Pa suffered a lot, Tak Sing Suk. He's greatly disillusioned about the Party."

"Your father sacrificed a lot for his country. He dedicated his whole life to China without thought of recompense. Yet he was persecuted. Life is never fair," Papa said.

One evening not long after the Tangshan earthquake, Papa's friend Stephen Kwan dropped by. Since meeting in police training school twenty-four years ago, Stephen Kwan and Papa had been on several beats together and worked together on many assignments. That day, Stephen came to talk about the investigations of the Independent Commission Against Corruption, the ICAC. I was studying in the sitting room when he came, and he didn't seem to mind my presence while he talked with Papa.

"Ah Sing, they're digging up three generations of dirt and making a big deal of everything," Stephen said.

"It's time someone does something about the Force, Kwan," said Papa. "It's high time."

"But it's usually the small fry who gets caught while the big ones get off easy!" said Stephen.

"Not this time, Kwan. It's going to be bad for some in the upper ranks too," said Papa.

"The problem is everybody was looking the other way before, and suddenly you have the Commission ransacking the whole place." Stephen puffed at his cigarette, then continued in a faltering manner, "Ah Sing, I may be in trouble. You see, on several occasions, I was given something, tea money, nothing big, that I had not bothered to return."

"I don't think they'll get to you, Kwan. They are mostly concentrating on those with big takes," said Papa. "Just play clean from now on."

"I'm still worried."

"I don't believe in looking back. It'll kill you to worry over it," said Papa.

"I can't help it, Ah Sing. I'm haunted by this witch hunt day and night."

The tension in the Force continued into the next year. Papa

stayed out late at police meetings, discussing solutions to the ICAC probes which, while necessary in the movement to stamp out corruption, were instilling paranoia and affecting morale in the Force.

"If they petition, I'll petition with them. If they march, I'll march with them. I'm one of the boys, and I'll stick with them. I believe in a chance to start over," he said to Mummy.

March they did to the Central Police Station, where a police delegation presented a petition to the Commissioner of Police to address the ICAC probes. Papa was one of the delegates chosen to represent the rank and file. A week later, the Governor announced an amnesty for policemen guilty of corruption prior to 1977, with the exception of cases involving big takes and serious embezzlement. The Junior Police Officers' Association was formed soon after, a legitimate voice for the junior ranks of constables and sergeants. Papa was elected a committee member of the newborn Association.

"Papa, do you suppose corruption is stamped out in Hong Kong?" I asked at the end of the police crisis.

"I'm very hopeful that things are going in the right direction." Then he added, "I've lived here for twenty-six years, and lately I feel a sense of belonging to Hong Kong that was never there before. I feel I've become a part of Hong Kong. I can now honestly call it my second home."

"And China is your first."

"China will always be my first."

I noticed the furrows on his forehead broadened with his receding hairline. I saw the grey on his trimmed short sideburns, the slight puffiness above the set jaw that defined his still handsome face, and shadows beneath those once bright and forever penetrating eyes. What had remained unchanged was that mole above his lips that I would touch as a child to hear a story. At forty-eight, Papa was showing his years.

"Are you thinking of *Yeh Yeh*, Papa?" I asked.

He nodded quietly, then brightened up. "Let me tell you

something."

"Yes?"

"Things are opening up in China, and the Hong Kong government is easing up on restrictions for civil servants to visit the mainland. I'm going to apply for permission to visit my father during the Chinese New Year holiday. You, Mummy and I will go visit *Yeh Yeh!*"

I had never seen Papa so upbeat, so high spirited, in the weeks before our visit to the mainland. Mummy had been well, and was shopping for dried mushrooms and scallops, preserved duck and sausages, as gifts we would take to *Yeh Yeh*. She bought a new padded Chinese jacket of blue satin for her father-in-law. Ever since she took me to China in 1965, she had been genuinely fond of the old man.

As soon as his application to visit China was approved by the Hong Kong government in mid-December, 1977, Papa wrote *Yeh Yeh* about our intended visit.

"How do you think *Yeh Yeh* will react, when he reads your letter, Papa?"

"He'll be speechless with joy."

"This is the moment *Lo Yeh* has been waiting for ever since you left, Tak Sing," Mummy said, looking as excited as Papa.

"And the moment I've waited for for twenty-six long years," Papa said.

An unusually cold, damp day in January, 1978, only a week to our departure for the mainland. School would go into recess for ten days, to welcome the Year of the Horse.

I finished classes early that day. I sauntered into the flat as soon as Ah Lan opened the door, and was surprised to see Papa home in the afternoon.

"What's up, Papa?"

He turned from the window to face me. In that moment, I knew something was very wrong. I ran over to him and instinctively put my arms around him. He rested his head on my shoulder and broke into uncontrolled weeping.

"Serena, I'm too late. Too late for your *Yeh Yeh*," he said between sobs. "I just got a letter from one of his friends. Father died ten days ago. They buried him with your grandmother, and I couldn't even be there for the funeral."

"Oh no! Papa, no!" I started to cry.

"If only he could've seen us before he went…. Why is Heaven so cruel? Why? Why?"

Papa turned from me, and with raised fists shouted out a resounding, heart-rending "Father!" that cut through the walls of our flat down to the street below, as though it wanted to find its way across the harbour, beyond the reverberating Kowloon Hills, and over the New Territories into Guangdong, until it reached the earthy mound behind Ka Hing, where my grandfather was laid to rest at last beside my grandmother.

I knelt between Papa and Mummy at the graves of my paternal grandparents near the village of Ka Hing, two days before the lunar New Year. We should have been rejoicing as a family with *Yeh Yeh*. Instead, we were there to pay our last respects to his memory. Papa had come home after twenty-six years, only too late to see his father, whose tombstone would bear the words Papa had ordered:

> *Father, your love is deep as the ocean,*
> *My impiety brings me life-long shame.*
> *Unable to honour you in this life,*
> *I can only repay you in the next.*

Later, when I asked Mummy why Papa used the word "impiety," she explained that a son would consider himself impious if he could not attend his parent's funeral.

"Papa shouldn't feel guilty. How could he have gone to *Yeh Yeh*'s funeral when he didn't even know *Yeh Yeh* had died?"

"I know. Your father should have no regrets," Mummy said

softly. Then, staring into space, she continued as if to herself, "but I – I learned about my mother's death from a cousin – I phoned – I wanted to attend – but my father said no...." Mummy's voice trailed off, as tears trickled down her cheeks.

"How long ago was that?" I was more surprised than disturbed by the news of my *Poh Poh's* death. Why hadn't Mummy told me? Not that I really knew my maternal grandmother. Above all, I was unable to come to terms with my grandfather's heartless refusal to let Mummy attend the funeral.

"Three years ago. I – couldn't talk about it then, not even to your Papa or Ah Lan. I couldn't."

Three years ago, 1975, the year Mummy overdosed.

40

The Ball

RICHARD HAS BEEN PHONING several times a week from England since he left Hong Kong in mid-May. He has started work with the *Somerset Reporter*. I love him and miss him so much.

The first time I fell in love, or thought I did, was when I was eighteen, in my first year at the university.

"Mummy, I'm in love," I said one day on coming home from classes. My eyes focused on my mother's knitting, as I watched the mechanical repetitive movements of her long graceful fingers.

"Anyone I know?" Mummy looked up at me, her eyes brightening with interest.

"No, you don't know him. He's someone I met in the student union office." I felt a little embarrassed after my initial outburst.

"Well, tell me about him," Mummy prompted eagerly. She secured her needles in the sweater she was knitting, and put the knitting back into the basket at her feet.

I told her how I melted when Jeffrey – that was his name – chanced to look at me one day in the student union office. Placing her arm across my shoulders, Mummy said, "It happened to me too. That was exactly how I felt when your Papa looked at me the first time in the classroom." She smiled to herself, brushing her cheek against my hair.

"Did you feel you had been electrocuted?" I asked.

"Yes, charged with electric shocks over and over again."

"What are the chances Jeffrey is feeling the same about me?"

"Time will tell. He'll make a move sooner or later if he feels the same way about you."

For weeks, Jeffrey Sun made no move. And when I finally ran into him at a union tea, he acted like a perfect gentleman, friendly but reserved.

"What shall I do, Mummy? What can I do?" I asked that evening.

A small smile formed on Mummy's lips, and she said quietly, "Ask him out, Serena."

"What?" I was shocked at my mother's forwardness.

"Invite him to a student function."

I thought for a moment, then a smile formed on my lips.

"How about the Marian Hall Annual Ball?" My hope for life-long happiness was revitalised.

Two weeks before the event, I braced myself and asked Jeffrey to the ball when I saw him sitting by himself in the cafeteria. But no matter how casual I tried to sound, with the implied message "I just need someone to take me to the official function and you happen to be the first person I come across," he must have sensed I liked him. And he graciously said yes. He would pick me up the evening of the ball from my home.

"The things we do for love," I sighed as buddy Beth and I walked to class.

"You've got to give it a push, when your happiness is at stake," Beth advised.

Jeffrey phoned the night before the ball. Papa answered the phone. My heart palpitated wildly as soon as I recognized his voice, so much so that I feared Papa could hear it. But what Jeff had to say crushed me with bitter disappointment. He would not be able to go to the ball, for his father had just suffered a stroke.

"Beth will be so disappointed. We were going to sit together," I fretted after hanging up, as though Beth was the reason for my tears. "Plus I'll have to forfeit the ball tickets."

"Not if you take Ming." It was Papa's voice.

Ridiculous as it initially sounded to me, Papa's suggestion saved the day. Ming had stayed with us for the time he attended

Ling Tao Secondary School, but moved into a rooming house on Stanley Street, not far from us, when he started at Hong Kong Tech, where he was learning the printing trade. With the sale of his gold bar, and a night job at a printing shop, he figured he could live on his own and put himself through college. We had become his family in Hong Kong. He would answer to the call of anyone in our household. About going to the ball, however, he did require a little persuasion.

"The dinner should be good, roast beef and chicken. Don't worry about the dancing. I'll teach you," I coaxed when Ming protested lamely.

On the night of the ball, held at the Hong Kong Hilton, Ming donned Papa's navy blue gabardine suit and black oxfords, and, with his fresh haircut minus the bangs, he looked quite smart, for the suit was a good fit although the shoes were half a size too snug. I wore an ankle-length maroon lace dress with an empire waistline with which I had intended to impress Jeffrey but instead probably won Ming's admiration, for I caught him staring at my dress, or me, many times during the evening. We shared a table with Beth and her date, Francis, who provided the entertainment, for he was talkative and danced like a wild man, with amusing affected stances.

"Poor Beth," I whispered to Ming, as I guided him around the dance floor to the band's rendition of *You Don't Bring Me Flowers*.

"You should say 'Poor Serena,' for here you are in your nice dress pushing an elephant around," said Ming.

"You're doing fine, Ming."

As the evening progressed, Ming was less of an elephant and became more agile with every step. He seemed to be enjoying himself, especially when the band played the popular *YMCA*, and he shook and waved in unison with everyone on the floor.

"This has been a lot of fun," said Ming as we were taxiing back to my flat. "I even forgot how much your father's shoes were killing me."

"I'm glad you let me talk you into going," I said, but secretly wished it were Jeffrey in the taxi with me.

41

Mummy

PAPA WAS PROMOTED TO inspector's rank in the fall of 1980, twenty-seven years after he started out as a constable. He remained with the uniform branch after his promotion, much to my delight, for I had always loved seeing my father in uniform. That winter, we moved into a thousand square foot unit in the inspectors' quarters on Breezy Path. Ah Lan thought it was a dream home, even though she had lived in a much bigger place, my maternal grandparents' house where Mummy grew up. For the first time, I could have my own room, instead of the small space partitioned off my parents' bedroom in the old flat. The excitement of moving into the new home raised Mummy's spirits. I had not seen her so joyful in a long time, and yet I was fearful the excitement of the move might be too much for her. What Mummy needed by then was ordinariness, nothing to stir up emotions regardless of its origin or nature. In short, she should neither be too happy nor too sad.

I came home to our new flat late one night after a concert at the University. I quietly tiptoed through the darkened hallway in order not to wake Papa and Mummy. As I passed their room, the door was ajar, and in the dark I could hear Papa's soft, deep voice.

"I want so much to make you happy, Lily. I want us to grow old together."

"We have no control of things in our lives, Tak Sing, although at times we think we do," Mummy answered.

There followed silence, except for the rustling of sheets. Feeling like an intruder on my parents' privacy, I tiptoed to my room.

That night, I stayed awake for a long time. *Mummy, why are you letting this senseless demon haunt you and rob you of your joy, cut away bits and pieces of you by and by, yes, take you little by little from us who love you? We do have control of our lives. Why won't you give it a damn good fight? Take hold of yourself, take your medicine, do whatever it costs to be well again, for your sake, for Papa's, and mine.*

And all I could hear were Mummy's desperate silent scream while I stood helplessly by.

I graduated from university with honours in June 1981 and secured a teaching job at Holy Cross Secondary School for that September. I would be teaching English to Form Five and Form Six students, a challenge I was ready to embrace with the enthusiasm and nervousness of a first-time teacher.

"You'll make a good teacher, Serena," Mummy said when I told her about the job.

"I guess it's in my blood," I said, feeling a special closeness to her.

Mummy had resigned from her own teaching post earlier in the year, following a serious relapse during which she had another overdose of sleeping pills. When she came home from the hospital three weeks later, there was a dullness in her eyes and a joylessness in her face that broke my heart. I cried myself to sleep many nights.

Papa spent every minute of his off-duty time with her, sensitive to her every whim, caring, devoted, hurting. But no matter how much he and I tried to understand Mummy, and assured her of our love and support, we could not reach the deep dark fathom of her mind. She had mostly become a silent being, and nothing we said or did seemed to interest her very much. She was slipping away, and we were unable to hold her back. I grieved to see her unhappy and breaking Papa's heart with her own pain.

One rainy night soon after I started teaching, Mummy came over to my room and woke me. I sat up immediately, ready to listen and talk, as long as she would open up. She seemed more in touch with me than she had been for months.

"I just dreamed my father had forgiven me and wanted me back, Serena, but then I woke and realized it was only a dream. Dreams are so cruel." Mummy started to cry. I put my arm around her and kissed her wet cheek.

"You'll always have Papa and me, Mummy."

"I know, I know." After a while, she said, "Serena, promise me you'll look after Papa if anything should happen to me. Promise me, will you?" Her voice was urgent and pleading.

"Of course I promise you. But don't talk nonsense. You're scaring me. I love you, Mummy," I cried. "I won't let anything happen to you."

She held me close to her bosom, as she had so often when I was a child. She kissed my forehead and rocked me gently as we both sat on the bed. That night, Mummy fell asleep in my bed. I lay down beside her, but stayed awake for a long time, listening to her peaceful breathing. I did not want the dawn to come, for it would take my mother away.

When tragedy strikes, we torture ourselves thinking *if only we had* and *if only we hadn't*, as if by turning back the clock, and being given a second chance to do things differently in the hours leading up to the tragic event, we could avert it and bring about a reversal of misfortune. Little do we see the tragedy as only the catastrophic end of a journey embarked upon long ago.

November 2nd, 1983. I had spent the last class of the day discussing Ophelia in *Hamlet* with my sixth form students. I took the usual ferry and bus home. Papa was on late shift. Ah Lan had gone to Yuen Long to attend a wake, and would not be home that night.

"Mummy!" I called, letting myself into our flat.

There was no answer, no sign of Mummy in the living room, den, kitchen, balcony, bedrooms. Of late, she had been afraid of crowds, of venturing out of the flat, or even answering the telephone. She could not have gone out by herself. With an uneasy feeling, I walked toward the closed bathroom door. Softly, I called out, "Mummy?" All was quiet from within. I turned the doorknob. I opened the door with the greatest apprehension, afraid of what might confront me. The room felt warm, steamy, clammy to my skin. A sour stale smell filled the atmosphere, at first unidentified, until my eyes focused on the tub, a tub of blood, blood mixed with water, dark near its source from where it was still pulsing, oozing, my mother's veins, her opened wrists, raw and gaping. The cursed instrument lay on the floor beside the tub, gleaming but for the red that stained its cutting edge. Mummy's motionless form clad in her silky nightgown was propped up inside the tub, her head tilted back, her eyes closed as if in sleep, her colours drained from her cheeks and partially opened lips, her lifeblood drained from her very being. I stifled the urge to scream, for fear of disturbing my mother. I put my hand to my mouth as nausea overcame me....

It was not until three days later that I was able to open Mummy's letter to me. Every word I read gnawed at my heart, until it was numbed by pain, and I could feel no more. I could not even cry.

My darling Serena,

A thousand poisonous snakes rattle in my head, and I cannot sleep. I am very tired, and I need to rest. Forgive me, my daughter, for what I am about to do. It is for the best, for you and your Papa, and for myself. Remember that I love you, and I always will, for I believe it is possible to love where I am going. How I wish to see you marry, and to hold my grandchildren in my arms, but I am afraid this is not to be. Look after your Papa for me when I am asleep.

Keep him from feeling lonely. Remind him that my spirit will be with him every day of his life.

I love you always,
Mummy

For a long time after Mummy's death, I felt angry with her for leaving me and Papa, and for tormenting me with the guilt that haunts those a suicide victim leaves behind. That anger helped allay some of my otherwise unbearable grief.

Papa never showed me Mummy's letter to him. I only knew he took comfort in it, for I had caught him on several occasions reading it silently when he thought no one was near, and then holding it close. His reaction to Mummy's death was one of stoic fortitude. No one would ever know the depth and intensity of sorrow in his heart.

"What is keeping me in the world of the living is the trust that your mother is still with me, loving me with a love that transcends death," he said to me on the day of the funeral. "Serena, I can feel your mother's presence, only she's on a different plane of existence now. When my father and mother died, I was overcome with grief. I experienced a helpless utter sense of irreparable loss, and I regretted deeply that I had not done enough for them while they were alive. But it's different with your mother. She couldn't have left me. No, she hasn't left me."

That night, Papa gave me the book he had written for me.

"Mummy read a great part of it the three years I spent writing it after your birth, but not the last two chapters," Papa said as he handed the book to me. "I kept them from her because I didn't want her to be reminded of her breakup with her parents."

"She must have thought you never finished it," I said, holding the book and opening it to the first page.

"In a sense, I never finished it. You have to give it an ending, Serena."

I noticed the age lines on Papa's face, the tired, forlorn eyes, the slight twitching of his lip. I held Papa close and whispered in his ear, "It'll be a good ending, Papa."

42

Retirement

PAPA, AH LAN AND I moved to this flat on Castle Steps after Mummy died. Papa retired in the spring of the following year, 1984, at the age of fifty-five, the retirement age in the Police Force.

"I have served the Force and Hong Kong for thirty-one years," he said to his colleagues at a banquet given in his honour. "I have treated the Force as though it were my second family. But it's time for me to pass my responsibilities on to a new generation. It's time for me to bring my career as a policeman to a close, give myself the chance to do the things I've wanted to do, and spend more time with my daughter."

The boys at Central presented Papa with a retirement gift – a two-foot-tall carved wood statuette of *Kwan Dai*, the belligerent but righteous red-faced god of war and patron deity of the police. Papa treasured the gift, placing it on the sideboard by the dining table. Ah Lan regarded *Kwan Dai* as a household god protecting us from harm. Every morning, she would light some incense in the little urn she placed in front of the statuette.

Most days, at the break of dawn, Papa would be up and taking his daily morning walk. On weekends, I walked with him along Bowen Road on the mid-level, where the air was fresh as the dew drops that had collected through the night on the hillside vegetation along his path. He would descend along a deep slope to Wanchai, to the Ying Wah Restaurant for breakfast, consisting of a pot of *po li*, a couple of buns filled with *charsiu*, and *har gao* in a bamboo steamer. He would sit for a long while, sipping his tea, taking a bite now and then of his *dim sum*, reading the *Sing Tao Daily*, and chatting with friends who passed by his table. In the afternoon, he would go for *tai chi* exercise in Victoria Park, then a few games of *wei chi* at the club in Causeway Bay. He usually came home for supper, unless I had a dinner engagement, which was seldom, for I wanted to spend time with him every evening. In spite of his undaunted trust that Mummy was still with him, I knew he must miss her terribly, more than he would admit.

It seemed peace had come to Papa in those early years of his retirement, and his days had become one long routine of orderliness and predictability, without the passion he embraced in his earlier life. It was not like him.

"Some of my friends are planning to move to Canada in the next few years. What about us, Papa?" I asked not long after his retirement. Ever since the question of Hong Kong's sovereignty became imminent with Margaret Thatcher's visit to Beijing in 1982, many Hong Kong people were worried that, with China's takeover of Hong Kong in 1997 upon the expiration of Britain's lease of the New Territories, personal liberties and the capitalistic lifestyle enjoyed in Hong Kong would be severely threatened.

"Serena, you will never understand what it means to leave your home, and the people and things you love, whether voluntarily or driven to do so, unless you have experienced it." Papa looked intently at me. I knew then not to bring up the subject of emigrating to a foreign country again.

One evening in the autumn of 1984, I came home to find a visitor with Papa.

"Serena, come meet someone I knew from long ago, Dr. Wong Wing Kay," Papa said as soon as I walked in.

The man was about forty, of medium build, casually well-dressed in a golf shirt and khakis.

"You are very fortunate, Serena, for you have the best father anyone can have," Dr. Wong said, as he shook my hand.

"Look at him now, an eye doctor educated in Canada. I'm afraid I'll have to consult you soon, for my age is creeping into my eyes these days," said Papa, stepping back and beaming at the man as though he was a long-lost son who had made good and come home.

"You studied in Canada?" I asked with interest.

"I went to the University of Western Ontario on scholarship, and practiced in Toronto for ten years after I graduated. I came back two years ago. I kept saying to myself I had to contact you, Sing Gor," he said, turning to Papa, "but with my practice and the family, I just let the days go by. Finally, this morning, I looked you up in the phone directory and there you are!"

"I'm very happy to see you doing so well, Ah Kay. I can't call you Kay Chai anymore, for you're a grown man and a doctor! How's your mother?"

"She's okay, suffering from severe arthritis though. She lives with us. She's one of the reasons we decided to move back to Hong Kong, for after several years in Canada, she was still homesick and hated the winters there."

"I gather you're married?" Papa asked.

"Yes. I met my wife while we were both at university. She's a nurse, but not working as such anymore, because we have two kids, a boy and a girl."

"It's unusual that you chose to come back when so many Hong Kong residents are leaving for Canada," I said.

"I'm doing the reverse, partly because of my mother, and partly because I feel it's time I give something back to Hong Kong. No matter how comfortable life was in Canada, I still felt like a displaced person. I could never forget I was in a foreign land. The minute I stepped foot on Hong Kong, I knew I was home."

When Dr. Wong got up to leave, Papa patted him on the back and said, "Your mother must be very happy now."

Nodding, Dr. Wong said, "Sing Gor, I still have the shoeshine kit to remind me of hard times, and of you."

43

Ming

W E ARE ABOUT TO ENTER the last week of British sovereignty in Hong Kong. Today, being Sunday, Ah Lan has made roast duck *congee* for lunch. She brings out two big bowls of the steaming gruel, complete with a plateful of crispy fried dough.

"*Hui gui* or not, we need to chomp," she says, as we sit down at the table. Ah Lan slurps noisily. "Ming liked this very much. Remember we always called him over every time we had roast duck *congee*?" Ah Lan dips a long fried dough into her bowl.

Ming had held a job at a print shop ever since he graduated from Hong Kong Tech in 1981. On some weekends, he would come visit, bringing a box of Mummy's favourite egg tarts when she was alive, or a couple of fresh ripe papayas which Papa liked, or Filipino mangoes Ah Lan enjoyed most, or, whenever they were in season, soft sweet persimmons, my kind of fruit. He always stayed for dinner, much to Ah Lan's delight, for she was very fond of Ming.

Since Mummy's death, Ming had been coming more often to keep Papa company. After dinner, the two usually sat in front of the television and watched some old *kungfu* movie, in which supernatural power and favours from the gods were as crucial to the fate of the protagonists as physical prowess and skills in the martial arts. I usually sat at the dinner table, marking my students' essays or preparing lessons for the week, content that Papa was enjoying the movie and Ming's company.

On one such occasion, after the evening movie was over, Ming took out two tickets from his pocket as we saw him to the door. "My boss has given me two front row seats for the Cantonese opera at the Lee Theatre for next Saturday night. It's the *Dream of the Red Chamber*. Would you like to go with me, Ah Lan?" Ming asked in his usual pleasant fashion.

"I wish I could," said Ah Lan, "but my friend's grandniece is getting married that day, and I can't miss the wedding banquet. Too bad, for I'd love to see it. What about Seenla? I used to take you to the opera and let you share my seat when you were little, remember?"

"I went mainly for the snacks at intermission. I can still remember the spiced gizzards," I confessed.

"Why don't you go with me, Serena. You may enjoy it, you never know," Ming said, looking suddenly shy.

I had never really enjoyed the Cantonese opera, the music a concoction of loud sounds coming from the clappers, the gong, the cymbals, the *erhu*, the *peipa*, and the high-pitched singing of Cantonese opera stars jarring to my ears. But seeing Ming's somewhat earnest expression, I softened and, without further persuasion, agreed to go.

I had known the story of *The Dream of the Red Chamber*, a classic novel written during the Qing Dynasty in the reign of Emperor Qianlong, a story of love and jealousy, murder and betrayal in a rich family with powerful connections. Consequently, I was able to follow the sequences of the opera, even though I wished the performers would take less time to sing and more time to speak their lines. The theatrical costumes and headpieces, especially of the actresses, were dazzling to the eye, glittering with sequins, beads and rhinestones. I enjoyed the breathtaking realism of the props, the revolving stage that changed the scene as it turned.

"Want something to eat?" Ming smiled at me as the curtain came down during the intermission.

I shook my head and laughed.

"Actually, I came for the show, Ming, not for the snacks," I said, wanting to be appreciative.

"I was hoping you came because of me," Ming murmured softly, awkwardly, unexpectedly, putting me in a sudden uncomfortable position. I looked up and he met my eyes with a tenderness that I had not noticed before. I averted my eyes. Heat crept into my cheeks.

Perhaps he meant nothing, and then perhaps he felt something for me that I had not known before. Thoughts raced through my head in that short instant, for I had to come up with a response satisfactory to myself and to Ming. I would never want to hurt him, and yet I could not give him any encouragement or reason to hope that what I felt for him was anything more than friendship and sisterly affection.

"You know I've always enjoyed your company, Ming. But I wish you had taken a girlfriend to this instead of your old sis," I said.

"You're not my sister," Ming said shortly.

"Well, you've always been a brother to me," I insisted, trying to laugh, but feeling rotten.

He bit his lip and looked away sulkily, while I studied the program booklet as though I was researching for a dissertation. We were quiet until the curtain rose again. I could not enjoy the second half of the opera. As we got up to leave the theatre, Ming remained sullen. I tried to break the silence.

"I got so mad that Jia Baoyu was tricked by his parents into marrying Xue Baochai when he really loved Lin Daiyu," I said about the love triangle in *The Dream of the Red Chamber*.

"Well, life can be cruel, you know. One can't always have what one hopes for," Ming answered sourly.

I grabbed Ming's arm as we descended the stairs to the theatre lobby, the way I would sometimes do when I took him shopping in his early days in Hong Kong. He let his arm hang limp beside him. When we reached the outside of the theatre, I let go of his arm and we walked silently to the tram stop, watching the traffic and the crowd as though for dear life. Once on the tram, we were separated by the throng of standing passengers. When I finally secured a seat, Ming did not try to weave through the crowd to stand over me. By the time we said goodnight in front of my building complex, I felt totally miserable.

I stayed awake that night, thinking of what Ming was going through. I was upset that something might have happened that was going to spoil our relationship. Wouldn't it be ideal if we could replace our friendship with romance? It would please a few people, people who meant the most to me and Ming — Papa, Ah Lan, and Ah Chu. Things would fall into place like the pieces of a jigsaw puzzle, forming a perfect picture that made sense. Sense. But something was in the way. I did not love Ming in the manner he would like me to, the way I guessed Papa, Ah Lan, and Ah Chu secretly hoped I would. I was not in love.

The next day, I wrote a letter to Ming, for sometimes the written word was easier to express than the spoken.

August 11, 1985

Dear Ming,

Thank you for last evening – the opera and your company which I've always enjoyed. Forgive me if I have hurt your feelings with something I said, for I would never want to hurt you in any way. Please don't let whatever might have happened last night interfere with what has always been beautiful and sincere between us, a reflection of that deep affection our fathers had for each other. I will always have your interest at heart, and hope you will find true happiness in someone who will be deserving of you.

Serena

Ming never replied to my letter, but the next time he came visiting with papayas and persimmons, he looked his usual

217

self, cheerful and obliging, Ah Lan's pet. It was as if nothing had happened between us the night of the opera. Perhaps nothing had.

For his fifty-seventh birthday the following January, Papa wanted dinner at Fun Lok Chai, his favourite restaurant, famous for its good food. It was a hot and noisy joint, where attendants wiped tables with suspicious-looking rags, carelessly pushing bits of bone and food left on the table from the meal before onto the floor, and invariably passed customers a roll of toilet tissue when they requested paper napkins.

"Reserve a table for five, Serena," Papa told me the night before his birthday.

"Why five, Papa?" I asked.

"Ming is going to bring his girlfriend to meet us!" Papa answered.

"I'm so glad Ming has a girlfriend," I said, genuinely happy and very curious.

"I've got to take a good look at this girl," Ah Lan was saying, as she appeared from the kitchen. "She's got *fook*, catching our eligible Ming."

"Everyone must order favourite dishes tonight," announced Papa the night of the party, as he and I and Ah Lan waited for Ming and his girlfriend at the restaurant. "Your sweet and sour pork, Serena, Ah Lan's steamed sea bass with ginger and onion, Ming's crispy roast duck."

"What about yourself, Papa?"

"Bitter melon and beef. I haven't forgotten that. We'll also get Mummy's favourite dish, mussels with black bean and garlic."

Papa's last statement, instead of casting gloom over us, was comforting to me. Looking at Papa that night, I knew it was no delusion in his mind that Mummy was still with him. Perhaps he really felt her presence and her love, and as far as he was concerned, she had never left him.

My thoughts were interrupted by the arrival of Ming with his girlfriend, a cheerful girl in her mid-twenties, simply but neatly dressed in a white cotton blouse and floral skirt. Her chubbiness was accentuated by her short stature, her ear-length hair resembling a black mushroom cap framing a round face with small eyes beneath thin fading eyebrows, and her puffy cheeks looking like two big buns when she smiled. Ming introduced her as Chan Kit Bing, also known as Kitty Chan.

In the course of the dinner, I found out that Kitty worked as a teller at the Hong Kong Bank. Throughout the evening, Ming was attentive to Kitty, piling food onto her plate, while she acknowledged his every gesture with a doting side-glance at him. Ah Lan could not help but stare at the poor girl, scrutinizing her every move, as though she was assuming the role of a future mother-in-law meeting her son's girlfriend for the first time. Papa leaned back, looking contented with the company, the food, and the atmosphere. The noise in the eatery had reached market level, market quality.

At the end of the meal, a waiter brought out a platter of small peach-shaped steamed buns filled with sweet lotus seed paste, symbolizing longevity. Finishing his longevity peach in one mouthful, and looking a little shy, Ming cleared his throat and addressed Papa.

"Tak Sing Suk, Kitty and I have decided to get married. The date will be determined by Kitty's parents after they have consulted the *Tung Sing Almanac*. Tak Sing Suk, I hope you will take my father's place as my witness at the marriage ceremony in the City Hall."

Everyone congratulated Ming and Kitty.

"Double celebrations tonight! Good luck to you both," Ah Lan said. Turning to Kitty and grabbing her hand, she added, "Ming *Siu* is a decent man, a good man. You are very lucky."

"*I* am very lucky," corrected Ming, smiling at his intended.

That night, after Papa had gone to bed, I found Ah Lan in the kitchen listening to Cantonese opera music.

"At least, things are happy for Ming *Siu* now," said the *amah* who would be seventy-one on the last day of the lunar year. "Finally, he has the sense to settle down."

I remained silent, not wanting to encourage Ah Lan to say more about the subject, for Ming had become a sensitive issue for me. Ah Lan seemed disappointed that I was not curious about her last comment.

"Let me tell you a secret now that he's getting married," she volunteered in a confiding manner, regardless of my apparent lack of interest. "He once told me when I asked him if he had a girlfriend that he was waiting for you, Seenla. He swore me to secrecy at the time. He had been secretly in love with you for a long time. Unfortunately for him, it was one-way traffic."

"I'm happy Ming has finally found someone who will be good for him," I said.

"True, although this girl is not pretty like you, she will make a good wife for Ming *Siu* - the way she seems to dote on him."

"Ming has made a very good choice," I said, as I left the light and noise of the kitchen for the darkness and solitude of my bedroom. A strange emptiness seized me.

"Seenla," Ah Lan called after me.

"Uh?"

"I still wish it were you he's marrying. It would make your Papa and this bag of old bones here very happy."

44

Guangdong

I HAVE ALWAYS CONSIDERED my trip to the mainland with Papa in 1988 as one of the high points of my life.

"I want to visit your grandparents' graves, and continue on to Beijing, Serena. I've never been to Beijing, and now is a good time to go," Papa said in the fourth year of his retirement. After a pause, he added, "I want to see Ah Chu."

We left Hong Kong soon after school was out in mid-July. We stopped overnight in Guangzhou. That night, I sat with Papa in the restaurant of the Guangzhou Hotel, looking out to a beautiful Chinese garden complete with a fountain and goldfish pond, an Oriental pavilion and life-sized statues of ancient lords and ladies.

"Guangzhou must have looked very different when you were here as a student, Papa," I said, sipping *oolong* tea and munching on a piece of crisp crunchy skin from a roast suckling pig. "It must have been a terrible feeling too, wanting to go home, yet prevented from doing so by a sense of duty." I was thinking of what Papa wrote in his book of his days in Guangzhou as a student.

"Sometimes, Serena, the call of duty is self-imposed. We chase after happiness, yet often we stand in our own way, because we do what we think we should, not what we would want to," said Papa.

We hired a taxi that took us to Ka Hing the next day. Rural Guangdong had not changed much in over twenty years, the same paddy fields, farmers working ankle-deep in water, white-washed farmhouses and distant hills all rushing past as our taxi sped on. My life seemed to be rushing past too. I felt like traveling back in time, seeing myself as an eager five-year-old going with Mummy to visit *Yeh Yeh*. The image of the dear balding old man, with eyes smiling at me, holding my hand as I pranced beside him, carrying me when I got tired, was still vivid in my mind. Then I saw Papa kneeling in front of *Yeh Yeh*'s freshly dug grave, crying inconsolably until there were no more tears to shed, refusing to get up long after the sun had gone down for the day. Strange how scenes from the past could blend into each other, as though the elapse of time played no part in the human drama of events in retrospect. As the taxi sped along the narrow country road, I looked out of the car window to hide my face from Papa, for I did not want him to see my tears. I was missing Mummy.

We arrived at Ka Hing in the early afternoon. The villager whom Papa had commissioned to keep my grandparents' graves clear of weeds and leaves had done a good job through the years. The tombstones looked tidy and neat except for the fading paint on the engraved characters. Papa and I went into the village, bought a tin of black paint and two Chinese brushes, and returned to the burial plot. Painstakingly, Papa repainted the words on his mother's tombstone, and I did the same on my grandfather's. When the job was done, the words looked as new and glossy as freshly engraved ones.

> *Greatness needs not come from heroic deeds*
> *That rouse the heavens and rock the earth;*
> *It can manifest itself in the silent love*
> *Of a virtuous wife and a good mother.*

****

> *Father, your love is deep as the ocean,*
> *My impiety brings me life-long shame.*
> *Unable to honour you in this life,*
> *I can only repay you in the next.*

Papa and I sat in front of the graves for a long while, until darkness shrouded the surrounding hills and fields, and all we could hear were the buzz of cicadas on the trees and the occasional barking of dogs in the village, and all we could see were the flickers of fireflies around the dark forms of the tombstones under the starless night.

"I just want to sit here a little longer, Serena, for I don't know when I'll come this way again," Papa said in a heavy voice.

"'Tis fine, Papa. 'Tis fine. I will sit here with you for as long as you wish."

45

Ah Chu

TIANANMEN SQUARE WAS THE MOST expansive open space I had ever envisioned, paved with thousands of grey stone slabs upon which recent history had unfolded. Regardless of sun or rain, there was an air of gloom in the cold austerity of the gigantic whitewashed buildings on its fringes, spartan, secretive, intimidating. At the south end of the Square, outside Chairman Mao's mausoleum, tourists and locals queued up to enter the sombre structure for a glimpse of the physical remains of the once Great Helmsman modern science had preserved and enshrined in a crystal coffin. At the northern end of the Square, Mao's portrait, much larger than life, hung from the exterior wall of Tiananmen Gate, an overseeing presence that could not be denied, as history was played out under its scrutinizing gaze. And everywhere between its extremities, crowds thronged the vast square, adults holding on to their children, and tour guides waving colour flags as they ushered forth their groups.

Our taxi driver let us off somewhere along the Avenue of Eternal Peace, and we walked towards the Square and Tiananmen Gate, beyond which was the Wumen Gate, marking the south end of the Imperial Palace Museum, the Forbidden City. At nine in the morning, the palace grounds were already filling up with tourists. Tour guides waving flags and umbrellas were guiding their groups through the palace buildings like mother hens leading their chicks, always afraid of losing stray members who had stopped to take photos or admire for one extra minute the thousand-year-old artifacts. Up and down stone steps that bordered dragon-sculptured ramps I walked alongside Papa, in and out of yellow-roofed palace buildings. I would have loved to lose myself among the ancient bronzes and potteries, historic clocks and jewels, scrolls of calligraphy and paintings by the old masters, but Papa was anxious to move on, to the northern section of the palace, once the emperors' private living quarters. I followed Papa's brisk footsteps into the gardens of the concubines, past artificial rocks and caves, bronze animals, through moon gates into decorative pavilions and buildings that once housed the inner chambers of the ladies of the court, beneath ancient shady pines and cedars. I knew Papa's heart was not in appreciating the grandeur of the palace or the beauty of the gardens. From Hong Kong he had written to Ah Chu at the address Ming had given him, citing a meeting place, a date and time. Although Ah Chu had not responded, Papa was confident he was about to see his best friend and blood brother again after forty-two years.

Papa glanced nervously at his watch as we sat down on a stone bench near the northern wall of the palace grounds. I scanned the garden as far as I could see. There were only a handful of tourists in that remote section of the Forbidden City at that time of day. The sun had emerged from behind a magnolia tree and I was feeling the scorch of its direct heat. I was about to suggest to Papa that we stand in the shadow of the wall when I noticed an intense expression on his face. I followed his gaze and saw a man heading toward us, slowly but surely. He was a tall and thin man, wearing a grey Mao suit and hat, and slouching slightly as he walked. When he was about ten yards from where we were sitting, Papa stood up and started to take slow, uncertain steps toward him.

They got to about five yards from each other, and Papa suddenly called out in a voice vibrating with emotion, "Chu!"

"Tak Sing!" the other responded.

They embraced for a long moment, then stepped back a little, studying each other intently, as if searching for the familiar features that time and suffering could not erase, and then both broke out into tearful laughter, punching each other on the arms.

I looked on, as the two aging men acted as though they had shut out the intervening years, and it was just yesterday when Ah Chu went off to Yan'an to join the Communists.

Papa then turned to me and quickly introduced me to Ah Chu, whom I would call Chu Pak, as my father's older brother. We strolled slowly in the garden of the east courts, with me feeling somewhat like an outsider, an intruder.

"Forty years?" asked Ah Chu.

"Forty-two," corrected Papa.

"It will take us a lifetime to catch up with each other and we only have a few hours," said Ah Chu.

"We'll be in Beijing for a week," Papa quickly informed him. "We are staying at the Holiday Inn."

"I see," Ah Chu nodded.

"Chu Pak, Tak Ming and Kit Bing have asked me to give you this," I spoke for the first time since I was introduced to him, producing from my handbag a small brown box.

At the mention of Ming's name, Ah Chu turned eagerly to me, his eyes lighting up. I noticed the lines on his thin dark face. Although he was only two years older than Papa, he looked at least ten years his senior. I presented the box to him with both hands, and he took it likewise, looking at it without opening it.

We sat down on the cement base that encircled the wide trunk of an old gingko tree. With trembling hands, Ah Chu removed the lid of the box to reveal a small ebony picture frame with two separate panels, joined and folded together like a book, hinged at the centre. A little brass clasp kept shut the two panels decorated with exquisite carvings of bamboos and peonies, embellished with mother of pearl. Ah Chu unclasped the panels. The inside surface of the left panel was solid wood carved with the characters: *Wo Wing Boo Mong.* I will never forget. The other panel was the picture frame but there was no picture. Ah Chu rubbed his fingers over the engraved words, perhaps disappointed about the missing photo. Immediately I took out from between the pages of my date book what he was looking for. It was a picture of Ming and Kitty taken at the Ocean Park in Hong Kong. Ah Chu laughed at the sight of the photo, laughed till he cried. A tear fell onto the photo. Quickly I blotted it away with a tissue.

"I kept the photo from the frame because you never know when they will search your bags. I didn't want them to see Ming's photo and ask questions," I explained.

"You can never be too careful here," Ah Chu agreed.

I slid the photo into the frame, and Ah Chu put it into the inner pocket of his Mao jacket, close to his heart. Beaming, he turned to Papa.

"Tak Sing, my wife and I are grateful to you for looking after Tak Ming all these years. We are very pleased with our daughter-in-law, and happy that a grandchild is on the way."

"Tak Ming is all that a parent could hope for in a son," said Papa. "And he made a good choice in marrying Kit Bing."

"What about your daughter?" asked Ah Chu, looking in my direction.

"Young people these days have a mind of their own. Man On hasn't found a match yet. Well, if she has, she hasn't told her old pa," Papa said, smiling at me. Then, patting Ah Chu on the shoulder, he continued in a light tone, "Chu, who would have thought we would someday be talking about our children like two old men!"

"We *are* two old men," said Ah Chu. Then, putting his hand on Papa's shoulder, he continued gravely, "I'm sorry about your wife. Tak Ming wrote me. I don't want to bring it up, but I have to tell you how much I grieved for you, and for your daughter."

"She gave up everything for me, everything," said Papa, putting his arm around my shoulders. Then changing the subject, he asked Ah Chu, "How's your wife?"

"She misses Tak Ming very much. We are hoping when things ease up a bit that he can perhaps come back for a visit."

"How has it been, Chu?" Papa finally asked.

Ah Chu looked up at the hazy sky, took a deep breath.

"I had never expected it to be easy from the start, when we

were fighting to free China from the Guomindang, but our cause made it worth all the hardship." There was a cutting bitterness in his tone of voice.

"Tak Ming told us you were – wrongfully treated during the Cultural Revolution, Chu Pak," I prompted.

Ah Chu was silent, gathering his thoughts before putting them into words.

"When the Cultural Revolution broke out, I was accused of being a revisionist with bourgeois sympathies, and sent to a labour farm where I was forced to criticize and re-evaluate myself. It was a very harsh time of physical and mental persecution. When I returned from the camp, I was allowed to keep my Party membership, but I was removed from my position as chief cadre of Zhoudu."

"Tak Ming told us," nodded Papa.

"For a long time, I had realized there was no future for Tak Ming in China. When he got into trouble for protesting against the government's suppression of tributes paid to Premier Zhou Enlai, he had no alternative but to escape to Hong Kong."

"Did the government hold his escape against you, Chu Pak?"

"I was interrogated about my son, but they were unable to get any information out of me. I played ignorant of his whereabouts. I owed Tak Ming's escape to a comrade of mine who harboured him and then helped him get to Shenzhen. Within two months after Tak Ming left, I was removed from my job in the office of a high-ranking cadre without any explanation. I would have been further persecuted, if it were not for the death of Mao Zedong a month after my dismissal, followed by the overthrow of the extreme element in the government."

"How were you treated under Deng Xiaoping afterwards, Chu Pak?" I was as much interested in the conditions under the Deng regime as in Chu Pak's own experience.

"I was given a job in the student welfare office at Beijing University. I worked there until I retired last year. These days, I have been making and selling bamboo toys at the Tian Tan market."

"At least, the government has left you alone since the end of the Cultural Revolution," Papa was saying.

"But I haven't left the government alone, Tak Sing. When the Democracy Wall went up in the late seventies, I was hopeful, but then Deng Xiaoping had it closed down, and dissidents arrested. In the mid-eighties, I was a supporter of Secretary-General Hu Yaobang. I took part in discussion groups and debates encouraged by Mr. Hu, to look for ways and means to bring democracy to the country and attack high-level corruption. Students joined in these discussions. Mr. Hu's dismissal last year was a big blow to us."

We had reached the Quainlong Garden in the eastern sector of the former emperors' living quarters.

"I fear these days I'm under surveillance. Perhaps we are being observed even as I speak," Ah Chu said in a low voice, with eyes on the ground.

His words sent a shudder through me.

"What are they looking for, Chu Pak?" I asked, casting my eyes warily around the Qianlong Garden that was filling up with tour groups.

"Any spark of democracy," replied Ah Chu in the same low voice.

We walked through the east side of the Palace Museum. I took a picture of Papa and Ah Chu in front of the Nine Dragon Wall, lively porcelain dragons set against a ceramic background of vibrant turquoise. I strolled beside them as the two friends spent the rest of the day within the walls of the Forbidden City. We walked through the palace buildings, looking at priceless paintings, jades, pottery and porcelain artifacts of bygone dynasties, treasures as remote to the common herd as their problems were to the imperial throne that hoarded them, until the government of the People's Republic made them property of the people. But all the while I realized that what my father and Ah Chu valued most was the little time they had together that day. They ate the buns I brought, although no one complained of hunger.

"Remember Ah Fong's rice cakes and fried dumplings?" asked Ah Chu.

Papa nodded with enthusiasm.

"I wonder if the *zheng* player is still at Tai Shek, and if her fiancé ever returned," Papa said.

"I did enquire about him when I first got to Yan'an in '46, but no one seemed to know about him," recalled Ah Chu. "He most likely perished on the Long March, like the majority of his comrades."

The rest of the day, all Papa and Ah Chu talked about were past times, old places, and the people they had both come to know and love as children. Ah Chu remembered fondly my paternal grandfather and grandmother, and Papa recalled Ming Suk and Ming Sum with great affection.

"Remember the *mui tsai* in the big house?"

"That was a world gone by."

They talked about the villagers and farmers of Ka Hing. They recalled wartime in Tai Shek.

"Chu, here's our phone number at the Holiday Inn. We'll be in Beijing until Friday. Call us. We have to meet again, and bring your wife next time," Papa said to Ah Chu inside the Shenwumen Gate at the north end of the Forbidden City, just before the palace closing time.

"I'll call you, Tak Sing," Ah Chu promised.

Before we parted, Ah Chu took from his pocket a small red cloth pouch. In it was a jade pendant in the shape of a sitting buddha.

"Please give this to Kit Bing, a little token Tak Ming's mother saved for our daughter-in-law."

He then took two other objects from his inner pocket. To Papa, he gave an extendable bamboo back-scratcher in the shape of a lion's paw.

"I make these *mui tsai* hands to sell," he said, referring to the back-scratcher. "They are great for old folks like us."

To me, he gave a whistle that he had whittled out of a piece of bamboo.

Papa and Ah Chu embraced outside the museum gate for one lingering moment. They were both crying visibly when they let each other go. We watched Ah Chu as he walked away. He turned to wave to us, wearing a smile showing a lot of teeth. Papa waved back. We looked after Ah Chu until he descended into the pedestrian subway and disappeared from view.

We stayed in Beijing the rest of the week. Other than a day trip to the Great Wall of China, Papa remained at the hotel most of the time, anticipating Ah Chu's call. He became restless as the week wore on. On the night before we were to fly back to Hong Kong, Papa finally received a call from Ah Chu. After talking a few minutes, he slowly put down the receiver and remained sitting on the edge of his bed, his back to me, his head lowered.

"Papa?" I asked quietly.

"He's not coming," Papa said in a small voice, without turning.

I pondered for a few seconds what I should do, then slowly I got up and went out of the room, closing the door gently after me, leaving my father to bid a silent goodbye to his dear friend.

46

The Vigil

JUNE 4th, 1991. A day of sad remembrance. A day that held special meaning for me.

The city was enshrouded in a funereal atmosphere of gloom. Everywhere, on buses, trams, ferries, the Mass Transit Railway linking Hong Kong Island to Kowloon through the cross-harbour tunnel, on the streets and in the markets, people seemed subdued, as though they were mourning death in the family. Not one, but many deaths.

I walked along the pedestrian flyover above the congested evening traffic of the Causeway Bay intersection in the direction of Victoria Park. Papa had intended to go with me, but he had come down with the flu. I was going to join the thousands at the candlelight vigil to remember those killed at Tiananmen Square two years before.

At the gate I received a candle in a holder and filed into the park, passing the dark bronze statue of the stern-faced British Empress who gave the park its name. Perhaps the park would be renamed after the handover. The statue would have to go, a reminder of the dark age of shameful servitude and foreign imperialism. I followed the silent crowd and headed for the centre of the park, toward the stage. Beside the stage stood a tall white plaster statue, a replica of the Goddess of Democracy at Tiananmen Square two years earlier, with arms raised to one side and hands joined in a fist, holding a torch.

The service began at sunset. I stood a distance from the stage, holding my lit candle, one flickering star amidst thousands. I was feeling the heat from the candles, and from close human contact. The stench that often came with a thick crowd on a hot and humid day was hard to bear.

"Remember Tiananmen! Let not your children and your children's children forget!" The voices of the Pro-Democratic Union broadcast from loudspeakers rang through the park. Events of June 4th, 1989 at Beijing's Tiananmen Square were recalled, events that would make the heavens weep. Students demonstrating for freedom, students on a hunger strike, tanks rolling in, soldiers of the PLA firing at the students, students retreating, screaming, falling....

Around me, some were dabbing their eyes. One young boy no more than four or five years of age sat on his father's shoulders, holding a candle reverently with both hands, participating in a ritual that as yet held little meaning for him. Not far in front of me, something caught my attention – a head of short wavy light brown hair standing out above a sea of darker ones all around. A foreigner in solidarity with us.

The atmosphere felt very oppressive as I heaved, trying to take in deep breaths to give myself more air. My head began to spin. People seemed to be going around me, encircling me in the centre, moving faster and faster until they became indistinguishable, like silkscreen images on a revolving Chinese lantern. My candle fell and went out. I did not want to stoop down to pick it up for fear I might not get up again. With an effort I kept my feet on the ground. I had to move away from the crowd to get some air, to regain my composure.

I made my way to an empty bench not far from the nearest gate, brushing everyone in my path. I plopped down on the seat and closed my eyes to rest. The air had not cooled down with the sunset. My blouse was drenched in sweat and stuck to my skin. My legs felt sweaty underneath my flared skirt, an unpleasant sticky feeling as they rubbed against each other. I discreetly parted my legs a little and tented my skirt to let some air in between my legs.

After a while, someone joined me at the bench, putting me ill at ease because of my all too relaxed manner of sitting. I shot a quick glance at the intruder who had sat down at the other end of the bench, and recognized him to be tall brown-hair himself. As I looked over at him, he acknowledged my presence with a faint smile. I nodded, not smiling.

"Bloody stuffy up there, wasn't it?" he started.

"Yes," I answered with emphasis, trying not to sound unfriendly, yet not wishing to say more.

"Same large crowd as last year. Uplifting, isn't it, to see the turnout."

"It sure is."

A pause. Then he began again,

"You know how people used to ask 'where were you when you heard the news of Kennedy's assassination?' Tiananmen's the new way to ask the old question." He was certainly in a conversational mood.

I could have smiled in agreement and left it at that. But, in spite of myself, I asked the expected question.

"And where were you?"

"In bed. The office called and got me out of bed. It was to be my day off, " he answered readily. Then, looking at me, he explained, "I'm a reporter with the *South China Weekly.*"

"That's exciting," I said, and for the first time I looked at him with more interest than as a foreigner who stood out above the crowd. I'd place him in his early to mid-thirties, and judging from his speech, British. "And did you cover news of Tiananmen?"

He nodded. "Oh yes, the funeral of Hu Yaobang, the deposed Secretary-General, the student demonstrations, the hunger strike, Gorbachev's visit. Actually, I'm here tonight partly as a reporter."

"The countdown to '97 must keep you on your toes these days," I said, "especially after Tiananmen." I seldom spoke much to strangers, but his work sounded interesting, and he seemed harmless, even pleasant.

"I was glad to be here, before, during and after Tiananmen," he said, looking thoughtfully at the crowd a distance in front of him.

He heaved a sigh and said half to himself, "I must say Tiananmen changed my perspective."

I was feeling better. Talking to that reporter kept me from being overly conscious of my physical well-being. By then, the vigil was almost over.

"I'd better leave before the stampede," I said as I stood up, gathering my purse.

"Actually I ought to be going too," said brown-hair, getting up. "Have to stop at the office."

Together we walked through the park gate, along the pavement and up the pedestrian flyover.

"So I can expect to read about the candlelight vigil in the *South China Weekly*?" I asked, curious as to what he would say about the vigil, and how he would present it.

"Next Saturday's," he replied. We had walked across the flyover and come down onto the opposite side of the road. "What I report, Beijing may not appreciate."

"Then I'll really have to read it," I said above the noise of traffic, as we reached a tram stop.

"By the way, I'm Richard Mills," he said, extending his hand, as a tram pulled up.

"Serena Lee," I replied, taking his hand as I looked up at him, almost a head taller than I. "And I'm a school teacher."

"I have the greatest respect for teachers," he said, sounding sincere. He had a firm dry handshake, a plus in his favour, for I disliked men with clammy hands whose handshakes were mere limp finger-pressing.

"Nice talking to you, Richard, and good luck with your reporting," I said, and stepped onto the tram.

"Cheers!" he called from the street.

I took a seat on the upper deck. The tram clanged its way toward Central, while a refreshing breeze caressed my face and ruffled my hair. I closed my eyes to take in the relaxing moment. Richard Mills crept unobtrusively into my mind, the wavy brown hair, the keen dark eyes, and thin lips forming a tight smile.

47

Christmas Bells

SEPTEMBER 1991 BROUGHT THE FIRST direct elections of the Hong Kong Legislative Council, in which the democrats took fifteen of the eighteen elected seats out of a total of sixty seats in the Legislative Council. At last, Hong Kong would have a truly elected Opposition in the Legislature. We had come a long way from the days when Hong Kong was ruled by a government under the jurisdiction of the Colonial Service. The feeling after the elections was one of euphoria, short-lived though it might be, for in everyone's mind was the fear that the Chinese government, like a lurking tiger ready to pounce, maul and devour, would kill our democratic beginnings after the handover. I felt particularly good about the democrats' victory, for I had helped all summer long in their election campaign, registering voters and passing out flyers for their candidates.

With December came preparations for Christmas, always a big tradition in Hong Kong, a religious holiday for some, and secular for the rest of us. Regardless, it was a time for partying and gift giving, and celebrations second only to the Chinese New Year. Even Ah Lan, who claimed to be a devout Buddhist, although she would pray to any household god, was caught up in the festivities of the season.

"For Christmas dinner this year, I've got this first class recipe for turkey stuffing from my friend who works for a *gweilo*," she said to Papa and me.

Ah Lan always came up with the best roast turkey every Christmas, even though it was never a common item in Chinese cuisine. With more than half the turkey left over from dinner, she would use its meat and bone to boil a tasty *congee*, popular for Chinese breakfast. I marveled at Ah Lan's resourceful mixing of east and west, her adaptability to the vicissitudes of the Hong Kong way of life, all the time holding her own. A real survivor she was, like so many people in Hong Kong, riding with the tide, refusing to be taken under by the current of the times. Ah Lan was a happy person by nature. She had been deeply saddened by events in her life, the most cruel being Mummy's suicide, but she had always been able to rebound with stoic fortitude and a renewed zest for life.

The evening after school adjourned for Christmas and New Year, I was to attend a Christmas reception at the Hong Kong Hilton, given by the victorious democratic parties, an appreciation-celebration, in the spirit of the season. I was never quite comfortable at big social gatherings, and I told Papa I'd be home for a late supper with him, after showing my face at the party.

The reception was one of pomp and glitter, men in tuxedos, women in eye-catching evening wear, waiters with trays of delectable hors d'oeuvres, a string quartet playing beside a tall sparkling Christmas tree. A few newly elected members of the Legislative Council came by to shake hands, careful not to miss anyone important in the crowd. The whole atmosphere was one of controlled formality, voices murmuring, occasional laughter loud but in a manner acceptable, heads bobbing, a few speeches made, of welcome, thanks, good intentions and hope for the future of Hong Kong.

At eight, I decided to make my exit. A good thing about these parties was nobody would care when I left, and nobody would miss me after I had left. I took leave of my acquaintances from the campaign office and inched my way toward the closest exit from the ballroom.

"So where were you when you heard the news of Tiananmen?" A baritone voice sounded from behind.

I turned to look straight into the face of Richard Mills.

"The candlelight vigil at Victoria Park!" I said in recognition after a moment's hesitation, as though I had to pick my brain to recall where I had seen him before. I refrained from pronouncing his name even though I knew it, for how was I supposed to remember the name of a stranger I had briefly met several months ago? "You're...."

"Richard Mills. And you're Serena Lee, I remember," he said candidly, putting me to shame for my pretence. "Imagine seeing you here." He looked pleased.

"I was a volunteer worker for the elections campaign," I explained. "What about you?"

"I'm covering the party for my political page," said Richard. "Are you leaving already?"

"Yes, I'm heading home."

"I'll walk you out," Richard said briskly, as he put his glass on a tray a waiter was carrying. We exited the reception area into the quiet of the thickly carpeted hall leading to the lifts. We reclaimed our coats at the coat-check and walked out into the clear crisp December air.

"And how are you going home?" Richard asked.

"I'm taking the bus, number twelve to mid-level."

"Let me give you a ride," Richard said immediately. "Buses at this time are not that frequent." He placed a hand lightly on my back, pointing at the same time toward the carpark by the Hilton.

"If it's not too much out of your way," I said, feeling shy all of a sudden.

As he drove his Renault up Garden Road, he told me he had served for six years in the Foreign and Commonwealth Office in London after graduation from university before casting his eyes abroad, looking for something that would bring some meaning into his life, as he put it. He found it when he took up the job of reporting for the *South China Weekly*.

"Are you ever homesick?" I asked.

"Sometimes, but I go home every summer." He glanced sideways at me. "I suppose your family's all here?"

I told him that my mother died eight years earlier, and I lived with my father and our old *amah*. He was deeply interested when I told him that Papa fled to Hong Kong when the Communists took over China.

The drive to my home seemed unusually short. Soon we would be at Castle Steps. I turned to Richard, thanked him for his trouble and wished him a Merry Christmas.

"Actually, I'll be working on Christmas Day. I have an assignment in Singapore over the holidays," he said.

"That's too bad. Wouldn't you be missed at home?"

"Well, my parents spend every Christmas with my mother's sister in Cornwall." He hesitated, and continued with a sour smile, "And I'm afraid I'm no longer on my former girlfriend's *missing persons* list. It's just as well that I'm working over the holidays. And you?"

"I stay home, keep my father company, especially now that he's retired."

I must sound strange to Richard – foreigners probably could not understand why an unmarried daughter would feel a moral obligation to stay home to look after an aging parent. In fact, Papa was one reason I had not dated seriously, apart from the fact that I hadn't met anyone I really liked, not in my dwindling circle of friends since university, and certainly not among the few male colleagues at the convent school where I taught.

"Your father's very lucky," Richard said.

"It's the other way around. I'm the lucky one. You'd agree if you knew my father."

Richard seemed thoughtful as he pulled up at the bottom of Castle Steps. He shifted the gear to park, and turned to me.

"When I come back from Singapore, think I can see you again?"

"I suppose." I was afraid he'd hear the palpitation of my heart.

He wrote down my phone number in his little notepad.

"By the way, Serena, you never told me where you were the morning you heard the news about Tiananmen," he said, frowning mischievously as I got ready to alight.

I stiffened and wavered, while he waited with a wondering look for what I had to say. Should I tell him? In spite of my usual reserve with male acquaintances, I felt comfortable enough with Richard, and liked him enough, to think I could tell him exactly where I was.

"I was – in the toilet, reading *Woman's Weekly*. My *amah* banged on my door to tell me the news."

Richard nodded soberly, lowered his eyes and tightened his lips. I knew at that moment he was drawing a mental picture of where I was, for I detected a glint of suppressed amusement in his eyes. I never wanted to see that man again.

48

The Escalator

R ICHARD MILLS DID NOT call in the New Year, after he had presumably returned from Singapore. Perhaps he had lost my phone number, or forgotten about me. What bothered me most was he had not appeared to me as one who would make light of his intentions. Rather, he had come across as a sincere person who had made me feel at ease, aside from the instance when he asked the 'where were you...' question. He seemed to be someone to whom I might open up freely. But I could have been wrong.

One evening in August, 1993, I left the headquarters of the United Democrats around seven. By that hour, the nine-to-fivers had vacated the busiest part of Central. Typhoon Shirley had failed to disperse some of the oppressive heat that had enveloped Hong Kong since June. I was thankful for the air conditioning in the office where I had volunteered to work every summer since 1991.

I dragged my tired feet along Queen's Road to the new outdoor escalator across from the Central Market, and got on it for the ride uphill. I loved the escalator, that unique engineering masterpiece, running from the Central District in the heart of downtown to Conduit Road at mid-level, with landings for getting on and off at intervals all the way. In the morning rush hours, it headed downhill in the direction of the business district. From late morning to evening, it reversed its direction, taking city workers to their homes on the hill. What amazing human progress since the days when, according to Ah Lan, for twenty cents, coolies would carry Mummy as a young girl up the hill from the waterfront in a sedan chair, a lift engineered by the strength and sweat of the human machine.

That evening, as I rode on the escalator, I was feeling a bit dejected, somewhat out of sorts. Perhaps it was the hot weather. Perhaps I was coming down with *gum mo*. Or perhaps it was the pang of loneliness that had seized me since spring. At thirty-three, I was becoming more sensitive to the passage of my prime. Most of my school friends had married, had had babies, a few had divorced. Some, including Beth who had married a doctor, had moved to Canada. I had stayed home with Papa, not just because of the call of duty, or it being Mummy's last wish, but also because Papa had always been the most important person in my life.

Leaning against the rail, I looked out to the bustling streets on the left and right of the escalator. Those back streets evoked happy memories of the days when I, as a child of eight or nine, walked down the stepped slopes with Papa to go to a movie downtown on his off days, and occasionally to his police station, one of the places I loved visiting. Those streets had kept their character over the years – billboards almost touching one another in mid-air, flower stalls with their sweet fragrances, old antique shops, jewelers, pawn shops, fortune-tellers, bakeries that gave off the inviting smell of fresh breads and pastries, and eateries with roast duck and barbecued pork hanging and dripping at the windows. And always, washing hanging from bamboo poles protruding from windows and verandahs, like flags of many nations.

The Central Police Station soon came into view as I neared Wyndham Street. Images of Papa, stalwart and handsome in his winter blue uniform, flooded back. Lee Tak Sing patrolling his beat, marching at ceremonial parades, speaking to his fellows at meetings of the Junior Police Officers' Association, promoted to the rank of inspector, receiving a silver plaque at his retirement ceremony.

Papa's retirement was a peaceful time in his life, until about a year after our visit to China, when, for a period of several months, he stayed out late and did not come home for supper many evenings. He was secretive as to his whereabouts. He always gave the explanation that he was out "with the boys" at *wei chi* tournaments. He even stayed out overnight on several occasions, although he always phoned so Ah Lan and I wouldn't worry. I suspected he had found a new girlfriend.

"He's entitled to one, Seenla," Ah Lan rationalized, when I voiced my suspicion to her. "*Siu Yeh* is only sixty-four and still very handsome. He may not have the dough, but some older women are not after money. They want the man." She covered her gold-toothed mouth with her hand and tittered.

"I suppose I ought to be happy for Papa if he has found a companion, but no one can replace Mummy, Ah Lan, and you know that! Papa would never love another woman!" I was close to tears, jealous that Papa might be giving his attention to some presumptuous brazen-faced foxy female who dared to think for a moment she could replace my mother. I intended to find an opportunity to bring up the subject with Papa and know the truth.

About that time, around midnight on a Saturday night, Papa, Ah Lan and I had just come home from my friend Josie's wedding banquet when the phone rang. I picked it up, wondering who might be calling at such a late hour. It was a woman's voice, asking for Lee Tak Sing. Papa looked disconcerted when he took the phone. I could hear grave okay's and hmm's coming from him, as he listened to the caller. Grudgingly I closed my bedroom door, so Papa could talk without worrying I could hear him.

"Is everything okay, Papa?" I asked soon after he had hung up. He looked upset and visibly shaken.

"Yes," he answered distractedly. Could he have gotten into trouble with a woman, or, worse, gotten a woman into trouble? No, not Papa. Yet, Ah Lan was right: at his age, Papa could still be attractive to women.

"You look really worried, Papa," I persisted.

He gave me an absent-minded smile and said, "An old friend has run into a problem, but nothing you need to worry about."

That night, he stayed up by the phone. Whether it rang again or not, I did not know, for I had drifted off to sleep in my room. When I got up in the morning, I found Papa asleep on the sofa. He never told me what the phone call was about, or who the woman caller was. And I refrained from asking further.

For a while, Papa continued to be out at all hours. But after a few months, his activities became more of his old routine again. If he had a new interest in his life, his passion must have cooled off. He still stayed out late occasionally, but I knew better not to ask. After all, I was not my father's keeper.

I passed the Caine Road landing on the escalator. A few people had stepped on and a few had got off in front and behind me. A man walked briskly down the steps that ran parallel to the escalator. His swift movement and foreign looks caught my attention for an instant. I looked casually over to him as he went past, and in that split second, I found myself staring at the face of Richard Mills. Instinctively, I turned my head, caught his eye and smiled in recognition, while the escalator firmly continued to put distance between us. I waved. I was not sure if he waved back, for I had almost instantaneously turned to face forward again. Stubbornly I stared ahead. The chance encounter with Richard ended as quickly and as suddenly as it took place, teasing and agitating me. The sight of him was adding insult to injury, for I felt more depressed after that, so much so that I started to cry.

Ever since the evening of the Christmas reception at the Hilton a year and a half ago, I had allowed myself to think occasionally of him. I had expected, and hoped, he would call. But Christmas passed, then New Year, and no phone call from Richard. Disappointment gave way to frustration, and eventually resignation that he would never call. I began to think the worst of him. Perhaps he was one of those, as the worldly-wise Beth said, who kept a little recipe box of names and phone numbers, indexed under GOODY GOODY, EASY OVER, BOOBY TRAPS, GOOD FORMALS, MOTHERS and other unimaginable and imaginative categories. I went to the extent of putting myself in his recipe box, making up a category for myself – PP, for PRISSY PRIM, or PAPA'S PET. And now the fleeting encounter on the escalator was a mockery, disturbing and cruel in arousing in me surprised elation at seeing him again, and then disappointment that he was gone as quickly as he had appeared. It might be another year and a half before I would run into him again, or never. I would probably never see him again, never again. It was just as well.

"Watch your step," a rather breathless, raspy baritone voice sounded from behind, and adrenalin rushed through my system in spite of my effort to appear calm. I could not let him see my tear-stained face. Without turning, I bit my lower lip to hide my confusion and my quiet joy. I looked down at my feet and stepped off the escalator onto the landing at Robinson Road, confident that he was getting off behind me. I turned to face him.

"I thought you had gone back to England for good," I blurted out with a half smile, perhaps in a slightly accusing tone, and regretted it immediately.

"I was home on leave for a year." He sounded still a bit breathless.

"Oh," I responded, surprised, and not sure what to make of the news. That could explain why he hadn't called. Perhaps he was back together with his ex-girlfriend. Perhaps he had found a new heartthrob while in England. With his good looks and pleasant disposition, he must have no problem dating girls. The recipe box came to mind again. Instead of asking him the reason for his long leave, I was silent. Richard must have sensed something was bothering me, for he was quiet as we walked out onto the street, keeping a respectable distance between us. I finally recollected myself sufficiently to ask which way he was going.

"Whichever way you're going," he answered quickly.

I was almost overwhelmed with the events of the last few minutes. We headed in the direction of Castle Steps. He walked briskly beside me.

"So you've been away," I said, feeling better about his long absence.

"Yes. My father died of a heart attack on Christmas Day, while I was in Singapore. I flew home for the funeral," he said.

"Oh I'm very sorry, Richard," I said, looking up at him and touching his arm to comfort, feeling ashamed that I had thought the worst of him.

He turned to look at me appreciatively, and touched my hand that was on his arm before we let go of each other.

"Mum was a bit of an emotional state, so I decided to stay on until things were better with her," he continued. "And in the meantime, a crony of mine got me a reporting job with the local *Mirror*."

I was satisfied, even happy, with the reason for his prolonged stay in England. "So much has happened to you since we last met," I murmured.

"So you're on summer holiday now. Keeping yourself busy?" he asked.

I told him about my voluntary work with the United Democrats for the past three summers. He regarded me with curiosity.

"Have you ever thought of taking a vacation? To Europe or some other place?" he asked.

I shook my head. "I don't want to leave my father, not that he's not capable of taking care of himself. But — since my mother died — in any case, he's not the traveling type."

Since Mummy died, the longest time I had been away from Papa was an overnight stay at a friend's villa in Shatin for my ten-year class reunion. It would be hard for Richard to understand my attachment to Papa. Still, he nodded at my explanation.

As we walked, we talked generally of the summer heat, of typhoons, and his latest assignments. All the while, my mind was in a turmoil. Should I invite him up to my flat for a cup of tea? What would Papa and Ah Lan think if I did? No, it wouldn't be proper to ask him up. I hardly knew the man. Most likely, this chance encounter would end the same way as the last two, and I would hear no more from him again.

When we were about to reach Castle Steps, he turned to me and said, "Serena, I'm sorry I haven't called since coming back. Things got very busy at the *Weekly*, and I was on several assignments in Southeast Asia the last few months." He paused, perhaps waiting for my reaction, but I was careful not to betray any emotion just then. He continued, "I really would like to see you again."

"It would be nice to meet other than by chance," I said in as calm a voice as I could affect, trying hard to still the butterflies fluttering inside of me.

49

Richard

THE PEAK IS ONE of the focal points of the first-time tourist as well as the lifetime resident crossing the harbour in a ferry from Kowloon Peninsula to Hong Kong Island. That pointed apex atop the highest hill on the island slopes gently on the east and steeply to the west, as if paying homage to the setting sun. Through the 156 years of British colonization, buildings have been constructed, demolished, and reconstructed all around it, and roads have been carved on its slopes; its pristine environment has been much threatened and violated, and eventually shrunk to the point of near nonexistence, but its outline has remained unchanged for centuries, dominating the island — a permanent landmark and an artist's dream.

Richard kissed me for the first time on the Peak, on the very top known as Governor's Garden, a quiet sunken sub-tropical haven lush with swaying palms and flowering shrubs. We had strolled along the paved pathways, and he had taken my hand as we went down a rather steep slope, and did not relinquish it until we sat down on the grass facing the south side of the island, looking past rocks and greenery to a reservoir in the valley below, and, beyond that, the blue green water of the South China coast. He put his arm around my shoulders and drew me to him, and I took comfort as I rested my head against his chest. I could hear and feel his heartbeat, and his soft breathing on my face, feel his lips on my forehead, eyes, cheeks, and lips, and I kissed him back with all the fervour checked for years and suddenly unleashed by this English reporter. If hell had broken loose at that instant, or the earth beneath where we sat had opened up, I would not have cared, for I was losing myself completely in the ecstasy of his embrace.

"Who is it, Serena?" Papa asked when I told him that I had met someone I really liked. "A reporter I first met two years ago and accidentally ran into again a few weeks ago. He's English. His name is Richard Mills." I winced as soon as I had blurted out in one breath the crucial information that Richard was a *gweilo*. I waited for Papa's reaction.

It took him a few good seconds to register what he had just heard. And then he looked unsettled, but almost immediately recovered enough from what I thought was initial shock that I was dating a foreigner to say in a calm, controlled voice, "Invite him home, Serena. I would like very much to meet him."

On the day of Richard's visit, Ah Lan busied herself in the kitchen all day, preparing a meal to impress "Seenla's *gweilo* boyfriend." She had researched among her market friends as to what dishes to cook for a *gweilo*, and decided on a menu of my favourite sweet and sour pork, stir-fried beef steak with sautéed onion, Portuguese chicken in a curried coconut cream sauce, and tender snow pea shoots with crabmeat. *Gweilo* liked desserts, Ah Lan was told, and so she made a mango pudding with fresh mango pulp and cream cheese, from a recipe she picked up from a friend who worked for an Indian family.

My heart was thumping hard as I presented Richard to Papa. Would they like each other? My future happiness was balanced entirely on that question. There were a few moments of awkward silence after I had made the introduction, when each man seemed to be assessing the other. I was a little disappointed at their initial reaction to each other, for I had hoped and expected it to be spontaneously cordial, if only for my sake. But if there was a cloud of uneasiness between them, it was dispelled almost as quickly as my thoughts formed. Papa was the first to clear the air.

"I am very pleased to meet you, Richard. My daughter has told me a lot about you," he said in slow but correct English, as he shook Richard's hand warmly. I felt more at ease after Papa's words of welcome, even though they were stock first words a father would say to his daughter's boyfriend.

Richard too got over his initial awkwardness and responded with equal warmth, looking Papa straight in the eye with an earnest sincerity that excited me as he said, "It's my honour to meet you, sir."

"And this is my mother," I said, as I led Richard to the main piece of furniture in the living room, the black lacquered credenza on which was the silver framed photograph of Mummy in the pink *cheongsam* and matching jacket. Inside the crystal bowl placed in front of her picture, a lone white water lily floated in water.

Richard stood in front of the photo and bowed, following the custom to show respects to the dead. Moved by his gesture, I put my hand on his shoulder, while Papa looked on quietly.

"She is beautiful," said Richard. Then noticing some characters etched on the bottom of the frame, he asked, "What does it say?"

"'*I alone love the lin flower because it arises from the soil and yet is pure and untainted,*'" I translated. "It's from my mother's favourite piece of classical prose. The *lin flower*, which is the lotus, belongs to the water lily family. That's why my father keeps a fresh water lily in the bowl all the time. They are hard to get, but he knows this florist who orders them specially for him."

Just then, Ah Lan brought out tea and shrimp chips. I was glad of the distraction, for the atmosphere was becoming a bit too emotional for comfort. The evening went well. Papa seemed genuinely interested in Richard, in his work as a reporter, and in his home in England.

"My father died a year and a half ago," Richard was telling Papa over dinner. "My mother was a nurse in Wells, until she retired. She lives by herself now in our family home in Somerset."

"Serena says you go back every year to visit," said Papa.

"I do. I enjoy our place. My grandfather bought it soon after he returned from the war."

"You must miss your mother and England," Papa said, looking intently at Richard.

"I miss my mother, and I look forward to going home every year, but I like Hong Kong. I find the people here extraordinarily interesting," said Richard as he tried to pick up a small piece of curried potato with his chopsticks, finally piercing it with their narrower ends.

"In what ways?" pursued Papa.

"Well, they are resourceful, hard-working, efficient in whatever they do, from the peddler to the bank manager. Hong Kong people can weather any trouble and come out on top. The place is beautiful, but it's the people that fascinate me most."

"I cannot agree with you more," nodded Papa, looking pleased. Whatever reservation he might have had about Richard when they first met seemed to have dispersed. They were talking in a relaxed manner to each other.

"Ah Lan, Richard says he loves your cooking," I said, as she brought out the dessert.

Ah Lan's wrinkled cheeks bunched into a big smile, revealing her gold tooth. At seventy-eight, she had slowed down considerably since her days looking after Mummy, but she still retained some of the energy that had characterized her all her life. Her biggest hindrance other than age was the osteoporosis that had plagued her for years.

After dinner, I suggested *mahjong*. "I'll teach you, Richard," I said, and pulled Ah Lan out of the kitchen to make a foursome, in spite of her protest.

"This noise is like firecrackers!" said Richard, as he arranged his tiles, counting the dots and the bamboos on them.

I could tell from the look on Papa's face that he was enjoying himself and enjoying the game, but more the fact that Richard was playing. Several times I caught Papa watching Richard and me, the way we talked to each other, the way we looked at each other.

"Richard, you have lost three hundred chips," I told him, counting what he had left at the end of four rounds.

"Not bad for a beginner," said Papa, who also lost to me and Ah Lan.

"Next time I play you, we play money," said Ah Lan, in her straightforward Cantonese, patting Richard on the back of his hand, grinning her gold-tooth grin at him.

Papa laughed.

"What did she say, Serena?" Richard asked.

"Never mind," I said, "but be ready to lose your pants if you play *mahjong* with Ah Lan again."

"Well, Papa?" I asked anxiously after seeing Richard off at the entrance to our building.

"He is a good man, Serena." His words were a happy surprise to me, for much as he seemed to like Richard, I had not expected him to make a judgment the first time they met.

"Does this mean you approve?"

"Serena, you know you don't need my approval when it comes to your happiness. As long as you are happy, I am content. But yes, I do approve of him." Then, in a teasing tone, he added, "And I'm relieved you've finally found your match. I was beginning to feel anxious, you know."

"Well, I have a very high standard, and it's all your fault, because I've been comparing every man I've met to you, Papa," I said, teasing him back, though my words were not far from the truth. "But I'm so glad you like Richard. What's more, he likes Hong Kong, and he likes his job here. There's no reason why he would want to leave."

Papa smiled at me thoughtfully, as he brushed a strand of hair from my cheek, the way he liked to do when I was a little girl.

50

The Peninsula

"I'VE HEARD ABOUT THE high tea here for a long while — never
dreamt I would be having it with you," I said to Richard.
I was nibbling on a dainty cucumber sandwich in the extensive
lobby of the Peninsula, not long after I brought him home to meet
Papa. The grand old hotel had long been a colonial institution,
where one could partake of extravagant and elegant high tea,
that ultimate English experience, with its three-tiered tray of tiny
sandwiches, petits fours, buttery scones, and the tea served in
fine bone china. Waiters and waitresses clad in black and white
uniform meandered among the tables and potted palms in the
lobby, below ornate gold-embossed ceilings and sparkling crystal
chandeliers, on carpets so thick that temporary indentations were
left where ladies' high heels had trod.

"I'd be jealous of any man taking you here," said Richard,
"other than your father, of course."

"My father would *never* come to the Peninsula for high tea,"
I laughed, thinking of Papa's idea of a good restaurant. I told
Richard what I read in Papa's book of the night he first arrived
in Kowloon on a train over forty years ago, how he passed by
the Peninsula. He was a poor homeless refugee then, an outsider
looking in, somewhat intimidated by the glamour and glitter
of the hotel. Now, more than forty years later, he was still an
outsider.

"I respect your father greatly, and I'm not saying it just to make
you happy."

"I'm glad you two seem to get along. I was a bit worried at first.

I was afraid Papa might think we were too different."

"Your father strikes me as a very open-minded person."

"He means a lot to me, Richard."

"You're doing far more for your father than what I'm doing for my mother."

"Has your mother ever asked you to go back, I mean, find a job back home?" At the back of my mind was the fear that, in spite of his soft spot for Hong Kong, he would have to go home one day.

"Not in so many words, but I know she'd love to have me home," Richard nodded. "My mother has never imposed her wishes on me. I've always been given wings, so to speak, always had the freedom to plan my own life." Then, as if he read my thoughts, he continued, looking at me softly, "I like my job here. And now you've given me another reason – the most important reason – to stay in Hong Kong. I have no intention of going back to England for a long while, Serena."

"What about after '97?" I needed the reassurance.

"The handover shouldn't pose a problem for me. I'll just find the job more challenging with self-censorship becoming more evident in the press circle. Actually, we've already been advised to use *discretion* in our political columns."

"Are you going along with the flow?" I asked, sipping my tea.

"As a matter of fact, no. When you censor yourself, you are accepting oppression without a fight, and giving up democracy of your own free will. That's the worst form of defeat. They can censor me but I won't censor myself."

"Do you suppose the Chinese government will curb our movements after the handover?"

"Probably. Who knows what they'll do." He hesitated. Then he leaned over and lowered his voice to almost a whisper. "Serena, there's something I meant to tell you, for I want no secret between us, but you must not repeat this."

"You have my word." I strained my ears, anxious to hear him above the soft piano music and the din of voices and jingling of bone china.

"I was involved in the operation to help dissidents escape, soon after the Tiananmen massacre."

"How?" I asked, my question condensed to a single syllable by the shock of Richard's revelation.

"They were smuggled across the border, by land or across the river. My job was to arrange for some of them to leave the colony."

"What did you have to do?"

"I got them visas, flights, literally got them on a plane to Britain, and I arranged to have friends to meet them in London."

"And the Chinese didn't know about you?" I was suddenly worried for his safety.

"No, they didn't," he answered. "But no one else must know about this, Serena, even though it was a thing of the past."

I nodded, thrilled with being drawn into the secret.

"Much as I marvel at what you did, admire you, adore you for this, I'm glad it's all behind you. I don't want anything to happen to you." Leaning over, I kissed Richard quickly. "Papa would be so proud of you, if only he knew."

51

The Proposal

"SEENLA, WHEN ARE YOU and Meesta Richee getting married?" Ah Lan asked soon after I brought Richard home to meet her and Papa, as she liked to put it.

"I don't know, Ah Lan," I answered. "Don't you think it's a bit too early to think of that? We've only gone out together for a short time."

"Don't mind Ah Lan telling you, but you are not young, and your Papa probably wants to hold a grandchild soon. Young people these days, they don't marry, just live together. I hope you and Meesta Richee are not going to do that."

"No, Ah Lan," I said, amused and exasperated. "We are not planning to live together."

Richard went home in May 1994 for a month. As soon as he stepped off the plane at Kai Tak on his return, he phoned me at my school.

"I have to see you tonight, Serena. I'm booking a table for us at the Peak Restaurant." He sounded happy and excited. Perhaps he had something to tell me from his visit home. Perhaps he had something to say to me.

That evening, before Richard came by to pick me up, Papa came into my room and, sitting on the edge of my bed, said thoughtfully, "Serena, I want you to be happy with Richard. You don't have to worry about me." Papa's words puzzled me. He hesitated and continued, looking intently at me, "I don't mean just tonight."

"You mean the rest of my life?" I asked tersely, upset at Papa's hint that I live my life without him. "Papa, I will never leave you, and Richard knows that. He's going to stay in Hong Kong. I want to be with you both. Why – why are you bringing this up all of a sudden?"

"Oh, Serena," Papa sighed, and in my mind I could just hear him asking, "what shall I do with you?"

A thought came into my mind just then, a mystery about my father that had been troubling me on and off for the past five years. Was Papa suggesting that I go with Richard, that he might live his own life?

"Papa, will you be mad if I ask if you've been seeing a girlfriend?"

Papa laughed hard. After a while, he sobered and said, "Serena, I have only loved one woman all my life, and that was your mother."

Papa did not exactly answer my question, but what he said was all I wanted to hear.

When Richard finally arrived to pick me up, he did not look as excited as he sounded on the phone. Instead, he seemed somewhat anxious and subdued. Nonetheless, we were happy to be together again, and as soon as we were in his car, he kissed me as though he was kissing me for the last time.

Later, Richard and I sat at the Peak Restaurant commanding a fantastic view of Hong Kong, for it was a clear night. The city below was shimmering with myriad lights radiating from countless multi-coloured neon signs, twinkling like diamonds, rubies, emeralds in a pitch-black mine. The harbour was aglow with nocturnal activities, ferries crossing its dark waters like electrified beetles, fishing junks each marked by a solitary light sailing out into deeper waters for a night catch, and anchored ocean liners outlined in glittering white lights. But my heart was not in the scene through the picture window, for I was anxious to hear what Richard had to say. Over dinner, he told me about his month in England, his mother, her dog, her garden, his lazy hazy days in his mother's Somerset home.

"Richard, you sounded as though you had something very exciting to tell me when you phoned this morning," I finally said, sipping my tea, feeling somewhat disappointed after my over-anticipation.

Richard squeezed my hand, and his hand felt cold.

"Serena, I told my mother I wanted to marry you and live in Hong Kong. She is accepting it quite well." I was elated. Before I could utter a word, he continued, "But a little problem has come up since I phoned you this morning, which may affect your decision."

"What happened?" Could happiness be so short-lived?

"I may have to leave Hong Kong when '97 comes around."

"Why?" I felt a sudden knot in my stomach as I braced myself to hear what he had to say.

He cleared his throat.

"Remember I told you I helped some dissidents after the massacre? I had thought that was over. Well, this afternoon, I received a phone call advising that I leave Hong Kong before the handover. According to my – contact, the people in the operation have good reason to believe the Chinese know about me and what I did back in '89."

"So you're on their wanted list. Are you still in touch with the people in the operation?" I thought he had washed his hands clean of the connection.

"Not really, except that I was contacted this afternoon by one of them."

"Your contact was quick in getting the news to you, as soon as you got back," I observed in a sour manner.

Richard nodded and was quiet.

Suddenly my world was crumbling. I would have to live in England if I were to marry Richard. I would have to leave Hong Kong, leave Papa. Papa would be alone, cared for by the aging Ah Lan, without me for the rest of his life, like – like his father was without him. History would be repeating itself cruelly, if I married

Richard. Yet, I loved Richard. *Mummy, I will never leave Papa. I will always look after Papa for you.* "*Serena, you know you don't need my approval where your happiness is concerned. As long as you are happy, I am content.*" *No, Papa, I cannot leave you, I will never leave you. Papa, you are breaking my heart. Richard is breaking my heart.*

Richard must have read what was racing through my mind, for he said, "I've been thinking perhaps we can persuade your father to come with us."

"Papa will never leave Hong Kong, Richard," I said, shaking my head hopelessly. "He left the mainland as a youth and spent forty-some years longing for his home in China. He has come to regard Hong Kong as his second home. He won't leave, Richard, and I can't leave without him."

"My situation may not be all that grave. Perhaps it's being blown out of proportion," said Richard. "After all, it's been five years since Tiananmen, and it will be eight years by the time '97 rolls around."

"Your source of information, is it reliable?"

"Very reliable," Richard replied gravely. "I can't say more."

"Then you shouldn't stay after the handover. You'd be risking too much," I said in a tight voice.

"We have quite a bit of time, Serena. Ninety-seven is still three years away. Things may change in the meantime."

"And what if things are as bleak as they look now? I can just visualize in three years' time you leaving for good, and you'll find some English girl, marry her, and – and give her babies, and – " The hypothesis was enough to fill me with jealous tears.

Richard put his arm around my shoulders, comfortingly kissing my forehead, and, lifting my face up to his, said gently, "My proposal is open. You don't have to give me an answer until you are ready, Serena."

Today the royal yacht *Britannia* steamed into the Hong Kong harbour. It will be the home of Prince Charles during his visit here to attend the handover ceremony. Although the handover is still a week away, two hundred soldiers from the People's Liberation Army are already in Hong Kong. Some five hundred more will enter three hours before midnight of July 1st when Hong Kong will revert to Chinese rule. The end of an era is at hand, as is the beginning of a new one.

52

Remission

THE STARK WHITE WALLS and smell of disinfectants at Mercy Hospital were especially disconcerting to me, for Papa was undergoing surgery for prostrate cancer. I sat in the visitors' lounge, looking out to the corridor, as hospital personnel in long white coats or nurses' uniforms continually crossed my vision. As the clock on the wall ticked away the minutes, I grew more and more tense and agitated. My students' essays lay on my lap, but I could not take in a word.

Across from the lounge, the elevator door opened and Richard emerged. The sight of him warmed my heart. I went to him and took comfort in his embrace.

"Still not a word," I said, my voice sounding strained and hollow. "He's been in there for three hours."

"He'll come out fine," said Richard.

Papa stayed a week at Mercy Hospital after his prostatectomy in the spring of 1995. He came home, high-spirited and feeling stronger by the day.

"I feel good. Serena worries about me too much, but I tell her I am feeling better than even before, all the attention I am getting," Papa said the first time Richard came by. They ate egg tarts and drank the dragon well tea Ah Lan had brought out. "I am so happy to be home. I don't like that hospital mush. I cannot understand why they give you western food."

"You look marvelous for someone who's just had surgery," said Richard. "I'll come by and challenge you to chess, when the

Legislative Council elections are over."

"I am ready," said Papa.

Later, as I walked Richard to his car, Richard said, "Your father seems in fine spirits and looks well."

I burst into tears. "The urologist told us they found cancer in a few lymph nodes. Richard, I'm so frightened."

Papa underwent two courses of chemotherapy that spring and summer. All that time, his good humour never left him. Ah Lan kept feeding him chicken soup to help replenish his energy. We were all very hopeful that the cancer would go into remission for a long time, perhaps forever.

With the chemo out of the way, Papa gradually regained much of his former feeling of well-being. Richard and I took him and Ah Lan for a sampan ride in Aberdeen on an early October day.

"In the forty-four years I have lived here, I have never taken a boat ride into the typhoon shelter until now. Of course, if I had been with the marine police, I would have come here often," said Papa, obviously enjoying himself.

Our sampan guide, a darkly tanned young *tanka* woman in a black *samfu* and a broad-brimmed straw hat, deftly steered her boat on the waterways among the anchored fishing junks in the typhoon shelter of Aberdeen, the fishing-village-turned-boom-town on the southern coast of Hong Kong Island. For over a century, Aberdeen had been the home of the *tanka* people, whose livelihood depended on their catches off the shores of Hong Kong and the surrounding islands.

I peeked into cabins of the anchored junks, resourcefully furnished with bare necessities, very bare indeed, cheap linoleum floors, worn rattan and wooden furniture, and strips of red paper with the inverted *fook* ideogram on the walls denoting the arrival of Fortune. A woman was cooking upon a deck on a portable coal burner. Another with a baby in a cloth carrier on her back was chopping vegetables on a wood block by the edge of the water. On another deck, a fisherman arranged his nets for the next haul at sea. They all looked up as we passed with as much curiosity as they themselves conjured. One sampan was selling steaming pots of food, mostly catering to the residents of the floating community. The *tanka* community was a dwindling world apart. Those who had remained in it, whether by choice or circumstance, lived in constant fear of the elements, yet had survived for generations, vulnerable yet enduring, like the rest of Hong Kong. To the city dwellers, the sampans and junks in the typhoon shelter were an ugly conglomeration of floating slums against the backdrop of a concrete jungle that had forever altered the once humble skyline of a fishing village.

Our sampan soon left behind the typhoon shelter and emerged into open waters, heading for one of the palatial floating restaurants in the bay.

"I ate at the Dai Lee once, at a dinner for a retiring senior inspector. These floating restaurants charge sky-high. But today, I treat you to seafood at the Gum Din," announced Papa, pointing to one of two ornate floating restaurants with pagoda-style roofs, "because I am very happy, and I want to be extravagant!"

The Gum Din was majestic. The interior décor was ancient imperial, with a rich red brocade wallcovering, dragon pillars, crystal and gold chandeliers and a grand throne covered with intricate wood carvings and elaborate embroidery of dragon motifs. The decorations were fit for an emperor, and so was the cuisine, concocted with the freshest harvests from the sea – boiled prawns in shell, steamed grouper, speckled crab with ginger and onion, braised baby squid and sautéed sea scallop.

"This is the best seafood I've ever had," said Richard as he struggled busily with a crab claw.

"This must cost you a cow," said Ah Lan in her colloquial Cantonese, as she sucked on the gills of the grouper. She did not mind the conversation carried on mostly in English. She was obviously enjoying herself.

"Today we celebrate Papa's recovery from cancer."

"And the result of the elections," said Papa, referring to the

Legislative Council elections that September, in which the pro-democracy parties triumphantly clinched a vast majority of the directly elected seats.

Holding up his little teacup, Richard proposed a toast to Papa's health, and to democracy in Hong Kong after 1997.

"And to Seenla and Meesta Richee, that lovers will eventually be united," said Ah Lan in Cantonese.

Papa smiled and nodded. Richard heard his name and mine spoken, Ah Lan-style, and understood. He put his arm around me and gave my shoulder a gentle squeeze.

"Well, let's make the most of the present while we can," I said, "for who knows what will happen after '97."

"As long as we do our own small parts for Hong Kong, there is hope," replied Papa.

As night fell, I leaned against Richard at the stern of the motor launch that was taking us back to shore, feeling the warm caress of the salt sea air, while Papa sat contentedly with Ah Lan in the enclosed cabin. If only I could capture that moment, right there, right then, and frame it for eternity.

Papa had been in a jolly mood since the outing to Aberdeen. His mind seemed to have affected his physical fitness, for in the last two months of 1995, he had ventured out on his morning walk again, along Robinson Road to the Botanic Gardens. I would accompany him on weekends, bringing a picnic lunch of sandwiches, soya milk and fruit. On one such occasion, when we were sitting atop the old battlement overlooking the large fountain, Papa brought up the subject of Richard.

"Serena, I don't mean to interfere, but will you tell me what you and Richard have in mind for the future?" he asked, taking a bite of a sardine sandwich.

"We're not sure, 'cause – " I hesitated, as I separated sections of an orange and offered them to him, "'cause it may not be safe for him to remain in Hong Kong after the handover." I knew it was time to confide in Papa Richard's problem. "He's blacklisted for helping to get dissidents out of Hong Kong after the Tiananmen massacre."

Papa looked intent and calm, without betraying any emotion on hearing what Richard had done for the cause of democracy in China. His reaction was not what I had expected.

"What Richard did was very brave and commendable. He's a fine man, one I would have no hesitation to give my daughter to," Papa finally said in a weighted and steady voice. "Why don't you go with him when he leaves? Serena, remember what I have told you so many times, your happiness is my first concern."

"Papa, I *don't* want to leave Hong Kong. This is my home, where I was born, where you and Mummy brought me up and gave me the best childhood anyone could have. You encouraged me to work for a democratic government in Hong Kong; you nourished in me a love for my homeland. I know how hard it was for you to leave yours. You can't tell me to turn my back on Hong Kong now, at its most urgent hour." I was in tears as I ended my barrage of words. I needed to convince Papa I was not staying behind because of him.

Papa patted me comfortingly on my back and looked at me with a smile in his eyes.

"Well, Serena, you certainly have succeeded in making your old father feel guilty that he has taught you so well." Then in a decisive tone, he added, "When the time comes for Richard to leave, I want you to go with him."

Papa wanted to have Mongolian hotpot for dinner on the eve of the New Year, 1996. I brought home several pounds of thinly sliced raw beef and pork, as well as fresh shrimp, fish balls and lots of Chinese cabbage for the grand meal. Richard was coming, and so were Ming, Kitty and their two boys.

Ming's two sons, John, a precocious seven-year-old, and William, a cherubic boy of two who had his mother's round face, were the centre of attention at the New Year's Eve dinner. Ming had taught the boys to call Papa *Yeh Yeh*, and it pleased Papa very much.

"Have you heard from his real *Yeh Yeh* lately?" Papa asked of Ming.

"Pa is quite well. He still makes those bamboo toys and sells them at the market. Ma is suffering from arthritis, otherwise she's fine. I'm hoping Kitty can make a trip back with the boys next year, when William is a little older."

"Don't wait too long, Ming, don't wait too long," said Papa.

We all sat around the table, around the big pot set on a portable electric burner in the centre, throwing our choices of raw meat, seafood and vegetables into the bubbling water in the pot. What a wonderful way to involve family and friends in a communal activity, warming the stomach as well as the spirit, especially on a cold wintry evening. We retrieved the cooked pieces from the pot with wire ladles, we ate, we tossed in more raw ingredients, all the while chatting and sipping the plum wine that Ming brought. Gradually, as the meal wore on, the water in the pot was transformed into the tastiest soup. Because of Richard's presence, conversation was conducted in various forms of English, according to the background and upbringing of the speaker, from pidgin to Queen's, except for Ah Lan who would make comments in Cantonese, but that did not bother Richard, for he had become accustomed to not understanding every word said in his presence.

"So China has named all the members of the preparatory committee for the handover," Ming said, opening up the subject of the latest in handover issues.

"I'm afraid we'll be seeing more and more of the Chinese factor before the handover," observed Richard. "The press is being too careful of what is printed these days. A lot of people I interviewed lately are afraid to say much."

"Things seem bleak. Just look, after all our hard work, the Chinese are going to replace the present legislature with an appointed provisional one," I said.

"Well, only time will tell what 'one country, two systems'

means, whether Hong Kong will really get a different treatment from the rest of China," said Ming the hopeful.

"One of my worries is that corruption may find its way back into Hong Kong," Papa spoke meditatively for the first time. "It is a vermin that has infested Chinese society for centuries. Even when no money and gifts are involved, there is always *guanxi*. You know people, you get the job. I hope the ICAC will continue to be effective, and not just a name, after '97."

"I have something to tell everyone," Ming said, clearing his throat, and casting a glance at Kitty. "Kitty and I have recently turned in our applications for immigration to Canada."

There was a brief moment of silence. Papa was the first to speak.

"Well, you are young and smart, and with your training and skills, you will make good anywhere, Ming."

"He is mainly thinking of the boys' future," Kitty spoke up.

"Much as I want to believe I will be safe in Hong Kong after the handover, for it has been twenty years since I took part in the demonstrations in Beijing, I'm still a bit worried what may happen when the Chinese take over Hong Kong," Ming said.

"People are leaving Hong Kong left and right, because they fear Communism. They fear for themselves, but more so for their children and grandchildren. They have good reasons to leave," Papa said, taking a sip of the plum wine. "You have an even greater reason to go, Ming, for as long as the Communists are in power, you can never be sure you won't be persecuted for what you did at any time in the past." So saying, Papa gave his blessing for Ming's decision.

"Canada will open up a whole new world for John and William. You've made the right decision, Ming," I said.

Kitty nodded vigorously. By then, the hot pot was emptied of food and soup. Both John and William were asleep. They would be going into the New Year in their dreams. Richard opened the bottle of sparkling wine he'd brought, just as the countdown to 1996 began at Statue Square. As the clock struck midnight, and the crowd at Statue Square blew horns and threw streamers, and sang *Auld Lang Syne*, Richard drew me to him and kissed me fervently. Toasts were drunk.

"To Papa's health!"

"To Ming and Kitty! For a bright future in Canada!"

"To Tak Sing Suk! May you enjoy good health and a long happy life!"

"To Ah Lan! No more aches and pains!"

"To Hong Kong's future! May Hong Kong survive the handover and continue to thrive beyond the next fifty years!"

"To Serena and Richard! This year is your year!"

The last toast was proposed by Kitty. Richard and I exchanged smiles tinged with sadness, for we did not know what the future might hold for us.

The spring and summer of 1996 were a happy time for Papa. I rejoiced over the fact that his cancer was in remission, and he seemed to have gained back most of his former energy. I ate supper most evenings with him and Ah Lan, who, ever since the New Year's Eve hotpot dinner at home, had finally agreed to take her meals with us. Richard joined us whenever he could, and I was happy to see how much Papa looked forward to his visits. Usually after dinner, the two men would challenge each other to a game of *wei chi* or chess. Richard had become addicted to the former game since learning it from Papa. Papa, on the other hand, was fascinated with chess, especially since its rules bear many similarities to those of Chinese chess. The two men had no problem communicating. In all the years Papa was in Hong Kong, his English, though far from being superior in grammar and syntax, had improved to the point where no effort was required to pick up his words and meaning. However, he had retained a strong Cantonese accent, and pronounced every syllable of every word carefully as an isolated entity. After all, Chinese is a monosyllabic tongue. And by ten o'clock, Papa would turn in for the night, and Ah Lan would confine herself in her own quarters with her Chinese opera music, leaving Richard and me to have some time alone. Richard went home to England for a month and came back in late August. By then, I was getting ready for the new school year. Kitty took John and William to Beijing in mid-August. According to Kitty, it was a heartwarming two weeks. Ah Chu and Chu Sum were the envy of neighbours and friends, especially because of China's policy limiting couples to having only one child. In October, Ming and Kitty's applications for immigration to Canada were approved. The timing was good for them.

"China has named the members of the provisional legislature to take office next July 1st," Richard called me as soon as he received the news. "Looks like they are wasting no time in replacing the present Council."

"As expected, but I had hoped China would ease up a bit." I felt disheartened, overwhelmed by the urgency of the news, and realized all too soon that the final countdown had begun.

Tonight Ah Lan has gone to bed early. She will stay up for the *hui gui* ceremony tomorrow. I sit on the sofa, watching the pre-handover festivities. Local singers perform popular songs in Cantonese and Mandarin. A dance troupe begins a lion dance, an auspicious act to herald *hui gui*.

Celebrations are taking place inside China too, to mark the return of Hong Kong. A young Chinese male soloist with a mop of dyed flaxen hair, in tight blue jeans and a T-shirt displaying the characters *Hong Kong* and the numerals *1997*, sings in Mandarin *"Hong Kong, welcome back to the motherland"* to the rock beat of a live band at Tiananmen Square. A ten-year-old boy is asked by a reporter at the Square what his thoughts are on Hong Kong's return to China.

"My greatest wish is to go sightseeing in Hong Kong!" he answers in a squeaky excited voice.

One more day.

53

Papa

SINCE LAST SEPTEMBER, PAPA had complained of back pain.

"I think my age has finally caught up with me. Ah Lan, I am experiencing what you must feel at times, probably worse," he told the old *amah*.

In time, Papa's back pain intensified. It kept him awake at night and often left him in crippling agony in the day. I took him to see his doctor, who ordered X-rays and bone scans to determine the cause of his pain. Early in November, I received the diagnosis I never wanted to hear — Papa's cancer had spread to his spine.

"They are going to give you radiation to relieve your pain, and chemo to shrink the tumors. You came out fine last time, and were in remission for a long while. There's no reason why you won't respond well this time. Willpower, Papa. That and the treatments will bring you back to health."

"Yes, Serena. I'll do my best," he said, looking tenderly at me.

"Promise me, Papa, that you'll be okay, you hear me?" I pleaded, as if his promise would pull him through.

"I'll try," Papa said, placing his hand on my shoulder. "I'll try."

In the weeks following his diagnosis, Papa visited Mercy Hospital for radiation and chemotherapy treatments. Richard and I took turns accompanying him, as our work schedules permitted. Up until January this year, Papa had continued to go to the cemetery to visit Mummy on Sundays. But the courses of chemotherapy were taking a heavy toll on him, leaving him drained of energy. He had to give up going to the cemetery.

By the end of January, the pain in Papa's back had gradually spread to his limbs and permeated his bones. Another bone scan confirmed our worst fear, that the cancer had spread further, beyond hope. Radiation could not relieve him of his pain. His doctor prescribed narcotics to numb the sensations.

Papa said to me one day in mid-February, "Serena, I'm in a lot of pain, and I'm tired, tired of fighting. I know my time is near."

The last sentence pierced my heart like a sharp knife. I was beside myself with tears. I embraced my father and would not release my hold on him.

"Papa, you can't give up. I won't let you go." I was close to hysteria.

"Serena, as long as you keep me and your mother in your heart, we will always be with you," he said, wiping my wet cheeks with his hand. "I have one wish though. I want to be here at home, close to you and to your Mummy, when I go. I can feel her presence here. Please don't put me in a hospital."

"I will never put you in a hospital, Papa."

Papa remained home, in spite of his doctor's strong recommendation for him to check into a hospital. To ease his pain, he was given a morphine drip with a device for self-monitoring the dosage. A nurse aide came by every day to check on the morphine supply. Ah Lan tended to his needs during the day, and I took over in the evenings and on weekends.

Richard was a frequent visitor, offering unfailing emotional and physical sustenance. Sometimes, I left Richard to stay with Papa in his room, while I graded students' work and prepared my lessons at the dining table. I was very grateful for Richard, for his unselfish dedication to Papa, his generosity with his time, and for his unconditional love for me.

By late February, Papa's pain had become excruciating, with little relief. He increased the dose of morphine, but it dulled his mind. I took a leave of absence from Holy Cross.

"A job I can always find again, but I only have one father, and he's dying," I said to Richard, who wholeheartedly supported my decision. I seldom left Papa's side after that. At night, I slept on a mattress on the floor beside his bed, listening to his hard breathing and agonizing moans, answering his every call.

Papa's condition worsened in the following weeks, so much so that his entire body felt like a house on fire, he said, with flames burning in every bone. Since the beginning of March, I had hired a nurse to tend to his needs at home. Friends kept suggesting that I put Papa in a hospital, but no, the hospital was not for my father. Papa would die at home, not in some cold hospital room with whitewashed walls and grey utility floors, smelling of antiseptics and ether.

"Serena, I want to talk," said Papa one evening, on one of his lucid days. His eyes rested on the photograph of Mummy which had been moved into his room, placed on the dresser across from his bed, so that he could see it all the time. Instead of the usual water lily in the crystal bowl, I had placed a pot of fresh Easter lilies beside the picture, for it was the season.

I pulled up a stool and sat beside him while he rested in the recliner beside his bed. Rubbing his swollen feet, I waited for what he had to say.

"You know, these feet remind me of my mother's, so out of shape, like those rice cakes at the Dragon Boat Festival, except hers were from broken bones when they bound her feet," Papa said dreamily, as his mind wandered back to long ago and far away.

I continued massaging his feet, keeping silent, for talking had a way of starting up my tears.

"Serena, that story I wrote you, you still have it?"

"Of course, Papa. I'll treasure it forever."

"Read it well. Keep it for your children, that they may know their roots."

I nodded, lowering my head.

"Richard — he's a good man."

"I know," I said, my voice hardly audible.

"Leave with him when I'm gone."

I kept my head lowered, unable to utter a word.

"Serena, go to the wardrobe and take out the tin at the bottom, in the back," he said after a while.

I retrieved the old tin once used for Watson's soda crackers. Papa told me to open it. Inside, wrapped in an old sock, was a bar of gold.

"My last gold bar," said Papa. "I've kept it for you all these years."

"It's from *Yeh Yeh*, isn't it?" I asked, placing the small ingot in my palm like a sacred object.

"All that he had worked hard for his whole life – shrunk into four gold bars. They have all been put to good use, except this last one I am saving for you."

"I'll treasure it always, like your book."

"Use it wisely when you have to. Gold is no use if hoarded."

He closed his eyes. After a while, he said quietly, "I want a cremation. No big funeral."

I rested my head on his knee and wept silently, without looking up at him.

"I want you to take your mother's ashes and mine to my village Ka Hing."

"Yes, Papa," I said, my heart so full it would burst any moment, tears falling like rain on Papa's feet. "I'll bury your ashes and Mummy's with your father and mother."

"No, Serena. I want you to take our ashes, go to the family burial mound, and from there scatter them to the wind, and let them fall on the earth."

"Why, Papa?"

"Because then I will be free again to roam the land I love, and this time I will be even happier, because I will have your mother with me. She would want you to do so too, I know."

"But I will not know where to find you and Mummy then," I said, feeling weak with crying.

"You will find us in your heart always, no matter where you

go, Serena."

Wiping the tears from Papa's feet and from my own face with my hands, I looked up at my father, into his eyes dulled with pain. I reached up and touched his mole, the way I did as a child when I wanted a story.

The next day, Papa slipped into semi-consciousness. His breathing was heavy and laboured. He never regained the lucidity he exhibited the day he spoke to me about his dying wish. On the evening of March 30th, Easter Sunday according to Christians, Richard and I were watching a *Star Trek* rerun in the living room, Ah Lan was making a sweet red bean soup in the kitchen for a nightcap, and Papa was asleep in his room. During commercials, I got up to check on him. I knew, when I saw the peaceful, painless expression on his face, the closed eyes, the slightly parted lips, that he had crossed over to the other side, and I had lost him forever.

54

Blood Brothers

M ING AND KITTY LEFT for Canada with their boys five days
after Papa's funeral. Two weeks later, Ah Lan handed me a
letter from China, postmarked in Beijing. I gave out a loud gasp
upon reading the letter. Richard and Ah Lan stared at me with
looks of apprehension and dread.

"Chu Pak is dead. He was hit by a car on the Avenue of Eternal
Peace while riding his bike," I told Richard, then repeated the
news to Ah Lan in Cantonese. "He died on March 31st."

"Why weren't we notified earlier? Why wasn't Ming told? It's
going to kill him not to have gone to his father's funeral," Ah Lan
rattled on, wringing her hands.

"This letter is from Chu Sum. She said the accident occurred on
March 30th, and Chu Pak was still conscious after he was hit. They
thought he might survive, but a brain hemorrhage he suffered a
day later killed him. Before he slipped into a coma, he bade Chu
Sum not to let Ming know about the accident until after he had
left for Canada. He did not want Ming to go back to Beijing and
risk everything."

"Ming will take it very hard," said Richard.

There was another letter inside the envelope.

"Chu Pak dictated a letter for Ming before he lost consciousness.
Chu Sum says it will explain everything to him."

"Poor Ming, *aaya*, poor Ming," Ah Lan murmured, wiping her
eyes.

I reread Chu Sum's letter to me.

"Richard, something Chu Sum wrote concerns Papa. Let me

translate it for you:

> *After Ah Chu had slipped into a coma, he kept murmuring your father's name. In his delirious condition, he said, 'Tak Sing's waiting.' At the time, I did not understand, for we had not yet received Tak Ming's letter about your father's death. When Tak Ming's letter arrived, I understood. While I feel very sad about your father's death, Man On, I am comforted to know the two friends are finally together again."*

A sudden chill came over me, the dawning of a revelation that was as comforting as it was uncanny. Hurriedly, I went to my room and brought back Papa's book. Like a researcher on the verge of a major discovery, I opened it to the page I was looking for. In a shaky voice, I translated the passage from Papa's book for Richard:

"'We, Lee Tak Sing and So Ah Chu, swear to the heavens that, from this moment on, we are brothers. We will never forsake or betray each other. We were not born in the same year, in the same month, on the same day, but we wish to die in the same year, in the same month, on the same day.' Chu Pak was hit by a car on the day Papa died, and they died within a day of each other."

The wish of the blood brothers had been fulfilled.

55

Lantau

RICHARD AND I LOOKED UP at the gigantic bronze outdoor figure of Buddha on Lantau Island, ensconced on his lotus pedestal atop the Temple of Heaven, a peaceful and benevolent Buddha, with downcast eyes and long earlobes, and a raised palm bestowing blessings on those who came to pay homage, worshippers and sightseers alike. We had come to Lantau for a weekend about a month after Papa died. We had made love in a little villa at the foot of the Po Lin Hill, in the shadow of the great Buddha, hungry and insatiable love, until we heard the distant gong of the temple that woke the monks for their prayer even before the first tint of red stained the eastern sky.

"I miss you already," I said in a muffled tone, as I lay beside Richard, my fingers walking lightly on his bare chest, my eyes resting on the gleaming opal set in antique gold he had placed on my finger, a ring once belonging to Richard's great-grandmother.

"Good, for then I know you will show up at Heathrow in August," he said, touching my nose playfully with his index finger. Our plan was for me to leave for England in mid-August, to give myself time to settle affairs after school was out, for I had returned to teaching after Papa's funeral. Richard was leaving Hong Kong before *hui gui*, on the fifteenth of May.

"I don't think there's anything that will keep me away from you anymore, Richard," I said, kissing him.

"I'll make it good for you," he said softly, gliding his hand down my spine as I lay on my stomach.

Richard's latest article appeared in an April 1997 issue of the

South China Weekly, attacking self-censorship in Hong Kong in the years leading up to the handover. Needless to say, his article had been toned down by the editors before going to print. As the Chinese factor became more evident with every passing day leading up to the handover, Richard felt it becoming a greater threat to the integrity of the press. He wanted a more honest journalistic environment, but he realized he could not fight the lurking tiger. Already, he had an interview scheduled with a Dartmoor paper.

"You know, Richard, it seemed Papa gave up fighting, let himself go to set me free. Ever since I told him you couldn't stay after the handover, he had wanted me to leave with you."

"But he also knew you would never leave him."

"Or without him. But he wouldn't survive being uprooted again."

Richard drew me to him, so that my head rested on his chest. He kissed my forehead and rubbed my arm gently.

"Serena, I think it's time you know the truth about your father, what you don't know." He took a deep breath and continued in a quiet voice, "He knew about my part in the rescue mission after Tiananmen long before you told him. I'm sorry I kept this from you, Serena. I wanted to be honest with you. I told you about my involvement as much as I could, but your father had asked me explicitly not to tell you about his."

"About *his!*"

"Your father was one of the key figures in the operation. He got some of the fugitives across the land border with the help of villagers in the New Territories." Richard paused long enough for his words to sink in. "You see, he knew many villagers from his days with the border police, and he was familiar with the border terrain. He knew where the weak spots were, areas that would be unguarded by the Chinese."

I took in the information silently, thunderstruck. There was no girlfriend, no round-the-clock *wei chi* tournaments. All that time, Papa was engaged in some high-risk rescue operation, helping dissidents on the run to escape imprisonment and possible death.

"He worked at night, best if moonless. He waited for them. Once they were across the border, he took them to villagers' homes to hide, until they could find asylum abroad."

"And he didn't tell me," I murmured, deeply hurt that I was kept from the truth by Papa, and at that moment jealous of anyone who knew about his involvement, jealous of the operation itself. "Why didn't he tell me?"

"He wanted to keep you out of it, and to keep you from worrying about him, because you mattered most to him, Serena. As long as you remained ignorant of the operation, you were protected."

"So you and Papa knew each other before I introduced you?"

"We had met twice before, in '89. He recognized my name when you mentioned it to him, but I only realized our connection when you took me home to meet him. I must say I was quite shocked." Richard thought for a moment and said quietly, "Serena, Ming was also involved."

I gasped. "Was that the real reason he went to Canada?"

"That's the biggest reason, for he has been blacklisted, like me, but Kitty did not know anything about it. She thought he was making overnight trips to Macau with his boss the times he was on rescue missions. That was what he told her. He knew quite well the route across the Shenzhen River, and he crossed over a few times to guide dissidents across the river."

"The same route he took when he first came," I said. Ming the wide-eyed country bumpkin, a one-time dissident, a refugee. So lately did I realize he was a hero, like Richard, and Papa. "And your part, Richard, was to get them out of Hong Kong."

"Yes, but I was just one of many with that job. You must remember we didn't act alone, Serena. We were part of an organization with the mission to find asylum for those the Chinese wanted after Tiananmen. It was a happy coincidence I worked with your father."

"Richard, it must have been very dangerous. I'm so thankful no harm came to you, or Papa, or Ming," I said, burying my face in his chest.

"One time, Ming was almost caught. I didn't know him at the time. There was this fellow in the operation who had smuggled some of the dissidents from Beijing to Shenzhen in lorries. He sent word to a guide who had just landed in Shekou that he was to make his way immediately back to Hong Kong. The guide did, just one step ahead of the PLA who got wind of the mission that night. Your father told me that guide was Ming, after I met Ming through you. But the fellow who tipped Ming off was not so lucky. They caught him and shot him that very night, June 17th, '89."

The date of the man's execution caught my attention. I was tingling with the thrill of a mystery unraveled.

"Richard, now I know what that phone call was all about, the phone call made by a woman, probably someone in the operation, to Papa, telling him of the trouble that night, June 17th, 1989. I remember that date because we had just come home from my friend Josie's wedding when Papa got that phone call."

"We lost a few good men working for the operation," said Richard. "They were all heroes."

"Unsung heroes."

"True, the more to be honoured because they never got the recognition they deserved."

We were silent for a while, listening to each other's breathing, each other's heartbeats.

"Still, I wish Papa had told me. And you were his collaborator, keeping it from me," I chided after some time. "Was Papa also blacklisted?"

"He said his identity was never known to the Chinese."

"Not that it matters now. Nobody could touch my father now." I raised my head to look at Richard. "No wonder you two got along so well. Right now, I'm mad you two kept me in the dark for so long, but I'm also awfully proud of you both, and of Ming." Then, as an afterthought, I asked, "Richard, was Papa the one who advised you to leave before the handover?"

"Yes, your father was my contact, and Ming's too."

"And how did he get his – intelligence?"

"From Hong Kong-based contacts he had worked with during the operation. He had stayed in touch with them since '89."

"How? I never suspected anything."

"They played *wei chi* too."

Through the window of our room on Lantau, we could see the giant Buddha with his downcast eyes, his hand bestowing a perpetual blessing on those who came within his shadow. Pure, serene, benevolent.

And Richard and I made love again.

56

Ah Lan

EVER SINCE I TOOK her to see the nursing home last month, Ah Lan has been busying herself with packing the belongings she has accumulated through the years. Her winter clothes she meticulously folds and puts away into her brassbound trunk smelling strongly of moth balls. She looks contented whenever she is in my presence, and says she is looking forward to going to the "old people home" where she will not have a care in the world. I know she is just putting up a front for me, not wanting me to feel guilty about sending her to a nursing home, for on a couple of occasions I caught her wiping tears from her eyes puckered with wrinkled skin, and the sight tore at my heart. I dread the day when I will accompany her out of the flat for the last time, ride with her in a taxi to the nursing home, leave her in the care of the nuns, and say goodbye to her whom I have loved dearly ever since I was a young child. That day will come all too soon, after *hui gui*, before I leave for England.

The cost of the nursing home is reasonable, since it is subsidized by a religious order. I have insisted on financing her stay, although Ah Lan says she can contribute with her life savings. The money I have received from selling the gold bar, plus the modest sum of money Papa left me, will go to paying the nursing home for the first two years.

Ah Lan and I went to see the nursing home soon after Richard left for England. It was a white two-storey building perched on top of a cement terrace. A sign at the bottom of the stone steps leading up to the building read BENEVOLENT HOME OF THE AGED. Slowly, hesitantly, I walked with Ah Lan up the steps to the gate, pausing often to let the eighty-two-year-old woman catch her breath.

We were taken by Sister Veronica, a Catholic nun of the Precious Blood Order, to one of the vacant rooms, a four-by-eight-foot cubicle, with a long piece of cloth tacked over the entrance in place of a door. A hard narrow bed with a straw mat and a bedside cupboard with a shelf above it made up the furniture in the room.

Out in the long corridor, old women sat, dressed in *samfu* and plastic slippers, engaged in games of *sky-nine*, or dozing, or staring into space or at everyone who crossed their vision, mumbling, talking sense or nonsense depending on the degree of clarity of their minds.

"Oh, and every morning at seven, we have group prayer in the chapel before breakfast. Lunch is at eleven, dinner at four-thirty, a snack of juice and biscuits at seven, evening prayer at eight, and by eight-thirty, every resident is ready for bed," said Sister Veronica, looking organized and in control. "We have programs for our residents. Every Christmas and Chinese New Year, school children come to perform for us. Sometimes, we charter a bus...."

Sister Veronica's voice grew faint and small as my attention wandered to Ah Lan, who was subdued the whole time we were being shown around. She nodded agreeably to every word Sister Veronica uttered, like a child completely taken in by the promise of candy and ice cream, except that, for Ah Lan, the lure was the prospect of structured and worry-free days in the sunset of her life. My heart was full at the thought of leaving her in a nursing home, no matter how benevolent. When children and grandchildren visited other residents at the home, Ah Lan would have no one to visit her or bring her things, a lonely old soul to whom her floor-mates might give a sampling of treats out of pity and the goodness of their hearts. And when the day came for her to leave the world, she would do so in the midst of caregivers who would be strangers, for I would be too far away in England to be at her side, and, even if I tried, I might not arrive until it was too late.

"Seenla, I like the old people home very much. I will go there when you go to England after *hui gui*, but, for now, let me stay with you and keep you company, since Meesta Richee is not here," said Ah Lan as we waited for a taxi outside the nursing home.

"I will miss you very much, Ah Lan," I said, my voice and heart at the point of breaking. "I'll come back to see you."

"As the saying goes, there is no endless banquet under the heavens. I have been blessed by *Kuan Yin* and Buddha, for your family have been like family to me. I am very grateful. I can only pray for you, and for Meesta Richee, that you two will have many sons and lots of money."

I had to laugh in spite of myself.

"Ah Lan, I hope the money comes true, but I don't know about the sons. Richard and I are both not young. We'd be lucky if we have any child, and we'd be happy with a boy or girl. As for praying, don't forget the nursing home is run by Catholic nuns. When you pray with the group, you are praying to their God, not Buddha or *Kuan Yin*."

"Oh what does it matter? Praying is always good, whether to God or Buddha or *Kuan Yin*, as long as you are sincere and have a good heart," said Ah Lan, with a wave of her hand, and a simple wisdom that amazed me.

"Come on, Ah Lan," I said as a taxi pulled up, "let's go home and play some two-legged *mahjong*."

57

Hui Gui

AFTER AN EMOTIONAL FAREWELL to his staff at Governor's House at about four in the afternoon, Governor Patten leaves his residence with his family in a motorcade in the drizzle for the British farewell ceremony at East Tamar on the harbourfront of Hong Kong Island.

The rain has become very heavy, drenching all the singers and dancers, the shadow boxers, the drummers, the marching bands, yes, even Governor Patten and Prince Charles as they stand at the podium to deliver their farewell speeches. The rain pours down, soaking the children as they sing *Children of the World*. But they sing on, regardless of blurry glasses, wet hair and raindrops dripping from the tips of their noses. On this late Monday afternoon, no one cares if he or she gets a little wet or very wet, or catches a cold, perhaps even pneumonia, not the Prince of Wales, not the Governor, not the performers, not the marching bands, not the children, and not the thousands attending the farewell ceremony. It is as if all present are caught in a web of emotion from which they cannot extricate themselves.

As Governor Patten speaks for the last time to the people of Hong Kong, he looks over to the public viewing stand, and rests his eyes there for a long moment. He addresses them in an emotionally charged voice, forceful and tight. In his speech, he salutes the men and women, most of whom came here with nothing, but who, with their courage, energy and hard work, have made Hong Kong into a success story. As I listen to the Governor's speech, I feel a surge of wonder, gratitude and affection for the people of Hong Kong – the like of Papa, the fighters, survivors, movers, regardless of their station, and social and economic status – who have built Hong Kong into what it is.

The rain continues to come down in torrents, as the Governor finishes his speech and Prince Charles walks to the microphone.

"Looks like this bad weather is trying to tell us something about *hui gui*," I observe to Ah Lan.

"As the saying goes, water is money. Maybe this rain will bring us good fortune after *hui gui*, not bad luck," says Ah Lan, always looking on the sunny side.

If nothing else, the rain reflects the sadness felt by many at the British farewell, as *God Save the Queen* is played, the Union Jack is lowered, and *Auld Lang Syne* is sung to the bagpipes of the Scottish marching band. Despite the unfair treaty at the end of the Opium War over 150 years ago that gave Hong Kong to the British, time has alleviated a lot of the grievance against the colonizer, and friendships have been built over the years.

Massive fireworks light up the harbour, sending showers of fiery explosives and billows of red smoke into the sky, such that the harbour is not unlike what must have been the scene of a sea battle in the days of the Spanish Armada. Intermittently, the camera flashes to the uniformed waxen-faced soldiers of the People's Liberation Army sitting tall and straight in army trucks and buses in Shenzhen, primly waiting to cross the border at Lok Ma Chau into Hong Kong.

It is the last hour before midnight as celebrities file into the hall of the Convention Centre where the handover ceremony is about to take place, representatives including the heads of state from the British, the Chinese and the Hong Kong governments. Soon, everyone who is to be present is seated in the big hall. Red catches my eye – the platform of red carpeting, the red outfits worn by some of the celebrities present, the red five-star flag of China, the red bauhinia flag of the Special Administrative Region of Hong Kong, red, the colour of celebration, the colour of energy, the colour of good fortune.

The Union Jack is being lowered in the big hall, and the five-star flag of the People's Republic of China hoisted, and suddenly I am gripped with an inexplicable sense of pride that Hong Kong is at long last reunited with China.

The band plays the National Anthem of the People's Republic of China, *The March of the Volunteers' Corps*, as Papa knew it as a boy in Tai Shek.

Papa's life had been affected so much by vicissitudes of the times. Mummy's too. If only, if only... so many hypotheses, yet one reality my father and mother would not have wished otherwise was their having fallen in love. If only Mummy didn't have to die.

"Your mother was like a lotus flower separated from its roots and native soil, and so she withered and died," Ah Lan once said to me. *Elegantly it stands alone, to be admired from afar, not touched up close.* She was touched by a poor man's love. And torn between two loyalties, like the ballerina in *The Red Shoes*.

Red, the colour of blood, the colour of sacrifice and martyrdom, the colour of love.

It is now after the hour of midnight on July 1ˢᵗ, 1997. Soon, Prince Charles and Chris Patten, the last governor of Hong Kong, will board the royal yacht, the *Britannia*, and sail out of Victoria Harbour, out of this brightest jewel of the Empire, on which the sun has finally set.

President Jiang Jemin of the People's Republic walks to the microphone and addresses for the first time the people of Hong Kong. He promises Hong Kong a high degree of autonomy and guarantees rights and freedoms according to the Basic Law of Hong Kong. Motherland is emphasized, the return of Hong Kong to the embrace of the motherland. *Hui gui.* Returning home.

58

Epilogue

Ka Hing, August 3rd, 1997

I REACH KA HING in the early afternoon of this steaming, muggy summer day, just ten days before I am to leave for England. The earth smells of fresh manure, trees are laden with dark green leaves, and the hills look a hazy purple in the far distance. Clouds have gathered since late morning, rain clouds, I hope, to bring some relief to the sultry summer heat. I ask the taxi driver to let me off at the east end of the village. I want to walk through the village to the northwest exit, beyond which is the temple, and further north of the temple is the Lee family burial mound where my paternal grandparents were laid to rest years before.

Ka Hing in 1997 is a declining village with a dilapidated exterior wall, one dust-covered main street with a few old shabby storefronts displaying a small supply of merchandise from yesteryear. A grocery store carries rusty canned food, packages of dry noodles, Camel cigarettes and bottled Coca-Cola. A small dingy shop sells sundry items, from rubber shoes and farmers' sandals to enamel utensils. The only eatery is a tented area with a food stall giving off an unwelcome odour of old cooking oil, nauseating to me, especially since lately I have been prone to morning sickness. I walk through the village, thinking of the days when Papa was there as a boy, when the village in its heyday was a bustling rural community, before war, revolution and migration to cities reduced it to this pitiful state.

Once outside Ka Hing, I climb a dirt slope leading to the temple whose exterior is in no better condition than the village. Roof tiles are cracked and broken, paint sadly peeled from decorative pillars and walls. When I came with Papa and Mummy in 1978, soon after *Yeh Yeh*'s death, I had gone into the temple with them, only to find *Kuan Yin* and all the other statues of deities destroyed by Red Guards during the Cultural Revolution. When Papa and I passed through ten years later on our way to Beijing to meet Ah Chu, we had gone into the temple again, only to find that nothing had been replaced in the intervening years. This time, alone, I decide not to stop inside. I hurry past the temple, walk briskly on until I reach the burial mound.

I am feeling very hot in my short-sleeved T-shirt and denim overalls. I wipe the sweat from my forehead with my hand. Catching my breath, I bend down to remove the long weeds that are cluttering my grandparents' graves. Then carefully I take from my backpack two ceramic urns that hold the ashes of my father and mother, and place them reverently on the white stone slab in front of my grandparents' graves. Three times I kowtow in front of the urns, in front of my grandparents' graves, each time my forehead touching the earth. Then I sit on a big stone beside the urns, like a sentry keeping guard.

I sit for a long time. Alone on the mound, except for the new life that I am nurturing in me, I experience a strange feeling of tranquility in my solitude, and solace in my sadness. It is as if I have finished reading a love story whose ending is far from fairytale, yet nonetheless has left me with a quiet sense of exaltation. The aftertaste of bitter melon is sweet and satisfying.

Finally, I stand up, kneel in front of the urns, and lift the lids. I take the urn containing Papa's ashes, touch it lingeringly with my lips, and walk with it to the edge of the mound. I scoop up a handful of the ashes, gritty to the touch, and, saying softly, "I'm doing this for you, Papa," let the ashes run through my fingers and fall to the earth beyond the edge of the mound. As I let the ashes sieve through my fingers, a warm gentle wind touches my skin and scatters the ashes across the slope. Goodbye, dearest

Papa. You are home, reunited with the earth you loved so much. Go wherever you wish to go. Roam free, for nothing can hold you back now. I repeat the motion of my hand until the urn holding Papa's ashes is completely emptied of its contents. Then I lift Mummy's urn. Having kissed it, I scatter her ashes across the earth in the same manner as I have done Papa's. As I let go of Mummy's ashes, I whisper, "Dearest Mummy, your desire was to follow Papa to the ends of the earth. Rest now in peace, for your wish has been fulfilled."

Having done as Papa had bidden, I stand atop the mound, looking across the wide expanse of the land that he had loved. Papa is home, and Mummy is with him. This is their *hui gui*. I ought to be sad, but I am not, not even lonely anymore. My eyes follow the white cabbage butterflies flitting among the dandelions, until they disappear into the brush below the top of the mound. I feel a drop of rain on my forehead, and another, and another. Quickly I take out the umbrella from my backpack and open it, just in time, before the raindrops become a steady drizzle. By the edge of the paddy field in the distance below, careless of the rain, some children are gleefully throwing a frisbee to a dog.

I must finish writing Papa's book.